C000113679

the fire prophecy

academy of magical creatures book one

MEGAN LINSKI & ALICIA RADES

Copyright © 2018 Megan Linski and Alicia Rades

All rights reserved. No part of this book may be reproduced in any form or by any electronic or mechanical means, including information storage and retrieval systems, without written permission from the publisher, except for the use of brief quotations in a book review.

The reproduction or utilization of this work in part of in whole including xerography, recording, and photocopying is strictly forbidden without the written permission of the publisher.

PIRACY IS FORBIDDEN AND ILLEGAL. Any piracy or illegal sharing by this work will invoke legal action by the publishers.

BISAC Category: Fantasy/Romance

This is a work of fiction. All names, characters, places and incidents are a product of the author's imagination and are used fictitiously. Any resemblance to actual persons, living or dead, business establishments, events or locales is entirely coincidental.

Cover Art by Orina Kafe Artworks.

For information about custom editions, special sales, ARCs, and premium and corporate purchases, please contact admin@academyofmagicalcreatures.com

Manufactured in the United States of America

MAP OF ORENDA ACADEMY
AND SURROUNDING AREAS

This book features a character with a rare disease. In the United States, a rare disease is defined as an illness that affects fewer than 200,000 people. Although our character's disease is fictional, 25 to 30 million people in the US are currently living with a rare disease, many of which are not clearly diagnosed or have no cure. To learn more about rare diseases, or to contribute to the research and education of these illness, please visit the Rare Disease Foundation.

ONE

Most of the world couldn't understand people like me.

I was never really normal— but I had never been *this different.* I came from a world where dragons exist and fairy tales are real, but it felt like all the magic had gone out of the world. Everyday, I saw mythical creatures glide across the skies with riders on their backs, witnessed people conjuring fire and controlling the earth and flying through the air.

Hell, even water obeyed my command. Waves rose and came crashing back down as I created them, and the ocean churned at my every whim. Rain poured from the clouds with just a blink of my eye, then froze into icy diamonds without me giving it a second thought.

But it wasn't the same anymore. It was no longer incredible or breathtaking. It just... was. I used to care about my powers.

I no longer cared about anything.

Except the rage. I was always angry or frustrated, sometimes for no reason, and it just never ended. I stopped having words to explain what happened to me long before I even comprehended what did.

I didn't know how to tell people. I just learned to deal with it.

I hated how people looked at me. I hated how I looked at myself.

They didn't understand what it was like to be on the brink of life and death constantly— fuck, I didn't even know. Not until after it happened. My entire life was turned upside down. I didn't even know who I was anymore. My life became nothing but questions. Was the man I was before just a lie? Or was the old Liam dead, and did this new, shitty one come to take his place?

I wished there was a way to make this better. And I wished he was here, so I could tell him I'm sorry, and that I wanted it to be me instead of him.

But he's not, and that's something I could never take back... something I could never fix.

Before, I hoped that someone could love me. For one incredible, amazing moment, I had someone that did. I actually believed for the rest of my life, I wouldn't have to be alone.

Now I knew that wasn't true. I was cursed to be an outsider, forever. And I deserved everything I got.

Grief is like being underwater, but never being allowed to come up to breathe.

sophia

TWO

"**S**ophia Henley, you're dead!"

It took everything I had not to bust a gut laughing. Amelia had threatened my murder enough times throughout my childhood that I knew her words were nothing more than an empty threat. Besides, all I did was admit to stealing a pair of jeans she'd left home while she was off at college. That was *hardly* a crime worthy of a death sentence.

I shot a smirk at my sister. "You'll have to catch me first."

I didn't give her a chance to respond. I sprinted forward, ignoring the burn in my legs as I raced up the mountain trail. The Salt Lake Valley was long behind us, with nothing but huge rocks and small shrubs covering the dry earth ahead of us. Pine trees dotted the surrounding mountain peaks. The higher I climbed, the narrower the dirt trail became, until I was running along a thin ledge. Sharp rocks jutted from the cliff to my right. It was easily a twenty-foot drop to the ground below.

Amelia would so regret saying that if I slipped and fell.

Good thing I was confident in my footing.

"Sophia!" Amelia shouted from down the trail. This time, it sounded like I was being sentenced for being faster than her. Because it'd be *so* unfair if I was actually better than her at something.

A high-pitched squawk filled the air above me. I glanced up to see

Amelia's parrot circling my head. I wasn't sure what kind he was. When I asked Amelia after she brought him home from college, she just said he was "exotic." I didn't have the heart to tell her that "exotic" wasn't a species. I didn't even want to ask how much she paid for the rat gremlin. She took him everywhere we went, though I wished he'd just stay in a cage. Amelia refused to buy one for him... said cages were inhumane.

He looked like some sort of parrot, but his beak was longer, and his feathers were a deep green, like the color of a luscious rain forest. I'd never seen anything like him before, especially not with his type of temperament.

The thing hated me, for whatever reason. Though I trusted my sister with my life, I didn't trust Kiwi.

I slowed. My chest heaved as I inhaled deep breaths.

"Sophia!" Amelia scolded once she caught up to me.

"What?" I asked innocently.

The path evened out, the sharp cliff behind us. Amelia plopped her butt into the dirt on the side of the trail, trying to catch her breath. The late afternoon sun beat down on us.

"When did you get so much faster than me?" she asked through heavy breaths.

"Right around the time I started walking." I shot her a teasing smile. I'd always been able to beat Amelia in a race— on land, at least. Amelia could totally school me in the water. Though, to be fair, I despised swimming.

She sighed and shook her head at me. "You're such a dweeb."

I scoffed and sat beside her. "I am not!"

She reached her sweaty arm around me and pulled me in close. "Of course you are. You're *my* little dweeb."

"Gross!" I protested, pushing away from her armpit.

"Come on, Sophia," she complained. "Give me a hug. I'm only home for a few days. I *miss* you."

I took a swig from my water bottle. "I'm not that gullible. You're just going to give me a wet willie or something."

Amelia laughed and wiped the sweat from her forehead. "We're not kids anymore."

I just rolled my eyes at her. It'd been four years since she moved out, but she was still my sister, which meant every time she visited I was subject to her teasing.

Kiwi landed in the dirt beside Amelia and immediately head butted a rock twice the size of his head. It rolled toward her hand. If I didn't know better, I'd say he was trying to offer the rock as a gift to her, but I was pretty sure he was just knocking his head against it for kicks. Despite what Amelia said, Kiwi wasn't exactly a bright bird.

Amelia sighed. "Forget about the pants. I just want to have fun with my little sister before I have to leave again for work."

Amelia had graduated college a few months ago and immediately got a job as a cruise ship attendant. She was only home for a week before she had to pack up and leave on her next cruise.

"I hate you, you know," I teased. "You have, like, the coolest job in the world."

Amelia shrugged, but she couldn't hide her smile.

"No, I'm serious," I said. "You get to travel the world on a cruise ship while I'm stuck at home for the next four years."

Amelia screwed the cap off her water bottle and held it to her lips. "Have you decided on a major yet?"

I shook my head as she threw her head back and chugged her water.

Honestly, I had no idea what I wanted to do. One day I was a kid, dreaming of becoming a wild land firefighter. The next my parents were telling me I had to get serious about a "real career." Before I knew it, I was filling out college applications and graduating high school without a clue of where I'd go next.

It seemed like everyone had their lives figured out but me. Amelia was going to travel the world on cruise ships, and my friends Emily and Leah were headed off to the same art school across the country. Even Kiwi— the idiot bird— seemed to know what he wanted in life. I didn't know what he was doing with that rock, but he sure looked determined.

Me? I was just hoping things would change once school started. I'd find my passion, and maybe a hot guy to share it with, and I'd make my mark on the world.

"It's okay," Amelia assured me, wiping water from the corner of her mouth. "You have plenty of time to choose a major."

"Yeah..." I grabbed a nearby rock and rolled it around in my hands, just so I wouldn't have to meet her gaze. I studied it intensely, taking note of the various shades of red woven together. It was cool enough to warrant a place in my rock collection. "It just feels like I'm going to spend four years exploring my options and still not know what I want to do."

Amelia rolled her eyes. "It's *normal* to feel that way, Sophia. You'll figure it out."

I glared at my sister. "Says the girl who's had her life figured out since she was five."

"That's not true," she countered. "I had no idea I wanted to work on a cruise ship."

"But you've always known what school you wanted to go to," I pointed out.

Amelia had gone to some school in Northern California that was so small it didn't even have a website. I was pretty sure the last four years of her life had been a scam, but she claimed she loved it there.

"The important thing about college is that you have fun—"

Amelia cut off when the sound of a twig snapping behind us reached our ears. Both of our heads snapped in the direction of the noise. My eyes darted between the bushes and shrubs on the mountainside, but I saw nothing. My shoulders relaxed, and I glanced to Amelia. Her eyes went wide in fear.

"Don't be such a wuss," I told her. "I hike this trail all the time by myself. I'm sure it was nothing."

Amelia kept her eyes on the landscape. "I just thought I saw..." She trailed off.

"Saw what?" I asked. Creeps didn't actually pop up out of the bushes, did they?

"Nothing." Amelia stood. "We should probably start heading back, though."

"But it's only half a mile to the top!" I countered.

"Which is, like, forever with this incline," she complained. "My legs hurt, and it's a long way back to the car. It'll be dark before we get back."

A half-mile was nothing, but it was my older sister I was arguing with. I'd never win.

"Fine," I relented. "But then you have to let me keep the jeans."

"No," she denied without hesitation, staring down at me and waiting for me to move.

I curled the rock I held into my fist and hopped to my feet. "You're a booger, you know that? You're a big, rotting clump of troll boogers."

"Wow," Amelia said flatly, like she wasn't at all impressed. "That's creative."

I smiled proudly, but my smile quickly faded when Amelia shot a nervous glance over her shoulder. The look in her eyes made my mouth go dry.

"You're okay, aren't you, Am?" All my teasing from earlier had disappeared from my tone. "You're not being stalked or something, are you?"

"What?" Amelia's voice rose at least three pitches above normal. The light laugh she threw in didn't sound the least bit genuine. "If I was being stalked, you'd know it."

I couldn't help but notice she hadn't exactly answered me. She started down the trail. Kiwi squawked and spread his wings to follow behind her. I remained quiet as we descended the mountain. Amelia didn't speak, either, but I noticed she had quickened her pace and kept glancing behind us.

It wasn't until night had fallen and we made it back to the parking lot that I finally spoke. I reached for Amelia's wrist before she could round Mom's crossover to the driver's side. "Are you going to tell me what's up, or not?"

Amelia's eyes scanned the dark, deserted parking lot. "Nothing's wrong. Just get in the car."

I planted my feet firmly on the pavement. "Not until you tell me—"

"Get in the car, Sophia!"

Amelia's tone hit me like a slap in the face. I rushed so fast to the passenger side door that she hadn't even unlocked it yet. Something was *definitely* up, and now that I had confirmation, I wasn't about to hang around to find out what it was.

The click of the lock hit my ears, and I swung the door open and scrambled inside. Kiwi flew in through Amelia's door, and she slammed it behind her.

"Amelia!" I demanded. "Talk to me!"

Amelia reached for her seatbelt and pulled it across her body. Her lips tightened as she turned the key in the ignition, but she didn't answer. The engine roared to life, and the headlights lit the bushes in front of us. My breath stopped when I caught sight of two small, shiny objects in the distance.

Eyes.

The creature was far enough away from the car that I couldn't see its body, but judging by how high its eyes seemed to hover above the ground, it was *huge*. Like, mountain lion huge.

"Am!" I cried. "There's something out there!"

Amelia gritted her teeth and spoke under her breath. "Yeah, I thought so..."

"Let's get out of here!" My heart slammed against my rib cage. In all the years I'd been hiking this trail, I hadn't seen anything larger than a big-horned sheep.

I racked my brain, trying to remember if sheep eyes glowed, but I was pretty sure they weren't nocturnal. Could it be some sort of canine? Maybe a deer? Yes! A deer. That wasn't so scary.

"No," Amelia said lowly, unclicking her seat belt and kicking her door open. "This ends now."

"What the— Amelia!"

"Stay here," she instructed. "Watch Kiwi."

Amelia slammed her door shut and headed straight for the bushes. What the hell was she thinking, going after a wild animal? If I didn't know better, I'd say *she* was the dweeb, but she wasn't this stupid.

I jumped out of the car behind her. "Amelia!" I hissed, keeping my voice as low as I could.

She turned back to me. The headlights of our car illuminated her. "I said to stay in the car."

"Are you insane?!" I wanted to rush over to her and drag her back to the car, but I still didn't know what kind of animal was out there. Fear stalled me, and I remained rooted in place next to the vehicle.

Amelia ignored me and stepped forward, disappearing into the darkness beyond the light of our headlights. She called out into the bushes, but I couldn't hear what she was saying.

Amelia's officially lost it.

The hairs on my arms stood. Kiwi let out a high-pitched shriek from inside the car and pecked against the windshield. Against my better judgement, I abandoned the safety of the vehicle and hurried forward behind Amelia.

"Come out, Naomi," I heard Amelia say. "Come and face me, you lousy piece of dirt."

"Amelia," I whisper-screamed.

Amelia had wandered so far into the darkness that I could only make out her silhouette.

"I told you to stay in the car!" her voice shot back.

She spoke with such authority that I almost considered turning back just so I wouldn't have to deal with her lecture later. Before I could make a decision, a shadow leapt from the bushes and slammed into her. My hands shot up to cover my mouth before a scream erupted from my lungs.

Amelia stumbled backward into the light, but tripped over a shrub and fell to the ground. She got to her elbows and scurried backward.

A low growl came from somewhere in the darkness. Every inch of my body shook, but I rushed forward and looped my arms under Amelia's to pull her to her feet.

"Am—" I broke off. I hadn't even helped her to her feet yet.

Up closer, I got a better look at the shadow in the darkness. It moved with finesse, as if every movement was calculated. The creature was stalking us, ready to pounce. It paced in front of us, its shoulder blades rising and falling with every step.

A cat.

But it wasn't the kind of cat you wanted to cuddle. This cat was bigger than me, with sharp claws and the kind of powerful teeth that could rip a human's throat out.

Amelia was right. I'm dead. We both are.

MEGAN LINSKI & ALICIA RADES

"Don't. Make. Any. Sudden. Movements." I whispered under my breath, completely frozen in place.

The cat in front of us was huge and covered in a coat of blonde fur. I'd never seen a cougar in real life before, but this seemed bigger, like some sort of African cat. Had it escaped from the zoo? I hoped that was the case and that it was used to humans... and that it wasn't hungry.

Against my instruction, Amelia jumped to her feet and dusted the dirt off her shorts, like she hadn't noticed the beast in front of us. Except... she stared right at it, almost like she knew the creature personally.

She turned from the cat and grabbed my arm. Her fingernails dug into my skin, but I couldn't bring myself to move for fear that it'd run after us. She tugged harder, and I had no choice but to stumble behind her.

"I told you to stay in the car!" Amelia scolded.

"I know, but—" A screech ripped out of my chest.

Amelia's hand fell from my arm as her body crashed to the ground again. The cat stood over her, baring its teeth. Before I could react, Amelia shoved her elbow up into the cat's nose. The cat immediately retaliated by swiping its claws at the arm she held protectively in front of her face.

Instinct overtook. I didn't even think about what I was doing when I drew my arm back and hurled the rock I still held at the cat. I didn't wait to see if I hit it. I bent and grabbed a thick stick in the dirt nearby and swung it upward to connect with the cat's jaw.

The dry stick snapped in half as it connected. The cat continued to stare down my sister, as if it hadn't felt a thing. I hurled the remaining half of my stick at its head. By sheer luck, I managed to hit it square in the eye.

The cat stumbled backward with a whimper, but before I could help Amelia to her feet, the cat turned its frightening gaze on me. I mean, it's one eye was winky, but that didn't make me feel any better. Sheer terror ripped through my gut, and my skin heated so much that sweat broke out across my brow.

A split second passed, then the cat lunged, launching itself through the air toward me.

My scream filled the air around us, and I threw my arms out in front of me. If I wasn't scared before, I was freaking *terrified* when a burst of red light shot across the space between us.

I didn't have the time to contemplate the strange phenomenon. I expected a blow to come, for sharp claws to rip into my skin and strong jaws to tear me apart, but instead, the cat twisted sideways and landed on the ground on its side.

I only let my shock last a split second. I rushed forward and grabbed Amelia's arm and dragged her to her feet. Together, we sprinted back to the car.

Amelia shifted into reverse before I even had my door closed. She tore out of the parking lot without looking back. Kiwi was going crazy, flying around the back seat.

"What were you thinking?!" I shrieked. "We could've been killed!"

"Forget about that!" Amelia cried. Her eyes darted between mine and the road. "Did I see you use *fire*, Sophia?"

"What?" Is that what that flash of red had been? Some sort of fireball?

"It was, wasn't it?" Amelia accused. "You're Koigni!"

"Koigni?" I practically yelled. "Have you gone insane?"

"No," Amelia bit back, obviously offended.

"You tried to pet a wild cat!"

Amelia's jaw tensed, but she softened her tone. "I wasn't trying to pet it."

"Then what *were* you doing?" I demanded.

"It doesn't matter," she said. "What matters is that Mom and Dad lied to me— to both of us."

I was momentarily struck silent. What did Mom and Dad have to do with this?

"They told me you were human— adopted." Amelia slowed the car to match the speed limit.

I swallowed hard. This had to be a dream, or maybe I'd been

drugged. Apparently, an African cat attack in the middle of Salt Lake I could believe, but there was *no* way my parents had lied to me for eighteen years about being adopted. Sure, I was the black sheep of the family, with lighter hair and paler skin, but we told each other everything.

Yet that wasn't the most disturbing part of what Amelia had just said.

"*Human?*" My voice shook. "What else is there?"

Amelia pressed her lips together. "How do I put this?" She took a deep breath. "Sophia, you're magical... like me. You're an Elementai."

My brow furrowed. Maybe Amelia wasn't insane. Maybe she was just high. Maybe we *both* were high.

"Elementai?" I repeated the word. It felt strange on my tongue, like it shouldn't be there. "What are you talking about?"

Amelia hesitated. "I'm sorry you had to find out like this, Sophia, but there's no other explanation. You're Koigni, a Fire Elementai. Me, Mom, and Dad are Toaqua, Water Elementai."

"What do you mean?" I demanded. Amelia had better start making sense, or I was going to lose it.

Amelia swallowed, like she didn't know how to break the news. "It means you're one of us," she finally said. "It means you have magic."

Liam

THREE

A long time ago, this school felt like home. Now all it'd become was a painful reminder of everything I'd lost.

The halls of Orenda Academy seemed dark and intimidating, not warm and friendly. Only every other torch was lit, because of summer, and the clouds outside from the impending storm covered up the sun. I kept my head down and focused on counting the stones two by two, avoiding the eyes of the judgmental paintings and tapestries.

They were all of Elementai and Familiars. I wasn't a part of them anymore.

Orenda Academy was huge. It took me a half hour to navigate through the castle and find the Head Dean's tower. I knew every inch of this castle by heart, yet my steps were slow and hesitant. I didn't know what Alric wanted from me. Not yet.

I would say being summoned by him scared me, but I wasn't scared. After what had happened, I wasn't afraid of anything anymore.

Just living.

I entered the tower and climbed the dozens of steps that spiraled upward to Head Dean Alric's office. I grabbed the dragon's head knocker and knocked three times. The great iron doors opened of their own accord, and I stepped into the office.

The room was circular and large, packed with books from the floor to the ceiling in bookcases that expanded upward, the sunroof shining light into the middle of the marble floor. A fireplace burned, and Hawkei memorabilia was placed in an organized fashion in glass cabinets.

Head Dean Caspian Alric, the master Elementai that ran the place, stood in the middle of the room with his hands clasped behind his back. Each part of his suit was impeccably ironed and cleaned, his shoes shined. Though he was ancient, he moved with all the grace of a young man. His short white hair and sculpted beard were trimmed to neurotic perfection. Even the wrinkles on his tanned face appeared to fall exactly into place.

His dragon Familiar was circling above the school somewhere. I could hear the power of her wings through the walls outside as she buffeted them up and down, her dominating roar quivering the tower.

Good. I didn't want to cross Valda today.

The four other minor Deans were situated around the room in four chairs. Dean Alizeh from Yapluma, the Air House, stared at me like I was in a zoo, while Dean Hestian from Nivita, the Earth House, wouldn't look me in the eye.

Alizeh's Familiar was a large yellow thunderbird that hardly glanced at me. I didn't mind— I didn't feel like getting zapped today.

Hestian's Familiar was a white stag that had ivy leaves twisting up its legs and around its massive antlers, which were twelve-pronged on each side and six feet end-to-end. The stag clicked its hooves on the floor, but said nothing more.

They *pitied* me. It was a sickening feeling that I hated.

I noticed that Madame Eleanor Doya, Dean of Koigni, was missing her lioness Familiar. That was weird. Naomi was hardly absent from Madame Doya's side. Wherever she was, no doubt the lioness was stalking some poor soul on behalf of Doya's bidding.

Whoever had been stupid enough to cross Madame Doya would certainly regret it.

Madame Doya was dressed elaborately, as she always was, in a purple velvet dress and furs. She had multiple rings on her fingers.

Her long red hair was curled, red lips puckered and tight. She had mastered resting bitch face better than anyone I knew.

My Dean from Toaqua, Professor Elliot Baine, was the only one who gave me an encouraging smile behind baggy and tired eyes. He had short cropped hair that was combed back, large square glasses, a thick and pointed nose, and a scraggly gray beard. He looked more or less thrown together, his suit sloppy with stains and shoes almost worn with holes, but despite his ragged appearance, I was glad he'd shown up.

His Familiar wasn't here, as she needed the ocean to survive. I was glad there was a fellow Water tribe member in here with me in case things got a little heated.

And I was already on my last nerve.

"What's this about?" I asked bluntly. It was more than a little rude.

Madame Doya raised an eyebrow, and the Nivita and Yapluma Deans shifted uncomfortably. Normally, a Third Year would get in trouble for mouthing off to their superiors... big trouble. A million punishments flew behind Madame Doya's eyes, but no one said anything.

I was testing them. I wanted to see how far I could push, how much I could get away with— just how *sorry they felt for me.*

Head Dean Alric didn't bat an eye at my attitude. By now, he was long used to it. "We've gotten notice of a missing child," he began. "Eighteen years ago, an infant was stolen from Koigni. We've recently located her in Utah, living with members of Toaqua."

"Toaqua stole a baby from the Fire tribe?" I asked in astonishment, before I shook my head. "No. It can't be true."

"It is true, *boy*," Madame Doya said in that condescending voice of hers, the one she reserved for literally everyone that wasn't from Koigni. "After all this time, we've discovered the missing child is alive and that she was stolen by none other than Robert and Susan Henley."

My stomach sank. I knew the family. Not very well, but well enough to know that yeah, they'd do something like this. There were multiple reasons that my tribe, Toaqua, would steal a Fire baby. Koigni and Toaqua were natural born enemies, and were always trying to one-up each other.

But what Alric said next floored me. "We believe the Henleys took the child to prevent a prophecy from coming true."

As if in unison, all the Deans spoke together:

"The fated Koigni child, born in the Summer Solstice in the Year of the Dragon,
Shall bring glory to the greatest House."

Hmph. I'd heard of the prophecy, but had always rubbed it off as F.A.S... that is, *fake as shit.* Who believed in corny stuff like that?

Apparently, Madame Doya did, because she looked pissed. "This girl is critical to the elevation and status of my House. She needs to be returned to Koigni, where she belongs."

"And you, Liam, are the perfect person to bring her back," Alric finished.

Oh, great. Here we go.

"Okay... a lost Fire baby," I said flatly. "And you want me to go looking for her... why? Why not send someone from Koigni?"

"The Elders don't want a Koigni. They specifically requested someone from Toaqua to smooth over the delicate situation," Dean Alizeh spoke up.

Yeah, that made sense. Better to send someone from the Henleys' own Tribe to convince them to hand over the girl than a fiery, pissed off Koigni, I guess.

"Fine. But why me?" I stuck my hands in my pockets and stared at them. "I'm just a Third Year."

"We know well of your... troubles, Mister Mitoh," Alizeh said, with a wayward glance at Baine. "It was suggested that you should be the one from Toaqua to go, as it might help restore some credit to your name."

This was ridiculous. Why was this my problem, and why did I care? I didn't want to get involved in things that weren't my business. I just wanted to keep to myself. That's all I'd asked for in the past few months.

On the other hand... this was my chance. An opportunity to win my place back in society, after the horrible mess I'd created. Status meant everything to the Elementai. I didn't care about stuff like that, but my family sure did.

I couldn't bear disappointing my parents more than I already had.

"All right. I'll do it," I said.

"Hopefully you're capable," Doya clipped.

You ever had a teacher who completely hated you? Yeah, that was Madame Doya. I was lucky enough to avoid her most of the time, because she mostly taught Koigni classes, but I had gotten stuck with her after bonding with Nashoma. We were put into Predator Familiars together, a class Doya and Naomi ruled like dictators.

That class had been hell. I'd barely passed.

At Nashoma's funeral, Doya had the nerve to come up to me and say that her time teaching me had been a waste. If I thought I couldn't hate her any more than I already had, she'd surprised me once again.

"We have complete faith you'll bring Sophia back to us, Liam," Baine said. He nodded to me for encouragement.

"Sophia?" It caught my interest. "That's her name? Sophia Henley?"

"She's not a Henley. At least, she won't be for much longer." Doya's tone was cool.

"We don't know if this girl is indeed the prophesied child," Alric said. "But we do know that she belongs here, at Orenda Academy. It's time to bring her home."

I nodded grimly. "Fine. Then I guess I'm your man."

They gave me an address, along with a free pass aboard the *Hozho* cruise liner before they allowed me to leave.

I felt dizzy when I went back down the stairs, but I ignored it. By the time I reached the hallway, I was determined to continue on, but a sudden wave of pain bloomed at the bottom of my back and spread throughout my body, causing my muscles to involuntarily spasm. I let out a cry of pain and gritted my teeth.

This. Sucked. I put a hand against the wall to steady myself and took deep breaths to try and regain my composure.

Come on, just hurry up and die already, I moaned inwardly. I leaned against the wall and waited for the vertigo to pass. It was always like this: agony would come up suddenly and without warning. One moment I was completely fine, the next, the room would be spinning and I'd feel my legs turn to water. One too many times in the past few weeks, I'd passed out.

How embarrassing would it be if some stupid First Year came along and found me on the floor? Or anyone, for that matter.

My dad wanted me to keep moving forward in life. But he didn't know what it was like. Most people who lost their Familiars died off right away. The ones that stuck around were older, past my father's age, and they only stayed for a few months. Young people like me usually kicked the bucket a few days after their Familiar was gone. Elementai couldn't live without their Familiars.

Not me. For whatever reason, my useless body stubbornly hung on. After Nashoma died, I'd gone from completely fine to completely disabled in a few short months and *it fucking sucked*.

After a few minutes, my vertigo went away and I felt like I could walk again, though I was significantly weaker. To distract myself from the harsh throbbing radiating throughout my body, I thought of the task ahead.

I had to go clean up a mess a bunch of stupid old people had made. Typical. This Sophia girl was probably a spoiled brat. I knew her sister, Amelia. I didn't exactly *not* like her, but that girl's middle name should be *bossy*. She loved ordering people around. I bet her younger sister was worse.

I wasn't exactly shocked to find my father waiting for me at the entrance to the school. His Familiar, a grizzly named Tatum, was blocking the hallway so I couldn't get around.

Fat-ass bear.

My dad was wearing a suit, too, which meant he'd been called in for a council meeting. He rarely got dressed up unless he had to. Toaqua went with the flow.

Dad had a thick nose, and tanner skin than I did. His long black hair hung loose far past his shoulders. If anyone looked like an Elementai, he fit the bill. Something I no longer did.

He never came up to the school, not unless it was important.

Somebody had probably told him about my summoning. Most likely one of my mouthy brothers or sisters.

Dad looked concerned, which I hated.

"How are things going, son?" he asked.

"You don't need to check up on me, Dad. I can handle things," I told him.

It was a lie, of course. I'd been such a mess over the summer, and he'd seen it all. I'm surprised he wasn't here trying to hold my hand.

"I wasn't checking up. Tatum and I were just passing through. Your sister wanted me to speak with Professor Lopez," he said.

Yeah. Right.

I resisted the urge to roll my eyes and said, "I'm guessing you know what this is about?"

Dad paused. His eyes narrowed as he said, "Yes. The missing Koigni girl has been found, I've heard."

There was an awkward pause. I pressed, "Dad, do you know anything about this?"

Dad cleared his throat. "There are some things, son, that are better left unsaid."

Tatum let out a growl of agreement, which just made me more suspicious. He was totally in on this somehow. I bet he'd helped the Henleys take her.

I didn't really care. My job was to drag her back, it wasn't in the details. Tribe politics bored me.

Dad changed the subject and said, "This is important, son. You must do everything in your power to convince this girl that Orenda Academy is the best place for her. Our family's reputation, and our House's, depends on it."

"I know, Dad." Being the firstborn son of the Water Chief had been fantastic, until I'd brought embarrassment upon the entire House a few months ago. After making sure I was okay, Dad's first priority had been coming up with ways to restore honor to Toaqua. As of yet, he hadn't managed to clean up the mess I'd made.

Dad was cautious with his next few words. "Liam, I know it hasn't been easy with Nashoma gone."

"Dad, I don't want to talk about it."

"I'm just saying, perhaps it is time to move on—"

"You ever try living without a soul?" I shot back at him, and he recoiled. "There's no *moving on* from that."

Dad stared at me, and I ran a hand through my hair. "I'm sorry, Dad. I'm just tired."

"I understand, son." He was letting me off too easy these days. "Go head home and relax. Your mother will help you pack for the trip."

I was twenty-one and didn't need Mom to pack my bags for me, but I bet she would anyway. She spoiled me. I listened to my father and headed out, blocking out the castle around me until I emerged into the evergreen forest that surrounded it.

But I didn't go to the ocean to head home. Not yet. Instead, I turned deeper into the woods, heading toward the burial ground.

Nobody was here, luckily. I moved around the burial mounds that were covered in flowers until I got to the newest plot, one that had only recently been constructed.

The hill was new, and was covered in dirt, not grass. A stone wolf's head totem stood before the gravesite. There were no other markings.

An empty plot was next to Nashoma's. We were supposed to be buried together. Not apart.

I knelt on the ground and took out a few offerings from my pockets. His favorite food, beef jerky, some wildflowers from outside his den, and a couple of incense sticks.

I muttered a prayer in the ancient language of our tribe as I lit the incense and scattered the petals over the grave. I don't know what I expected. Some sign from the ancestors, some indication that Nashoma was here— but I felt nothing, and saw nothing.

I was totally alone. And fuck, it felt that way.

I hung my head. "I'm sorry, Nashoma," I whispered. "I don't know why I'm here anymore."

I couldn't help being bitter. My life meant nothing.

I'd lost everything.

sophia
FOUR

A pparently, I *was* magic, but that was all Amelia had bothered telling me. It was an hour-long drive out of the Salt Lake Valley and back home to our cozy small town, but Amelia barely let me get a word in the whole time. By the time we got home the night of the lion attack, she'd worked herself up so much that I couldn't understand her ramblings. She threw around words like *Hawkei* and *Nivita*, as if she knew an entirely different language. I couldn't understand a word of it.

She blew up at Mom and Dad the second we walked through the door. "How could you lie to us?!" she demanded.

They acted deeply offended, like they couldn't believe Amelia would accuse them of such a thing.

Despite my desperate need to understand what was going on, Mom and Dad exiled me to my room to "deal with Amelia in private." I'd lain on my carpet with my ear pressed the vent in my floor and a blanket draped over my body, trying to hear everything downstairs. I couldn't hear most of what they were saying, and the bits and pieces I caught didn't make any sense.

"She can't go to Orenda," I heard Mom say. "She's a Koigni raised by Toaqua. The Elementai would have her killed."

I tried to tell myself that the events of that night hadn't actually happened, that I was drunk or something, but no matter how much I

21

tried to convince myself otherwise, I couldn't get over how *real* it felt. How my heart pounded at the sight of the lion. How my skin heated when the fire shot out of my palm. How Amelia looked at me like I wasn't her real sister.

And who knew? Maybe I wasn't...

Sometime during the night, I drifted off. I woke to the morning light and peeled my face off the vent grate. A glance in the mirror showed evenly spaced white and red lines across my skin where the grate had dug into my skin. That was going to take a while to smooth out.

I was still dressed in my athletic shorts and t-shirt from the day before. I was in desperate need of a shower, but clean hair and a change of clothes could wait.

I tossed my blanket to my bed and left the room in haste. I nearly tripped over our cat in the hallway. The stupid feline jumped out of the way and hissed at me. He shot daggers my way, like I'd seriously offended him.

If I wasn't used to Oliver's constant need to avoid me, I might've been intimidated by the thirty-pound beast and his razor-sharp claws, but he just turned from me and continued down the hallway.

The house was eerily quiet this morning, which gave me chills because there was *never* a silent moment when Amelia was home. I padded softly down the stairs, listening for signs that anyone else was awake. I was usually the last one up, so it'd shock me if the rest of my family was still in bed.

I reached the bottom of the stairs and heard the cling of dishes in the kitchen. I crossed the hall and peered into the room. Mom, Dad, and Amelia all sat around the table, quietly scooping cereal into their mouths. They *looked* like my mom and dad. Mom, with her dark brown hair piled on top of her head and the first signs of age touching the corner of her eyes. And Dad, with his salt and pepper hair and a shadow of scruff along his jawline. They looked the same as every other day, but they moved like robots.

I hesitated in the doorway. What could I possibly say to them?

So, I'm adopted? You lied to me? Spill it, Mom and Dad. If those are, in fact, your real names.

Mom glanced up from her cereal bowl and caught my eye in the doorway.

"Sophia," she said with a wide smile.

She was acting far too cheerful. Another reason I knew last night wasn't just a dream.

She stood and pulled the chair out from beside her. "Sit down, honey. I'll grab you a bowl."

My initial reaction told me to do as I was told. I wasn't one to touch conflict with a ten foot pole if I could avoid it. But I knew I couldn't avoid it this morning. No matter what I did, I needed to tackle this issue.

Dad eyed me like he couldn't believe I hadn't accepted my mother's invitation to join them. Amelia looked half-surprised, too, but she mostly avoided everyone's gazes. Another red flag. How many were we up to now?

Mom turned from the cupboard. "Sophia? Aren't you going to join us for breakfast?"

I crossed my arms. "The only thing I'm hungry for is answers."

Mom's brow furrowed as she set my bowl on the counter. "What do you mean, honey?"

I glanced to Dad, hoping he would respond to my request, but he only dug into his cereal like he hadn't heard me.

I swallowed. "Amelia told me I'm adopted."

Mom let out a laugh so loud that it made the rest of us jump in unison. "Oh, honey, Amelia was only teasing. *Of course* you're not adopted."

Mom was a terrible liar— even worse than I was.

Amelia shot to her feet and slammed her hands against the table top. A loud *bang* filled the air. Bruno, who I hadn't realized was lounging under the table, jumped to his feet and scurried out of the room. The dog, who looked more like a coyote than anything, nearly ran me over on his way out.

"Can we cut the bullshit?" Amelia snapped.

Mom and Dad exchanged a glance, but they didn't back down.

"You can't keep this from her forever!" Amelia yelled, her eyes darting between the two of them.

Finally, Dad sighed and straightened in his chair. "She already knows, Susan. We might as well tell her what we can."

Mom's lips tightened. "I hoped it would never come to this..."

"We knew it would, eventually." Dad turned to me. "Amelia is right. We adopted you."

The confirmation was like a knife through my back. I didn't want to believe it was true. It wasn't just that this family wasn't my own. It was the fact that all three of them had lied to me my entire life. Even Amelia, who I'd grown up spilling every last deep, dark secret to, had lied to me. I trusted my family with everything, but now... a knot tightened in my chest until I could hardly breathe. My knees shuddered, and I held myself up against the door frame. I wanted to scream, to spew all the hateful words that were racing through my mind, but I was afraid that if I opened my mouth more than just words would escape.

Mom rushed to my side and took my arm. "Sophia, honey. Sit down, please."

I hardly noticed her leading me across the kitchen to the empty chair closest to the door. I sank into it, but my mind raced so fast that it hardly felt like I was in the same room as them.

They lied to me. Who lies about this kind of thing?

"Why?" I heard the word escape my lips, but it took me a moment to realize that I'd spoken it. "Why would you lie to me about something like this? If I'm not your daughter... where did I come from?"

Mom and Dad looked to each other again. Their stalling was getting on my nerves.

"Just tell her," Amelia demanded. "Tell her, or I will."

Dad frowned and scooted his chair closer to me. "Sophia, everything we've done has been to protect you."

I pulled my hand away from his when he reached out for me. He didn't get to comfort me. Not right now. "Protect me from what?"

"From the Elementai," Amelia answered.

Mom shot her a heavy glare, but her expression quickly softened when she turned back to me. "You were placed in our protection when you were a baby. In our world, it's forbidden for a Toaqua to raise a Koigni. We wanted to raise you as our own, and we knew that we would care for you well, but we couldn't do it in our society. That's why we left."

"Toaqua? Koigni?" I repeated. The words didn't sound real.

"We come from a group of people with the ability to manipulate elements," Dad explained. "There are four Houses of Elementai. Toaqua— that's us— are able to manipulate water. Koigni can manipulate fire, while Nivita control earth and Yapluma control air. You have the power of Fire, Sophia."

"No." I denied the truth immediately. If my family was running some sort of prank, they obviously hadn't thought it through very well. "I can't be from the Fire House. I'm scared of fire. Everyone knows that."

I can't be from the Fire House. My own words echoed in my mind. I said them like it was possible I'd come from another House. Was I actually entertaining the idea that I *could* be one of these Elementai?

Mom shook her head slowly... regretfully. "We only let you *believe* you were afraid of fire."

"What?" I asked in shock. *Another lie.* "But I fell into a fire pit when I was a kid. You wouldn't even let us have bonfires, or a fireplace, because you said I was too afraid of them."

"We only said that to keep you away from fire," Mom admitted.

"So that I wouldn't control it and freak people out?" I demanded. Is that what I was? A freak?

"No," Dad insisted. "Elementai don't get their powers until they're older. Yours are still very weak. We made up the story about the fire pit to curb your fascination with it. Fire can't hurt you."

Explains why I have no burn scars.

My blood boiled at the confession. What else had they lied to me about?

I lifted my gaze to meet Amelia's from across the table. "This is all true?"

Her eyes filled with apology. She nodded.

"Why didn't you tell me, Am?" I whispered.

"You think I didn't *want* to tell you I could control water?" Amelia replied. "In case you don't remember, Mom and Dad lied to me, too! I had no idea you were Koigni. I thought you were a normal human, until yesterday."

I got to my feet and paced across the room. How could I possibly accept what they'd just told me? Magic didn't exist.

I whirled back toward them. "What else should I know about the Elementai, about the Koigni? What did I need protection from?"

I stared at Amelia, but she didn't seem to have an answer for me. Mom and Dad had both gone pale.

Mom was the first to speak. "None of that matters. The fewer questions you ask, the safer you'll be."

"Safe from what?" I demanded.

Nobody answered me. My jaw clenched so hard I was afraid I might crack a tooth.

Finally, Mom stood. She pulled me into a hug. I wanted to push her away, but her hug was both a betrayal and a comfort. No matter what she lied about, she was still my mom, and nothing beat a mother's touch.

I still hated her right now.

"Sophia," Mom whispered into my ear. "I'm sorry we can't be more honest with you. You're just going to have to trust us."

The thing was, I wasn't sure I'd ever trust my parents again.

THREE DAYS HAD PASSED, and I was still avoiding my parents as often as I could. They didn't want to open up to me, so I refused to open up back. Amelia, at least, was sympathetic. She found me sitting on our old swing set in the backyard. We hadn't used the thing in years, but right now, it felt like the only thing that was normal.

It was pouring rain, and I was soaked.

I didn't want her sitting next to me. I wanted to be alone. But Amelia wasn't the type to give people space when they needed it. She took the swing beside me and opened her hands. The rain had stopped. I looked up and noticed that Amelia had made some sort of force field around us so that the rain slid off thin air and stopped pouring on me.

"That's kind of creepy," I said flatly.

"You'll be able to do creepy things, too." She smiled at me, but I didn't smile back. Instead, I scowled at Kiwi on her shoulder because I'd rather look at him than stare her in the eye.

"Come on, Sophia," Amelia encouraged. "You have to talk to me eventually."

"How can I talk to people who lie to me?" I bit back.

She frowned. "That's not fair."

"Really?" I said sarcastically. "Then why don't you tell me what really happened the other night?"

"It was a mountain lion attack," Amelia insisted, just like every other time I dared to bring it up.

"I've seen pictures of mountain lions," I said. "That thing was bigger."

"It just looked bigger because of all the adrenaline." She wouldn't budge on the topic, but I could still tell she was lying. If she really thought it was a mountain lion, she wouldn't have gone to investigate it.

"There are still other things you lied to me about," I pointed out.

"You're being unfair," Amelia said. "I knew you were adopted, but I didn't know you were one of us."

"Exactly," I emphasized. "You knew I was adopted, and you didn't say anything."

"It wasn't my secret to tell," Amelia said.

I bit my lower lip. "But we tell each other everything, Am."

"You don't understand," Amelia argued. "I couldn't tell you about the Elementai. Everything in our world has to be kept secret... for our survival."

I paused, considering this. "What's your world like?"

"It's *ah-mazing*," Amelia sighed with a dreamy look in her eyes. "It's incredible. It's everything you ever wanted. Imagine the best dream you've ever had, and then multiply that by a hundred. Orenda Academy was my home, and it'll be your home, too."

My home? "What do you mean?"

"You get to spend four years learning how to use your powers and how to take care of magical creatures," Amelia stated simply.

27

"Magical creatures?" I asked warily. My first thoughts flickered to the fat naked plant babies that came screaming out of the dirt in *Harry Potter*.

"Yes," Amelia said with a smile. "It's an Elementai's duty to take care of all animals that have magic. You'll learn more when you get to the academy. You'll bond with your Familiar, and—"

"My Familiar?" I asked. It was like she was speaking in riddles again.

"Your creature," Amelia clarified while stroked Kiwi's feathers. "Kiwi is mine. Bruno is Dad's, and Oliver is Mom's."

"Wait. Mom and Dad have Familiars?"

"Yes. Every Elementai has one."

"What is it?" I asked.

"A Familiar? It's your lifetime companion," Amelia explained. "The most important relationship you'll ever have."

I still didn't really understand Familiars, but if mine was anything like Kiwi, I'd take it back. The thought that creatures like dragons, unicorns, and griffins really existed made me feel worse. How had I gone my entire life knowing nothing about who I was? This was too much information at once.

"I'm probably going to bond with a plant," I said dully.

"Don't say that. Your Familiar is going to be so awesome. I just know it," Amelia said.

"So... what exactly did you learn at this school? Like, Water Math?" I asked.

Amelia laughed loudly. "No, Sophia. You learn how to use your powers, and how to use them to work together with your Familiar. You'll be in Fire classes, learning how to use your Fire magic."

I didn't know if I wanted to learn Fire magic. I would burn up my plant.

Amelia smacked herself in the head. "That's right! You're Koigni! You're going to have classes with Madame Doya."

"Madame Doya?" Her name sounded harsh, even when I said it. "The title sounds so formal."

"We only call her *madame* because she's on the Elder Council," Amelia explained. "She's really young to be an Elder, too. Like, Mom and Dad's age. Anyway, she's a total bitch. I had her for one class, and we never got along, mostly because she's so mean. She's probably going to hate you, too, because you're my sister. But maybe not, because she's the Dean of your House. She loves her little Koigni pets."

"Oh, great." I already had a strike against me. Madame Doya sounded horrible, like the kind of person who would find pleasure in whipping students if it were allowed.

Amelia was rambling now. "I loved Orenda Academy. There were so many hot guys from the other Houses, but I never got a chance to hook up with them because it was forbidden."

"Huh?" I really didn't want to hear about my sister hooking up, but the forbidden part sounded intriguing.

"People aren't allowed to mate between Houses. You can only date people within your own element class," Amelia explained. "You'll learn all about it once you get there."

Amelia made Orenda Academy sound perfect the more she talked about it. Yet there was so much I still didn't know. I wasn't good with the unknown. I was good with comfortable. *Nothing* about the Elementai made me feel comfortable.

There was still this voice in the back of my head telling me that Amelia was pulling my leg. But I knew that all of this... whatever it was... was real.

Eventually, I stood and headed inside. Amelia followed me in with Kiwi, and the force field around us trailed us to the front door. It shut off once we stepped inside, and the rain that had piled on top of it splashed down onto the porch steps.

"Do you really think I'll fit in at Orenda Academy?" I asked my sister as we entered the kitchen.

"No, because you're not going." Dad's sharp voice cut across the room before Amelia could answer. He had a coffee in his hand, but nothing else. He'd been watching us.

"How can you say that?" Amelia asked, disgusted. "She's an Elementai. It's where she belongs."

"She can't go. We'll find another way," Dad said, before he turned his back and left the room.

Whatever that meant.

"I guess that settles it," I said, defeated. "It doesn't matter what I know or don't know about Orenda Academy, because Mom and Dad won't let me go anyway."

Amelia just smiled... like she knew something I didn't.

My sister and I ate dinner in front of the TV every night since the lion attack. Mom and Dad didn't say anything about it, even though they had a strict no-food-in-the-living-room policy. They just let me avoid them. I wasn't sure if they were giving me my space or if they were avoiding me as well.

Amelia and I were curled up on the couch with our dinner when the doorbell rang the following night. Amelia didn't even blink and kept her eyes on the TV.

I stretched my foot across the couch and nudged her. "Get the door, Am. You're closer."

Amelia frowned. "*You* get it. I don't even live here anymore. I'm a *guest*."

I groaned, but set my dinner plate on the coffee table and rose to my feet anyway. I ran my fingers through my ponytail. I hadn't bothered with makeup today and was sure I looked like a slob. It was probably just a neighbor or something, so I guess I didn't really care what I looked like.

At least, I didn't until I opened the door. The guy standing in front of me looked nothing like one of my neighbors. He looked more like a security guard. A *hot* security guard, only without the uniform. He was tall, at least a half a foot taller than me, and made of muscle. His skin was a deep brown, and his straight black hair hung past his shoulders. His eyes were dark, and his jaw strong. He stood with his feet in a wide stance and his hands crossed in front of him, like he was here on some sort of official business.

He could officially business me. I mean, if I didn't faint into his arms like a crazy fangirl first. Did he have a fan club? Because I'd totally join.

"Sophia Henley?" he asked. Even his voice was hot.

Oh, God. He knows my name.

I stood in the doorway, my mouth agape. A million questions raced through my mind. Who are you? How do you know my name? Why didn't I put makeup on today? Did I even brush my hair? Why do you look like a god?

"Uhh..." That was all that came out of my mouth. I was officially an idiot.

"Who is it, Sophia?" Amelia called from the living room.

The guy's eyebrows rose at the confirmation of my name.

"I... uh..." *Good. You got one word out. Try another.* "Yeah, I'm Sophia. And you?"

"Liam," he said in a clipped tone, like he was in too much of a hurry to introduce himself properly. "I'm here to escort you to Orenda Academy of Magical Creatures."

What?!

"Amelia!" I shouted, never taking my eyes off Liam.

"What?" Amelia rushed into the hallway. Alarm settled on her face until her eyes fell upon Liam. Her expression immediately softened, but it held a hint of confusion. "They sent a student?"

"Yes," Liam said, though he didn't care to elaborate.

I stepped back from the doorway, suddenly feeling like I should be slamming the door in this guy's face. Mom and Dad *did* say they were trying to protect me from the Elementai, and here one was, standing on my front steps uninvited.

"Am, what's going on?" I asked in a shaky voice.

She didn't have a chance to answer before Mom and Dad entered the hall from the kitchen.

"Girls, what's—?" Mom's voice cut off when she caught sight of Liam in the doorway.

"Mr. and Mrs. Henley," Liam greeted with a nod of his head, like he already knew for certain who my parents were. The least he could do was say their names with some respect considering he was at their house, but he sounded more bored than anything, like he was forcing himself to be formal.

"Come inside," Amelia offered.

"Hold on," Dad objected before Liam had a chance to move. "What's this about?"

"I'm from Orenda Academy," Liam said. "I've been assigned to escort Sophia—"

"No," Mom cut him off. "Absolutely not. If you think we're going to let some Koigni come and take Sophia—"

"I'm not Koigni!" Liam spat, as if the word was poison on his tongue. "I'm Toaqua."

"Can we *not* have this conversation out in the open?" Amelia grabbed a handful of Liam's shirt and dragged him inside. She slammed the door behind him.

I whirled toward my parents. "I thought I wasn't going to Orenda Academy."

I still hadn't decided if it was something I *wanted* to do. Amelia kept saying it was where I was meant to be, but according to my parents, I'd be facing some unknown danger there. I wasn't exactly excited about throwing myself straight into harm's way without knowing what I'd be up against, no matter how much I wanted to spite my parents.

"You aren't," Mom said with certainty. She turned to Liam. "How did the school find out about Sophia?"

Liam's jaw tightened. "I don't know. They didn't tell me."

"I did." Amelia stepped forward. "I told them about Sophia."

Mom's hands clutched over her chest, horrified. "Amelia, what have you done?"

"I realize you're trying to protect our family from a lifetime of shame," Amelia said, "but Sophia has to go. She has to find her Familiar. If she doesn't—"

"You don't know what will happen if she goes to that school!" Dad roared.

Everyone's eyes went wide in stunned silence— except Liam, who still looked bored. My dad was always a gentle person, so to hear him yell... it was unusual, to say the least.

Dad's tone softened. "There's more going on here than you realize."

"Then tell us!" Amelia demanded.

Dad's gaze dropped. "It's... complicated."

"How can you say that?" Amelia cried. "Nothing's more important than your Familiar bond. You should both know that. How could
you hide this from her? What were you planning to do when the day
came for Sophia to bond and she didn't have a Familiar to bond with?"

Mom and Dad both dropped their heads. I steadied myself against
the banister in the hallway, trying to keep my heart from racing a
million miles per hour. I couldn't stand that they were fighting over
me. If I knew what to do, I'd step in and end this argument right then
and there, but the fact was, I had no clue if I was supposed to side with
my parents or with Amelia.

"We knew it would happen eventually," Mom said in a near whisper. "We just... didn't know what to do about it. We were hoping we
had more time."

"She's eighteen!" Amelia shouted, as if it was obvious their time
was up.

Liam cleared his throat, and all eyes turned to him. "If I may... the
Elders are aware of your crimes."

Crimes? Oh, crap. Were my parents criminals?

"They're willing to pardon you if you let Sophia come to Orenda
Academy," Liam continued. "That being said, she *will* be attending
one way or another. I suggest you take the deal the Elders are
offering."

My head swam with the information Liam just revealed. They'd
get me to that school *one way or another*. What were they going to do?
Hold me prisoner? Take me by force?

This was all too much. My knees could no longer hold me up, and
I sank onto the bottom stair next to the door.

"If you don't mind, I'd rather not get involved with your family
affairs," Liam said. "I'll give Sophia time to pack her bags and say her
goodbyes. I'll be waiting at the coffee shop three blocks from here. If
she's not there in three hours, I'll be forced to contact the Elders. If
you decide to run, they'll be shortly behind you."

Was he *threatening* us? Ugh, this guy was a total jackass. Cross me
off the fan club list. I wasn't going anywhere with him.

Liam turned on his heel and swung the front door open. We all

33

stared, dumbfounded, behind him. It wasn't until the sound of the door slamming stopped echoing in my ears that Amelia finally broke the silence.

"I can't believe you two," she snarled at my parents.

I didn't hear their reply, because I shot to my feet and raced up the stairs. I needed a moment alone to absorb what just happened.

In the safety of my own room, I finally had a chance to run everything over in my mind. I tugged my hair tie from my ponytail and paced back and forth across the room.

"I'm an Elementai. My parents are criminals. I'm being forced to go to Orenda Academy; otherwise, my parents will be punished," I whispered to myself. Saying it out loud didn't help ease my nerves.

How did my world change so much in just a matter of a few days?

A light knock came at my door. Before I could tell whoever it was to give me a moment of peace, Amelia poked her head into my room.

"Hey, Sophia," she said softly.

I fell onto my bed and buried my face in my hands. "What's happening, Amelia?"

I heard her cross the carpet and felt the weight of her body as she sat beside me on the bed. I expected her to hug me or something, but I wasn't sure I wanted her to. Though she'd been the most understanding about all of this, she was still a part of it. She didn't touch me, though.

"I know I don't have any clue on what you're going through," Amelia said. "But I really think you need to follow Liam to Orenda Academy."

"Why?" I asked, my voice muffled in my hands. I could just run away... somewhere the Elementai couldn't find me.

"Because you need to find your Familiar," Amelia pressed.

"I don't care about that," I said.

"I know you can't understand yet how important this is for you." Amelia's voice was soft, sad. "But if you can't do it for yourself, do it for Mom and Dad."

I finally lifted my gaze to meet hers. "What will they do to them if I don't go?"

Amelia swallowed. "My guess is they'd kill their Familiars. It's the worst thing that can happen to an Elementai, to lose your Familiar. Worse even than death."

This was so wrong. The Elders or whatever couldn't force me to go. Except... they could, and they were.

Bruno and Oliver would be killed, and Mom and Dad would never be the same. I couldn't do that to them, even though they had lied to me.

"Just keep your head down like you always have," Amelia advised. "Steer clear of Doya, and don't get yourself into any trouble. That should be easy for you."

True, considering I'd pretty much been invisible my whole life. I had every intention of staying invisible.

"Here." Amelia shoved a pair of folded jeans toward me. I hadn't even realized she'd been holding them.

The jeans we'd been fighting over.

"Am, I can't," I declined.

"Take them, Sophia," she demanded. "Take them, and think of me every time you wear them."

I couldn't believe this was happening. I didn't even realize I'd made a decision until I reached out and took the jeans.

"I should probably say goodbye to Mom and Dad," I whispered.

"No," Amelia insisted. "Even though they lied to you, they still love you. They'd risk their lives— and their Familiars— for you. You have to leave before they realize it."

My heart broke into a million pieces, but instead of feeling pain rip through my chest, I only felt numb. That numb sensation was probably the only thing that got me to rise from the bed and begin packing with Amelia.

Orenda Academy, I hope you're worth it.

Liam

FIVE

I hated coffee, but I needed it to keep me awake, because I'd been up for the past three days.

I rubbed my face and stared at the stain on the table in the coffee shop. At this hour, no one was in here but me. I'd been waiting *forever*. I told Sophia to meet me here hours ago. What was taking so long?

Elders be damned. I wasn't going to waste my time waiting for some spoiled prep to figure out she wanted to grow up and join the real world. I was about to get up and get back on the ship to Orenda Academy when the door opened.

In stepped Sophia. She had a duffel bag full of clothes and a lost puppy-dog look.

She was hot, I guess. Long, chestnut brown hair, chocolate eyes, and a body that was totally bang-worthy. She caught my gaze. Ripples ricocheted in a shock wave through my stomach.

Then I remembered who I was, and everything inside me shut down. No girl wanted to be with someone like me— a crippled failure who'd lost their Familiar. Besides, she was Koigni, I was Toaqua. *Never going to happen.*

Amelia wasn't with her this time, thank the ancestors. Sophia sat down at my table and went to speak, but I got up and ordered her something. She looked like a chai latte kind of girl. I pressed it into her hands, and she looked down at it.

"Thanks." She looked up. "But I don't drink—"

"You're going to need it," I told her. "The walk to the ship is cold."

"Ship?" she echoed.

I resisted rolling my eyes. Never mind. I didn't think she was hot. She was annoying, and completely clueless. I couldn't stand people who weren't on top of things, and Sophia was about a hundred pages behind everyone else. I'd be babysitting a toddler until we got back to school.

She reminded me of a little kid. And that's exactly what I'd call her.

"Follow me, *pawee*." I stood up. She trailed me, sipping at her latte. I carried her duffel bag, though the weight of it instantly brought my fatigue surging back.

"Do you need help?" She caught me struggling.

"I got it," I told her as we exited the coffee shop and started down the street. I wasn't about to let her think I couldn't carry a duffel bag. Though it was getting *really hard* to keep faking it. A duffel bag full of clothes felt like a military backpack weighing me down.

Being disabled was a real pain in the ass.

We got out of the city limits and into the desert. Sophia hesitated when she reached the town sign. She touched it, then looked back at her old home.

"Well, come on," I said. I was trying not to gasp for breath, and trying to act normal, but it was hard. "I'm not going to abduct you."

Sophia snorted and shoved past me. "You couldn't abduct me if you tried."

Sadly, she was probably right.

We walked a mile into the desert, which might as well have been ten miles for me. I kept up a brave face so she didn't notice that my body was screaming. When the lights of the town had dissolved behind us, I dropped the duffel bag and struggled not to drop to my knees, looking up.

I took the golden pass out of my pocket and waved it in the air. Sophia looked at me like I was crazy.

We waited a few minutes. The desert was chilly at night. Sophia shivered. I told the cold to piss off.

"What... what are we waiting for?" she asked reluctantly.

"That," I told her. My eyes never left the sky as the clouds parted. Sophia jumped as the blaring horn of a ship coming into port echoed all around us.

Her mouth dropped open, and I grinned. From the sky descended a massive cruise liner, over a thousand feet in length, equally as tall and weighing two-hundred thousand tons. The ship was painted white, with elements of stark gold here and there. Sophia went to run, but I grabbed her arm and held her in place as the massive ship descended. It could fit over ten thousand passengers, along with two-thousand crew members, but there were rarely that many people on it. Elementai only used it when they wanted to go on vacations, mostly, and when the government insiders needed to get back home.

It wasn't meant to transport students, yet here we were.

The ship came to a slow park in front of us, the bottom suspended about a hundred feet in the air, before two Elementai on the ship's sides waved their hands. The earth jutted up above us and formed steps, a staircase made out of desert dirt, rock, and sand that met the cruise ship's platform. Two Familiars, a pegasus and a toucan, both landed on the ground beside the earth staircase and bowed to us.

"Welcome to the *Hozho*, the Elementai's premier cruise ship," I told her. "It's how we'll be getting to the Academy."

"It... it..." Her mouth bobbed up and down like a fish's.

"Yes, *pawee*, it can fly," I told her. "Hurry up."

Sophia grabbed her bag before I could (thank the ancestors) and ran after me. I began the climb up the long, torturous staircase, which was the last thing I needed after that walk.

"Why are you going so slow?" Sophia complained behind me.

"Shut up." I was already out of breath. We finally reached the top, and an Elementai reached out her hand.

"May I take that bag for you and deliver it to your cabin, miss?" she asked Sophia.

"Um," Sophia started.

"We'll be staying overnight. It's a long flight to the Academy," I told her. *Not to mention this big-ass ship doesn't move very fast.*

Sophia handed off her bag, and I gestured for her to follow me. The staircase was pushed back into the earth. The doors closed behind us and the *Hozho* rattled as it rose into the sky once more.

Sophia clung to the railing like a cat, shaking and terrified. I rolled my eyes this time.

"Come on." I grabbed her arm again and hauled her after me, from the deck and into the inside of the ship. Sophia's head went from this way to that as she tried to take in all of her surroundings and failed. The carpet was lush green with swirling designs, and the walls were wooden paneling with gold railings. We passed all sorts of shops, such as rare jewelers, clothing stores, and places that sold souvenirs and chocolates.

I think the Elementai with their Familiars is what impressed her the most. She had to be careful to avoid accidentally stepping on anyone in the crowded hallway. Elementai had birds on their shoulders, or small animals like rabbits or chinchillas in their arms. Dogs followed at the heels of their Elementai, while big cats like tigers and jaguars stuck together, yowling as if they were having some sort of conversation. Sophia had to press to the wall to let a moose with antlers that were as wide as the hallway pass by. Above us and imbedded in the ceiling was a huge inner tube filled with water. Water creatures, like manatees and otters, swam to where they needed to go.

Once, a unicorn shoved her out of the way. Sophia went to pet it, but I grabbed her hand.

"Don't touch another person's Familiar without permission," I told her sharply. "It's not allowed."

Yep, like watching a toddler. I dragged her out of the hallway and onto the deck, where it was more quiet. All around us was the murky grey of the clouds and a touch of condensation, a hint of the Toaqua on board doing their job.

She gasped when I led her to the main lobby. A crystal chandelier hung from the center, opening up to a massive ballroom with stained-glass windows and a shiny wooden dance floor. A classical band played soft music while attendants checked in guests. I gave our passes to the Elementai at the front desk, who handed us two key cards.

Sophia wasn't paying attention. She was twirling around on the dance floor like a princess in a fairy tale.

"It's gorgeous," Sophia said, looking around.

"It's something." I'd been riding the *Hozho* since I was a kid, but it still never failed to impress me. They were always adding more and more onto it. I was pretty sure there was a movie theater and an ice rink somewhere in here. Personally, I'd been fine with the waterpark. I'd been on this ship a million times over the years, and I still hadn't seen everything.

The ship bobbed up and down like a real cruise liner would, only it rode the air currents instead of the waves. I was a Toaqua, so I was immune to getting seasick, but Sophia looked a little green.

"Come on. Let's get something to eat," I told her.

"But I just had dinner," she protested.

"Yeah, well, good for you. I didn't." I led her to my favorite restaurant— known for native Hawkei food. It was late, so we didn't have to wait for a table. We sat on the deck outside the restaurant and watched the tiny hydras and dolphins playing in the pool below. Their Elementai swam and chatted in the water. They were Toaqua, so they manipulated the water to splash each other, causing mini-waves.

Their happy screams made me remember what I'd lost.

"You want anything?" I asked, looking up from my menu.

She shook her head. "No, I'm fine."

"Well, that's not happening," I muttered. She needed some food in her, to combat the sickness. Riding the *Hozho* on an empty stomach was a recipe for disaster, and I wasn't going to be holding the trash can all night for this girl. I'd seen her plate when I'd gotten to her house— she'd barely eaten her dinner. She had to be starving by now.

The waiter came back, and I said, "I would like the salted salmon with a side of buffalo stew. She'll have some acorn bread and ginger ale."

"Liam, I don't—"

I gave her a look, and she shut up.

I handed the waiter our menus. He came back with the acorn

bread a moment later, and I nudged it toward Sophia. "Go on. It'll help."

She nibbled on it, and I noticed the green in her skin subsided. She ate half of the loaf, and I grinned. She'd lied about not being hungry.

When her ginger ale was half-gone, she put down the drink and sighed. "Thanks. I do feel a little better now."

I smiled. "Good."

By this time, my food was out. I was a gross eater, a true carnivore, but there was no shame in it. I really didn't care if people thought I was nasty. I inhaled the soup and started tearing into the salmon with my bare hands seconds after, chewing loudly. There was sauce smeared on the side of my cheek. Sophia stared at me with a disgusted look on her face, her nose wrinkled and lip curled.

I was starving. That was the only thing worth sticking around for anymore, the food.

I put the plates aside and wiped my face. Sophia was giggling.

"What?" I asked, throwing the napkin down.

"Nothing." The waiter took the plates away, and Sophia stared at me. "So, I've been meaning to ask you a few questions."

Oh, goody. "Like what?"

"Well, for starters... how the heck is this thing flying around, and why hasn't anyone noticed it yet? It's a huge cruise ship!" she belted.

"The Yapluma use the power of Air to keep the ship flying and afloat, while Toaqua move clouds in front of the liner so it isn't spotted by outsiders," I informed her. "The Koigni keep the boiler room running, so the rudder has control over where the ship is directed. The Nivita help it land and build the staircase. We all work together to make the ship possible."

"That's weird. Amelia made it sound like the different Houses hated each other," Sophia said.

She's not wrong. "Amelia was exaggerating. Yapluma and Nivita are opposites as Air and Earth, but they get along fine. Like I said, we all need to work together to stay alive and underground."

"I'm guessing Fire and Water don't mix?" Sophia asked.

There was a rolling in my stomach, and I shook my head. "No. To be honest, it would be weird for people at school to see you, a Koigni, talking to me, a Toaqua, outside of class."

She nodded glumly. "My House sounds terrible."

I wanted to high-five her, but I gave a diplomatic answer instead, because it's what my dad would expect me to do. "Our entire world is about unity. We need each other to keep our society running," I informed her. "That's why most of the Elementai live together, in the area around Orenda Academy."

"I thought Elementai would be all over the world." She sat upright.

"No. There are some Elementai spread around the earth and throughout the world governments. They're put there to keep our world secret. But most of the Elementai live together in Northern California, which is where we're going. It's... unheard of for an Elementai to be away from the tribe like your family is." I eyed her.

"Tribe?" she questioned.

"All Elementai come from one ancient tribe, the Hawkei. We still follow their customs and live in the same area they originated from long ago."

"Like Native Americans?" She stared at me blankly.

"There are many indigenous societies. All of them have their own traditions and are very different. The Hawkei are no exception," I said.

"I've never heard of the Hawkei before. They weren't in any history books I read," Sophia replied.

"We don't let in outsiders for a reason. Keeping our culture and stories secret is one of the only reasons our people are still alive." I crossed my arms.

"Amelia said something like that." She looked away from me. "But... I notice all the Elementai look different."

I sighed. "We... that includes you... have married and intermingled with many different cultures throughout the centuries."

"Oh." She sipped at her latte again. It was taking her forever to finish it. It was getting on my nerves. She didn't ask any more questions about the original tribe, which made it obvious she was the type of person that didn't care about history or tradition.

Oh, we were going to get along *splendidly*. And by splendidly, I meant not at all.

"Are there other... magic people in the world?" Sophia asked. "Or are there just Elementai?"

"There are a few groups who have magical powers. But none of them can bond with animals like Elementai can, and their magic is different. Only we control the elements. Our kind doesn't associate with them. We keep to ourselves."

"I feel like I'm so far behind." She dropped her eyes.

Tell me about it. "You'll catch up, *pawee*. I promise."

"Why do you keep calling me that?" Her eyebrows knitted together. "*Pawee?*"

"It means *little child*," I told her, smirking. "Because you act like such a kid."

"Thanks," Sophia said sourly. It made me smile more.

What I didn't tell her was there was another meaning behind the word, too. But that was a secret.

I stood. "It's nearly midnight. We should really get to bed. The ship will come into port early tomorrow."

Sophia followed me out of the restaurant. The traffic had started to die down, and many Elementai had returned to their cabins. We were basically alone out here.

I rounded a corner before Sophia did. I stopped in my tracks when I saw a large lioness prowling the deck, her eyes searching for something.

Naomi. I'd seen her, but she hadn't seen me... yet.

I didn't have anything to hide. I was bringing Sophia back, like Madame Doya wanted. There was no reason for her Familiar to bother me. Even so, just being around Naomi made me feel like a criminal— like I had something to hide.

Dad always said to follow my instincts. I wasn't about to question them now. Before Sophia knew what was happening I latched onto her, then dragged her behind a collection of lifeboats with parachutes, hugging her tightly to my body.

Sophia screamed. I slapped my hand over her mouth and whispered, "Be quiet! Someone's coming!"

Sophia's eyes widened when she saw the cat, then she went silent. Naomi stopped in front of the lifeboats, then raised her nose to sniff the air. Her lip curled, and she made a rumbling noise of discontentment before she moved on, her steps heavy with intent.

I didn't breathe until the lioness was gone. What was Naomi doing here? Madame Doya was at the school. Why were they separated?

Sophia kept quiet until I let her go. We stepped out from behind the lifeboats, and Sophia cried, "What the heck is that stupid cat doing here?"

"You know her?" My eyes widened.

"Yeah! That cat attacked me and my sister when we were hiking in the woods the other day," Sophia explained.

"Was anyone with her?" I asked quickly. "A woman?"

"Not that I know of," Sophia said slowly. "I just thought she was wild. She must be a Familiar. She seemed really focused on my sister."

My mind raced. What the hell had Amelia Henley been up to while she was at school?

"That cat is Madame Doya's Familiar," I told her. "I'm assuming you don't know her."

"No. But Amelia mentioned her." Sophia tapped her chin with a finger, thinking. "You mean to tell me that the lion who attacked me and Madame Doya are bonded?"

"Yes."

"But... Amelia told me it was just a mountain lion," she said quietly. "She should've known that was Madame Doya's Familiar. She took classes with her."

"Naomi is an African lioness, not a mountain. Amelia knows who she is. She lied to you." I had to be blunt. Sophia deserved to know the truth.

"She lied? Again?" Sophia deflated. Her face went into a pitiful, upset look.

"There has to be a reason for it." I struggled to recover, because even though I didn't like Amelia, I knew Sophia loved her and I really didn't want to get in the middle of family drama. "Maybe she was just trying to protect you."

"Maybe." Sophia chewed her lip. "But why not tell me the truth? What was she trying to protect me from?"

I hesitated. "Your guess is as good as mine."

This wasn't good. Madame Doya and Naomi couldn't be separated. If they were apart, it meant that they were looking into something important. Amelia had been poking her nose in places where it didn't belong, and I didn't like it.

Sophia crossed her arms. "Why would Madame Doya send her Familiar after us?"

I could think of a few good reasons, but I shrugged and said, "I don't know."

She didn't seem satisfied with my answer.

I led Sophia to her cabin. She used the keycard to get in. Inside, there were dozens of little Familiars making everything perfect. Hummingbirds plumped the pillows and straightened out the sheets, while monkeys and lemurs polished the mirrors and floors. They bowed to us as we came in before they scuttled away. I noticed that the Elders had spared no expense in Sophia's room. It was one of the nicest suites on the ship, with a King sized bed, a mini-bar, a living-room area collected around a fireplace, and a window that showed the clouds sailing by. She even got a kitchen, something my suite didn't have. Her duffel bag had been placed on the dresser. I noticed a pair of her pajamas had been neatly folded and set out for her immediate use.

She took a peek in the bathroom and squealed when she saw a Jacuzzi big enough to fit four people. There was also a vanity and a widescreen TV inside the room. I'm pretty sure her toilet was one of those weird ones that talks to you.

I myself was looking forward to getting into my own Jacuzzi tonight and not coming out for a really, really long time. My body was sore.

A raccoon wearing a sailor's hat and an apron pushed a little cart into the room. He handed Sophia a warm towel scented with lavender and a tiny box of chocolates.

"Thank you," she told him. The raccoon tottered out with his cart and shut the door behind him.

"Now that's what I call service," she said in a bright voice. She squealed happily before jumping on the bed.

By the ancestors, this girl was lame. And really cheesy. Why couldn't she just be cool?

"My room is right across the hall if you need anything," I told her. I really hoped she didn't come by. My duty was done, as far as I was concerned.

"I think I'm just going to hit the hay," she told me. I resisted snorting. She got off the bed and stood in front of me. "Thanks for showing me around, Liam. I really appreciate it. This ship is incredible."

Don't get used to it. "Like I said, I'm right across from you if you need anything."

She beamed at me, and I felt funny again, but it was probably just my nausea kicking in. I always felt sick after I ate these days. I headed across the room to my suite and filled up my tub, grabbing a beer out of the mini-fridge. I wasn't supposed to drink anymore, because it would probably make me feel worse, but screw it. Maybe the alcohol would help me sleep for the first time in days.

I laughed a little when I thought of Sophia. She was so naive. If she thought the ship was awesome, she hadn't seen anything yet.

Just wait till she got to the castle.

sophia
SIX

The cruise ship horn blared, sending a wave of disappointment over me. Liam and I stood on the deck as the ship descended into port the next day.

"What's wrong?" Liam asked with a heavy sigh.

"This ship is just so magical," I replied. "I'm not ready to leave."

He scoffed.

"What?" I asked. Had I said something wrong?

He just shook his head. "You've got a lot to learn, *pawee*."

Liam pointed over the railing. I peeked over the edge, and what I saw took my breath away.

"Welcome to Kinpago," Liam said.

Below, the clouds parted. Tall mountain peaks rose around us, but they were different from the mountains back home. These were covered with tall trees and lush greenery, and the caps were painted with snow. In the distance, a waterfall cascaded down the side of the mountain. To my other side, the ocean reached out to the horizon.

A city with winding streets stretched far across the valley. The buildings were short, no more than two or three stories high, and most were hidden beneath a thick layer of trees. There were all sorts of houses, but they were unlike any houses I'd ever seen. They were almost like elaborate huts, with stucco walls and thatch roofs. The streets were dirt, and there weren't any cars, just carriages pulled by an array of creatures like pegasi and unicorns. Thousands of people were down there, venturing in and out of little shops. It looked like a city straight out of a fairy tale.

"Get your bags," Liam said. "It's time to go."

Minutes later we descended a long flight of stairs made from earth. I couldn't take my eyes off the city in front of me. From this vantage point, there seemed to be a unique charm to it. I had the urge to explore the entire valley.

The air was chilly, in stark contrast to the dry desert air I was used to. I pulled my cardigan tighter around me as we made our way down the steps.

"You cold?" Liam asked.

"Yeah," I said. "It's a lot colder here than back home."

Liam shrugged. "You'll get used to it. Plus, you're Koigni, so it should be easy for you to stay warm."

I barely heard what he said, since the city once again stole my attention as we got up close. At the base of the staircase vendors lined the street, like we were walking straight into a magical farmer's market. I saw one group in a unicorn-drawn carriage. Another guy rode on the back of a huge beast that looked like a bear with horns. Large plants of all shapes and colors, bigger than even some houses, bloomed out of gorgeous painted pots. Streamers and banners, along with little stringed lights, criss-crossed over our heads and connected to various buildings. Every shop looked different, some with hand-painted signs, and others with ones that looked like they were made of metal. It was like everywhere I looked there was a different color, or something else going on. There were so many different smells, like bread cooking, and cinnamon and other spices. I heard music coming from all directions, along with laughter and conversation. It was so loud I had trouble hearing myself think.

"You're in the center of the city, where you'll find most of the stores, restaurants, and shops. All your magical needs can be supplied here," Liam said, like he wanted to get this over with. "Behind us near the cruise port are offices and shopping centers. Each part of Kinpago is split into various cultural districts, though the Hawkei district, the one we're now in, is the largest. For example, the Latin district is directly on the left, three blocks down, and on the other side is the Gay Quarter. About a mile down Main Street is Chinatown. You can find Little Bavaria on the other side."

Liam rattled on and on about all the areas of Kinpago, so quickly that it was tough for me to keep up with him. It seemed like every country from around the world was packed into the crooked streets and small spaces. People of all colors and nationalities crowded the streets, dressed in everything from casual daywear to traditional clothes from various places around the world.

Were they really all descended from the Hawkei tribe? Everyone looked so different. I'd never been in a place so culturally diverse...

"I didn't realize Kinpago would be so big," I said, glancing around in wonder.

Liam shrugged. "There are maybe ten, fifteen thousand people per tribe."

"Tribe?" I asked. "There are more than just the Hawkei here?"

"No. We're all Hawkei," Liam answered, sounding irritated. "I'm referring to the four Houses. Earth, Water, Fire and Air."

"Oh," I said, but I was quickly distracted.

The only things more beautiful than the people were the Familiars. They came in all shapes and sizes, their fur purple and blue and sometimes multi-colored. Elephants with rainbow manes and purple skin walked beside cats that had scales. A four-legged mammal the size of a horse, but that looked like a weasel with a large furry white mane and feathers, blinked at me before its Elementai called her, and she vanished before my very eyes.

I was pretty sure there weren't even names for some of these gorgeous creatures. They were things I hadn't even imagined seeing in story books.

In the middle of the street, a man in a beautiful outfit that was embroidered with beads and decorated with feathers danced to a couple of street musicians playing on flutes and drums. I wanted to stop to watch, but Liam grabbed my wrist and dragged me behind him.

I resisted his hold, my pace slowing to take it all in. A nearby booth buzzed with small critters. They were the color of emerald tiger beetles with wings like dragonflies. They glowed a soft yellow, blinking on and off like fireflies.

"Fortune Fairies!" the guy behind the booth shouted. "Get your Fortune Fairies! Said to bring you good luck and change your future."

I took a step toward them, but I didn't make it far before Liam tugged on my arm.

"Hey!" I protested. I just wanted to see what they looked like up close.

"Don't waste your money," Liam said. "Fortune Fairies are easy enough to catch on your own. Besides, they don't bring fortune to everyone."

While he spoke, my eyes fell upon white winged stallion ahead of us. My breath left my chest, and I stopped right there in the middle of the street. Children swarmed the pegasus and petted its soft white fur. The sign in front of its stall advertised pegasus rides. Nearby, a kid cried because his mom wouldn't let him "ride the pony."

I turned to Liam, who didn't look happy that I'd stopped again. "I thought you weren't supposed to touch someone else's Familiar."

"You aren't," he confirmed. "That pegasus isn't bonded yet."

I wanted to ask if it would ever bond, but before I could, a voice cut through the crowd.

"Mr. Mitoh!" a male voice called.

"Not interested, Jones," Liam replied.

I turned to see who he was talking to, and another wave of amazement overcame me. At this point, I was probably going to pass out from sheer overwhelm before we made it to the school.

An older guy with a lot of muscle stood on the other side of the street, holding the reins on two massive beasts. The front half of the beast looked like a stag, with a long nose and pointed antlers. The back half resembled a bird, with strong legs, sharp talons, and massive feathered wings. It even had a beautiful plumed tail spanning out behind it.

"What *is* it?" I whispered in wonder.

"They're peryton," Liam said, like they weren't interesting in the slightest. "Half-deer, half-bird."

What was this guy's problem? Was he so used to this place that he could no longer appreciate the magic in it?

"Mr. Mitoh," Jones repeated in a whining voice.

"We don't have the money," Liam told Jones before he could get another word in, though it sounded like a lie.

"Not to worry," Jones responded, taking no notice to Liam's rude tone. "These peryton have already been reserved, courtesy of Elliot Baine. They're to take you up to Orenda."

"Baine. Thank the ancestors," Liam mumbled under his breath.

His shoulders relaxed. He led me closer to Jones until we were close enough to touch the peryton. The one closest to me stared down with his big dark eyes. He was a large beast, but there was a gentle quality in his eyes. I was just about to reach out and touch him when a set of hands wrapped around my waist and swept me off my feet.

I let out a yelp on instinct.

"Up you go," Jones' voice said in my ear.

Before I knew what was happening, I was straddling the peryton with my knees tucked under his wings. Jones placed the reins in my hands, then adjusted the strap on my duffel bag so that it draped securely across my body.

"You're in good hands with Bud here." Jones patted the peryton's neck. "Just hang on tight, and don't startle him."

"But wait—" I started to say.

Jones smacked Bud's behind, and the creature lurched forward. My stomach dropped, and a shot of adrenaline rushed through my chest as we launched into the air. A scream tore out of my lungs. Within seconds, the market was far below us, and the people looked like nothing more than ants.

"Relax!" Liam shouted over the sound of the air whipping past my ears. He looked more comfortable on the other peryton's back than I'd ever seen him in the short time I'd known him. I think even a slight smile graced his expression.

I quieted, and the fear in my body slowly eased. Even with the flapping of the peryton's wings, I felt strangely secure on his back. Laughter bubbled up from my chest.

I think I can get used to this.

We flew over the city and toward the ocean, but we didn't reach it before the peryton shifted course, soaring parallel to the mountain range. As the town disappeared behind us, a large clearing came into view.

A castle bigger than the state capitol back home stood at the center. Pointed stone towers stretched into the air above the trees. The walls were long, sturdy, and thick. Hundreds of ornate, stained glass windows were placed here and there. Within the castle walls there were keeps that stretched high above the towers, while gargoyles of various Familiars sat perched along the castle's walls. The castle itself was surrounded by a series of narrow rivers and tall waterfalls. The sunlight glistened off the water droplets at the base of the tallest waterfall, creating a rainbow. A large, open patch of grass stretched out in front of the school's main doors, filled with flowers and elaborate fountains. There were hundreds of kids and Familiars down there, chatting excitedly with each other as they entered the school.

A roar caught my attention. My stomach lurched as I saw dragons — *actual dragons*— soaring in a circle around the castle. They weren't alone. Other flying magical creatures, like griffins and manticores, flew above the castle and played with each other, pretending to fight or making loud noises like they were chatting.

Holy crap. Amelia made Orenda Academy sound magical, but she didn't tell me I'd be attending something this spectacular.

Our peryton circled around a courtyard near the tallest tower. Birds of all different sizes and colors soared above the courtyard, while creatures followed behind their Elementai as they crossed the lawn. I caught sight of another pegasus, and I saw what I swore was a huge feathered serpent slither behind someone and into the open doors at the front of the school.

Bud swooped down so fast that I was afraid we'd crash straight into the ground, but he pulled back at the last second and landed gracefully at the center of the courtyard. Liam's peryton landed behind Bud, and he slipped off its back with ease. Meanwhile, I was acutely aware of all the eyes on me.

Liam reached up to help me off the peryton's back. I placed my hands on his shoulders to steady myself, shivering slightly as his hands touched my hips to lift me off. As soon as I landed, the perytons took off again and went back the way we came. Once I was on the ground, Liam let go of me like I was a hot potato.

Liam started for the grand double doors, but I remained rooted in place. The whole courtyard had gone quiet. At least a hundred pairs of eyes locked on me.

"Is that her?" someone whispered.

Liam hurried back to my side. "Are you coming?"

I still couldn't move. It didn't seem right when I was being oggled at like a zoo animal. "Why's everyone staring?" I asked under my breath.

"We don't often get outsiders," Liam explained.

Great. I'd already been pegged an outcast.

"You know, they'd stop staring if you followed me to your dorm," Liam said.

I was just about to take him up on that offer when a girl with long black hair and manicured eyebrows stepped forward. She wore skin-tight black pants that showed off her curves, and a orange top that accented her chest. Her liquid eyeliner and perfect contouring made it look like she spent hours every morning painting on her face. A group of five stood behind her— two girls and three guys. They all had the same tan skin and I'm-hot-and-I-know-it look. A large, beautiful red bird landed on the girl's shoulder. Her tail feathers were so long they trailed on the ground, and she had a feathery plume on her head, which accented black eyes.

"You must be Sophia Henley," the girl said with a smile. "I'm Haley. I'm from your House, Koigni."

Despite the look of disgust on Liam's face, I shook her outstretched hand. It was only polite.

"So, is it true?" Haley asked in a tone that had *gossip* written all over it.

I glanced to Liam warily. "Is what true?"

"For the ancestors' sake, she just got here," Liam snapped at Haley. "Could you let her get settled in before you start interrogating her?"

Haley narrowed her eyes at him. "I wasn't asking *you*. I think Sophia can speak for herself."

"Yeah, I can," I agreed.

Liam growled.

"But I have no idea what you're talking about," I added.

Haley crossed her arms. "Rumor has it *you're* the one the prophecy talks about. If the prophecy is to be believed, that is."

She had to be kidding. I mean, prophecies weren't a real thing. Then again... I had no idea what was real anymore after what I'd seen recently.

"Like you said, it's just a rumor," Liam reminded her. "No one even believes the prophecy. Someone made it up just to scare the Houses."

"Maybe Sophia can confirm it for us," Haley argued. She looked to me for a response.

"Look..." I didn't know what to say. This girl was talking crazy. "No one mentioned a prophecy to me."

"See?" Liam said. "Now, would you let her rest? She's had a long journey."

Haley's lips tightened. "I don't take orders from people like you."

Liam's nostrils flared. He opened his mouth, but I cut in before things could escalate any further.

"Actually," I said, "I'd just like to get checked into my dorm. But maybe later you can tell me more about this prophecy."

I wasn't betting on it. Haley didn't seem like the kind of girl I'd hang out with. She held her nose so high that she'd drown in a rainstorm. Liam left without saying another word. I hurried to follow.

"What does she mean by *people like you*?" I asked once we were out of earshot.

Liam hesitated, but answered anyway. "In our society, the stronger your Familiar is, the higher you stand on the social ladder. She's Koigni *and* her Familiar is a phoenix. She outranks just about everyone at this school."

"That seems unfair," I said. "Shouldn't social status depend on your intelligence and accomplishments?"

Liam didn't get a chance to answer. A fluffy red critter darted between his legs. He stumbled and cursed under his breath. The creature stopped several feet away and sat, curling its bushy tail around itself. *A fox.* It looked up at Liam with bright eyes.

"Sassy!"

A curvy girl in the strangest outfit I'd ever seen approached us. She wore a bright green tutu, with striped pink tights and blue sneakers. Her shirt was black with purple polka dots. At least five thick bangle bracelets hung from each wrist. She wore her hair in pigtails, a giant sunflower pinned to her head between them. Her hair was strawberry blonde. She stood out, even when you stripped away the quirky Dr. Seuss look.

"Leave the poor guy alone, Sassy!" the girl scolded the fox. She bent to scoop up her Familiar, but the fox leapt from her arms and made a break for it.

The courtyard buzzed with conversation again, but there were still a lot of eyes on us. Quirky Girl didn't seem to notice— or didn't seem to care— as she chased Sassy between a group of nearby people. She dove forward to catch her Familiar, but it dodged out of the way. She sprang to her feet and didn't seem to notice she was covered in dirt. Haley's group pointed and laughed.

"Sassy, if you don't get back here, you're sleeping in the woods tonight," Quirky Girl threatened. "You know what are in the woods, don't you? Big dragons!"

Sassy darted between the legs of a tall, muscular guy. He stood on the outer edge of a small huddle of students who were no longer paying attention. Quirky Girl dropped to the ground and stuck her head *right between the guy's knees.*

Liam tried to stifle his laughter next to me. I just watched in horror. *How embarrassing.*

"What the—?" The guy glanced beneath him.

Quirky Girl dragged her fox out of the crowd and rose, as if totally forgetting anyone else was there. The top of her head smacked right into the center of the guy's crotch. Like, full sunflower pressed firmly onto dick.

I cringed. It was like watching a trainwreck. I couldn't take my eyes off it.

"What the hell?" the guy cried. He jumped away from her and grabbed one of his friends to use as a human shield.

Quirky Girl's eyes widened. "Oh, my ancestors! I am *so* sorry. I was just— my Familiar is—"

"You need to put that thing on a leash, *Imogen*." Haley clipped each syllable in the girl's name as she made her way over. Her cronies followed behind her.

Imogen got to her feet. "That's cruel, and you know it."

"That thing is a hazard!" Haley snapped. "People who can't control their Familiars shouldn't have them."

"She is not!" Imogen pulled the fox closer to her chest. "She's just playful."

"Come on," Liam said from beside me. "Let's go."

"Hold on," I objected.

I dropped my bag at my feet and bent to my knees beside it. I dug inside for an extra tote bag I'd brought with me. I thought it would come in handy if I wanted to haul stuff with me to the beach or something. It was light blue, with bright pink flowers all over it. It would suit Imogen perfectly.

Liam groaned when he saw me pull it out. I ignored him and walked across the courtyard, abandoning him with my stuff.

"That *thing* needs someone to actually train it," Haley was saying when I approached.

I cleared my throat. "Um... Imogen?"

The whole crowd turned to look at me. Whereas everyone else's expression hardened when they saw me, Imogen's softened.

"Would this work?" I held the tote bag out to her. "You can keep Sassy by your side, but she can still jump out and run around when she wants to."

Imogen's face brightened. "That's brilliant. Thank you so much."

I opened the bag, and Imogen gently placed Sassy inside. She swung the bag over her shoulder and twisted from side to side, as if she was modeling it. Sassy peeked out of the top of the bag, looking positively content.

Haley looked me up and down. She was *not* pleased with my solution.

"Better?" Imogen asked her mockingly, like it didn't matter to her at all what Haley thought.

Haley pursed her lips. "I hope it suffocates."

The crowd drew a collective breath, but the following laughter told me more people agreed with her than were shocked by her heartlessness.

"And *you*," Haley pointed at me. "Be careful about who you stick up for. It could reflect badly on our House. I'll let it pass this time, because you don't know any better."

"Your House has enough of a reputation," Liam said from behind me. I hadn't realized he'd followed me. "I don't think the friends Sophia makes is going to change anything."

Haley stared him down but turned to me instead. "Just know that you've been warned. Blood is thicker than water around here."

Haley turned on her heel, and the crowd dispersed.

Liam handed me my duffel bag. "Can we *finally* go?"

I glanced to Imogen, who was petting Sassy and looked thrilled with her bag.

"Yeah," I said, slinging the strap over my body.

"Wait!" Imogen called when we were several paces away. "Thank you!"

"No problem," I told her, waving back to her and Sassy.

Imogen grabbed Sassy's paw and helped her wave to me. I turned away and followed Liam across the lawn, finally entering the castle.

He led me up the big stone staircase to a pair of doors three times my height. If I thought this world couldn't get any more magical, I was wrong. The doors opened up to a huge white foyer that stretched five stories high with a big gold chandelier hanging in the center. Balconies on every level wrapped around the foyer. The marble floor was dotted with large area rugs and big comfy chairs. Ahead of us, a huge grand staircase led to the second level. Tapestries and elaborate paintings hung from every inch of the wall, and a fireplace big enough to hold a dragon burned in the center. Suits of armor stood at attention around the doors and the fireplace.

"What... how...?" I couldn't manage to find the words as I tried to take in the splendor of it all.

Liam didn't slow his pace. How could he not just stop and stare? I hurried to keep up with him.

"It's a castle," I managed to get out. Because apparently I was really good at stating the obvious.

"Yeah," Liam said with a shrug.

"But— but how?" I stammered. "Did you magic it here?"

Liam looked thoroughly unamused. "No, we didn't *magic it here*. It was gifted to the Hawkei long ago."

"Oh," I said flatly. I wished he'd explain more, but Liam kept silent.

Liam led me down a long, wide hall on the second level. Tall arched windows outlined in elaborately carved stone lined one side of the hallway. Between them stood more statues of Familiars, except this time, they were accompanied by statues of Elementai as well. On the opposite wall hung large dreamcatchers, woven blankets, and feathered headdresses. It seemed like the castle was a mix of old medieval architecture and Native American historical pieces. Everywhere I looked, there was something more beautiful to stare at.

Liam's pace slowed the farther we walked. He stayed silent the whole time.

"Thanks for sticking up for me back there, by the way," I said to break the silence.

"Yeah, well, don't get used to it," he growled.

What the hell?

"A simple *you're welcome* would suffice," I responded.

"You're welcome," he said flatly.

Moments later, Liam stopped in front of a set of large doors. The handles were golden and were crafted in the shape of flames. They were intricate and nearly looked like the real thing.

"Look," he said, "we're from different Houses. I shouldn't be sticking up for you, and you shouldn't be sticking up for Imogen. We only work together when we have to. Haley is right. You'll alienate yourself from your House if you keep acting this way. My advice is to find yourself a Koigni friend and stick close to them."

Any ounce of happiness I'd found in the magic of this place instantly disappeared. I knew Amelia said you couldn't date outside your House, but you couldn't be *friends*, either? What kind of society was this? I thought Liam said these people were all about unity. They seemed full of bullcrap to me.

"This is your dorm." Liam gestured to the doors beside him. "It's where I leave you. Good luck." That was all he said before he started down the hall the way we came.

"Wait, Liam!"

He turned back to me, his brow furrowed. "If you have any questions, ask a member of your House."

The unspoken words in his tone were clear. I wasn't his problem anymore.

Liam turned his back on me. Nerves twisted in my gut. How could he just leave me alone?

I took a breath and stepped toward the doors. I glanced down the hall one last time to watch him go. My heart broke a little. Liam hadn't exactly been friendly since we met, but at least with him, I hadn't been alone. Now the one person here who'd helped me make any sense of this place was abandoning me.

Jerk.

I gripped the door handle and pushed. I half expected that Liam had lead me to the dungeons, but I stepped into a common room. Sunlight spilled in through a tall window, and through a sunroof that opened up in the ceiling. There were four fireplaces, each with plush red chairs surrounding them, and two rows of study tables in the center of the room. A flat screen TV hung on the wall. Two long hallways split off in either direction, which I guessed led to the dorms. The room was swathed in colors of deep red, orange, and yellow. It seemed cozy and warm.

At least thirty people were inside. All eyes turned to me, and the whole room quieted.

Was it going to be like this every time I entered a room?

I swallowed. I must've looked like a deer in the headlights. No one bothered to step up and tell me what to do. Was I supposed to claim a room, or just hang out in here until my advisor showed up?

The doors banged open behind me. I jumped.

"You can all relax," Haley said in a bored tone as she entered, followed in toe by her posse. "She's not the one. She's just a bastard."

Wait... what? I was *so* not interested in indulging in any drama. I was planning on keeping my head down like Amelia told me to. But I had to say *something*. I mean... what the hell?

"*Excuse* me?" I snapped.

Haley crossed the room to the closest fireplace, and her phoenix fluttered behind. The two boys sitting there immediately got up, and Haley's group took their place.

Haley tossed her dark hair over her shoulder and looked at me with a shocked expression. "Oh, I didn't mean it in a bad way."

Since when was that word *not* meant in a bad way?

"I just meant... your mom was Toaqua, wasn't she?" Haley asked. "You're Koigni, so she must've whored around with some Koigni guy or something."

I was too stunned to move, even though every fiber of my being told me to punch the girl in the face.

"You don't even know my mother," I snarled.

Haley shrugged and turned away. A part of me wanted to reach out and pull a chunk of her hair out, but the rational part told me to walk away.

"At least *my* mom raised me right. I'm not sure you can say the same."

It wasn't until everyone in the room inhaled a collective gasp that I realized I'd said it out loud. *Mortified* didn't even begin to describe how I felt. I wasn't the kind of girl who said things like that.

Haley just gaped at me, so shocked she couldn't even respond. I wasn't about to stick around to hear whatever she came up with. I whirled around and rushed through the doors I'd just entered.

The problem was, I didn't know where to go from there. Even if I missed orientation, I would've thought *someone* would greet me with a welcome packet or a quick tour. This place wasn't very welcoming, to say the least.

I slumped down the hall and dropped my bag on the floor. My whole body shook as I leaned my shoulder up against the stone wall. The events of the last few minutes repeated over and over in my mind. It was like high school all over again. I thought I was done with that.

I stared down the hall, my eyes passing over each magnificent statue and tapestry. I couldn't believe I was here. I already missed my parents. I wondered how they took the news the night I left. I hoped they were safe and that Amelia had convinced them not to come after me.

Speaking of Amelia... I reached into my bag and grabbed my phone. I found Amelia's number in my contacts and hit the call button. I just wanted to hear her voice. Maybe she could answer some of my questions, like where to pick up my class schedule. We hadn't had much time to talk about that kind of stuff once I stopped acting like a turd and actually listened to her.

"Hello?" Amelia's voice was like music to my ears.

"Hey, Am—" I cut off when my phone flew upward out of my hand. "What the hell?"

I whirled around, expecting it to be some sort of hazing ritual led by Haley. Instead, I came face to face with an older woman. She had curly red hair, long lashes, and high cheekbones. Her green velvet dress hung to the floor, and she wore a ton of jewelry. The fumed expression in her eyes gave her away immediately.

Madame Doya.

She looked just as mean and ornery as Amelia described her.

And I just swore at her. *Woops.*

"Sophia?" I heard Amelia's faint voice on the other end of the line. "Why are you calling me? Didn't I tell you—?"

I didn't get a chance to hear the rest of what she said, because Madame Doya hit a button on the screen, and the call went dead.

"We do not allow students to have communication with the outside world," she stated sternly.

I gaped at her. "But... you have TVs?"

She pursed her lips. "Students are allowed access to streaming services and local channels. Once you graduate, you may access telephones and the Internet, but not until you are trained in proper communication channels. We can't take any risks. This phone should've never been allowed on campus."

"I was only calling—"

"It doesn't matter who you were calling," she cut me off. "The rules are in place to keep our society safe."

Of course. This wasn't a school. It was a prison.

So, basically high school...

I dropped my gaze, because I was a goody-two-shoes who never talked back. Yes, I admit it. Despite the anger coursing through my body, I fell victim to her authority.

"Yes, ma'am," I whispered.

"Here." Madame Doya shoved a folder in my direction. "You'll find your class schedule in here, along with your dorm key and a map of the school."

I took the folder. That was it? That was my entire welcome?

Madame Doya stared down at me past her nose, like she didn't know what else to say. She cleared her throat. "Welcome home, Sophia."

I stared after her as she breezed down the hall toward the main stairs, all the while trying to force down the lump in my throat. What she'd said bothered me to the core. This place was the furthest thing from home. I'd momentarily let myself become distracted by the magic of this world, but the truth was, I would never belong here. My own House didn't even want me here.

I was completely and utterly alone.

Liam

SEVEN

I tried to tell myself that I didn't feel bad when I left Sophia in front of the Koigni dorms, but I kind of did. She seemed so lost and helpless when I abandoned her at the doors and turned away.

But I couldn't go in there with her. She was from the Fire House. Time to stop holding her hand.

The Water dorms were swathed with sapphire and silver, Toaqua House colors. Pools were embedded everywhere in the floors, and Water Familiars dove in and out of them, along with Elementai. The lighting in here was bright and fluorescent, until you went down the right corridor, which was darker and more relaxing, like a spa. Unlike most of the cushy furniture throughout the rest of the castle, the furniture in here was made of wicker and waterproof. Everything got wet. It was like a constant summer party in here. Toaqua could never stay dry for long.

"Hey, Liam, jump in with us!" Wyatt waved to me in the water. He was hanging onto his walrus Familiar, who was tugging him around. Wyatt had been one of my best friends, before. I hadn't seen him all summer.

I wasn't in the mood. "No thanks." I turned my back on them and headed to my dorm. I heard mutters behind me, but I ignored them. I wasn't a part of them anymore.

My room was clean, which I was sure was going to last about a week. By next Friday it'd have clothes and shit all over it. There'd be so much clutter it'd be difficult to walk. I wasn't really an organized guy.

I found my schedule sitting on my bed. Baine must've dropped it off. I picked it up and opened the letter. Usually, students above First Year level got to pick their classes. But I'd been so depressed over the summer that I told the school they could pick for me. I glanced at my schedule. They were a bunch of random classes. Medical Care of Familiars, Advanced Toaqua Magic III, Magical Herbs and Plants, Survival Instincts, and Basket Weaving.

Fricking *Basket Weaving*.

There was nothing that specified any course of study. It was so obvious they didn't know where to put me. But I really couldn't blame them. I didn't know where to put me, either.

Last year I'd been *so looking* forward to signing up for Hunters and Gatherers. But that was out of the question. For that kind of class, you needed a predator familiar to hunt with.

Which I no longer had. I knew what my schedule would've looked like if Nashoma were still here. Interhouse Diplomacy, Ceremonial Tradition, Communing with the Ancestors, War and Negotiation.

Classes to prepare the Son of the Chief to one day take over.

But I knew my chances of becoming Chief of Toaqua were long done. That was my brother Ezra's job now. Dad would never let a Familiar-less Elementai take the role of chief after he stepped down, even if I was his first-born.

Most of the students were staying in their dorms tonight, but I still had a few things to get from home. I left the Toaqua dorms and headed back to the main entrance.

On the way through the courtyard I saw that Haley was outside again, gabbing with two of her clones. Her phoenix, Anwara, was sitting on her shoulder. A jaguar and a winged python, Familiars that had to belong to Haley's friends, were playing on the grass. Haley's Familiar was watching the other animals with interest. Her eyes gleamed longingly as she watched the winged snake and the jaguar wrestle. She seemed a bit lonely.

Anwara nudged Haley with her head, then bounced a little on her shoulder, fluffing her feathers. She clearly wanted to play.

"Anwara! Cut it out!" Haley snapped, and Anwara shrunk on her shoulder. "Why do you want to go and make a fool of yourself? Sit still and behave!"

Anwara hung her head lowly. She didn't coo. Haley went on bragging loudly about the advanced classes her mother had gotten her into while Anwara watched the other Familiars play with a bit of a tear in her eye. Haley's friends pretended like nothing had happened.

I felt a wall of rage rise in my chest. I *hated* people who mistreated their Familiars. I would do anything, anything at all, to have just five more minutes with Nashoma, and here Haley was treating her poor phoenix like it was some designer purse to show off, one that was born simply to do her bidding.

I gritted my teeth but didn't say anything. I'd already caused enough trouble with Haley when I stuck up for Sophia.

The last thing I wanted was another lecture from Dad. Even worse, if I kept messing with House lines, the Elders would get involved. I knew I was already in their line of sight.

If I didn't want to mess things up more than I already had, I needed to keep my head down.

ORENDA ACADEMY WAS RUN like any other college. I had classes scattered throughout the week on different days and times. Mondays and Wednesdays were loaded, with three different classes, while I only had two classes on Tuesdays and Thursdays. I liked night classes, but the stupid school had signed me up for mostly mornings and afternoons. I hated myself for not picking my own schedule as I dragged my ass out of bed Monday morning and stumbled into the shower.

I showed up late to Advanced Toaqua Magic III. It was held right on the beach. Baine was already lecturing when I showed up. His Familiar was swimming far beneath the surface somewhere out at sea. Everyone else was gathered in a circle around him with their Familiars. As a Third Year, I was the only one without one. I hung back and tried not to be seen.

Which Professor Baine was insistent on screwing up. "Liam!" he announced the moment he saw me. "You're just in time. Come on. We're practicing shields today. Amy, you can be his partner."

Amy wrinkled her nose, but quickly rearranged her face when she saw me looking. We moved toward the ocean until our ankles were deep in water.

I barely had time to get my shield up before Amy clenched her hand, causing a jet of water to rise up from the ocean. She sent it hurtling toward me at a high speed, directed toward my face. I raised up my hand in a sharp manner and a wall of water came up, stopping Amy's jet midstream.

I knew the tribe had resentment toward me for what had happened over the summer, but damn. This was a bit much.

Amy snarled. She started tossing bits of water at me faster, one right after the other in fast succession. They nearly looked like bullets with how fast they were going. They got larger, stronger. Yet my wall held. It didn't break, or waver, and I smirked. I still had it.

Amy couldn't break my shield, and she was getting pissed. Whatever. Even though I was now weaker than almost everyone in my tribe, I was still really good.

I just couldn't keep it up as long. Amy's hits kept getting harder and harder, and I was starting to sweat with the effort of keeping the wall steady. I couldn't spar like the rest of them anymore, and I hated myself for it.

"That's enough, Liam," Baine said sharply when he saw me leaning over my knees, trying to catch my breath. "Take a break."

People were staring. He was coddling me and embarrassing me in front of everyone. I wanted to kill him.

I let the wall drop spontaneously, and it splashed Amy. She jumped back and glared at me, but I didn't say another word.

"Amy, you can take turns sparring with Jack and Lira," Baine told her, like I wasn't even there. Amy gladly left me behind, and Baine walked over to me.

"You know better than to push yourself. I've told you this before," he said.

"I can keep up with everyone else, and do even better," I growled through gritted teeth. "I'm more talented than anyone here."

"But I don't have to remind you what you lack." Baine shook his head. "One day, you're going to have to face the truth, Liam. Your greatest weakness is your biggest strength, and you need to learn how to implement it to your advantage."

"Advantage." I snorted.

"You think you're better despite your illness. I know you are. But prove it," Baine said, with force. "You're smart enough to find a way around it. But if you keep trying to be like you were before, just like everyone else... well, you and I both know it's not going to work."

Baine turned his back on me to help the rest of the class. I was breathing hard, but it wasn't from exhaustion.

It was from rage.

Forget this. I wouldn't be looked down upon because I was different. I was ditching. I grabbed my backpack and headed out of there without another word. My next class wasn't for another hour, but I didn't care. I wouldn't be seen as the *weak one*.

I was thinking about ditching Basket Weaving too, but I really couldn't afford to get into anymore trouble. If I skipped too much, I'd get kicked out. I hardly cared, but I knew what my tribe would think, so I forced myself into Professor Amber's classroom at eleven.

Her classroom was one giant wicker basket perched on top of a tower. Inside, tons of blankets and rugs were scattered all over the floor, alongside giant pillows. Incense holders hung from the ceiling and created a smoky atmosphere. I had to resist gagging when I saw Amber's Familiar, an orangutan, actually playing a wooden flute for ambiance.

This class was full of gossiping girls. Not one single male soul in here but me. I sat on a pillow before a loom and let myself be engulfed by the estrogen.

What a hippie class. At least it was an easy credit. And I got to sit down.

Professor Amber waltzed in. She was wearing a long skirt, covered with a draping shawl and actual feathers weaved into her curly hair. She danced... literally danced... into the room with bare feet while she twirled her arms above her head like some sort of witch.

"Greetings, fair children," she sang. "I am Professor Amber. Welcome to Basket Weaving." She bowed to us, and her Familiar mimicked the movement.

"Today, you will be learning the art of storytelling through the magical art that is weaving. In this class, you will understand how to intricately bind together the forces of thread and straw into a unison of sensual and delightful purpose."

Professor Amber made making a basket sound sexual. She sat down at her loom.

"Pay attention, everyone," she said while taking out a collection of threads. "This technique is to be used for your blissful understanding and pleasure."

Yep. Definitely sexual.

She demonstrated the technique. The girls watched in interest and I tried not to fall asleep. She then handed out thread to all of us in baskets, and stood at the head of the room.

"I will be playing the drums and the gong for sound healing while you work. Feel your soul heal through the vibrations that are played," Amber soothed.

I was ridiculously spiritual, but this was even pushing it for me. I winced as she struck the heavy gong again, then got to work. I had nothing else to do for these two hours.

After a while, I fell into a kind of stupor. Weaving the blanket wasn't difficult on my body, and it didn't require that much concentration. It was repetitive work, one that required me to focus, but not think overly hard. It was sort of nice... like being there, but your body is just existing, doing the same movements over and over, and the rest of you is floating.

Kind of like being high. Maybe.

"Liam, your weaving is so perfect!" Professor Amber praised. She snapped me out of my concentration. I found that everyone was staring at me jealously as Amber displayed the loom, and my blanket, to the class. "Never have I seen a beginner make such a beautiful beginning of a piece!"

I looked around the room and saw that while the thread on everyone else's looms looked choppy and loose, my stitches were tight and uniform. I blushed so hard everyone could probably see it through my dark skin. I had to resist punching my loom.

Professor Amber continued to brag loudly about me to the rest of the class until it was over. I shot out of there as quickly as I could when we were finally released. I was definitely switching this class the minute I could. *Stupid-ass Basket Weaving.*

I wolfed down lunch and headed to my last class of the day. Magical Herbs and Plants was held beside the greenhouse, off a small connecting room called the Alchemist's Lair. Inside were circular stone tables with small wooden bowls, pestles, and vials. Each desk had an alchemy brewing station. Professor Perot strutted around with his peacock Familiar, teaching everyone what the different plants in the greenhouse meant and how to use them.

I scowled. This class was for Elementai who wanted to be medicine men and women, healers. Something I definitely wasn't interested in.

Yet I didn't know my place in society anymore... which Baine had made clear this morning... so I figured I could at least try it. Professor Perot taught us that plants like burdock, clovers, chickweed and dandelions could be consumed in a food shortage emergency, something that was in high stock around here. The lecture was long, but interesting. I was happy when I successfully made a poultice for stopping bleeding wounds out of clay and cayenne pepper.

Magical Herbs and Plants wasn't going to be so bad. It might even help. Alchemy was going to be something I needed after I graduated. Familiars and Elementai got hurt all the time, mostly by magical afflictions. If some sort of potion or plant could help them feel better, or create some sort of spell that could save them in a pinch, I wanted to know.

If I couldn't help myself anymore, maybe I could at least still help my tribe.

I left Magical Herbs and Plants feeling more positive than I had in months. This semester was going to be easy. I turned to head back to the Toaqua dorm to, you know, brood and be alone.

And maybe work on my basket weaving in private. But I'd die before I told anyone that.

I halted in place when my eye caught Sophia in the middle of the hallway. She was looking at her folder, shuffling through her papers like mad and turning on the spot. It was obvious she was lost and trying to find her way around. No one stopped to help her, not even anyone from her own House. That was typical of Koignis. You had to keep up, or they'd literally throw you to the flames. They didn't take well to weak members. The Koigni House valued strength and power above everything. Something Sophia *did not* emulate.

Sophia looked really upset. Tears were welling up in her eyes, and her bottom lip was trembling. She was two seconds away from a breakdown.

Oh, by the ancestors. I needed to go save this girl, before she embarrassed herself in front of everyone yet again. People didn't let things slide around here. They'd remember it forever if she broke down in the middle of school.

But before I could, I hesitated. How far had I actually gotten in life by being *nice?* Being nice was only for two things. One: making hurting people feel better. And two: using it to get what you wanted. Nobody ever got anywhere by being *nice*. If being polite didn't work, you had to take what you wanted by force.

Sophia had to learn that, or she'd get eaten alive out here.

I stood there watching her, wrestling with a decision. She wasn't my problem anymore. Yet, she was.

People were funeral pyres. Every single one of them was scrambling to light the nearest match as quickly as possible, and then, once they were on fire, they complained that the fire burned.

I was no exception to this rule.

Nope. If I had learned anything about people, it was that you could give them a hundred options, and every time, they'd always pick the worst decision they possibly could.

Sophia was a bad decision. But she was one I couldn't help but make.

I rolled my eyes and stomped over there. Her expression cleared as I came into view. Without a word, I yanked the folder out of her hands, opened it, and scrolled through her schedule. Typical First Year stuff. Except...

We had Medical Care of Familiars together tomorrow. *Fuck.*

"Your first class is Beginner Koigni Magic I. It's down the hall, to the left. The door is by the statue of the dancing sprite. If you hit the cafeteria, you've gone too far." I threw the folder back at her. She scrambled to catch it, and papers got jumbled in her arms.

"Th— thank you," she stuttered.

"Don't mention it," I told her sharply. "Like, ever again."

I shoved my hands in my pockets, turned around, and stormed off. Which I was getting exceptionally good at doing lately.

I glanced behind my shoulder, just to double-check on her. Well, she seemed a bit more organized, at least. She had a clearer direction of where she was going.

I sighed. Sophia was sweet, but she needed to learn how things ran around here. She couldn't keep being lost and confused. She had to find her place at Orenda Academy, fast.

And I needed to learn how to stay away from her.

sophia
EIGHT

I was grateful for Liam's help in finding my first class, but it would've been more helpful if he'd told me what a *sprite* actually was. I wandered down the hall, my folder shaking in my hands. I gave myself an hour to explore the castle and find my first class, but it looked like that wasn't going to be enough time, even with the map in front of me.

I was starting to think Liam gave me the wrong directions just to get in a good laugh. It wasn't hard to doubt the guy when he acted like a total ass.

What was with him, anyway? He always had a stone-cold look on his face and often breathed heavily, like he had no concept of simple relaxation. He acted like just being alive was difficult. Weird.

Eventually, I hit the cafeteria Liam had mentioned. I turned around and headed back the way I came, looking for any signs of a dancing statue. I ran my hand across the fabric of my jeans— Amelia's jeans— hoping they would bring me luck. So far, I felt so out of my element that I wasn't sure they weren't cursed.

I need you, Am. I wish I didn't have to do this without you.

My eyes finally fell upon a statue of a woman wrapped in flowing fabric. She rose on one bare foot, the other off the ground and her hands in the air.

This must be it.

I glanced into the open door beside the statue. The room was one of the biggest I'd seen so far in the castle, with a high ceiling and a massive fireplace along the far wall. The area in front of the fireplace was empty, and there were scorch marks along the hardwood floor. Several large couches faced the empty area. I guessed the space was for training and the couches were for observing. Tables and chairs were set up in front of a chalkboard in the opposite corner of the room. Tall bookshelves lined the classroom area, and candles burned all around the room.

A red-headed woman sat behind a large desk near the chalkboard, shuffling through papers. Besides that, the room was quiet. I was the first one here.

Madame Doya looked up from her desk. She had that same hard look on her face as the first time I met her. I was starting to think it was a permanent expression.

"Can I help you?" she asked, like she had no intention of actually helping me.

I glanced down at my schedule, as if one more glance might help me make sense of everything I'd been trying to understand since yesterday. "Um... yeah. Is this Beginner Koigni Magic I?"

"It is," she answered. "But you're early."

Since when did teachers chastise you for being *early*?

"I— uh— wanted to make sure I was on time," I said lamely.

Madame Doya looked up at me with tight lips, but simply nodded and gazed back down at her papers. "You may take a seat and practice conjuring a flame in your palm until the rest of the class arrives."

Practice conjuring fire? I thought that was what this class was for. To teach me how to do it.

"What are you just standing there for?" she snapped without looking up from her desk.

I sank into the closest chair two rows back. "I don't know how to conjure fire yet."

Madame Doya's head snapped upward. "Excuse me?"

I fiddled with a corner of my folder. "I mean, I used my fire once, but it was an accident. I didn't know I was supposed to know how to use it before class started."

Great. I was going to be light years behind my classmates.

Madame Doya frowned deeper— if that were possible considering the ever-present downturn of her lips. "You should know how to conjure a basic flame by your age."

"My dad said my powers would be weak until—"

"Your dad?" Madame Doya interrupted. "It was my under-standing that you'd never met your father."

What? Who would tell her a lie like that?

Realization dawned. She was talking about my biological father.

"I meant my adoptive father," I said. It felt so wrong to call my dad that.

"Robert Henley is *not* your father," she stated in a tone that stung.

"Oh, I, um..." What was I supposed to do? Agree with her?

Madame Doya stood from her desk. That was the first time I noticed the creature lounging at her feet. My blood ran cold as a huge African cat with blonde fur stood and followed Madame Doya over to one of the nearby bookcases. I swore the cat *scowled* at me, like it knew something.

It does, I told myself. I licked my dry lips, but my tongue felt like sandpaper. This was the cat that had attacked Amelia and me just days ago. Naomi. I knew it. I urged to demand an answer from Doya about what her Familiar was doing hundreds of miles away, stalking my sister and me in the Salt Lake Valley, but fear blocked my words. I didn't want to draw any more attention to myself than I had to, and I had a feeling that the more I dug into that, the more danger I'd put my family in.

Madame Doya didn't seem to notice I'd gone completely tense at the sight of her Familiar. She pulled down one of the thickest books I'd ever seen and flipped it open. She walked over to me and dropped the book so hard onto my desk that I jumped back a few inches.

"Your father's name was Anthony Greyson, and your mother's name was Lucy Greyson. They were both highly respected members of the Koigni House."

Madame Doya pointed at the page in front of me. I glanced down at it, but continued to watch the lioness out of the corner of my eye. She stood still but stared back.

Names and birthdates lined the page. It was a genealogy chart, and sure enough, the names Anthony and Lucy were written beside each other, with a line connecting them to the name Sophia Greyson. My birthdate was written below the name. It wasn't exactly a shock considering my parents admitted I was adopted, but it still didn't feel right to see my name written that way, connected to a man and woman I'd never met.

"Your *adoptive father* was nothing more than a thief," Madame Doya accused in disgust. "He stole you away from this world when you were only a baby. You must learn to accept that fact."

I sat there dumbstruck. She couldn't actually believe my parents *stole* me, could she? I mean, apart from the whole lying-about-being-adopted thing, my parents were the best. I was sure that whatever happened when I was a baby, the Greysons wanted my parents to have me. And I didn't care what anyone else said. Robert and Susan Henley were the people who raised me. They were— and would always be— my real parents.

God, I missed them. And thanks to Doya, I couldn't even call them to tell them that.

I forced down the lump in my throat, but my voice still came out small. "Do they— Anthony and Lucy— know I'm here?"

"They don't know anything," Madame Doya said coldly, "considering they're dead."

"What?" I asked breathlessly. I wasn't sure I'd heard her right.

"Your parents died shortly after you were born." Madame Doya spoke without emotion, as if she wasn't delivering earth-shattering news.

I sat still for several beats, absorbing the information. "What does this mean? Am I the prophesied one?"

Whatever it meant to be the prophesied one. With all that talk the day before, no one cared to tell me what the prophecy actually said.

Madame Doya's nostrils flared as she inhaled a deep breath. "I believed you could be, but anyone capable of fulfilling the prophecy should actually be able to *do* magic."

What was it with this woman? She knew how to deliver a blow with the most minimal of words. Talking to her felt like being thrown into a lion's den without a weapon. At this rate, this lady was going to chew me up and spit me out by the end of next week. She petrified me.

Voices from down the hall met my ears, and a group of students entered the room. I turned to see Haley at the front of the group, her phoenix on her shoulder. I noticed she was the only first-year Koigni in the group with a Familiar. She stopped talking the moment she laid eyes on me.

Madame Doya slammed the book on my desk shut, stealing my attention from Haley. She scooped the book up in her arms and began her way back to her desk. The lioness followed.

"Everyone please take a seat," Doya said in a bored tone. "We'll get started shortly."

To say I was behind my classmates was an understatement. These people could light a fire in the palm of their hand with a snap of their finger. Literally. I didn't even have the snapping-my-fingers part down.

Haley showed off by lighting up the wood in the fireplace from halfway across the room and sending it whirling up the chimney like a fire tornado. If that was the kind of thing Koigni could do on their first day, I wasn't sure I wanted to see what they were capable of after four years of training.

Maybe by then I'd be good enough to burn Haley's perfect eyebrows off, if I was lucky.

"Come on, people!" Madame Doya yelled across the training area. Apparently, my classmates weren't doing as well as I thought. "This isn't Nivita magic. We're not moving mountains here. All I'm asking is to see you sustain a flame for ten seconds. It'd be nice if some of you could conjure a flame at all."

She shot a glare my way. It didn't go unnoticed. Haley followed Madame Doya's gaze and smirked.

Maybe if Madame Doya actually tried *teaching* us something instead of just yelling like a drill sergeant, we'd have made some progress since the beginning of class. I didn't dare ask her how it was actually done. I probably wouldn't get a direct answer, anyway.

"I want to move on to fireballs by next week," Madame Doya said. "At this rate, it'll take us a month, and everyone but Haley will be repeating this class next semester. Sophia!"

I immediately froze from where I stood near the fireplace, my fingers pinched together in preparation to snap them. I knew it wouldn't work since I'd already tried a hundred times since class started.

"What are you doing?" she demanded.

I blinked a few times, unsure how to answer. "I'm trying to conjure fire..."

"Yes," Madame Doya emphasized with raised eyebrows. "Which you have yet to do."

I swallowed hard. "I... I'm not sure how. I didn't have Koigni parents to teach me." Surely everyone could understand that.

"Everyone back to their desks," she instructed.

The class hesitated.

"Now!" she boomed.

Everyone scurried back to their seats. Madame Doya walked so lightly that she seemed to float across the room. She stopped at her desk, where her Familiar lay on the floor, and grabbed one of the candles burning there. She brought it to her face and blew the flame out. Everyone watched with interest as she turned and started her way down the aisle of desks. My heart pounded with every step of her feet. She headed straight toward me.

I prayed she would pass me by, but she stopped beside me. My mouth went dry as she set the candle in the middle of my desk.

"Light it," she commanded.

What?

I just sat there, glancing between her and the candle. Was she serious?

"You should be able to conjure a flame for a simple candle," Madame Doya insisted. "Perhaps you need a little pressure to push you in the right direction."

Everyone's eyes were on me. I could feel it even without having to look up. Haley snickered from across the room.

"What are you waiting for?" Madame Doya asked. "Light the candle."

I stared at the charred wick. Anything not to look her in the eyes. A slew of emotions surfaced— anger, embarrassment, fear. The list went on. It made my blood boil. I thought for a moment the candle might actually light from the power of my emotions. But the seconds ticked by, and all that happened was a tension headache formed in my head.

Whispers spread across the room.

Why won't she just light it?

She's not going to get it.

Is she even Koigni?

Hot breath passed by my upper lip, and my eyes burned. I focused every inch of attention I had on that candle wick, and nothing happened. Why wasn't the damn thing lighting? Why wouldn't Doya tell me how to actually do it?

Because she finds pleasure in tormenting you, for whatever reason.

I must've reminded her too much of someone she hated.

"Enough!" Madame Doya's voice cut off the whispers and snapped me out of my concentration.

But I couldn't take it another second. When I looked up, all eyes were on me. It felt like the walls in the room were getting smaller and smaller, and they would crush me if I didn't make it out *now*.

And so I did the only thing I could do.

I ran.

I wasn't sure what came over me. I'd never ditched class before, and certainly not when I'd already attended the first half of it. I mean, who *does* that?

Me, apparently.

"We've got a runner," someone teased as I rushed out the door. I couldn't even think straight enough to tell if it was Haley.

I was already winded by the time I reached the end of the hall. To be fair, it was a long hall, and I was sprinting pretty fast, but I continued forward. I had to get as far away from that room as I could.

&

I RACED out the first doors I found, down a long flight of concrete steps and onto a worn path carved through the forest. I only slowed when I was far enough into the trees that I felt safe from other students or staff spotting me.

I needed to get into nature. It was the only place I felt safe, felt normal.

The sound of running water traveled through the forest. The farther I walked, the louder it became. Finally, I reached the water I'd been hearing for the last five minutes. A tall waterfall rushed down the side of a cliff and followed a narrow river over rocks and down the mountainside. White water sprayed into the air, sprinkling the trees hanging above the river. A narrow footbridge with rails crossed over the water, but I abandoned the trail and sat on one of the rocks closest to the bank.

I curled my knees to my chest and rested my chin on them. My mind raced, and fury coursed through my veins. Madame Doya should've been fired for how she treated students. And Haley shouldn't have even been in Beginner Koigni Magic if she was that good. They singled me out because I was new, because I was an easy target. I didn't want to be here. It was—

The sound of a creature trilling in the trees above me distracted me. I looked upward and spotted a small, fluffy white creature the size of a fat squirrel jumping from branch to branch. It moved so fast I couldn't catch a good glimpse of it. All I saw was that it had white fur and a fluffy tail almost as big as its body.

I shot to my feet on the rock, completely alert and captivated by the critter. It trilled again. Its voice was melodic and exotic. Whatever the creature was, it wasn't like anything I'd ever seen before.

I followed the critter with my eyes. The way it stretched out its arms and swung from branch to branch was effortless and adorable. I had the strangest urge to climb up the tree and swing from the branches with it. I actually cracked a smile.

The creature reached the end of a branch hanging over the river. I caught enough of a glance to see it was male. He stretched forward to grab a branch on the next tree, but it was a few inches out of his grasp. The animal glanced behind himself, as if calculating what he had to do to make the leap. He scurried back along the branch and stopped. He set his eyes forward, then sprinted away from the trunk of the tree.

The creature kicked off from the end of his branch and soared through the air. He grabbed ahold of the leaves on the tree he'd been aiming for. The whole branch bowed, and then the leaves he held snapped off the tree.

My stomach lurched as the critter flipped through the air and landed in the water with a hard splash. The water rushed so fast that when he came up for air a second later, he was already several yards down river from where he fell in.

I couldn't explain why I did what I did. I didn't even give it a second thought. I just jumped. One second I was standing on a boulder along the bank, and the next I was in the middle of the river, with shoes on and everything.

The current caught me as soon as I jumped in. I was *so* not a water person, but my parents had forced me into swimming lessons as a kid, so I wasn't completely useless. But I'd underestimated how fast the current flowed. The water rushed over my head and pushed me over rocks that cut into my skin. I tried to dig my feet into the river bottom to slow myself, but each time I manage to gain a hold on a rock, the current swept me off my feet again.

Finally, my head broke the surface long enough for me to inhale a deep breath. The current slowed, and the river grew wider and deeper. Up ahead, tiny white hands shot out of the water, and then they were gone again.

I kicked my legs and pushed myself forward. Not far ahead, the river turned back into rapids. Huge boulders stuck out of the water, threatening death to anyone who came too close. If I didn't reach the critter soon, I was going to die. *He* was going to die. And I couldn't let that happen. I couldn't explain the overwhelming sensation that told me that if I somehow survived without him, it just might kill me anyway.

A high-pitched cry filled the air and echoed off the mountains. The creature resurfaced and tried to swim upstream without making any headway. Dread filled my entire body.

I stretched my arm forward and stroked as fast as I could toward him. Relief washed over me when I finally reached him. The critter grabbed onto my arm and climbed onto my back, leaving both of my arms free to swim to shore.

It took all the strength I had to get us to dry land before the rapids hit, but I crawled to shore in one piece. I fell onto my stomach, heaving in heavy breaths as my heart pounded against my rib cage. I wasn't sure I'd ever been closer to death. And all for...

What was it?

Whatever it was, it was worth it, I decided.

I rolled over, and the creature jumped off my back. I expected him to run away now that he was safe, but when I twisted my head, he was still there, so close that all I saw was a coat of white fur. He shook his fur out, covering my face in another layer of water droplets.

I sat up to wipe the water off my face with the back of my hand, then looked down at him. Oh, my heart. It was the cutest thing I'd ever seen. I thought my heart might explode.

He had big, fur-covered ears like a fennec fox, with a fluffy tail, chubby cheeks, and a small black nose. Two tiny, rounded horns protruded from the top of his head. His paws were miniature and adorable. The thing that got me, though, were his eyes. I'd only ever seen eyes that big and round in cartoons and on stuffed animals. But here he was in real life, staring up at me with sparkling blue eyes that took up half his face. The creature's expression softened, and I swear he *smiled* at me.

I was so entranced by his stare that it didn't even register how strange it was that he reached out for me. I extended my arm back. His tiny paws grabbed my fingers, and he hopped forward to rub his face into my hand. His eyes never left mine.

Around us, time seemed to slow to a stop. My entire body froze. I was certain even my heart had stopped beating, and I knew for sure I wasn't breathing. Something in that moment changed everything. It was like I'd been missing something my whole life, and when the tiny critter's gaze locked on mine, a piece of my heart had been returned to me. It was like I'd lived my whole life going through the motions just to lead me to this moment.

Time started to move forward again, but neither me nor the creature moved. My senses ignited, rooting me in place. A light, warm breeze brushed across my skin and through my hair. I felt a heartbeat pulse through my skin, but it didn't feel like my own. The sound of the birds chirping met my ears. They sang a tune that sounded a lot like the lullaby my mom used to hum to me as a kid. The birds' voices came together as a choir, singing in perfect harmony. As I stared down at the creature, the taste of my father's homemade cherry pie washed across my taste buds, and the smell of Amelia's apple-scented shampoo filled my nose. It didn't make sense what these reminders of my family were doing here out in the woods hundreds of miles from home, but one thing was certain. I'd never felt more at home in my life. My entire body tingled with glee, and tears rose to my eyes from sheer overwhelm.

The creature's eyes glistened, mirroring my own. He never looked away, as if he too was captivated by the magic in the air.

I forgot all about what happened in Madame Doya's class earlier. I forgot about wanting to leave this place. I forgot about *everything*. It was like nothing but me and the little creature clinging to my finger mattered. For the first time in... forever, I felt truly at peace.

The critter trilled again, pulling me from my daze. The warm wind died down, chilling me to the bone, and the sound of the birds I'd heard no longer reached us.

The critter nudged me again. I laughed and scratched behind its ears. He let out a low rumble, like a cat's purr. I was pretty sure he liked it. The more I petted him, the more I laughed, but inside, my mind was fixed on the strange moment that just occurred between us. Had I imagined it, or was there something bigger going on?

"What's your name, little guy?" I asked out loud.

He made a small noise that sounded a lot like *Esis*.

"Esis?" I asked, as if he could actually communicate with me. "That's your name?"

Obviously, he didn't answer, but he let me pet him like he was happy with whatever name I gave him.

"Okay, Esis." I scooped his tiny, fragile body into my arms, cradling him into my chest. He clung onto my shirt in a surprisingly comfortable position. I giggled and stood. "You're not going to let me go, are you?"

Of course not. Why would he? The mere suggestion didn't make any logical sense.

He let out another noise that sounded like he was rolling his tongue. I loved the little noises he made. They were the cutest sounds in the world. I wanted to keep him.

Screw whatever rules their might be. I *would* keep him. He was mine now, and I was his.

I stared down at the small fur baby in my arms. He had his foot in his hands and was chewing on his toes. How had my heart not exploded yet?

"I'm going to take you up to the school and find someone who can check you over," I told him. "I want to make sure you're all right."

I glanced around the forest, wondering how I was going to find my way back to the castle. I started upstream, hoping to meet up with the trail I'd come down.

Water squished through my sneakers, and goosebumps broke out on my arms. It seemed to take forever to walk through the brush upstream. I was starting to think maybe I was following the wrong river or something when the bridge I'd seen earlier came into view. I hurried along the trail and back up to the castle.

I wasn't sure where I was headed, but I knew I wasn't going back to Madame Doya's room. I'd find another professor to send me in the right direction. The hall was empty when I entered, but it wasn't long before a familiar voice met my ears.

"What happened to *you*?" Haley sneered when I passed a hall on my left. She and her group of five were hanging out around a serpent statue, gossiping. I hoped it wasn't about me, but it probably was. "Did you get into a fight with a Toaqua?"

I gritted my teeth. "No, actually, I jumped in to save—"

"*That?*" Haley turned her nose up when she spotted Esis in my arms. "You saved a dust bunny?"

Her cronies echoed her laughter. I was officially royally pissed off. Esis made a noise that sounded a lot like a comeback. Good. At least *he* knew how to stand up to her.

"I—"

"What's going on?" A woman's voice cut me off.

I whirled around to find Madame Doya standing behind me. She looked me up and down, clearly displeased by my soaking appearance. Her Familiar stood beside her. Naomi's lips curled back over its teeth as she glared at me. I pulled Esis closer to me, just in case the lioness thought she was hungry for a snack.

I spoke before Haley could. "This little guy fell in the river. I wanted to get him to a vet— or whatever you have around here— to make sure he's okay."

Madame Doya eyed Esis. "You can take him to Professor Fawn, but it's hardly worth it."

"What do you mean?" I asked.

"No one knows what that creature is, so even if he could be treated, we wouldn't know how to treat him," Madame Doya explained, like Esis' life was about as important as the dirt on her pointed heels.

"Thank you," I said, just to end the conversation. "I'll go find Professor Fawn." Not like I had any idea where to find him— or her— but I'd do anything to get out of this hallway.

"I bet she bonded with it," Haley muttered under her breath before I could even take a step.

I paused, wondering what exactly that would feel like. *Had* I bonded with Esis?

"What's it like to bond with Familiar?" I asked Doya, expecting a disapproving glance and curt answer, which is exactly what I got.

"It's different for everyone," she replied.

Even without a clear explanation, somehow I knew... the moment we'd shared in the woods left no doubt. Esis and I had bonded. Which meant I was never letting him go.

The lioness stepped forward and let out a low growl. I instantly took two paces back.

"Calm down, Naomi," Madame Doya scolded, placing her hand on the lioness' back.

Naomi glanced back at her and dropped her head. Madame Doya raised an eyebrow, but her lips turned down.

"It seems that you *have* bonded," she said, eyeing Esis with disgust. "I expected better from a member of my House."

What the hell did *that* mean?

"Now it makes sense why she can't produce a flame," one of the girls in Haley's group said to the other. She spoke under her breath, but I heard every word.

My jaw tightened. I knew I couldn't snap back, not in front of Doya.

"If you bonded, I guess that means you'll be competing in this year's tournament," Haley said with a smirk.

"Tournament?" My voice shook. She was only saying it to scare me, right?

Madame Doya sighed, like she couldn't believe how uninformed I was. I blamed her for that, considering she was the head of my House.

"Yes, the tournament," she bit, like it was obvious. "Each student who has bonded by the end of September every year will be entered into the Elemental Cup to prove their bond with their Familiar and their place in our society."

That didn't sound too bad.

Madame Doya scowled at me. "I suggest you don't make skipping class a habit. You'll need all the help you can get preparing for this tournament considering your current... circumstances. Your competition will be fierce."

Madame Doya glanced to Haley, who had a smug expression fixed on her face. I knew instantly she meant that Haley would be in this year's competition with me.

I bit back the string of nasty words that danced on the tip of my tongue. "I'm not too worried about the competition."

88

Haley's face fell. "You *should* be worried. You'll never survive with *that* Familiar."

The blood drained from my face when no one countered her. Haley wasn't just insulting me. She was serious. I realized... this was a *deadly* competition.

It was clear that if I didn't learn how to use my fire, this tournament would kill me.

Liam

NINE

I wasn't looking forward to Medical Care of Familiars. But it wasn't like I had a choice whether or not to go.

The class was held in a large medical room tied onto the medical wing. Medical equipment hung on the walls, and long desks with sinks were placed among the room in uniform manner. The room was stark white, and the fluorescent lighting in here was so bright it was enough to make you go blind. It looked like the literal inside of a hospital. I'd spent enough time in one over the summer, so it churned my stomach to look at.

I was late again (a bad habit that I was developing, but fine with), and most of the class was already here. I saw that Haley and her morons were in this class, too. But my attention only lingered on them for a moment, because my eyes went directly to Sophia.

There was a tiny animal sitting on Sophia's shoulder. It was white and looked like nothing but a big fur ball rolling around her torso. Sophia giggled as she played with it, and the little puffer let out tiny mews as she tickled it.

It made her happy. Which made me happy, I guess.

"You've bonded!" I said as I walked up to her. She saw me coming and grinned. My heart skipped a beat, but I ignored it. Feelings were for losers.

"Yep." Sophia was stroking the little critter on her shoulder, who had calmed as I'd approached. "Isn't he just so cute and fluffy?"

He was, even though I didn't know *what* he was. "What's his name?"

"Esis," she responded cheerfully. "I just got him yesterday. I found him in the woods."

Like I'd found Nashoma. "Is that a ball of lint?" I asked, smirking.

"Stop it!" She recoiled away from me, holding Esis. "Don't pick on him!"

"I'm just teasing. He's cute." I reached out to scratch Esis under the chin. His eyes rolled back and he grinned, thumping his foot.

I looked at Sophia. "How did Fire class go yesterday?" I didn't even know why I was asking.

Her smile fell. "Terrible, actually. Everyone else can make fire snap from their fingers. I tried, but it didn't happen."

"You can't even make a flame?" I asked, surprised.

Sophia looked down in shame. "No. I can't even light a candle."

Hoo boy. She was gonna have one hell of a time during the tournament with Esis. His survival skills seemed nonexistent. She'd better hurry up and master Fire quick, before she became one of the casualties.

Thinking of Sophia dying made me really sad. So I didn't. I was just glad I wasn't required to join the tournament because I'd lost Nashoma. Competing against Sophia wouldn't be fun, but being on a team with her would be a nightmare.

"Don't worry. This class will be easier," I told her. I was reassuring her. Why, I didn't know.

"Liam!" someone said behind me. I turned to see Jonah next to me, his hippogriff Familiar following behind him.

Jonah was huge. And I mean *huge*. He was easily six-foot-five, and towered over everyone else at Orenda. His brown hair was up in a man-bun, and a thick beard grew halfway down his chest. He wore a red plaid shirt with loose dark-wash jeans, and boots I'm pretty sure a dragon could fit into. His arms were as big around as tree trunks, for crying out fricken loud.

Jonah had bonded over the summer. Jonah's hippogriff, Squeaks, was dancing around and knocking stuff over behind him. I'm pretty sure she had ADHD, because no matter what the class was Squeaks couldn't stand still. She was as big as a draft horse and brown in color, with ginger feathers that gleamed in the light. Her eyes were yellow, her beak pitch-black. I had to step out of the way to avoid getting my foot stomped as she continued her frantic dance, hooves tapping a beat.

Jonah and I hadn't really talked since what had happened with Nashoma, though he and Squeaks had come to the funeral a few weeks later. I shook his hand and bumped my shoulder against his.

"Hey, man. What's up with you?" Jonah asked.

"Not much." I shrugged. "Same old shit."

"I was worried you wouldn't come back this year," Jonah said. "I'm glad to see you didn't give it up."

Sophia was eyeing me curiously. I forced a laugh and said, "I stayed to annoy you."

"Always, buddy." Jonah's eyes followed Renar (a tall, thin guy who I always thought had a face that looked like a rat's) as he entered the classroom and sat at one of the desks in the front row.

"You preoccupied? Because, you know, I can always leave you two alone," I poked.

Jonah's attention was still on Renar. "Yeah, yeah, you're hilarious. Hang out later?"

He didn't wait for me to answer before he crossed the room and slid into the seat beside Renar, talking lowly and nudging him with his shoulder. Squeaks muscled her way in beside him and sat down next to the desk.

I rolled my eyes. That was Jonah. He was always after the D.

"I thought people from different Houses couldn't be friends?" Sophia asked me in a low tone, a small smile on her face.

"Shut up," I mumbled to her as the professor entered. Sophia didn't get it. A Toaqua guy being friends with a Yapluma dude was no big deal. Not like Sophia's and my friendship would be. Water and Air could mix. Water and Fire... no go.

"Gather 'round, everyone!" Professor Costas said, and eventually, the chatter quieted down.

I focused on Costas. I'd had her before. She wore a long white coat, with a stethoscope hanging around her neck. She was short and looked cute, but she'd seen her fair share of blood and gore.

"Welcome to my class," Costas started. "Now, I know many of you are wondering why this class is necessary, as for most of you, you will be staying within the ranks of the Elementai, and will be near enough to emergency medical care."

Professor Costas paused to gaze around the class. "However, some of you will be taking positions within the tribe that will require you to be away from home and away from other Elementai. When you're out in the field, you won't be able to get to medical care quickly. In a majority of cases, you will be alone and must rely on yourself to save your Familiar's life. Which is why the majority of this class will be held outside, away from the equipment you undoubtedly won't have while exploring the wild. Follow me!"

Professor Costas led us outside, to where a collection of really creepy life size Familiar dolls were lying around. They were in various shapes and sizes of animals, and were meant to practice on.

I was feeling a little glum. Maybe if I had taken this class last year, I could've saved Nashoma.

Also waiting outside was Costas' Familiar, Hera. She was a hydra, a large reptile with nine heads, green in color and very intimidating. She walked on four legs with large, rounded claws, and was about as big as a small house. Venomous fangs protruded from the mouth of each head, along with a collection of poisonous spines along the creature's back all the way down to her long, whip-like tail. From what I'd heard from other people, Hera was a real sweetheart.

I'd believe that *after* I'd spend enough time with her to know one of her nine heads wasn't going to eat me.

"Pair up, everyone!" Costas yelled loudly. "For this, I'll need you to work in teams!"

The best people were gone in seconds. Jonah immediately paired up with Renar, which I saw coming. Everyone else already had a partner, which meant I was stuck with Sophia.

She immediately gravitated toward me, and of course, I took in the sorry orphan, because I was a sorry orphan too. We sat next to a doll that looked like a tiger, and Costas held up a bandage with splints.

"Listen up, and pay close attention. I will be instructing you on how to create a splint for broken bones," Costas started. She demonstrated on Hera, and I tried to watch. but I noticed Sophia was nodding off, her eyes following Hera around the gardens instead of listening to Costas' instruction.

Learning to set bones was useful, but it was tough work for the first day of class. Sophia couldn't wrap the bindings tight enough, and I think she ended up breaking the doll's leg worse than what it originally was. I face-palmed at least five times.

Esis didn't make things any easier. He kept on running around over the doll, squeaking and tumbling like he didn't see the point in wrapping up a broken limb. At one point he sank his little teeth into the wrappings and started tugging at it, trying to play. Sophia laughed, but it wasn't funny to me.

At least we weren't the only ones struggling. Haley got frustrated and ended up throwing her doll, which made me chuckle under my breath. Jonah was sitting around and letting Renar do all the work. While Renar was binding up the doll's leg, I caught Jonah looking at his ass. I got Jonah's attention, pointed to Renar when his back was turned, and made humping movements with my hips.

Jonah went red and flipped me off. I laughed.

"What's with you guys?" Sophia questioned, raising an eyebrow.

"Jonah's been crushing on Renar forever, but he hasn't made a move," I explained.

"Hm." Sophia nodded, then went back to wrapping the mangled doll's leg. Esis stared at me, his eyes getting bigger... and bigger... and bigger.

By the time I ripped my gaze away, I'm pretty sure his giant pupils were covering the rest of his face. That thing was an alien or something.

By the end of the class, bandages were everywhere. A couple of girls were crying in frustration, and Haley was bitching. Most everyone had given up.

Costas' face was thin and brittle. She obviously wasn't impressed.

"The majority of you will need to study up. This is not an easy class. If you perform like you have today, you are going to fail. Tomorrow, we'll be learning how to perform CPR on your Familiar, and next week we'll get into poisons. Class dismissed."

People scattered out of there. Professor Costas was a hard-ass, but at least she was fair. She was far from Madame Doya. I looked down at our doll. We'd managed to fix the leg back to normal, and the bandages were wrapped tightly now, but I'm pretty sure if it had been a real tiger Sophia and I would've killed it.

Sophia looked happy, though. "We actually make a pretty good team, don't we?"

Esis let out a *mew*, and I told Sophia, "Don't get your hopes up."

We stood up to leave. We didn't mean to walk together, that's just what happened.

Near the entry to the gardens, Haley was taking out her frustration on another Koigni First Year. "You know Costas was talking about you, Taylor," she said. "You're never going to pass."

Taylor was in tears. I think she was Levi's little sister, which would make sense— Haley and Levi dated over the summer before he realized what a bitch she was and thankfully dumped her. But that meant his little sis had to spend a whole semester of enduring Haley's torments. Poor girl.

"Leave her alone, Haley," Jonah bit at her, laying a hand on Taylor's shoulder. "Yours looked worse."

Haley's eyes narrowed, and she sneered. "Aren't people from Yapluma supposed to be thin and small? How do you expect your hippogriff to lift your fat ass, Goliath?" Haley goaded, and her friends roared at the insult.

"He's another abomination, like Sophia," Kelsey, Haley's second-in-command, added. "His mom probably slept around with some Nivita guy. This is why Houses shouldn't mix. You get all these freaks running around."

"Right? Sophia's so inbred she can't even light a candle. Her magic's useless, just like her stupid Familiar," Haley said, shooting Sophia a nasty grin.

Haley and her friends roared. Esis puffed up into a little ball of fury, hopping up and down on Sophia's shoulder and stomping his tiny feet. Sophia tried to comfort him— his tiny cheeks swelled up as he made a quick *whoosh* sound. Sophia looked troubled, like she didn't know what to do.

Jonah moved closer to Taylor and whispered, "Are you okay?"

Taylor slapped his hand away. She backed up, wiping away more tears. "Stay away from me." She took off as fast as she could, and Haley grinned. She knew she'd won.

Haley then looked at me. She dug around in her bag for something, and then threw it at me. "Here. I thought you might need this, Liam. Finish the job, since you're no good to the tribe anymore."

It hit me. My insides cringed as my hands caught what she'd tossed. A rope.

Sophia's face was red with rage. Sophia didn't understand what Haley's comment meant, not really, but it still pissed her off. She opened her mouth to say something.

But I wasn't dealing with this. Haley's actions didn't deserve a reaction. I stuffed the rope inside my pocket, then grabbed Sophia's wrist to pull her away before a bigger scene was made. Jonah turned his back on Haley to look for Renar, but he was already gone.

"I'm getting really tired of people picking on me," Sophia grumbled as we walked away. There was a large stone fountain with a statue of a thunderbird taking flight on top of it. Nobody was around, and Sophia paused to catch her breath. She was furious.

"So then do something about it," I told her. "Fight back."

"Fight back?" She gave me a condescending look. "You just dragged me away before I could say anything."

"Because you've got to fight in the right way. You can't just say whatever you want. Haley's mean, but she's also super smart," I told her. "Not to mention she'll go running to Madame Doya the minute you open your mouth. You've got to fight with actions, not words."

Sophia sighed. "I guess you're right."

She sat on the edge of the fountain. "This sucks. I was so happy when I found Esis. It was like everything was going to be okay," she started.

I nodded. I knew the feeling. "And?"

"And... then Madam Doya ruined it." She made a face.

"Typical of her."

"I'm supposed to be some prophesied child, but I can't even make a tiny flame. Everyone talks about unity, but it's just crap. No one wants to help me. And now there's this tournament, and..."

She sighed in defeat. "I don't know, Liam. I don't know how to do this."

The thought crossed my mind to help her. I wasn't supposed to be teaching a Koigni how to use a flame. I didn't even know how to do it myself. But the thought of Madame Doya's bitchy face as she gazed down in Sophia in disappointment was enough to make me act. "You'll show her. Come on, follow me."

I started walking toward the forest, where we wouldn't be seen. She followed. When we were deep enough into the trees, I motioned for her to put down Esis. She put him up on a tree branch. He looked down at us in interest, large ears forward.

"If you want to beat Haley, you have to show her you're better than her at magic," I started. "Nothing she could say will trump that. It'll eat away at her."

"How? She's the best in my class, and I'm the worst." Sophia's shoulders slumped. "She's had years of practice."

"You need someone willing to teach you. Not just yell at you," I started, before I paused. "And I guess that sad sack is me."

"You?" She raised an eyebrow. "But you're Toaqua. How do you know how to conjure fire?"

"I don't. I'm just guessing. But it's all elemental magic, right? Can't be too difficult."

I showed her. I hovered my hand over the ground, and dew droplets rose from the dirt, leaves and grass to form a ball of water in my hand. I moved it back and forth, weaving my hands like a wave as the water swished in the air from this side to that.

"Let your magic flow through you. It's an extension of your body. You are connected to the earth and everyone in it. Everything is a living thing, and is willing to help you. Use that connection to summon your power."

Sophia tried. She raised her hands and tried to conjure magic, but all that resulted was a look that made her seem like she had to shit.

"I don't get it," she said. "Can you explain another way?"

I thought for a moment. Harnessing water was all about self-control. You had to let peace and harmony flow through you steadily before you gathered it into a powerful force. Water sustained life, but it could also take it.

Fire was different. Fire was raging and angry and was fueled by strong emotions unbound by any force. Koigni were strong and ill-tempered. They burned off of pride. It was one of the reasons Haley was so good.

No wonder Sophia couldn't create a flame. She was too meek, too gentle. She had to get pissed. I literally was going to have to light a fire under her ass.

"Think about Madame Doya. How she humiliated you in front of everyone, and how badly you want to prove her wrong," I said. "Meditate on how that feels."

Sophia scrunched up her face. Moments passed, and became minutes. I wondered if we'd be out here for hours.

Suddenly, a ball of flame appeared brightly in her palm. She opened her eyes, mouth falling open in delight, but the flame only lasted a few seconds before vanishing.

"Did you see that?" she screeched happily, bouncing. "I did it!"

"You did. You see? It's not that hard." I shrugged. "Madame Doya's just a terrible teacher."

"Yeah." She grinned and looked up at me. "Thanks, Liam. I just hope I can do it again in Madame Doya's class."

"You've got it," I encouraged. "Just trust in yourself, and the ancestors will guide you."

"Ancestors? I don't believe in anything like that," Sophia said. "All that spiritual stuff is really silly. My parents didn't raise me like that. Believing in the afterlife is for people who can't stand on their own."

Esis looked at his Elementai like he couldn't believe what she'd just said, ears back and little lips trembling. I went to bite back something sharp before I held my tongue. Here I was helping this girl, and she was blatantly disrespecting our religion, our culture. She just didn't understand what it meant to be part of the Hawkei.

No good deed goes unpunished, I suppose. *Now* she was acting like a superior Koigni. Great fricking timing. This was why the Elders didn't allow outsiders.

Esis came down from the trees. But instead of going to Sophia, the squirrel reject went for me. He landed on top of my head and screamed in what seemed like a victory as he perched on top of my skull.

"Dude, get down." I tried yanking him off, but it didn't work. Esis was set on riding on top of my head. He'd made a nest in my hair and was clinging onto the strands to hold on, making loud cooing noises like he was the captain of this ship.

"He likes you." Sophia grinned.

"Yeah, well, I don't like him." I gave up and let him sit there. It wasn't like he weighed anything. We started back to the castle, where hopefully I would find a vice grip to pry the little bugger off.

But then there was more than the sound of our footsteps crunching the earth. Someone was giving an audible shout.

A cry for help.

"Did you hear that?" Sophia looked at me.

I paused to listen for a second, then nodded when I heard the voice again. "Yeah. Someone's in trouble."

Esis took off. He leapt off my head and started jumping from tree to tree toward the screaming.

"Esis, wait!" Sophia cried. We broke into a run to keep up with him. He became a little white dot in the leaves, zig-zagging this way and that.

Sophia was ahead of me. She didn't look where she was going, and someone stepped onto the path, who Sophia slammed into.

"Oof!" the figure cried. Imogen again.

"What are you doing here?" I asked her as she untangled herself from Sophia. I helped both girls up and stared at Imogen. She was wearing these large bunny ears that looked like antennas poking out of her hair. Sassy was nearby, rising on her hind legs curiously.

"I had some free time and was out looking for wolpertingers. Sassy loves to play with them," Imogen said. "We were adventuring until we heard screaming, and we came this way."

I was pretty sure whatever Imogen said didn't exist, but I went along with it. Another voice broke through the woods.

"Oy! There you guys are!"

From behind us and with a bunch of twigs in his hair came Jonah, grinning like a wildcat.

"Jonah? What the fuck?" I asked. Squeaks was having a hard time getting through the trees. The hippogriff crushed bushes and knocked over saplings on her struggle to get to Jonah, squawking her irritation at him.

"I saw you and Sophia go into the woods together, and I got curious." Jonah waggled his eyebrows. "But then... I got lost."

"Typical." I rolled my eyes. Jonah wasn't very good with directions.

Esis was hopping up and down in the tree ahead of us, peeping and wanting us to keep up. There was another scream.

"Let's go," Sophia said, and she led the way.

"Isn't it so interesting how we're all going on such an adventure? I think we're going to be very good friends," Imogen said pleasantly amongst the backdrop of the horrified wailing.

"Yeah. We're a fucking group, all right," I mumbled. The Kogini girl who couldn't conjure fire, the gay Yapluma guy who was too big to be from Yapluma, the weird Nivita girl who creeped everyone out, and me, the Familiar-less cripple. This joke was too damn perfect. If anyone saw me together with all these people at the same time, I'd be a laughingstock.

The trees eventually ended and cleared. Below us was a large cliff about fifteen feet tall, and at the bottom was a thick black tar pit, sticky and deep.

Tar pits weren't unusual around here. There were quite a few dotted throughout the woods. Most people knew to stay away from them, but apparently not this time.

The yelling was coming from Professor Perot. He was submerged in the middle of the pit up to his neck, the only thing being free his arms and his head. His peacock Familiar, Baxtor, was fluttering around the pit trying to get Perot out. But he had changed. Baxtor's body had morphed into a bird representing a cloud. His body, feathers and plumage were transparent and white, and he fluttered over Professor Perot frantically. With each beat of his wing, he tried to summon the winds to get them to lift Perot out of the muck, but his magic just wasn't strong enough. All the rampaging air managed to do was buffet the trees around and knock a few limbs down. The lower Perot sank, the weaker Baxtor got. He was sinking too, struggling to keep himself aloft as Perot gasped for air.

Perot's eyes caught us on the cliff. "Children!" he shouted. "Go away from here! This isn't something you can see!"

"We'll get you out!" I yelled back.

"It's too late! Leave!" Perot coughed, the thick tar rising up to his chin.

He already considered himself a goner. Not on my watch.

"We need to find a teacher," Jonah said. He went to run back the way he came, but I snagged him by the arm to hold him back.

"There's no time. He'll be dead by the time we get help. We're going to have to work together," I said.

I raised my hands. My power searched the tar pit below for some sort of liquid. It was in there, but it wasn't much. I gritted my teeth and tried to make the liquid beneath Perot move upward. I managed to budge him up for a moment, but once I let go, he sank right back down.

"There isn't enough water in there for me to manipulate. Tar is earth. Do you think you could try, Imogen?" I asked.

"I can." She took a deep breath and stepped forward. She raised a hand toward the tar pit. We stood around her in a circle, waiting for something to happen. The tar pit bubbled and rumbled, but nothing else happened. Imogen gasped and dropped her hand.

"I can't." Imogen wiped a bit of sweat from her brow. "I'm sorry, Liam, but I'm just a First Year. If I had a bit more experience, I could."

"Fire won't help. If I try to burn it, he'll be killed in seconds," Sophia said.

"Air is already useless," Jonah said grimly, staring at Baxtor.

"We're going to have to figure out another way." I put my hand to my mouth and thought. We had ten minutes, maybe, before Perot went under. But if our powers didn't work to get him out, what would?

"There!" Sophia interrupted my train of thought by pointing to a loosely hanging tree branch Baxtor had blown free. She walked up to the branch and ripped it off, handing it to Jonah.

"Jonah, can you get your Familiar to dangle this over the professor? Maybe she can yank him out," Sophia said.

"Worth a shot," Jonah replied. He handed the branch to Squeaks, who took it with her beak. She flew over Perot and dangled the branch over him.

"Professor! Grab the branch, and she'll pull you out!" Sophia cried.

Professor Perot reached up to grab the branch. Once he had ahold of it with two hands, Squeaks pulled. His upper body rose out of the tar, but from the waist down, he was still stuck. No matter how hard Squeaks pulled, she couldn't yank him free.

"It's not working," Jonah said. He appeared tired at Squeaks' struggle. "She's not strong enough."

Sophia looked desperately at me. I got an idea. "Here." I pulled the rope Haley had thrown at me out of my pocket. It was just long enough. I tied a loop, then handed the end of it to Sophia, Imogen and Jonah. "We'll slide down the embankment, then get this around him. With all of us, we should be able to pull him out."

Sophia nodded. "Right."

This was way dangerous. We had an equal chance of falling in and getting trapped ourselves. But there wasn't really any other plan. I slid down the embankment first, on my back, then Sophia followed, trailed by Imogen and Jonah. At the bottom was a thin strip of dirt we could stand on. Perot saw what we were doing, and his eyes widened.

"Don't risk your own lives, children! I'm not worth it!" he yelled.

"Yes you are," I said firmly. "Let go of the stick for a moment. We'll lasso you and pull you to shore."

Meekly, Perot did as he was told. I concentrated, focusing my eyes on him. We only had one rope. If I missed, it was game over.

I tossed the rope, and thankfully, it looped around Perot. He adjusted it so it was around his waist, then reached up to grab the branch Squeaks was dangling again.

"All together!" Sophia shouted. "Pull!"

We yanked on the rope. It wasn't an easy task. Perot really was stuck. Even with all of us pulling, he remained trapped.

"Harder!" Sophia shouted. "I know we can do this!"

Her confidence wasn't helping me, but it obviously did something for Jonah and Imogen, because Perot began to move through the tar toward us. Baxter flew forward and latched his talons under the branch Squeaks was holding, helping her pull up. Sassy lunged forward and sank her teeth into the rope to help Imogen pull. Esis hopped up and down on the cliff above and cheered us on.

"It's working!" I shouted. Perot was getting closer and closer to shore. "Keep pulling! He's almost there!"

With a monumental effort that was gonna pull out my back, all of us yanked at once. Perot came free of the tar pit and landed onshore, heaving. Squeaks dropped the branch and Baxter flew forward, landing on the shore and pecking at Perot's head.

"I'm fine, Baxtor," Perot breathed. "I'm fine."

"Professor, are you all right?" I asked him. "What were you even doing out here?"

"I was looking for magical mushrooms for our class next week, before I tripped and stumbled down the embankment," Perot said. "I didn't see the pit, and fell in. I would've died if you and your Familiars hadn't come along."

Perot was obviously very weak, and his clothes were stuck to his body. Sophia moved forward and said, "Come on. We've got to get him back to the castle."

Shadows loomed overhead. We looked up and saw that Madame Doya was there with Naomi, as well as Head Dean Alric. Valda landed by his side, staring down the pit. She was an amethyst dragon, with brilliant gemstone eyes that stared down in concern at Perot. Her large leathery wings blocked out a portion of the sun as she stared down at us.

"Perfect timing. Thanks for all the help," I grumbled.

"Perot! Can you stand?" Alric called down.

"I... I am strong enough to make it up the embankment, but not to walk much after," Perot said.

We helped Perot up the hill before we climbed it ourselves. By this time, I was exhausted. I still had a long walk back to the castle before I sank into my nice, warm bed. With help from Alric, Perot climbed onto Valda's back, and she spread her wings to take him to the medical wing.

Now that Perot was out of the pit and safe, Baxtor changed back into a regular peacock. He cooed as he followed behind Valda to safety.

"You children are remarkable. Thank you for risking your lives to save Perot's," Alric said to us. "I'm afraid the situation would've ended quite differently, if you weren't involved. Madame Doya and I were just on our evening walk before we heard the shouting. I daresay we wouldn't have reached him in time."

The guy was practically astounded that we'd stuck out our necks to rescue a teacher. People had morals every now and then, didn't they?

Madame Doya didn't look happy. In fact, it looked like she was almost displeased we'd saved Perot's life.

"It's nothing. Don't mention it," Sophia said, smiling.

Don't mention it? Are you kidding? I wanted to scream at her. Wasn't there some sort of award we'd get for this? Really?

"Yes. Well." Alric forced a grimace at her. "I think it'd be best if you returned to your dormitories. I also think it best if we keep this between us, and prevent gossip from spreading."

Jonah nodded like a brainless doll, and I took the first opportunity I could to get the hell out of there.

Great. We weren't even going to get any credit for this. All because of Sophia.

Sophia, Imogen and Jonah followed me back to the castle. I expected us to split up at the door, but they kept trailing me, along with their quirky Familiars. Esis was sitting on Sophia's shoulder again, and was singing some sort of peppy tune.

Ancestors, it was like the soundtrack to a sitcom or something, and I was living it.

"You guys want to eat together?" Sophia gestured toward the dining hall. Her cheeks were a bit pink. "I... well, I usually eat alone, but it'd be nice if you'd like to join."

"I'm in." Jonah rubbed his stomach and threw an arm around Squeaks. "Me and Squeaks are always down for some grub."

Imogen's smile spread wide at Sophia's invite. "Sure! Liam, you want to come?"

I was starving, but I wouldn't be seen with them. I wanted some alone time. "I'm not hungry. I'm heading back to my dorm."

I turned my back before they said anything else. Sophia's face was crestfallen. I felt bad about being a dick, but still. I knew that I'd messed up.

It was one thing to be polite and be acquaintances. Maybe even friends. But being in a life-or-death situation was an entirely different story. I didn't want to be that close to anyone. I was supposed to be the lone wolf.

I'd formed a bond with these people, which was a critical mistake.

§&

THE NEXT DAY, Sophia was still following me around like a puppy dog, which was irritating. She couldn't stop talking about how amazing it was that we'd saved Perot. Since I wasn't getting some type of reward, I just wanted to forget about it.

"You were pretty cool yesterday," she commented after she'd caught me coming in from Water class, and I groaned. "You're a good leader."

"Don't say that. I don't like helping people," I growled.

"You helped me earlier." She leaned against a window in the hallway. Esis was in her arms, and he did that weird staring thing with his eyes again when he looked at me, his little mouth forming a tiny grin. That fluff ball was gonna give me nightmares.

"Totally different."

"Uh-huh. Sure it was." Sophia's tone was so smug I no longer doubted she was a stolen Koigni child.

"You were the one who came up with the plan," I said. "I just helped."

"What I said earlier is true. We make a good team."

"Oh, yeah. Fire and Water. Great mix." I rolled my eyes. "Think whatever you want, Soph."

I didn't mean to call her that, but I did. She brightened like a lightbulb, and I wanted to hit myself. By the ancestors, it was so hard not to let her in.

"Out of the way!" a teacher's loud shout caught my attention. Baine was clearing a path through the hallway, shoving students aside and directing them to get to the wall. A massive group of professors were behind them. Their faces were drawn and grim, not worried but accepting a dark fate. Students froze like statues, clinging to their Familiars as they saw what was behind the teachers.

Some creature was in the back of a wagon pulled by a black chimera. I couldn't tell what it was, because the animal was covered in a black, velvet shroud. It was utterly still, and didn't move.

The sight of the black shroud caused my body to convulse. I gagged, and almost threw up. Pangs of agony shot through my spine and spread throughout my back, and the room turned wavy. I got light-headed. My body shuddered violently, and I turned away from Sophia so she wouldn't see, pressing my head against the cool rock and shaking.

"Liam?" I felt Sophia's soft hand on my back. "Are you okay?"

I took a few deep breaths and blinked back tears. "I'm... fine." I forced myself to regain my composure and turned back, forced myself to watch the gruesome scene, where I already knew what had happened.

Behind the cart was a boy. Carter. He was from Yapluma. A guy was on either side of him, helping him walk. Carter's face was ashen, and his steps were staggering. The guys more or less carried him as he dragged his feet, his eyes dull and lifeless. All the color had gone out of him. It looked like someone had sucked everything out of him that made him... himself. He said nothing, eyes staring straight ahead, dried tears on his expressionless, void face. Saying he looked half-alive would be a compliment. Carter was more or less a walking corpse. It was the scariest thing to witness.

He was nothing. A shell. There wasn't anything left.

I'd looked the same way when they brought me in. I *felt* the same way. I was the only one in this hallway who knew what Carter was feeling, because not so long ago I had been the one trailing behind that cart, staring at the lifeless form that had been Nashoma, buried under that black shroud.

I jumped when I felt someone coming up behind me. It was Imogen. She snuck between the two of us and kept her voice low.

"You guys hear the news?" she said.

"What's going on?" Sophia asked, confused. I kept quiet and let Imogen explain. This was too painful for me.

"It's Carter. He and Tiara had an accident in Flight class," Imogen whispered.

My stomach sunk. "What happened?"

"Carter misdirected her. They hit a tree, and Tiara spun out into the target they were supposed to fly through. It impaled her through the heart," Imogen hushed. "She died while they were trying to get her back to the medical wing."

Imogen sighed. "Poor kid. He did so much, too. Volunteered for the community, captain of the sports teams and everything. All that's done now. But at least he accomplished something while he was here."

I felt like I was going to throw up again. Sophia was really pale. Horrified screams began echoing down the hallway. The girls turned their heads, but I just closed my eyes and wished it was over.

When the wailing got louder, I was forced to look. I knew him. James, from Nivita. He was beside himself. A couple of girls tried to comfort him as he sobbed. His screams shook the walls as tears streamed down his red face. He was cradling his small dragon Familiar in his arms tightly. He couldn't fly on him yet, but I think that they were in Flight class with Carter and Tiara, too. I bet they'd watched the whole thing.

"Poor James," Imogen said softly. "It's just so sad."

"Are James and Carter really close?" Sophia asked.

"They're best friends," Imogen said lowly. "Or they were. James knows he's gonna have to say goodbye soon. Carter's a goner."

"What do you mean?" Sophia asked, and my heartbeat quickened. "He's okay, isn't he?"

Imogen shook her head. "No. He's not. Elementai can't live without their Familiars, and vice versa. Carter's as good as dead."

"You mean... if you lose your Familiar, you die?" Sophia hushed her voice as the procession passed us by.

Imogen waited until the group was gone before she nodded solemnly. "Yep. It's how it works. You can't survive without your soul."

There was a lump in my throat that was hard to swallow. *Yeah. Except for me.*

"How... how long can you survive without your Familiar?" Sophia said, pulling Esis closer to her.

Imogen shrugged. "If you're older, a few weeks. Months, maybe. But students rarely last a few days. I'll be surprised if Carter makes it through the night. The bond is still too fresh. Nobody outlives their Familiar for long." Imogen shot a look at me. "Well, except for Liam."

"*What?!*" Sophia physically jumped into the air, and I cringed. "Liam's Familiar is dead?"

"Thanks for reminding me," I said sourly. That comment hurt. It felt like she'd slapped me or something.

Her jaw fell slack. "Liam, I..."

"You mean you didn't know?" Imogen's eyes went wide, and she gave an apologetic look toward me. "I'm sorry, Liam. I didn't mean—"

"It's okay, Imogen," I told her quietly.

"You lost your Familiar? I didn't know you'd bonded." Sophia's face is shocked, and in pain. "How?"

"I don't want to talk about it," I said immediately. I didn't want her to press. But she was Sophia, so she did anyway.

"But I—"

"*I don't want to talk about it, Sophia.*" My tone was so harsh she physically recoiled away. I took a walk before she could ask more questions, and before I said something I would regret.

⁊

109

CARTER DIED SOMETIME in the night, as I knew he would. He wasn't strong enough to survive for long after Tiara died.

Lucky bastard.

The school was a little somber the next morning, but mostly normal. It wasn't unusual for students or Familiars to cork off around here. People died every year in the Elemental Cup, after all. Students were given resources on what to do if they were struggling, Carter and Tiara's funeral date was announced, and that was it.

I avoided Sophia. I couldn't face her now that she knew what was wrong with me. I caught her chasing after me a couple of times to apologize, but I managed to duck out and get away from her every time.

I knew the moment was coming where she'd be creeping outside the Toaqua dorm, waiting for me to come out. So I more or less held myself hostage in my room so she wouldn't be able to find me. I knew I could only run from her for so long. We had class together, after all.

That didn't mean I wanted to see her a moment before I was forced to. It hurt too much to face her.

When Ezra told me that Baine wanted to see me, I knew I had to leave my room. I hoped Sophia didn't bump into me on the way. But my brother looked worried. He wouldn't tell me what it was about when I pressed him. I strolled down to Baine's office, thinking that this was finally the moment where I'd be expelled and they were making my House Head tell me.

Baine was hunched over his desk, papers and books scattered everywhere. Little fairies, glowing bright with white light, zoomed around him and made chirping noises. He ignored them, face grim, as I weaved my way around the various trinkets and objects scattered around the room. A carved staff, a few totems, lots and lots of artifacts from his travels around the world were placed in every open spot available. Statues, paintings and scrolls were literally stacked against the walls in piles. Baine had been an explorer for the Hawkei before he became a teacher, venturing through ancient crypts and tombs for the Elders.

I had no idea why he gave up such a cool position just to grade papers for lazy college kids. Maybe, after all those years, he just gave up on whatever he was looking for.

By the ancestors, it was such a mess in here. Baine was a disgusting slob. No wonder he hadn't found a woman to put up with him.

"You wanted to see me?" I asked as I came to a stop at his desk. My shoe crunched a papyrus map and kicked a small golden sculpture. I hoped they weren't important.

"I wanted to warn you before your summons came," Baine started.

"Summons?"

"For the Elemental Cup."

My entire body turned cold. I think I literally shivered— even the fairy lights in the room seemed to dim. "Why would they be summoning me? I'm not competing."

"Yes, you are." I hoped this was some sort of sick joke, but Baine was completely serious. "The Elders have decided that despite your loss, you will be competing in the Cup anyway. It's the only way for you to prove your worth to the tribe. If you don't participate, you'll be exiled. You know what that means, Liam."

I was going to be sick. *This* was sick. I got that the Cup was some sort of coming-of-age ceremony for every Elementai, and that the Elders wanted everyone to compete.

But without Nashoma, I'd *die* out there. And probably get my teammates killed, too.

"I can't enter the Cup! I don't have a Familiar anymore! Nashoma's *gone*," I argued.

"I'm sorry, Liam. But the rules are absolute," Baine said firmly. "It doesn't matter that you lost Nashoma. All Elementai who've bonded with a Familiar over the previous year are required to enter the tournament in order to continue their education at Orenda Academy. That includes you. I'm sorry. You don't have a choice."

A pit of horror formed in my gut, growing larger with each passing second. It didn't matter that my Familiar was dead.

I was being forced to enter the tournament anyway.

sophia
TEN

Life at Orenda Academy was lonely, especially now that Liam was avoiding me, but Esis made everything better. He was my constant companion everywhere I went and cheered me up every time I felt like I was missing home. It was like he could feel my emotions and knew exactly how to make me happy. Usually, he just snuggled into my hair, but one night he actually fanned my hair out on my pillow and gave me the most amazing scalp massage. I didn't care what anyone said about my furry little bundle of joy; he was one of the most amazing, intelligent creatures I'd ever met.

But even Esis couldn't ease my anxiety when it came to dinner time. I stepped into the cafeteria with Esis on my shoulder, knowing I had nowhere to sit. The room was vast, with hundreds of tables situated in rows throughout the room and modern-day booths lining the outer wall. Near the main entrance sat a buffet line piled with some of the most delicious food I'd ever tasted. On the opposite side of the main doors were heating trays with foil-wrapped burgers and wraps that people could take back to their dorms.

The cafeteria was bathed in natural brown tones, with soft lighting that made it look like a fancy restaurant. Along the far wall, a huge mural depicted each House's element from left to right. The orange Koigni fire faded into green trees for Nivita, which swirled into purple wisps for Yapluma and finally blue waves for Toaqua. I'd noticed that there seemed to be an unwritten rule about sitting closest to your element in the mural, with Koigni always sitting toward the left of the room, Toaqua on the right, and Nivita and Yapluma in the middle.

As I stepped into the buffet line I eyed the Koigni section, knowing that if I was going to stay in the cafeteria for dinner, I'd probably have to sit over there. The room was packed with people and their Familiars and buzzed with conversation. I didn't notice a single empty table in the Koigni section. I contemplated whether I should introduce myself to someone or just claim one of the empty tables in another section. It was like I was in middle school all over again.

I made it through the buffet line and stared out at the crowd. I decided to take the easy route and just sit at an empty table when a guy passed by me and his elbow knocked into my shoulder. My tray jumped in my hands, and my plate went flying. The ceramic clattered to the floor, and my potatoes and gravy went everywhere.

"Watch where you're going," the guy snarled before continuing on his way to the Koigni section.

Of course he's Koigni, I thought as I bent to clean up the mess.

Esis jumped down from my shoulder and began licking at the mashed potatoes on the floor.

"Ew, Esis. Don't do that," I scolded, pulling him away from the potatoes. He already had most of them cleaned up.

"Here you go." A pair of hands shot out in front of my face, offering me a pile of napkins.

I glanced up to see Imogen dressed in a floral dress that suited her figure but had *way* too many ruffles on it. Her hoop earrings nearly touched her shoulders, and her hair had been twisted into three separate braids. Her heels were shiny blue like metallic nail polish, with four-inch heels whose points split into three different directions in the shape of bird talons. They looked like something from one of those runway shows where the models wear the most ridiculous things but the outfits never hit the market.

"Thanks," I said shyly, taking the napkins from her.

Imogen gestured to Sassy in the tote bag that hung from her shoulder. "Sassy and I were just going to sit down. Do you want to join us?"

"Sure," I answered far too quickly while I mopped up my spilled food.

"Excellent." Imogen clapped her hands together. "We sit over there, in that booth."

She pointed to a large booth in the corner of the room. Toaqua occupied the tables surrounding it, but Imogen didn't seem to notice.

I stood with my pile of dirty napkins piled atop my tray. "I'll join you in the buffet line. I need a new plate, anyway."

Several minutes later, we slid into our booth in the corner. I sat across from Imogen and faced the wall. I felt more comfortable not being able to see the eyes I knew were on me. Esis jumped down from my shoulder and sat beside me. He placed his little hands on the edge of the table, but he could barely see over the top of it. I was going to need to get this little guy a booster seat.

"How are you liking Orenda Academy so far?" Imogen asked.

"Oh..." I glanced down, completely taken off guard by the question. "It's, um, okay."

"Oh, right," she said wrinkling her nose. "You're Koigni. You probably have Doya. The professors make all the difference. I'm really bummed I didn't get the guy I wanted for my cultures studies class. He's a total dreamboat... I mean, for an old guy."

I just nodded along.

"How many classes are you taking?" she asked.

"Not many," I answered. "I'm only taking the minimum amount of credits, which I guess is good because I'm going to need the extra time to practice my Fire."

"I know what you mean," she agreed. "Beginner Nivita Magic is already kicking my butt. And I have it almost every day of the week."

"Me, too," I said. "Beginner Koigni Magic takes up most of my schedule, then I'm in Medical Care of Familiars a few days a week. I have my first Dragonology class tomorrow."

"Ooh!" Imogen said in excitement. "I'm in Dragonology, too!"

I smiled. It'd be nice to know someone in each of my classes.

"So, what's the dealio?" Imogen asked, discretely dropping a piece of meat to the floor, which Sassy promptly followed and scarfed up. "Is that all you're going to eat?"

I glanced down at my meat and potatoes. "Are you kidding? This looks delicious."

"Sure, if you're bored of traditional Hawkei food," she agreed. "But you aren't even taste-testing half of what they have at the buffet. Are you going to get adventurous, or what?"

I tucked a strand of hair behind my ear. "I tend to play things safe."

"Ah," Imogen said in understanding as she took a bite of food. "Well, not today, girlie. Here, try a bean."

Imogen pushed a long purple bean pod onto my plate. It was slathered in some sort of oil and spices and didn't look appetizing in the slightest.

"What is it?" I asked, unable to keep the skepticism out of my voice.

Imogen shrugged. "We call them magic beans. The ancestors blessed them ages ago, and they prospered in this area. They're like a green bean."

I poked the bean with my fork and held it up to examine it. "But it's purple."

"So? Purple vegetables are delicious," Imogen said. "Beets, eggplant, carrots..."

"Um... carrots are orange."

Imogen shook her head. "Carrots weren't orange until the 17th century. Now, eat up."

Trusting her judgement, I put the bean to my mouth and bit into it. To my surprise, it was juicy and delicious, like the best green bean I'd ever tasted.

"Good, right?" Imogen asked with raised eyebrows as she dropped another piece of meat on the floor for Sassy.

"Delicious," I agreed. "But... are you supposed to be doing that?"

I glanced around the dining hall and couldn't help but notice that Imogen was the only person feeding her Familiar regular food. Other Familiars just sat there watching people eat.

Imogen lowered her voice. "Not really, but you won't tell, will you? Sassy's a fussy eater."

I shook my head. "I won't tell."

"What about him?" She cocked her head toward Esis. "What does he eat?"

"I don't know," I admitted. "I talked to this guy at the Familiar nutrition center, but he didn't know anything about Esis' diet. He suggested he might like bugs, but when I tried to go digging for worms, Esis turned up his nose at them. The only thing I've gotten him to eat so far is burgers from the takeout line."

Esis was barely the size of my head, but I swore he ate more than I did. I was pretty sure there was a black hole in the pit of his stomach somewhere. The trashcan full of wrappers in my dorm room was proof of his appetite. I wasn't sure where all the food went. I was just grateful I didn't have to pay for it and that all our food was sponsored by the school.

"As long as he doesn't starve, that's all that counts, right?" Imogen said.

I smiled. I could really get used to Imogen's positive attitude.

AFTER THAT NIGHT dining with Imogen, I didn't have to sit alone in the dining hall anymore. Imogen was there every night, and she always stood and waved me over as soon as I filled my tray. At first I thought it was strange, like she was trying to draw attention to herself, but I'd come to realize that was just part of Imogen's over-the-top personality. She honestly didn't even notice the attention.

Strangely, I felt comfortable in her presence. It was easier to ignore the eyes on us with her around.

Three weeks passed, and Liam had managed to avoid me the entire time. He'd skipped out on our Medical Care class the first week following the tar pit incident. When he returned the next week and Professor Costas instructed us to pair up, he didn't even look at me. He headed straight for his lumberjack friend, Jonah. I got stuck with a first-year Toaqua who wouldn't even look me in the eye.

But, thanks to Liam, I was actually making progress with my Fire. I sat on the rocks next to the river almost every night practicing conjuring and manipulating flames. Esis perched on a rock beside me.

He clapped and trilled as if he were my own personal cheerleader. I hoped that with enough practice, Madame Doya would stop looking down her nose at me in Fire class. So far, no such luck.

"It's just a piece of wood!" Doya shouted in class one day. "I'm not asking you to set the entire forest on fire!"

The class stood in a line facing the room's massive fireplace. A small log atop a cast-iron firewood grate five feet in front of each person. We were each to light our log on fire from a distance. Madame Doya paced down the line of students, analyzing each of us as she went. Naomi prowled behind the logs, watching for any signs of flame.

I laser-focused my attention on the log in front of me. I did as Liam had instructed and focused on pulling my anger to the surface. I didn't like that I was angry all the time these days. I'd grown up learning how to control my emotions, but I had to throw all that out the window if I was to survive at this school.

"It's embarrassing you're trying so hard, Hudson," Doya scolded the guy next to me. "This should be simple for you."

I couldn't help it when my gaze flickered from my log. Hudson looked like he was suffering from a hernia. Poor guy.

"Stand straight, Tabitha," Doya yelled to a girl at the other end of the room. "Conjuring fire takes confidence."

Just as she said it, Haley's log burst into flame. Haley squealed in excitement and high-fived Kelsey beside her. The phoenix on her shoulder ruffled its feathers in delight. Haley's eyes caught mine on hers, and her face instantly fell. She glanced to my log and smirked.

Tiny little hands grabbed my ear. Esis tugged on me until I finally tore my gaze off Haley. He made three quick noises and pointed to my log. He settled back into his spot on my shoulder and wrapped my hair around his body. It was hard to find my anger when he was a constant comfort.

The smell of burning wood filled the air as two other logs lit up in flames. Beside me, the bark on Miranda's log was slowly shriveling as embers burnt the delicate outer layer.

"Sophia!" Madame Doya's harsh voice called.

There it was, that noise that was sure to get my blood boiling. I could already feel my skin heating.

"Yes?" I asked, trying to sound cool and collected. I didn't want to give her anything else to yell at me about.

Madame Doya held her nose high as she made her way over to me. "We don't have all day. You're bonded now, which means your powers should be easier to access. I expected your log to light long before any of your classmates'."

"Yes, Madame Doya," I said through gritted teeth. "I'm doing my best."

"Then why, dare I ask, is your log not on fire yet?"

My teeth gritted as I focused on my log. I *was* going to light this bitch on fire if she didn't stop pestering me. Nothing was ever good enough for her. Madame Doya stood there, observing. I could feel her eyes on me as all the tiny little hairs on the back of my neck stood up. Naomi stopped behind my log. She gave it a good sniff before turning her face down in dissatisfaction. She was almost as bad as Doya.

I felt my magic rise within me, but I didn't know how to direct it across the space between me and my log. Still, I tried. I pictured my magic flowing through the hardwood floor, because I thought it'd be easier than air to go through.

The smell of burning hair filled my nose. A second later, Naomi leapt backward. I just barely caught sight of the patch of singed fur on her paw before she burst into flame. Literally.

Esis buried his face in my hair, and I stumbled backward, completely shocked. The back of my knees hit into one of the couches, and I fell onto it. My eyes widened. Every inch of Naomi's fur lit up with orange flames. I could still make out the shape of her face through the fire, but the blonde fur was nowhere to be seen, as if the fire had replaced it all.

Holy guacamole! Had I lit Naomi on fire? I didn't mean to!

Except... Naomi didn't scream. She didn't back away in pain. It was like the flame engulfing her body didn't hurt her at all. Instead, she stood rigid, her flaming eyes fixed on me.

"I'm sorry!" I cried. "I— I didn't mean to."

The whole class watched as Madame Doya stepped forward and placed a calm hand on Naomi's flaming body. "Calm down, Naomi."

Naomi's ragged breathing slowed, and the flames died down. Her blonde fur returned, untouched, but she never took her eyes off me. I was frozen in shock, though my heart hammered. What had just happened?

Madame Doya whirled toward me, her lips tight. "We do not harm other people's Familiars, Sophia."

Except that Doya looked like she was two seconds from ripping Esis off my shoulder and snapping his neck in revenge. I held him closer to me, just in case she decided to try anything.

"I'm sorry," I repeated, stumbling over my words. "I don't know what happened."

"I think it's obvious," Madame Doya raged. "You burnt Naomi's paw."

I did what?

"So... those flames... I didn't do that?" I asked slowly.

Madame Doya furrowed her brow. Then, realization dawned. "You can't even light a simple piece of wood on fire. Naomi is a fire lion. It takes much more power than you're capable of to engulf a creature like her."

I stared at Naomi just so I wouldn't have to look Doya in the eye. Naomi's gaze was almost as equally terrifying. When my eyes jumped to the other side of the room, I saw that Haley was standing with her arms folded over her chest, a look of amusement on her face. I should've burnt her instead.

Madame Doya turned to the other students. "We'll pick up here later this week. I expect everyone to be able to accomplish this task by the end of class on Thursday. Class dismissed."

Everyone scrambled across the room to grab their things and hurry out the door. I was still shaking in shock, though Esis tried to comfort me by rubbing his fluffy belly against the skin on my neck. It helped a bit, but I wasn't about to waste any more time. I wouldn't be left alone in this room with Doya.

I hurried to my feet and grabbed my bag at my desk. I filed out of the room with everyone else. In the wide hallway, I felt like I could finally breathe. Students broke off in both directions. Some headed to the cafeteria, others to their next class, and some back to the Koigni dorms.

I tried to stay away from the dorms as often as I could. The Koigni common room wasn't a welcoming place, and when I tried to find some peace and quiet in my own room, there was usually someone giggling in the hall while the scent of smoke wafted from under the crack in my door. They thought they were hilarious. I thought they were idiots.

I quickened my pace toward the doors at the end of the hall, but I stopped dead in my tracks when I caught sight of a man with dark hair and a strong build.

Liam.

He leaned against the big stone lip that outlined one of the tall castle windows. He was surrounded by a group of five other people. A large, multi-colored bird that fluttered around like a hummingbird hovered above one girl's head. A guy almost as big as Jonah was petting the ears of a stag that appeared like it crawled straight from Mother Earth's lair. It had forest green fur, with twisted antlers that looked like bark-covered tree branches sticking out of its head. I wasn't great at spotting the differences between Houses yet, but judging by the guy's size and his Familiar, he was definitely Nivita.

Liam faced away from me, but I could tell by the way his shoulders shook that he was laughing at something the Nivita guy said. Of course. Because he only acted like he had a stick up his ass when he was around me.

He didn't notice me. Now would be a perfect time to finally catch him and apologize. My feet started moving in his direction before I even decided to approach him.

I cleared my throat. "Liam?"

No way was he escaping on me this time. I totally had him cornered.

Liam turned around... only it wasn't Liam. I mean, he *looked* like Liam. He had the same muscular build, same long black hair and dark skin. He even had the same eyes. But the shape of his nose and his jawline were off by just a hair.

Liam Clone smiled at me. Inside, I was screaming in embarrassment. Instinct told me to flee, but before I could, Liam Clone spoke.

"Sorry to disappoint you." He smirked.

121

I took a step back. "I'm *so* sorry."

He shrugged. "Hey, it's okay. I can pretend to be Liam if you'd like." Liam Clone stood straighter. His eyebrows tightened, and the corners of his lips turned down as he deepened his voice. "I'm Liam Mitoh. I swear by the ancestors that I will sulk around until the day I die."

I totally lost it. His voice was spot-on, and he looked *exactly* like Liam when he scrunched his face up like that. I could almost believe I was looking right at him. Liam Clone's face relaxed, and he laughed along with me.

"That was a *really* good impression," I said, giggling.

"I would hope so," he replied. "I've had a lot of practice imitating my brother. It gets on his nerves."

"You're Liam's brother?" I shouldn't have been shocked. I mean, the guys were practically identical twins.

"Yep. Ezra," he introduced, sticking his hand out.

I shook it. "Sophia."

"Ah." He nodded his head in recognition. "*You're* the pain in his ass."

Esis drew in a breath of surprise. He didn't take well to crude language.

My shoulders slumped involuntarily. "He calls me that?"

"Not directly," Ezra said with a roll of his eyes, like it was just a joke.

Still, the statement bothered me. What if Liam hated me? I mean, it explained why he'd been avoiding me. I wasn't sure what I'd done wrong besides mention his Familiar, and I'd been trying for three weeks to apologize for it. Was it really that bad?

"Hey," Ezra said softly. The laughter in his voice had vanished. "I didn't mean it like that. I just—"

"Ezra," the Nivita guy interrupted. Ezra looked at him. "We've got to head to class, but we'll catch you later, okay?"

"Yeah, no problem." Ezra waved as his friends headed down the hall.

He turned back to me, but I knew he was just going to say something about his brother. I didn't want to talk about Liam, so I spoke before Ezra could.

"That guy with the stag is Nivita, isn't he?" I asked.

"Yeah," Ezra confirmed with a shrug.

"I thought people from different Houses weren't supposed to be friends." I'd been sure that was one of the reasons people stared at Imogen and me so much at dinner.

"Where'd you hear that?" he asked. "My brother?"

I nodded, though Haley had mentioned it, too.

"Don't listen to him," Ezra said. "He takes things like that way too seriously. He makes a bigger deal out of most things than they are."

"Oh," I said flatly. Liam sure sounded serious about... everything.

Ezra's gaze traveled past me, and his eyes lit up. "Speak of the devil..."

I turned around to see Liam— the real Liam— headed down the hall toward us. He took one look at me and whirled around in the opposite direction. He wasn't even sneaky about it. It was obvious he saw me.

"What's up with him?" Ezra thought aloud.

"He's mad at me," I admitted in a small voice. "He avoids me every chance he gets."

Ezra looked amused. "My brother can be a real... *eh-hem*... sometimes. Come on. He's not getting away this time."

Ezra jogged forward, calling out Liam's name. Liam quickened his pace but didn't look back, pretending as if he hadn't heard him. I followed quickly behind. Ezra reached Liam and draped an arm around his shoulder.

"Hey, brother," Ezra said casually just as I caught up with them.

"Hey," Liam replied without emotion.

"Sophia tells me you've been acting like a dick lately."

"I did not!" I objected.

"Yeah, well, it's true, isn't it?" Ezra glanced between both of us, grinning.

Liam stopped walking and stood rigid. He still hadn't looked at me. "Maybe you should mind your own business, Ezra."

"Maybe *you* should learn some manners," his brother bit back.

"Sophia said she's been trying to apologize, and you've been avoiding her. The least you can do is let her say what she wants to say, and then the two of you can go your separate ways."

Liam's nostrils flared. He and Ezra stood eye-to-eye, staring at each other. "Fine."

Liam looked down at me expectantly. It suddenly occurred to me that I had no idea what I wanted to say to him. I just knew I had to say *something* or I'd never get the chance.

I swallowed. "I'm sorry."

"Is that it?" Liam asked with raised eyebrows. He turned to leave.

"No," I said quickly, stopping him. "I'm sorry I freaked out about your Familiar. I know it really has to hurt, and I get why you're upset. My reaction was uncalled for. I hope we can still be friends... if you're okay with that."

Liam's features hardened when I said the word *friends*. I wasn't sure if he'd ever considered us friends. The realization broke my heart. I waited for him to actually admit it out loud, but before he could say anything, a voice cut through the silence.

"Liam. Sophia. Just the two people I was looking for."

A man with messy gray hair and salt-and-pepper stubble approached us. His eyes were young and free of wrinkles, though they looked tired. I guessed he was around my parents' age, despite the premature graying of his hair. The man wore khakis and a baby blue button-down shirt tucked into his slacks. He had one of the sweetest, caring smiles I'd ever seen. He seemed like the kind of person who was always under constant stress but told the best dad jokes.

I immediately noticed Imogen and Jonah following behind him. Jonah's hippogriff glanced up at a small dragon statue and almost tripped over her own feet.

"What is it, Baine?" Liam suddenly seemed less annoyed.

Baine. Where had I heard that name before? I quickly recalled that he was the one who sent the peryton for Liam and me to get to school.

"We were headed to lunch," Baine said, gesturing to Jonah and Imogen beside him. "Would you like to join us?"

"He says he has great news!" Imogen bounced on her toes. Sassy peeked out from the bag hanging from Imogen's shoulder.

"What kind of news?" I asked curiously.

"We can talk about that once we get our food," Baine said kindly.

"I'm not hungry," Liam declined.

Baine shot him a look I didn't quite understand. "You should come along anyway. How about you, Ezra? Are you hungry?"

"Nah," Ezra replied. "Thanks for the invite, but I'm actually going to be late for History of the Hawkei as it is. I'll catch up with you later."

Ezra strolled away casually, walking in a cocky manner with his head thrown back. As he walked down the hallway, about ten different people from all Houses waved or acknowledged him in some way. It was clear Ezra was the golden boy— the Academy's most popular student. He had this air around him that was hard to resist. It didn't matter what House you were from, it was obvious people loved him and wanted to be around him.

Unlike his brother. He and Liam were totally different.

He said he was going to History. Why wasn't I enrolled in that class? I was sure it'd be helpful. The library didn't exactly have many published books on the Hawkei. I'd tried looking for them and didn't find any.

"Shall we go?" Baine suggested, like he wasn't giving Liam a choice. We followed behind him.

"So, what do you think of Baine?" Imogen whispered to me from several paces back.

I shrugged. "I don't know."

"He's hot, right?" She wiggled her eyebrows.

My eyes darted to the back of Baine's head. "*He's* the professor you think is hot?"

Imogen blushed.

"Ew, Imogen. He's like... fifty."

Imogen grinned. "Yeah, fifty shades of sexy."

I almost gagged. "If you're into the disheveled look..."

"He's not disheveled," Imogen argued. "He's... sophisticated."

"When you said an older guy, I thought you meant in his thirties. Not old enough to be *your father!*"

Imogen smirked. "All I'm saying is that if I needed to sleep with someone to boost my grade, I would—"

"Dear Lord," I cut her off as we reached the cafeteria. "Please don't finish that sentence."

Imogen just shrugged and hurried into the line.

Baine suggested we eat outside, so we all grabbed premade wraps from the takeout line. These weren't like the usual wraps I ate back home. They were made with a fried flatbread and filled with beef, beans, corn, and a delicious seasoning that was the perfect blend of sweet and spicy. I wasn't sure if the cooks at Orenda used magic in the food here, but sometimes, I wondered. It even beat my dad's cooking, and he was the best cook I knew.

I pushed the thought away. I couldn't bear to think about my parents. I missed them too much.

"What's wrong?" Imogen asked. "You don't like the wraps?"

"They're great," I replied, glancing down at the wraps in my hand, one for me and one for Esis.

Baine led us outside to a grassy hill with a clear view of the ocean through the trees. A pleasant breeze passed through my hair as I sat. I handed Esis his wrap, and he jumped down from my shoulder. He pulled the plastic wrap off and gobbled his food down before I'd even bitten into mine. I giggled at him as he snuggled into my lap.

"So, what's the news?" Imogen asked eagerly as she plopped down in the grass beside me.

Sassy rolled around in front of her. Imogen pulled a plastic container from her bag, and I nearly gagged when she opened it. The thing was stuffed to the brim with fluffy white carcasses. She pulled out a dead mouse by the tail and tossed it into the air. Sassy caught it in her mouth before it hit the ground. On the other side of Baine, where Jonah and Liam sat, Squeaks gave a jealous squawk.

"I'm sorry," Imogen said gently to the hippogriff. She turned to Jonah. "Do you mind?"

Jonah answered with a full mouth. "Go ahead."

Imogen tossed another mouse into the air. Squeaks swallowed it in one gulp.

"Ew, Jonah," I complained. "Can you not chew with your mouth open?"

"Sophia hates it," Imogen said with a teasing smile. She knew I couldn't stand the guy who usually sat two tables away from us and always chewed like his parents had never taught him proper table manners.

Jonah took another huge bite and chewed loudly, taking extra care to keep his mouth open as much as possible, like he didn't care in the slightest. A smirk touched the corner of his lips.

Liam scowled at Jonah's gross display. Imogen just giggled.

Baine leaned back on one hand. "It's nice spending time with friends, isn't it?"

"Get to the point, Baine," Liam groaned. He hadn't taken a single bite.

Baine sighed. "I was getting there. You do consider each other friends, don't you?"

"Of course!" Imogen said, before Liam could deny it.

He would've. I just knew it.

"Good," Baine said with a nod of his head. "Because the four of you will be spending a lot of time together. I've requested you be placed on the same team for the Elemental Cup. I will serve as your mentor."

"What?" Liam exploded, shooting to his feet. "This is bullshit! First I'm forced to participate. Now I'm placed on the reject team?"

Esis' ears perked up. He didn't like that comment. Neither did I.

Jonah rose to his feet beside Liam. "Calm down, dude. I understand that you're feeling—"

"You don't understand shit," Liam snapped. "At least you have Squeaks. You might actually survive out there with her. For me, this is a death sentence."

"There's a reason I put you four on a team together," Baine said calmly. "I'm aware of what happened at the tar pit. Based on what I heard, you four worked together well. No one's going to let you die in the tournament, Liam."

"Yeah," Imogen agreed. "We won't leave you behind."

"That doesn't matter," Liam growled. "I still don't have a chance."

"You do," Baine countered. "Do you know what the leading cause of injury during the tournament is?"

Liam's jaw tightened, but he didn't answer.

"Death and injury occur when teams don't work together," Baine explained. "Accidents occur when there are disagreements, when a team member runs off thinking they can get through an obstacle alone, or when someone tries to show off their strength instead of working together. If you let your team members help you, they won't let you down."

Liam's hands clenched into fists. "I'm not sure I can believe that."

The look Liam shot me was like a knife through the heart. My chest compressed. He had to know I would do everything I could to help one of my teammates.

The thing was, I didn't think it was that he didn't trust me. He didn't think I was capable.

"Liam's right." My voice barely broke through the lump in my throat. "This isn't a good team. We'll never work together."

It killed me to say those words. I didn't even realize how true they were until they came out of my mouth.

"I'm sorry," Baine said regretfully. "I didn't realize you felt that way about each other. But there's no changing teams now. You're stuck with this team until the Elemental Ball."

"There's a *ball*?" I asked. Lovely. Because a dance was *just* what I needed when the one guy I might've said yes to hated my guts.

"Yes," Baine replied. "It takes place following the tournament. It's a celebration to present the participants as full members of the tribe."

"Please," Liam scoffed. "It's a party to celebrate the winners. We all know that."

Jonah frowned. "We have no chance of winning with that kind of attitude."

"Who said I wanted to win?" Liam asked.

I couldn't help but feel that Liam had a point. I just wanted to survive. My jaw clenched as my anger once again surfaced.

"You're all capable of winning," Baine assured him. "But you'll have to set your differences aside. You must choose to work together."

"Why? What's the point?" Liam snapped.

"I agree." I couldn't believe I'd said the words until they escaped my mouth. As soon as I started, I couldn't shut them off. "I was *forced* to come here. I left my family and my entire life behind. Now I'm told I have to team up with the guy who dragged me here if I want to live?"

This was bull. All of it. I just wanted to go home. I wanted to see my family again. I didn't even care about Amelia's teasing or Dad's stinky socks. I missed Mom's hugs and Dad's deep belly laugh. I missed driving into the city to shop at the mall all day with my friends. I missed my own bed and all the memories I left behind.

The only good thing about Orenda was Esis... and maybe Imogen. I'd thought there was more to Liam, too, but now I wasn't sure.

Baine looked completely dumbstruck. I'd surprised everyone with my outburst.

"The Elemental Cup tests and secures your bond with your Familiar," Baine said slowly. "It also tests your ability to work with other Elementai and determines your place in society. It's my understanding that you're here for a reason, Sophia. That reason being the very thing you left behind."

My parents.

I knew exactly what he was saying. If I didn't play my part, I'd no longer be able to protect my family. I recalled how Amelia said my parents' Familiars could be killed for my parents' crimes. If what Imogen told me was true, that Elementai didn't live long without their Familiars, my parents were as good as dead. I'd never let that happen.

I had only one choice. Suck it up, work with Liam, and make sure he doesn't quit on us.

Liam whirled around and started back toward the castle. I scooped up Esis in my arms and instantly chased after him. I didn't look back to see if anyone else was following.

"Liam, wait!" I called.

Liam stopped abruptly and spun to face me. "I just want to be alone right now."

He pierced me with his dark eyes. Though his eyebrows were

tight, there was a softness in his eyes when he looked at me. My gaze flickered to his lips. I had the sudden urge to brush my lips against his, to take away his pain and make everything better.

What am I thinking? Liam would never kiss me. He hates me.

"You want to survive, don't you?" I blurted.

Liam hesitated. "Yeah, I guess so."

"So do I. Whether we like it or not, we need each other. Can't we just try to get along?"

When he didn't say anything, I added. "For Imogen and Jonah's sake."

Liam's features softened. "If we have any chance of making it through that tournament, there's something we need to do first."

My curiosity piqued. "What's that?"

Liam sighed and glanced around, like he didn't want to talk about it out in the open. "Meet me by the fountain next to the greenhouses tomorrow at dusk. We can talk then."

Liam

ELEVEN

I headed down to the fountain the minute the sun was starting to cast the earth in a warm autumn glow. Ezra cried out something when I left the Toaqua dorms, but I ignored him. This was important. I couldn't be distracted right now from what I was trying to tell Sophia.

She was about to get a huge wake-up call.

When I saw her, I paused for a moment to observe. She was working on homework, crouched over a pile of papers that was sitting on an open textbook on her lap. She sat on the ground with a muddled expression I couldn't decipher, the fountain towering over her and looking like it was about to attack. Esis was on her shoulder, peering at her homework like he was reading it, too.

I noticed something strange. Sophia kept switching her pen from one hand to another, writing with both, chewing on her bottom lip like she couldn't grasp what the book was trying to tell her.

"Can't decide which hand to write with?" I asked as I approached. She looked up and grimaced a bit when she saw me. She obviously was in a mood. Esis, though, peeped and grinned like he'd never been more ecstatic to see me. Weirdo.

"I'm ambidextrous," Sophia said. "I play with my hands when I get agitated."

Hm. She could use both hands equally. Dad once told me that was a sign of a strong Elementai. Maybe she *was* someone I needed to watch out for, and not someone who was weak. "Why are you anxious?"

"It's just... this work. I don't get it." Sophia huffed a stray strand that had fallen out of her ponytail away from her eyes. "The Elementai world is confusing, but Koigni magic is the most frustrating of all. There's no rhyme or reason to it."

"What do you mean?"

"For me, everything has to be even. Symmetrical," Sophia explained. "I don't like when things are out of order, and Koigni magic, it's all feeling. Chaos isn't my thing. I can't handle it."

I didn't say anything. Even after my help, Sophia was still struggling. She wanted perfection and organization. But fire was rampage and chaos. Sophia kept suppressing the part of herself that she was most— probably on account of being taught to suppress it by Toaqua parents, whether she knew it or not.

She'd been raised like a Water child, and she clearly wasn't. You couldn't put a square peg in a round hole. At some point or another, she was going to have to embrace who she was.

Maybe she would, after today.

"Come with me," I said. I jerked my head in the direction of the forest. Sophia slammed her book and threw it in her bag. She went to fling it over her shoulders, but I shook my head.

"Leave it," I told her. "It'll be here when you get back."

"You've still got your bag," she countered.

"It's got things we need," I insisted. "Just do as I ask."

She did. I turned into the forest with my hands in my pockets, and she followed, Esis wrapped tightly in her arms.

We walked for about ten minutes before we came to the base of a mountain. It towered above us like a proud warrior who refused to move in spite of outstanding odds against it. A range of smaller mountains dotted the area around it and spanned along the seashore, but the one in front of us was the most prominent. It was craggy and spiked, and a thin dirt path wound its way up to the summit. The very top had snow dotted upon it, but we wouldn't go that far.

She looked at me. "Up?"

"Up," I responded. "It's a mile climb. There's a well-worn path. You can make it," I told her.

"Shut up. I go hiking all the time. I know I can make it," she muttered under her breath.

I laughed under my breath before I took the lead. I was feeling well today, so I'd picked tonight to make this hike. There was no guarantee that I'd be able to tomorrow, and this couldn't wait. Sophia needed to know.

I was out of breath pretty quickly, but I continued to put one foot in front of the other as we ascended the rocky slope. It was slow going, and we were silent. Sophia kept looking at me like she was concerned, and I hated it.

I stumbled for a moment. She reached out to catch me with the hand that wasn't holding Esis, but I shoved it away.

"I've done this a million times. I don't need your help," I grumbled.

She scowled. "You're sick, aren't you?"

"Define *sick*." God, she made it sound like I needed to be on bedrest. The nerve of this woman.

She tilted her head. "What's wrong with you?"

A part of me jerked inside, and I said, "No one knows."

She was looking at me in a way that physically hurt. I didn't want her stupid pity. I was just as normal as she was. Just had a broken body.

I wanted her to see me that way, too. But I felt like that was wishing for the moon.

When we finally reached the top, an inner peace washed over me and I was able to breathe normally again. This was my favorite view, hands down. The mountaintop looked down upon the entire forest and all of Orenda Academy. The castle was far below. From here you could see the masses of magical creatures flying around it. The summit we'd reached was a relatively flat space, a decently sized area of a few hundred feet that was encapsulated in a circle. The ground was nothing but dirt and rock, with a few remnants of wooden bowls filled with incense people had brought up here. The sky had turned to a burning orange now, streaked with lines of red and purple. It cast the mountainside in a bright glow of warm, muddled colors mixed with elongating shadows.

At the center of the circle was a large totem pole. It had the symbols of each of the Houses, Fire, Air, Water, and Earth stacked upon each other, with Nivita on the bottom as a growing leaf, Toaqua depicted as a rushing wave within a water droplet, Yapluma as a gust of wind, and Koigni symbolized by a singular flame.

Koigni was only topped by one other totem. Anichi... the Soul House. Anichi was commemorated with a complicated swirling design, meant to symbolize the spirit.

Sophia stared at the Anichi symbol like she didn't know what it meant. She was going to hear the whole sad story today. Esis hopped out of her arms and skittered around the totem pole, looking up at the Anichi totem with an unhappy expression.

It was lonely up here. And quiet. I put my bag on the ground and turned to face her.

"What is this? Why did you bring me here?" she asked.

"Sit down, Sophia." I gestured to the dirt below the totem.

"What, on the ground?" She gave me a skeptical look.

"Yes, Sophia." I gave her a hard look. "Today would be nice."

She sat. I took out a tiny placemat that I made in Basket Weaving (yes, I was proud of it, thank you) and set it on the ground before I placed another group of items upon it. A stick of sage, a leather pouch mixed with various incenses, a small leather drum, and silver bells on a wristlet. Lastly was a wooden smudging wand, with eagle feathers splayed out in a fan across the top and small designs carved into the wood. The wand was old, and had been made with the feathers of my grandfather's Familiar. It'd been a present from my dad when I turned eighteen.

Usually this type of thing would require more people. There'd be dances, multiple chanters, and songs that would go on for days. Elementai would be wearing ceremonial outfits, not jeans and t-shirts. People didn't just up and summon the ancestors on a whim— and definitely not on a Tuesday.

I could get in trouble for this. But this was my birthright. It was something that I wasn't going to let be taken away from me.

Sophia stared at me. Esis had left the totem to crawl into her lap. I sat on the ground and let my wrists hang off my knees.

"The first thing you need to understand is that there weren't four original Houses," I said. "There used to be five."

"What?" Sophia reeled back. "How? What happened to the fifth House?"

"Let me start from the beginning." I cleared my throat. "Hundreds of years ago, the Hawkei had no power. They were just normal human beings, a tribe of people who sought to live in peace like anyone else. And, for a long time, they did."

My tone turned dark. "Then the colonizers came. They brought all kinds of diseases our bodies couldn't fight off. They hunted down our food and stole our land. They hated us for our brown skin and customs that they considered strange. At first, we thought coexistence was possible, but more and more settlers kept coming, and they didn't want peace. They wanted us gone. There weren't enough of us to fight back. A war meant certain extermination. We were dying."

Sophia looked down at the ground. Her expression was sad, and a little muddled.

"Our shamans pleaded with the ancestors to save us from our fate. Suddenly, the skies opened, and from them flooded a dazzling array of magical creatures, hundreds of them in number. When they reached the ground our spirits fled out of our bodies and attached themselves to the creatures. Once the bond was set, we found we could control the elements— Earth, Water, Air, Fire, and Soul."

Sophia's eyes were as wide as Esis' now. The little guy perched on Sophia's arm, his ears up and listening intently.

"Though we had our creatures to defend us now, and our magic, we still knew we needed to hide. So we walked until we found a special place of seclusion, a world that was so far removed the colonizers didn't dare venture through it. The forests and mountains surrounding it were filled with deadly animals, thick tar pits, and treacherous mountains. The weather was harsh and changed constantly. There was no gold and little room for farming. The strangers didn't want it. The land was dangerous, but we would make it work. We had our magic now, and we had our Familiars."

"Then what happened?" Sophia was immersed in the story. Esis' little tail waggled, and I smiled slightly.

"We knew we had to diversify to survive. You've noticed that there are a variety of races within the school. The Elders believed the more footholds we had in cultures around the globe, the better chance we had if the colonizers found us again. Nivita and Yapluma went to places like Africa, South America and Asia to find partners and bring them back here. At first, it was for diplomatic reasons, but then people started falling in love. Koigni worked on mating with influential and rich Europeans to gain power. Toaqua is the most traditional House, so we stayed behind to manage the tribe... which is why I look like me and you look like you." I grinned at her.

"I always wondered about that." She cuddled Esis. "Sometimes I don't think I've got any Hawkei in me, because I can't see any traits."

"Don't believe that. You've got Hawkei blood in your veins just as much as I do," I told her. "If you didn't, you wouldn't be able to summon fire. You wouldn't have been able to bond with Esis."

Sophia stroked Esis' head, and I continued. "Arthur Cedrick was a settler from Europe, but he wasn't like the others. He was a friend to the Hawkei. He'd been outcasted from his family and from his town because he preached that the Hawkei and the settlers needed to live in peace. When he had nowhere else to go, the tribe took him in. He used his large family fortune to build a castle here, to remind him of those that he missed growing up in Scotland. He had no known heirs and offered the castle as a gift to the Hawkei before he passed away. The Elders used it to create Orenda Academy, a place where Elementai could come to learn how to use their magic. The castle had been specially designed by Arthur's daughter, Anna, who wanted the estate to go to the Hawkei and crafted it specifically for use of our powers."

"I thought you said Arthur had no known heirs? How could he have a daughter?" Sophia asked.

"Anna died before Arthur. She had some sort of disease. Her illness was so strong not even the Anichi could heal her, only prolong her life for a time," I explained. "Arthur was so grateful for extending her life that he left us everything he had."

"So Anichi could heal?" Sophia asked.

"Anichi was the strongest House. They had control of the spirit, of healing," I told her. "They ruled each of the five Houses equally. They had the power to heal Anna, at least for a time."

"If they were the strongest House, how come they aren't here anymore?" Her eyebrows knitted together in confusion.

"Something horrible happened. Koigni... destroyed them." I closed my eyes and shook my head. "Koigni was jealous of the power that Anichi had and wanted it for themselves."

"That's awful." Sophia frowned.

I nodded. "Koigni was looking for something, some sort of object that only the Anichi had and that gave them the power to rule. Whatever it was became lost to legend, but the stories say that whoever had possession of this item could control the fate of the Hawkei— even control the ancestors."

Sophia held her breath, and I continued. "A great war broke out between the Anichi and the Koigni. The other Houses tried not to get involved, which ended up to be a grave mistake. Toaqua's, Nivita's, and Yapluma's inaction led to the demise of Anichi House. Koigni completely destroyed them. Healing magic was gone with the Anichi. So was whatever the Koigni were looking for."

I paused. This part was hard to explain. "The Koigni felt like they were in charge now, but the destruction of Anichi brought upon the Elementai a terrible curse. Without the healing House, we could no longer heal ourselves or our creatures if disease or terrible injury came to one of the tribe. Neither could we communicate with the ancestors as easily as we once could, because with Anichi remained that gift. We no longer had a ruling House, so each of the Houses became divided. We began to fight amongst ourselves, which led to more death and slaughter. We were killing each other faster than the settlers ever had, and worse yet, we were at risk of exposing ourselves to the outside world."

The wind blew, casting a few strands of hair in front of my eyes. I swept them away and said, "It became clear that after Anichi was destroyed that if we didn't stick together, the Elementai would die out. So we became forced to rely on each other for survival. We stopped mating with outsiders, and the Elders ruled that people could only marry within their own Houses. We stayed within the confines of the village instead of venturing outside, except for rare occasions. Once Anichi was gone, everything changed. Elementai could no longer survive without their Familiars as they could before. Our world had become different."

I stopped speaking. I stooped down to slip the bell wristlet over my wrist and to pick up the drum.

"What are you doing?" Sophia asked, totally confused.

"You need to see that this is more than just a story," I told her.

I started playing a steady beat on the drum. Every time I brought my hand down, the bells on my wrist jingled, until the drum and the bells were creating a harmonious rhythm.

Sophia didn't know the Hawkei language, but I did. I made low chants in my throat, repeating a song that my father had drilled into my head from the moment I could understand language. I made the words mingle in time with the drum. Sophia watched curiously, mesmerized as I continued to cry out to the ancestors.

Calling them down.

After a few minutes, I put down the drum and stopped chanting, but still, the music continued. Other voices were there to replace mine now, humming a far-away song that was getting closer and closer with every second.

"What's that music?" Sophia looked around, scared. "Where's it coming from?"

I didn't answer her. Somewhere in the distance, an eagle cried, and I thought I heard a howl drifting on the wind. The sounds mingled with the dancing bells and the beating of the drum. The whispering got louder, approaching us from every angle. Sophia squeezed Esis and scrunched up into a tiny ball.

I needed a piece from every House. Air was already all around us. I scooped up a bit of dirt and threw it into the wooden bowl for Nivita, then summoned what water I could from the ground. It formed in my hand, and I kept it tightly within my concealed fist before I threw the incense bag inside the bowl. I looked at Sophia.

"Fire, Sophia," I told her. "I need fire."

Despite her fear, she focused her intention on the incense bag in the bowl and lit it up. Her flames burned the bag quickly, sending smoke into the air and the smell of the incense floating around the mountain. The herbs burned quickly, turning to embers within moments. Before the embers could die out completely, I lashed out my hand to grab them, and Sophia gasped.

Ignoring the burning in my palm, I clenched the smoldering embers tightly before I flung them upward into the setting sky.

From the embers burst all colors, every shade possible known to creation. These colors flooded outward and upward, encircling the area and creating a spinning whirlwind around us that felt like the inside of a tornado, a column that spun up as far as the eye could see and into the sun. The entire mountaintop lit up with its glory. Sophia's hair whipped around her face as she jumped to her feet in alarm. Esis leapt out of her arms and onto the ground, squeaking and wiggling in delight.

I too rose as the colors spread. From them emerged shapes and figures. Magical creatures. Dragons spiraled above, gigantic winged beasts like chimeras and large birds at their sides. An enormous fire-bird with ruby feathers and a orange beak cawed triumphantly, and a jet of flame shot across the sky. Within the whirlwind of color, other creatures spanned, running upon thin air like it was the ground. There were feathered serpents, perytons, alicorns, and species that had long since gone extinct. Aquatic creatures like leviathans and megalodons swam around Fire animals such as manticores and blazing pegasi. Among them were creatures such as big cats, like lions, panthers and lynxes, woodland creatures such as deer, bear, and raccoons, reptiles and fish transforming into their elemental forms as they ran by— Fire and Water.

Some of these creatures I didn't even know the names of. There were hundreds, so many that they made a swirling wall on all sides that blocked out everything except the colors that painted the wind. It was hard to distinguish them all. One creature with a thin neck, a small face and long limbs that was entirely made of water swam by me. Its companion, a twin to it in everything except that it was made of fire, blazed by and intertwined itself with the Water creature. They danced in unison as they returned to the stampede of charging animals.

A group of white stags circled Sophia, jumping around her before bounding off into the air. She gasped, pressing a hand to her mouth when a humpback whale swam by. Sophia gaped at the performance of the ancestors, tears streaming down her cheeks. She reached out to touch them, but their spirit essence floated through her fingers without any sense of actually being there.

I laughed as a pack of wolves ran through me, ruffling my hair. They transformed into Water canines and became a singular wave, sweeping throughout the area like it was the ocean.

A wyvern spiraled down from the sky and landed in front of Sophia. As he did, he changed shape to resemble a muscular warrior wearing a feathered headdress. Another creature, the firebird, landed in front of Sophia to become a red-headed woman wearing a ballgown with a corset. A blazing hound made of flame came to a stop in front of her to morph into a man with a cowboy hat, and a white griffin landed beside him to transform into a beautiful woman with long black hair that reached her ankles. They bowed to Sophia. She took a few steps backward, unsure of what she was experiencing.

My ancestors came down and started landing in front of me, too. They were wearing all types of clothing from various time periods, changing from animals like kelpies, krakens, and gigantic sea monsters. A pale-faced girl, her dark hair in two braids, stood near me and gave me a gentle smile. They bowed to me, too, and I nodded my head in return. Once I acknowledged them, they changed back into their animal forms and took off into the dazzling array, joining again with the crowd that was ever enclosing around us, the sound of their song welling in our ears.

I thought I saw an eagle soaring far above, out of my reach, and I wondered if it was my grandfather. The song was swelling louder and louder, and I knew it was time to bring this to a close. With a singular movement, I swung my arm over my head and downward. I opened my palm and allowed the water residing in my hand to splash upon the burning incense that was still inside the bowl. The smoke went out, and in a few seconds the ancestors retreated into a slit in the sky, taking the colors and the song with them.

When the ancestors were gone, Sophia and I were left in complete darkness. There was nothing above us except the littered array of bright stars against a dark sky. Night had come. Silence thickened the air between us, and it was harsh and ringing now that the loud chanting and drum beats were gone.

Sophia was shaking. I didn't know what to say to her, but she spoke.

"That was... beautiful." Her voice cracked. Esis waddled over to her to put a paw on her shoe, and she looked down at him.

"That's our destiny," I told her. "I don't pretend to have all the answers to life, or to even know where the rest of the human race goes after death. I don't even know where the ancestors go. But they're here with us, and that's our meaning. You don't die until your purpose in this life is done. Once it's accomplished, you move on to be with the rest of our kind. Elements, Elementai, and Familiars, all united as one in perfect harmony."

Her face was still pretty white. "Who were those people that bowed to me?"

"They were your guides. Those particular ancestors that came down to greet you agreed to watch over you and specifically be involved in your life before you were born," I said. "Every Elementai has their own ancestor guides."

"They changed. From human to animal," she said.

"Our Familiars fuse with us and our magic when we die. We truly become one," I explained.

Sophia sniffled. She wiped her nose and looked at me.

"Do you understand now? Our people were almost *exterminated*. Everything that meant anything to us was taken and destroyed. Our culture and religion is all we have," I told her. "That's why the Houses need each other to survive. I know you think this is all stupid political bullshit, and everyone's trying to one-up each other all the time."

I sighed. "And, yeah, a lot of it is that. But underneath it all is a pact for survival. To be frank, if we all don't work together, we're still facing extinction. And all of us agree that our creatures deserve better than that. If we're gone, there's no one left to take care of them. And you know as well as I do they wouldn't survive in this modern world. Not without someone to protect them."

Sophia nodded. She wiped away remnants of the tears that were still drying on her face and picked up Esis. "Yeah. I... I get it, Liam. I understand why you brought me up here. It took something like this to make me realize who I really am."

Esis purred happily. She kissed him on the top of the head, and I gathered my things.

"Ready to head down?" I asked.

"Yeah." She chuckled. "I'm starving, actually. I haven't eaten much all day."

"I'll sit with you," I blurted before I could stop myself. "It's no big deal. I haven't eaten, either."

Sophia grinned. *Stupid, stupid.* Just a few weeks ago I was refusing to be seen in the cafeteria with her, and here I was changing my mind.

We started heading down the mountain. I noticed that Sophia was unusually silent, even more so than when we'd started heading up here. "Something bothering you?" I asked.

"Nothing. It was just..." She hesitated. "There was a wolf standing there, staring at you. He was sitting by your side the entire time we were on the mountain."

Talk about a punch to the gut. It was nearly enough to knock me off my feet. My eyes burned, and I struggled to catch my breath. All the air had just gone out of me.

"He was your Familiar, wasn't he?" Sophia said softly.

There was a lump in my throat. "Yes."

"You can't see him?" She sounded sad.

"No." My reply was heavy.

"Oh." She looked down. "I'm sorry."

"It's okay."

She brought her beautiful face back up to look at me. "What was his name?"

"Nashoma. His name was Nashoma."

She was quiet for a moment. "Do you mind telling me what happened?"

The words were hard to get out. "He died for me."

Sophia didn't press any further. She just clung tighter to Esis.

"And yes, before you ask," I added, "I'm the only one of my kind. No one else in our history has ever survived their Familiar's death, not since Anichi was destroyed. Not even one."

Sophia didn't answer right away. For days afterward, I couldn't figure out why Nashoma had sacrificed himself for me, as his death would cause my own, too. He knew that. Every Familiar did.

But I hadn't died— I'd survived, and managed to go on without him. Though how he could've known that, I didn't understand.

Maybe he'd known something I didn't.

While I was still lost in my thoughts, Sophia added, "Well... for what it's worth, I'm glad you're still here, Liam. You've been a good friend to me. I like having you around."

A small part of my spirits lifted, and I gave her a tiny grin. "Thanks, Soph."

We continued our descent, but we were closer together this time, walking so our bodies almost touched. I felt fine right now, but a part of me knew I'd be paying for this walk the next morning. I only had so much energy to give these days, and I'd spent a lot of it climbing up and down this mountain.

Sophia, though. She was worth it.

I almost wanted to reach out and hold her hand, because, you know, I'm a masochist who loves torturing myself. My fingers reached out for hers, but I brought them back before she noticed. I called myself a wuss and reminded myself that we had rules.

"Can any Elementai do that?" Sophia asked abruptly, snapping me out of my stupid internal debate. "Like, if I learned how to do it, could I summon the ancestors, too?"

"There are only a few Hawkei who can summon the ancestors. The Elders, chieftains, and firstborns of chieftains," I explained. "My dad is Chief of the Toaqua tribe, so I have the ability to call them."

"Do you know anyone else who can?"

"Haley can. She's the firstborn of a chief," I said. "Her mother is Chieftess of Koigni."

"Of course she is." Sophia made a bitchy face. "What else has she got that I don't have?"

"Well, for starters, her tournament team is probably phenomenal. Madame Doya already chose her for her front runner, and Doya doesn't take losers. Most likely, she has the best pick from every House."

"You're not helping me feel better, Liam. You called us the reject team," she said sourly.

"Because we are. We're the kids that nobody wanted, so we got stuck together," I said.

"Baine wanted us. He specifically chose us for his team," Sophia argued.

"Baine's being sympathetic. Or stupid. He's about three fries short of a Happy Meal. It's not a compliment that he's our coach. People complain about getting him every year." I crossed my arms. "I just want to get this thing over with and come out on the other end with all my limbs intact."

"That's not good enough. I want to win, and rub it in Haley's stupid face," Sophia snapped.

"That's Koigni thinking. You need to get it out of your head that we have a chance of winning this thing," I shot her down immediately. "The only thing I'm concerned about is making it out alive, because people do *die* in this tournament, Sophia."

"What if we just refused to do the tournament?" Sophia asked me. "What then?"

"No one is truly forced into the Elemental Cup. People have walked before," I tell her. "But if you walk, you become an outcast. You're banished from the tribe and never allowed to speak with any Elementai ever again. Even worse, your Familiar will be taken away from you. You won't die, because your Familiar is still alive, but you'll be separated forever. An Elementai that is too cowardly to enter the tournament is considered unworthy to have a Familiar."

"How did this whole thing get started, anyway?" Sophia asked. "Did the Elders just decide to throw a contest where people die for fun?"

I smirked. "No. Before the Familiars came, the Hawkei had a

coming-of-age ceremony for every person in the tribe. They were expected to survive in the wilderness for three days alone. After Anichi fell, that ceremony turned into the Elemental Cup. This tournament is every Elementai's way of proving they belong here. That they're valuable to the tribe."

"Well, I think it's sick that we should have to prove we deserve to live." Sophia's face was scrunched up in a snarl.

"You don't understand. Back then, weak people would bring the tribe down. They'd take up resources and harm everyone's way of life. It was considered honorable to give your life for the tribe's," I argued.

"Things aren't like that anymore," Sophia said harshly. "We have more resources now. We should change."

I took a deep breath. "Look. I get that you don't like it. And I can understand it's barbaric and dated. But this is your way of proving that you and Esis can contribute to our society, and that you're strong enough to help raise magical creatures."

"What about you?" She raised an eyebrow, challenging me. "What do you think of all of this, especially considering your situation?"

My situation. It didn't take her long to make me blissfully happy and piss me off again all in the same hour, did it? "I get that people like me would've died out there, a long time ago. But I'm not turning my back on my tribe."

"Not even to save your life?"

"No. If I'm being forced to do this, I'm going to show everyone that I still belong here. That I'm not useless," I growled. "And since you're doing it, too, you should use it as your opportunity to show that you're really one of us— a true Elementai, not an outsider. Don't do it for Haley. Do it for yourself."

Sophia's expression cleared. She glanced at Esis and stroked his fluffy fur. "Yeah. I get what you're saying. I'm no coward. And after everything you've shown me today, I want to prove that this is where I belong. And I'm definitely not giving up Esis. Anyone who tries to make me can go straight to hell."

"Good," I responded sourly. My face went back to that shriveled-up pout that I hated and that I only realized that I did now. It'd been set like that for months, and I hadn't even realized.

Sophia had shattered that statue today, and bringing it back now was terribly uncomfortable. But I didn't want to smile right now, because she'd poked the bear. Irritating.

"What, now that we're heading into school you're going back to being emo?" Sophia asked, laughing as we reached the bottom of the mountain.

"I'm not emo," I grumbled, and we headed back into the forest. "You're pushing your luck."

"Oh, really? What are you gonna do?" She punched me in the shoulder and drew herself up. "Give me one of your salty comments, Water boy?"

"Shut up." I laughed under my breath. I nudged her with my shoulder, and she nudged back.

It was by accident, but when Sophia leaned against me, I didn't pull away this time. We were leaning on each other the entire way back to the castle. Esis happily cheered and left Sophia's shoulder to hop on my head again.

When we saw the spires of the castle coming into view, it was like we were electrically jolted apart. Both of us retreated from one another until we were at least a few feet away, like it was a crime to be seen together.

I guess it kind of was.

Esis, though, didn't come off my head until Sophia pried him away. He took a good chunk of my hair with him, too, the little shit.

"So... dinner?" Sophia asked reluctantly, as if she was scared I was gonna bow out on my promise now.

"Dinner," I confirmed. I followed her into the cafeteria. It crossed my mind that people might talk if they saw us eating together, but I pushed it out of my head. They could look. We were tournament partners now, after all. We had to talk to each other to strategize. People wouldn't think too much of it. We had an excuse.

Far too convenient of an excuse. Don't get too close, I reminded myself.

It was too late for that. I really liked Sophia.

Which meant that I was totally screwed.

sophia

TWELVE

Orenda Academy was starting to feel more and more like home with each passing day following our trip up the mountain. If it wasn't for Madame Doya's class and the fact that I still worried about and missed my parents, I might actually feel like I could stay here forever.

"Sophia!" Madame Doya snapped one Thursday during class— just like almost every day. She had led us outside to a clearing in the forest. Dry pine needles and leaves littered the ground. We hadn't even started the lesson and she was already yelling at me.

The sound of my name snapped me out of my thoughts. I'd been focused on how things had changed since Liam took me to meet my ancestors. He had returned to being my partner in our Medical Care of Familiars class, and I'd even caught him smiling a time or two over the past several weeks. For the most part, Haley had left me alone, and the other Koigni in my dorm had grown bored of playing pranks outside my door.

Imogen and I continued to hang out when we weren't in class. We spent most of our time outside the castle, either walking the mountain trails or scouring the beach for cool rocks. As a Nivita, Imogen could sense the minerals in the rocks and knew where to find the pretty ones before I could even see them. Esis had a blast digging through the rocks to help. He always managed to find the shiniest rocks on the beach. The ledge of my dorm window was filling up with rocks far too quickly.

I was making progress with my Fire, but it was easier in class, where Madame Doya made my blood boil. Still, that didn't seem good enough for her, despite the fact that I was outperforming all my classmates besides Haley. Two other girls and a guy had since bonded with their Familiars, and their skills were catching up. But until they did, I was maintaining the notion that Doya had absolutely nothing to yell at me about. She, apparently, didn't get the memo.

I forced myself to hold her gaze. "Yes?"

"I want you and Haley up here in the front," she instructed with tight lips, as if I was wasting her time. A low growl bubbled up from Naomi's throat beside her, warning me to hurry up.

The crowd of students parted. I stepped forward. Esis sat cradled in the hood of my sweatshirt but tugged on my ponytail to get a better look. Haley crossed her arms and smirked from beside me. The phoenix on her shoulder held her head high, mirroring Haley's attitude. Above us, the October sky was overcast, and it looked like it might rain.

Doya projected her voice across the clearing. "In today's exercise, we will be extinguishing fire rather than conjuring it. You will each be paired up, and each pair will take a turn putting out their fires. You must work together quickly and efficiently. We don't want to start any forest fires."

Doya shot a narrowed gaze my way, as if she believed I was most prone to letting things get out of hand. Naomi mimicked her. Anger settled in my gut like a bag of rocks. How much more could I possibly prove myself to her? I'd already shot flames from my palms, generated heat without a flame, and shaped my Fire into a sphere, all before ninety-nine percent of my classmates did. Plus, I was the only one who managed to set my hair on fire without singeing a single strand. Miranda had ended up needing a pixie cut to get rid of the damage, and I was pretty sure Haley had cut at least two inches off her hair.

Granted, I lost one of my good ponytail elastics that day, but that was a small price to pay for the victory. Doya had just looked down her nose at me but didn't say anything. I considered it a compliment.

"Haley and Sophia, you're up first." That was all Madame Doya said before she stepped aside.

In the blink of an eye, a band of fire lit a mere two feet in front of us. Pine needles cracked as the flames licked several feet into the air. The needles burned so quickly that the flames were already spreading across the clearing at an alarming rate before I had a chance to react.

I'd already resigned myself to the fact that Madame Doya would never give us any clear instruction. She used a "throw-them-into-the-lion's-pit-and-watch-them-fend-for-themselves" type of teaching style. I didn't bother asking how she expected us to complete this task.

I turned to Haley. "Any ideas?"

Haley's gaze was already narrowed at the fire, and her brows constricted as if she was thinking hard. "Yeah," she snapped. "You could help me."

The more Haley concentrated, the bigger the flames grew. I took several steps back, but I could still feel the heat radiating across my face.

"We don't have all day," Madame Doya chastised. "If you let the whole clearing burn, no one else will get a chance."

I listened to her words, but only to drive my anger at her. It always seemed to help me do better in her class. Behind me, Esis kneaded the back of my neck. I brushed his small paws from my skin.

"Not now, Esis," I whispered, but he ignored me and continued to press his paws into my muscles. It was surprisingly relaxing, which was *totally* not what I needed right now. Like Liam had said, Koigni magic took strong emotions, and I needed to channel everything I had right now.

I concentrated on the fire. Its warmth didn't just touch my skin— its energy permeated down through my muscles and into my bones. My body buzzed to its frequency, but it was different than controlling my own Fire. Doya had conjured this fire, and though it felt similar to my own, there was something slightly off about it. It seemed angrier and more brutal, as if I could feel Doya's emotions pulsing through the flames.

The fire continued to spread, roaring and crackling. Dark smoke rose into the air.

"What are you doing, Sophia?" Haley snapped. "Help me!"

I blinked to clear my vision and focused on the fire. My mind raced with possible solutions, but so far, we'd only learned how to *conjure* fire, not extinguish it. We'd been using traditional means until now.

I imagined the flames dying down, burning to nothing but embers, but they didn't. I tried to pull the flames together, to create a fireball that would keep them from spreading, but that only separated a fireball from the other flames that continued to rage through the clearing.

"Stop it, Sophia!" Haley yelled as she took another step back, as if it was entirely my fault the fire was growing.

The flames burst higher, like they were exploding with Haley's anger.

That's it! I realized.

Fire was made of rage and fury. It thrived off untamed emotions. Extinguishing it would require just the opposite.

I took a deep breath and focused on the soothing massage Esis was giving me. I ignored Haley's remarks and Doya's hard gaze, letting everything around me fade until it felt like I was alone in the forest with Esis and the fire.

I willed the energy sizzling through my bones to calm, but it pushed against me.

Haley.

"You have to calm down," I told her. "Anger and frustration will only make it worse."

"Yeah, because that's so easy," Haley said with an eye roll.

I forced my annoyance down. Haley didn't deserve any of my energy anyway.

Just stay calm, I told myself. *Nothing good will come out of anger today. You can do this. You can control it.*

Images flashed through my mind as I tried to focus on the things that would calm me most. I pictured Amelia's smiling face, which only made me smile since I was wearing her jeans today. I thought of my parents. A pang entered my chest, the same one that hit every time they crossed my mind.

Not working, I told myself.

I quickly switched focus. Instead of focusing on the things I'd lost, I focused on those I'd gained. I thought about Esis, about his soft paws on the back of my neck, the way he purred when I held him in my arms, and the way he looked at me with his big blue eyes as if I were the only person in the world he could ever love. My heart swelled at the thought of him.

My thoughts flickered back to last week when I was sitting in one of the big comfy chairs in the castle foyer waiting to meet up with Imogen for lunch. Esis was jumping from armrest to armrest, tagging my fingers that I wiggled in the air above him. I giggled until my gaze lifted and I spotted Liam passing through the hall at the top of the grand staircase. Our eyes met for a moment, and my heart flipped in my chest when I witnessed a ghost of a smile touch his lips.

The flames in front of me shrank from several feet high to mere inches. I held the fire back, keeping it from eating away at any more dry debris. It fought against me, the energy pressing against my chest like a snowplow. I threw my walls up, blocking the pressure out and funneling my calm energy into it. The fire eased more and more until there was nothing left but embers. I forced the final bit of Fire energy off my chest with a calming breath, and the remaining embers sizzled away to nothing. A large circle of black, charred debris at least ten feet across stood as a reminder of our exercise.

Haley breathed a sigh of relief. "Whew. I did it!"

She glanced to the other students proudly. Kelsey gave her a thumbs up, but Hudson and Tabitha both looked at me like they knew I'd been the one to extinguish the flames by myself. I looked to Doya, expecting some sort of praise, but she just pursed her lips and looked away from me. Beside her, Naomi shot daggers my way.

"Ben. Kelsey. You're next," Doya barked.

She ignited another fire as soon as they made it to the front of the group. I turned in complete shock and found my way to the back. My mind raced as I watched group after group struggle with the task. Doya had to put most of the flames out herself, save for one group toward the end who'd I'd seen whispering and strategizing before-hand. Clearly, I was outperforming most of my other classmates. What about that wasn't good enough for Doya?

The calmness I'd felt during the exercise quickly washed away. My frustrations grew the more I thought about it. Doya hated me since the first day I showed up in her class. It was more than just her normal distaste for students, too. Did she hate Amelia so much that she had to take it out on me? What had Amelia done to her? Or was there something else going on here?

I had the entire class period to mull it over in my mind. By the end of class, I was bound and determined to figure out what the reason was. That disappointed look she liked to give me had punched one too many holes through my gut.

I hung back by the edge of the trail we'd come as soon as she dismissed the class. She'd just put out the last group's fire and didn't see me standing in the trees until she spun around. Her face immediately fell.

I was going to say her name, but that look sent the words right back down my throat. *Maybe I shouldn't do this.* Esis tugged on my ponytail, snapping me back to attention. I was *totally* doing this, whether it risked her tossing me out of her class or not.

"Class dismissed, Sophia," Doya said with a sharp edge to her tone.

I forced my voice to remain even. "I know, but I'd like to talk with you." I purposely didn't ask her permission. She'd probably deny me the opportunity and tell me to find her during office hours.

Doya sighed and started down the trail with Naomi at her side. "Fine, but make it snappy."

I hurried along behind her. I only took a second to gather my courage. Anything more than that and she'd for sure yell at me again. Honestly, it was impossible to please this woman.

"Why do you hate me?" I spit out the words before I had a chance to second guess myself.

Madame Doya whirled around, her velvety dress and red hair swirling around her. She spun so fast that I nearly rammed into her. I took a step back, my heart thumping like a bass drum against my chest. I couldn't believe I'd actually worked up the courage to say it.

"Excuse me?" she bit. Naomi growled protectively.

I swallowed hard, though my pulse continued to pound through my ears. There was no backing down now. "It's pretty obvious that you hate me. I just don't know why."

Madame Doya scoffed and turned her back to me to head down the trail. "Do you honestly think I treat you differently than any of my other students, Sophia?"

I thought about the way she praised Haley whenever she executed a task with precision. She didn't exactly praise many other students, but most of them weren't as good as Haley, either. I was *certain* there was no one else in class she yelled or snapped at more than she did to me.

"Yes," I stated confidently.

"I'm hard on you because I want to push you to be better, Sophia," Doya said from in front of me. "I expect much more from you than the others."

She was lying. I completed most of the tasks she required from us. I had a sure shot at passing this class. What more could she expect? Why would she even care?

"Why?" I pressed. "Is it because I'm bonded? Other people have bonded, and—"

"No," she said in a clipped tone. "It's because..."

She trailed off, like she didn't want to answer. "It's because you show more promise."

I couldn't see her expression as we walked along the trail, but I could hear the lie in her voice. There was something she wasn't telling me.

"I know that's not true," I said, my heart finally slowing. "I came into your class knowing nothing. I had about as much promise as a slug."

We emerged from the trees and reached one of the staircases at the edge of the castle's lawn. I took two steps at a time until I was beside Doya. Naomi climbed the stairs on her other side, giving Esis the stink eye as he chewed on the string of my hoodie.

Doya kept her gaze fixed forward on the castle. "That may be true, but look how far you've come."

I wasn't sure if that was meant to be some backhanded insult or a compliment. I guess it made sense why she thought I had promise. It also made sense why my Koigni classmates weren't fond of me. I came in with less potential in my entire body than they had in their pinky fingers, bonded with the cutest, most harmless Familiar around, and I still showed them up. I bet they were starting to think there was some truth to that prophecy after all.

Which reminded me...

No one had actually told me yet what the prophecy said or what I had to do with it. Every time I asked Imogen, she just said she didn't know *exactly* how it was worded and didn't want to give me false information. Which was quickly followed up by *"Besides, it's just an urban legend."*

Which, coming from Imogen, sounded like a complete lie. If anyone believed in the prophecy, Imogen would. She believed there were freaking *wolpertingers* in the forest, which Jonah kindly explained to me didn't exist. Urban legends were kind of her thing.

I'd resigned myself to believing that meant the prophecy was bad news for me and that maybe I didn't *want* to know what it said. But I was feeling bold today. The question slipped out before I could stop myself.

"What does the prophecy say about me?"

Madame Doya stopped dead at the top of the stairs. I took another step toward the castle before realizing she and Naomi had both frozen up. I turned to her.

Esis dropped my hoodie string and straightened.

"That's why you're hard on me, isn't it?" I asked. "You want me to be better than everyone else— even Haley— so I can fulfill the prophecy?"

Doya folded her hands like she often did, but the muscles in her forearm bulged beneath her sleeves as her fingers tightened together. "That may be part of it," she admitted, though she kept her emotional walls up as she spoke.

Of course it was.

"It's going to be kind of hard for me to fulfill this prophecy if I don't know what it says, won't it?"

Honestly, I didn't know where my confidence came from. Usually,

I'd avoid Doya at all costs. I half expected her to snap back at me, scolding me for my attitude.

Instead, she glanced toward the sky. "It's going to rain soon, Sophia. I can't stand out here all day talking about this. I have another class soon."

I side-stepped to block her path. "Why are you keeping this from me?" I demanded. Koigni magic tingled through my skin as my anger surfaced. *Oh, that's where the confidence is coming from.* "Do the Koigni *want* me to fail?"

Madame Doya blinked rapidly, as if I'd just slapped her in the face. "No. Of course not."

Naomi snorted, like I'd offended her.

"Then why aren't you helping me?" I demanded.

"I *am* helping you!" Doya all but roared. "I'm doing what I was assigned to do. I'm teaching you how to use your magic."

Well, damn. I wasn't expecting that answer. Yet it wasn't enough.

I crossed my arms. "Whose job is it to tell me about the prophecy? Because whoever was supposed to do that screwed up and forgot."

A muscle fluttered in Doya's jaw, and she glanced around. The closest people were way across the lawn near the courtyard. They couldn't hear us from here.

Madame Doya caved with a sigh and lowered her voice. "The prophecy says that you will be the one to bring our House, the Koigni, to glory. *The fated Koigni child, born in the Summer Solstice in the Year of the Dragon, shall bring glory to the greatest House.*"

Wait. That was a good thing? Weren't the Hawkei better off with a democracy where *all* the Houses had a say in things, not one where the Koigni controlled everything?

"That's it?" I asked. It seemed so simple.

"Isn't that enough?" Doya snapped.

"I don't know," I replied in uncertainty. "I thought the prophecy would be more... dangerous."

"Of course it's dangerous," Doya barked like I was an idiot. "The other Houses don't want this prophecy to come true. They're watching you, Sophia. If you value your life, you will push yourself harder in my class— in all your classes. And take pride in the House you were born into. It's the only one you have."

My hands shook at her words, and Esis' fingers tightened in my hair. That sounded *bad*.

My voice quickly lost its confident tone. "Does the prophecy say anything about how I'm supposed to do this?"

Doya glanced around again to make sure no one was within earshot. She spoke firmly. "There is more, but I expect you will not repeat this part to anyone, as it is for Koigni ears only."

Naomi glared at me. I swore she raised an eyebrow in my direction. After a beat, I realized Doya was waiting for my response. Honestly, I didn't know if I could keep the information quiet. Depending on what it was, I would be tempted to tell Imogen.

But something told me I wasn't prying the information from Doya's lips without complete and utter honesty. I was playing by her rules.

"I won't tell anyone," I promised.

Doya took a breath. "You will have to find a powerful item that will serve to fulfill the prophecy."

"A specific item? Where am I supposed to find it? What does it look like?" So many questions raced through my head. Chief among them... was the prophecy even worth fulfilling?

"I don't know." Madame Doya's features hardened, quickly turning her back into her usual unhelpful self. "I'm not the one who will fulfill this prophecy. You are. But for the ancestors' sake, Sophia, tread carefully. The other Houses have not yet confirmed you are the one, but as soon as they do, you better be ready. They would rather see you dead than see the Koigni in their rightful place of power."

With that, Madame Doya turned and hurried across the lawn toward the back of the castle. Her dress billowed out behind her, and Naomi prowled in her wake.

I stood at the top of the steps, completely stunned. A shiver crawled down my spine as my eyes traveled toward the courtyard. People from all Houses swarmed the lawn. It suddenly occurred to me that any one of them might want me dead. And I hadn't even done anything wrong yet.

Yet. Key word. Did that mean I *would* fulfill this prophecy? Would *I* be responsible for the downfall of the other three Houses?

It didn't seem possible, but I couldn't shake the feeling that the ancestors wouldn't have delivered this prophecy if it weren't true.

⁂

"GIRL, WHERE HAVE YOU BEEN?" Imogen demanded with a smile when I met up with her in Dragonology later that day.

I'd spent the last three hours poring over books with Esis in the library, searching for any further information about the prophecy. But as I'd already come to find, the library was useless when it came to Hawkei history. I'd learned they much preferred passing down stories orally rather than writing them down. Who knew how much the prophecy had been twisted since it was first foretold?

"Sorry I'm late," I said vaguely as I joined her in the back of the class.

The sky above us had darkened since earlier, but it hadn't started raining yet. I'd asked Imogen once why the Elementai didn't just control the weather around here, and she told me they didn't like to mess with it because it could damage the ecosystem. Plus, you never knew if another Elementai was messing with the weather a few miles away. It was strictly forbidden, except in controlled cases like the cruise ship and during the tournament.

Dragonology took place in a clearing along a ledge between the castle and the ocean. It made for a perfect view of the beach. We'd spent the first half of the semester in the classroom studying dragon anatomy and taking care of Aisha, a baby dragon whose mother had abandoned her because she was born with a limp wing. She reminded me a lot of Squeaks. Today was our first class outside, and it was our first chance to meet a full-grown dragon up close and personal. As excited as I was about this opportunity, my mind was elsewhere.

I stared down the mountain toward the beach. Students prowled the rocky shore near the pier, but it wasn't the crowd that caught my eye. A quarter mile down the beach from them, a guy with long black hair sat alone on a big rock. He stared out across the vast water and twisted something beige around in his hands, almost like he was knitting a sweater. I'd recognize those broad shoulders and silky black hair anywhere.

Liam.

A whistle sounded from beside me, pulling me out of my daze. I turned to Imogen.

She wiggled her eyebrows and sang, "Somebody's got the hots for *Liam.*"

"Shut up." I swatted at her. "I do not. Besides, I'm not allowed to date anyone who isn't Koigni."

Which meant my love life was going nowhere. Koigni guys were all assholes.

"Says who?" Imogen challenged. She placed her hands on hips, on top of the floral skirt she wore over skinny jeans.

"Um... everyone?" I pointed out.

Imogen rolled her eyes. "So you can't marry him. That doesn't mean you can't have fun."

I suppressed a smile. "You're naughty."

Imogen smiled proudly. "Live a little."

An involuntary frown crossed my face. I wasn't the kind of girl who broke the rules, not even for a guy like Liam.

"Seriously, come here." Imogen grabbed my shoulders and shook me. "Just relax. Let all that tension go."

Esis cooed from my shoulder, but his voice vibrated. I didn't feel much like smiling, but I couldn't help it.

"Okay, okay," I said through suppressed giggles. "I'm relaxed."

"Good, now—"

"Everyone." The sound of Professor Curt's voice cut Imogen off. "Meet Kalina."

He gestured to the trees and stepped aside. Aisha, who he'd taken a fondness to, sat on a rock near him and scratched the back of her blue ear with her hind leg.

From out of the thick forest stepped a beautiful dragon coated in shiny red scales. Long horns protruded from her head, and short spikes traveled the length of her spine and down her tail. She only took a few steps out of the trees before lowering herself to the ground and folding her bat-like wings across her back. She held her head high and looked positively comfortable despite the thirty pairs of eyes staring back at her.

"She's magnificent," I whispered in wonder.

Esis huffed like he was offended.

I'd seen plenty of dragons since arriving at Orenda Academy, but I'd never been this close to one before. None except Aisha. Aisha was the size of a medium dog, while Kalina was bigger than a pickup truck. She held herself in a way Aisha never would. She was basically a work of art.

"Don't be shy," Professor Curt encouraged. "Kalina is my Familiar. She will not harm you— unless I tell her to, of course." He let out a light laugh. "But I assure you I won't. It's perfectly safe."

Imogen bent and scooped up Sassy in her arms, who'd been playing with her shoelace the whole time. "Let's go meet a dragon!"

Imogen pushed through the group and was the first to approach Kalina. I followed closely behind her with Esis on my shoulder. Kalina sat as still as a stone when Imogen approached. She held Sassy up to Kalina's face, as if introducing them. Sassy promptly let out a loud sneeze, her whole body tightening under the pressure. Kalina drew her head back in surprise, but she quickly stretched forward to give Sassy a good sniff.

Imogen cradled Sassy in her arms. "Oh, sweetheart, are you allergic to dragons?"

Whispers broke out behind us, but I was so used to it now that it barely registered.

Sassy reached out a paw to touch Kalina's nose. If she wasn't careful, her paw would fit straight up Kalina's nostril.

I giggled at the thought, which drew Kalina's eyes to me. She stared at me with a look in her eyes I couldn't quite place. Admiration, maybe? Whatever it was, it was inviting.

"Come on," Professor Curt said, motioning for me to step forward. "She likes you."

I wanted to pet Kalina, but she was so large and confident, it was intimidating. She could literally bite my arm off. I stepped forward anyway and gently reached out my hand. Kalina bowed her head, allowing me to pet the space between her eyes. Her scales were soft and warm.

"Good, good," Professor Curt said. "Anyone else?"

Several other students rushed forward to marvel at his beautiful Familiar. Imogen and I were pushed aside.

"You're fine, Sassy," Imogen said, bouncing her in her arms. "You've never had any problems with Aisha, have you?"

Imogen held Sassy up to Aisha's face. The baby dragon immediately stuck her tongue out and dragged it across Sassy's cheek. We both laughed.

"I think they like each other," I giggled.

"Of course they do," Imogen agreed. "Who wouldn't love this little red fur ball?"

From my shoulder, Esis stretched out a hand, as if he wanted to touch Aisha. I bent to Aisha's rock until they were close enough to touch. Esis grabbed her small horn and climbed onto her head. She spun in a circle, nipping playfully at him as he slid down her back. Sassy squirmed in Imogen's arms as if she wanted to play with them.

"Oh, my gosh!" I exclaimed. "They're too cute."

Behind us, a guy scoffed. I threw a glance over my shoulder to see Brandon, a Koigni senior, and his Familiar, an orange cat the size of a lynx, staring at us.

"Is there a problem, Brandon?" Imogen snapped at him.

He shot her an unamused expression. "That dragon's not *cute*. There's a reason its mother abandoned it."

My gut twisted at his blatant disregard for another being's life. What did Aisha ever do to him?

"Screw you, Brandon," Imogen shot back at him. "You wouldn't know cute if it bit you in the ass."

I stifled a laugh. Sometimes Imogen's bold personality was a blessing.

"Yeah, well—" Brandon started to retort, but Imogen turned away, ignoring him. He huffed but apparently couldn't come up with a strong enough comeback, because he let it drop.

Esis reached the point behind Aisha's shoulder blades, right between her wings. He stretched out to her limp wing like he was about to climb out onto it.

"Hey, there, buddy," I said, scooping him up off the dragon's back. "We don't want to hurt her."

Esis' small claws dug into the fabric of my sweatshirt as he tried to pry himself away from me.

"Whoa." I held onto him tighter. "What's up? Where are you going?"

Esis struggled harder until his hands were clamped around the exposed skin on my hands, digging in so deeply that I thought he might draw blood. Instinctively, I yelped and dropped him in the dirt.

I rubbed my hands while Esis scurried up the rock and returned to Aisha's back. "Ow, Esis. What's gotten into you?"

Esis grabbed Aisha's wing again and pumped it, as if encouraging her to take flight.

"Esis, she can't fly," I told him, as if he could understand. I noticed for the first time that Aisha's wing looked straighter and stronger than normal. Maybe she'd eventually grow out of her deformity.

"Relax," Imogen insisted. "They're just having fun."

Except I could tell something was wrong. Esis had never jumped out of my hands like that before.

Esis trilled and continued the flapping motion. Aisha stood high on her rock and began flapping her good wing.

"See?" Imogen said. "Just having—"

The words died on her lips as Aisha's body lifted into the air. Esis cheered in victory the same moment my stomach dropped to the ground. I should've been happy for Aisha, considering none of us ever thought she would ever fly, but I wasn't. I was terrified for Esis as I watched them climb higher. Aisha dropped several feet between each flap of her wings, as if she was simply limping along. Sheer terror filled me as a slew of possibilities rushed through my mind. Esis could fall and get hurt! I couldn't let that happen.

Behind me, all infatuation with Kalina died as everyone's attention turned to Esis and Aisha as they rose above the trees.

"Esis!" I ran after them. If he fell, I'd be right there to catch him.

Professor Curt didn't seem at all concerned with my Familiar's well-being. He just laughed in disbelief and said, "That's my girl, Aisha. You're flying!"

I rushed into the trees to stay under them. I tried to keep an eye on them, but I only caught glimpses of blue scales through the canopy. The top of a tree moved as Aisha's toes grazed it.

"Esis!" I cried.

Oh, God. Ancestors. Whoever. Don't let my little guy die! He means the world to me.

His trill of excitement echoed through the trees.

"Esis! You get down here *this* instant!" I screamed.

To my horror Aisha caught the top of another tree and her body slammed into the next one. It pulled her from the air like a giant monster reaching for its prey, and she and Esis went tumbling to the ground. Twigs snapped on their way down, and pine needles rained to the forest floor. They both landed in the dirt with a sickening *thud*.

My gut immediately tightened like I'd been punched. I quickly rushed forward to where Aisha and Esis lay sprawled. Aisha's bad wing was even more twisted than before, and blood trickled out of a wound on her face. The red liquid was in stark contrast to her blue scales. Her eyes were closed, and I wasn't sure she was breathing.

Beside her, Esis lay still. My heart hammered ferociously against my rib cage. I skidded onto my knees beside them. My hands shot out to cradle Esis, but before I touched him, his eyes popped open and he sprang up to his feet. Dirt coated his white fur. Though he normally dusted off, he ignored it this time. He ignored me, too, pushing my hands away when I reached for him. His eyes locked on the cut on Aisha's face.

I froze as Esis stood beside her. He was barely the size of her head, but he bent over her like he was the stronger, wiser of the two. He placed his tiny little paws on either side of her wound and then closed his eyes.

My eyes widened as Aisha's cut began to knit itself together right in front of my eyes.

"Esis," I whispered. *What kind of magical creature are you?*

I didn't have a chance to finish my thought aloud before someone cleared their throat from behind me. I whirled around to see that Imogen had followed me. She held Sassy in her arms.

"Imogen, I— I—" I glanced between her and Aisha, who was starting to wake. The cut had completely vanished, and her scales were perfectly intact, as if nothing had happened at all.

I didn't know what to say. This changed everything. It meant that Esis wasn't just a helpless Familiar after all. He was *powerful*. So powerful that if anyone got wind of this, they might take him from me.

Like Doya had said, I needed to tread lightly. This kind of thing just might get us killed.

I could barely think straight, but there was no denying Imogen's expression. Her usual smile had vanished, and her mouth hung open slightly. She didn't even blink.

"Imogen, please—" I couldn't finish my sentence before Professor Curt and the rest of our class rushed up behind her.

Professor Curt knelt beside me to inspect Aisha's injuries, but I never tore my gaze from Imogen's eyes. Before I could rise from the ground and drag her away to talk about what had just happened, she'd whirled around and bolted past our classmates and out of the trees.

It was in that moment that the skies decided to open. Rain fell to the ground in large, heavy drops, soaking my clothing and Esis' fur within seconds. Students scattered but I remained frozen, staring through the trees where Imogen had just ditched me.

A chilling fear traveled down my spine. *Imogen saw.* She saw Esis heal Aisha. She knew as well as I did that Esis wasn't all he appeared to be. The only question was, would she honor our friendship, or would she turn us in to the Nivita Elders?

I wasn't sure how long Esis and I had before another House confirmed the prophecy and decided to kill us for it.

Liam

THIRTEEN

Survival Instincts had been held in the woods almost every time I went to it, but since it was pouring out today, it'd been moved into Professor McCauley's main classroom, located in the dungeons.

Professor McCauley wasn't one to be afraid of "a little rain," but when there had been a tornado sighted nearby, Head Dean Alric put his foot down and forced us to relocate inside.

McCauley had ranted that young people today were coddled before she started her lesson. Made me laugh.

Good thing, too. I could keep the rain off of me, but I didn't want to hear the rest of the class whine that it was too wet. I guess the Yapluma would get their kicks when the rest of us were carried off by a twister, though.

Although... I would almost rather be outside in these dangerous conditions than inside McCauley's creepy classroom. There were no windows down here, and besides the wooden desks, the only decor she had were multiple arrays of skeletons, both human and Familiar. They were mounted throughout the room in various poses before dark tapestries that depicted gruesome scenes. Every day was Halloween when McCauley was concerned.

"When you are in a survival situation, the first thing you need to do is stop and assess your surroundings," Professor McCauley boomed. "It is better to create a plan and execute it than to hesitate too long and lose precious seconds. If you panic, you will most certainly end up dead."

McCauley's Familiar, Bram, was lurking around the room and making people shiver. I ignored him and tried to focus. Professor McCauley's Familiar was a wendigo, and it was creeping out the majority of the people in this class. It was easy to tell why. The wendigo had the skeletal body of a horse, with wolf's paws and a reptilian tail. The head was merely the skull of a deer, the antlers intact. Its black skin was drawn tightly over its skeletal form, and its bones clicked together as it wandered around the room.

Bram hissed and gnashed his sharp teeth near a student who'd fallen asleep. The guy woke up screaming, and the class laughed. I was pretty sure the dude pissed himself.

Bram chuckled like he was pleased before he moved on. The thing looked like it could survive in the wilds alone without a problem. In fact, Bram looked like he could survive, kill, and maim everything within a hundred miles of wherever he'd been abandoned.

McCauley was pretty creepy herself, and had to be close to a hundred by now. She matched her Familiar in looks, taut skin stretched over thin bones. The two of them appeared to be walking skeletons. McCauley dressed in all black, only increasing her frightening appearance.

They should've retired from teaching to become crypt keepers years ago. I was pretty sure McCauley was gonna outlive me.

This wasn't McCauley's class— Professor Devante usually taught Survival Instincts— but he and his wife had just had a baby, so McCauley was filling in for this semester.

Not that I minded. Professor McCauley had sneered at everything that had tried to kill her off so far, so obviously she knew a thing or two about staying alive.

"Water is more important to find than food in a survival situation. Depending on the situation, you will either need to find a source or have a Toaqua draw it up for you," McCauley preached.

Water was easy. I could supply it if we ran into a pinch, and Sophia had fire.

Unless one of us died, and the rest of us were screwed.

"If there is adequate access to water, the human body can survive around twenty days or so without food. Keep in mind, however, that by this time you will be very weak, and it will only take a matter of days without food before you become useless and unable to harvest or hunt." McCauley scanned the room with piercing crow eyes. "Therefore, daily nutrition becomes very important, for both you and your Familiar."

McCauley took a tray and began passing it around the room. "These types of plants are local to the region, and edible. You can find them in many places on earth. Memorize their appearances and names."

When the tray passed to me, I focused on it. Cattails, the inside of conifer bark, acorns, wild blueberries. Not exactly the most delicious, but when you were hungry, anything looked good.

I passed the tray behind me, and McCauley said, "There will be a quiz next time you come in. Anyone who doesn't pass I don't expect to last long. Class dismissed."

People gathered their things and headed out. McCauley's comment was obviously directed toward the tournament. Besides me, there were at least four other people in here who were going to be competing. I knew she was watching us and expecting us to do well.

I passed a bunch of squealing girls in the hallway complimenting one of the girls on her brand-new Familiar. I wasn't sure what it was, but it looked like a pink pom-pom. At least she had a year to bulk the thing up before she was forced to compete.

I winced as the girls squealed again and continued on. I thought Survival Instincts was going to be a blow-off class, but now that I was forced to be in the tournament, I made myself pay attention. And it was a good thing, too. I'd already learned how to make a quick shelter.

I no longer skipped class. I'd need every piece of information available to keep me and my team alive out there.

I heard someone else giggling— and I knew that voice. Around the corner was Sophia. She was leaning against the wall with a bunch of books in her hands. Esis was perched on top of them. Ezra was with her, grinning coyly. They hadn't seen me.

I was about to turn around and go the opposite way before Sophia said to Ezra, "Seriously, your Liam impressions are the best."

"Aren't they?" Ezra snorted. "It took months of perfection to get just the right scowl."

I slunk against the wall at Ezra's comment, hiding. Ezra and Sophia were *talking about me*.

The little bastards.

I was about to round the corner and confront them before a question from Sophia stopped me in my tracks. "So... what was Liam like? Before he lost Nashoma?"

What was I like? What made her think she had the right to ask that question?

I decided to hold back and listen in. Eavesdropping wasn't right, but hey, it was way better than playing the fool.

Ezra laughed. I imagined him looking up, because any time someone asked him a question the idiot always had to glance skyward, like the answer was on the ceiling. "What was he like before Nashoma? Well, let's see. His favorite thing was swearing. Still is. I think he started saying the F-Bomb when he was like, ten."

Sophia laughed, and I smiled. Yeah, that pretty much described me.

"He laughed a lot. He was always up for an adventure, whatever it was. He loved exploring. He wasn't a big sports guy, but he enjoyed being active. Hiking was one of his favorite things."

"I love hiking, too," Sophia said quietly.

"And he loved helping people," Ezra added. "He'd jump in any time to lend a hand. He had the biggest heart."

"Seriously?" Sophia's tone was doubtful. "None of that sounds like Liam."

"Is it really that hard to believe?" Ezra sounded amused. "Word around school is that he's the reason your Fire started emerging, and pretty strong, too."

Dammit. Should've known that would get out somehow. The damn trees had ears around here.

"It's just..." Sophia paused. "He was pretty blunt about it when he told me he hated helping people."

"Don't believe him. He's just being a jerk. It's like his default setting is grumpy nowadays."

Sophia and Ezra laughed together, and I scowled. *Thanks, assholes.*

"Nashoma just amplified those traits," Ezra said. "He became super brave. He was never afraid of anything. And he was a really good leader. Better than I ever could be."

Doubt that, Ez. People adored my brother. They rotated around him like he was the sun. I'd never been like that— popular.

"And now he's not the same," Sophia said.

"Now..." Ezra sighed. "He's secluded. He doesn't like being around anyone, not even me. He goes to class and then locks himself up in his dorm. I can't talk to him without being insulted."

Ouch. That was kind of true, but it hurt. I had been a dick to Ezra lately, along with everyone else.

"He seems very spiritual," Sophia commented. I think she was trying to direct the conversation into a more positive light.

"He is. He's super religious. Not that it isn't true, or anything, but I think Liam was more into our culture than any of us because he took the responsibility of being firstborn so seriously. It really hurt him when our dad told him he wasn't going to be chief anymore."

Fuck yeah it did. Second most painful day of my life was when Dad brought me in to tell me he was passing on the chief hood to Ezra. Fricken sucked.

"You said he was a good leader, but that he likes seclusion," Sophia mulled. "What does that mean?"

"He's always kind of been a lone wolf, pun intended," Ezra said. "Even before he lost Nashoma, he found it hard to let people in. He'd shoulder other people's problems but never share his own. It's just how he is."

"I bet he would've made a really great chief," Sophia said.

That small bit of praise made me want to fly. It was nice Sophia believed in me.

Until she said, "How do you feel about being chief?"

I imagined Ezra shrugging. "I don't know. It is what it is."

I knew he wasn't into it. But it wasn't like he had a choice now. My one bad decision had cost me Nashoma, but it had also cost my tribe its leader, and my brother his future.

"Do you... do you think he wants to make it through this tournament?" Sophia asked. "He said he didn't want to die, but..."

Sophia made a good point. Yeah, I didn't want to die. But I didn't really want to live, either. I was caught in the middle.

Ezra's voice became heavy. "I don't know. We were super close before Nashoma died. Then once it happened, it's like he couldn't see me anymore. He just... forgot about me."

A surge of guilt rampaged throughout my insides. Ezra and I had been close. We'd practically hung out every day, even after I started at Orenda. That had changed pretty quickly over the past few months.

I made a mental note to hang out with Ezra more often. I didn't realize it until now, but I missed him.

"Are you excited to find your Familiar?" Sophia asked him, trying to change the subject. "I wasn't sure, but once I found Esis, it's like my entire life changed. I'm so happy now."

"I don't know." Ezra's tone was guarded. "Not really."

Not really? What the hell was that supposed to mean?

"I get scared, you know," Ezra said, quietly now. "After seeing Liam go through what he did, if having a Familiar can cause you that much pain, I'm not sure I want one."

Double whammy. If I was guilty before, I felt like melting into the floor now.

This was my fault. My grief over losing Nashoma had pushed my brother into thinking having a Familiar was a terrible thing. But though my time with Nashoma had been so short and the pain afterward so intense, I wouldn't have changed a thing.

Not for anything.

Ezra paused. "Why are you asking about Liam, anyway?"

Yeah, pawee. Why are you trying to dig up dirt on me?

She hesitated. "We're tournament partners. It's my job to know as much as possible about him. I depend on him for my survival out there."

It was a great excuse, but I didn't buy it. Neither did Ezra. I could hear it in his voice. "Well, if the rest of us can't get him to open up, maybe you can. He really likes you."

"You think?" Sophia's voice sounded hopeful.

"Oh, yeah. I know my brother. He's really mean to the ones he likes the most. It keeps them from getting too close." I heard footsteps. "I've got to get to class. Catch you later."

"Yeah." Sophia went the opposite way, I assumed. I turned the corner and saw them going in different directions.

Sophia's hair was bouncing up and down on her shoulders behind her. I longed to explain to her that I really wasn't as big of a prick as she'd been told.

But I couldn't, you know, because I was.

I took a step forward to go after her, but then thought better of it. I needed to spend my free hour alone.

BANG, BANG, BANG.

I was jolted out of my dreams at the loud noise and wrenched awake. Somebody was trying to bang down my door at eight o'clock on a Friday morning.

I moaned and rolled over in bed. I was going to kill whoever was out there. Fridays were my days to sleep in, and my body fricken ached all over. Twelve hours of sleep hadn't done anything to dull the pain that'd been coursing through me last night.

"Liam!" I heard Jonah's voice outside the door. "Let me in, man!"

People from other Houses weren't usually allowed in dorms that didn't belong to them, but people made an exception for Jonah—mostly because he was friends with my family, and also, because the female RA's from my dorm loved having a gay best friend around. As long as no teachers found out, it wasn't a big deal.

He was going to bust the door off its hinges. I staggered out of bed and wrenched the door open.

"I swear to the ancestors, Jonah, you're gonna die," I snapped immediately.

Jonah looked down once at me in my boxers. "Good morning, sexy."

"Are you checking me out? Because I'm seriously not in the mood," I growled.

"Baine called us in for a training session for the tournament," Jonah said. "We gotta go. It starts at nine, beachside."

"Oh." It was like Baine to ruin a perfectly good Friday. "Fine."

I slammed the door in his face, threw on some clothes, and staggered outside without combing my hair.

Jonah offered me a doughnut. "Breakfast?"

The sight of it made me feel like puking and devouring it at the same time. Chronic illness was fucking stupid. "Yes." I grabbed it and shoved it down my throat.

"You've got jelly on your face," Jonah sang out. He was way too chipper in the morning.

I waved my hand as we walked by the pools. A huge wave welled up out of them and crashed down on Jonah, soaking him from head to toe.

"What the hell?!" Jonah yelled at me as Toaqua people laughed. "Was that really necessary?"

"Was it necessary to ram on my door to wake me up, Paul Bunyan?" I snapped.

"You wouldn't have woken up any other way," Jonah said back.

I rolled my eyes, because I knew he was right. I raised my hand and the water soaking him was drawn out of his clothes and hair, leaving him completely dry again. I opened my palm, and it splashed on the floor over his boots.

"What'd you do that for? Maybe I *liked* looking soaked and seductive," Jonah said.

By the ancestors, I couldn't deal with him this early in the morning.

"Why are you even studying to be an Elementai, Jonah? Why don't you just become a model for some sex toy catalogue instead?" I asked.

"If only." Jonah sighed dreamily. I slapped myself in the forehead.

It'd been a joke, but seriously, I could see Jonah leaving school for such an opportunity.

Squeaks was waiting for us outside of the Toaqua dorms. She squealed happily when she saw Jonah, and followed us outside. She stumbled over her big feet a few times and knocked over a couple of statues on our way out. I shook my head. If I ever met a more clumsy hippogriff than Squeaks in my life, I'd protest for the species to continue.

It was still cloudy outside, but the storms had passed late last night. When we got to the beach, Squeaks tripped and went head over heels into the sand. While Jonah helped her up, I looked around for Sophia. She was there, sitting on a large rock by the shore.

Imogen wasn't with her, which was odd. Those two girls were hardly apart lately.

"Hey," I said as I approached her. Sophia looked up, and I asked, "Where's Imogen? It's almost nine."

"She isn't coming," Sophia said. "She has a cold."

"You heard from her?" Jonah asked.

Sophia went slightly pink. "Uh... no. I haven't talked to Imogen since yesterday. A Nivita girl from her dorm hall told me that this morning, before I left."

This was irritating. Our first training session, and Imogen was skipping. Usually I wouldn't care if someone didn't show up because they got sick. Like, stay in bed, because I don't want that shit. I hated when classmates showed up with a cold or the flu. All you were doing was making people miserable and spreading it around.

But this was survival, and we only got so many chances to get this right before we were literally tossed into the threshold of hell. She'd better be puking out her guts right now, because having a cold wasn't a good enough excuse for, you know, learning how to avoid death.

"That's okay," I forced myself to say. "She needs to take care of herself and get strong for what's coming."

"You don't seem to think that way when it comes to yourself," Sophia said.

"I have different standards for myself. If I stayed in bed every time I felt ill, I'd never leave my room," I told her.

Jonah and Squeaks nodded solemnly behind me, in unison. It was a little weird.

"What about Sassy?" I asked. "Is she gonna show?"

"I don't think so." Sophia shook her head.

She couldn't even send Sassy? This was getting interesting. I was starting to think that Imogen not showing up was because of something that happened between her and Sophia and not this imaginary cold.

Drama was the last thing we needed right now. These girls needed to get it together.

"Imogen should be here. There are only two more sessions after this," Jonah said.

"What?" Sophia's expression became surprised.

"We only get three training sessions with Baine," I told her. "More than that is considered cheating."

"Great." She wrinkled her nose. "I guess we should make the most of it."

We waited on the beach for Baine to show up. But nine o'clock came, and then nine thirty, and Baine was nowhere to be seen.

Okay, this was majorly annoying. First Imogen wasn't coming, and now Baine was late to his own damn training session. We were so going to lose.

"I'm about ready to head back to my dorm," I said. It'd been annoying before, but now it was seriously pissing me off. Did Baine even care if we survived?

"Let's just wait a few minutes longer." Sophia looked around. She was getting nervous.

"Hold on a minute, guys..." Jonah looked around, and Squeaks' head swiveled on her neck. "Do you hear something?"

I paused and listened closely. There was... the rushing of water— the approach of an oncoming wave.

"Jonah, get Sophia up in the air!" I screamed.

I ran toward the forest and paused at the edge while Jonah took Sophia's hand tightly. He pushed his free palm toward the ground and the two of them rose into the sky, hovering far above the beach. Sophia clung tightly to Esis as she was sent soaring into the skies.

Squeaks followed them, beating her wings so she could match their height.

Then it came. Trees bowed over as a massive wave came rushing out from the forest. I immediately threw my hands up in front of me, fingers wide, to prevent the wave from knocking me over. The water swelled around me and rushed back into the ocean, but it was hard. I struggled to keep my balance, and my strength, as the force of the powerful wave threatened to bowl me over.

Jonah saw that I needed help and curled his fingers into his palm. Immediately I felt the wind pick up around me and it spun quickly in a circle, protecting me from the water. Sophia was looking around above me, unsure of what to do.

The wave was getting stronger, harder for me to fend off. Eventually, the water broke through Jonah's shield and crushed my magic. I was dragged underneath the wave and rushed out to sea. I heard Sophia screaming.

I couldn't tell which way was up. But I knew I needed to breathe. Summoning what magic was left within me, I pushed my hands downward and the water around me shot me up like a rocket. I broke onto the surface. I felt Jonah's Air magic around me as I was lifted to the clouds, where he, Sophia, and Squeaks were levitating.

The wave below us had vanished, returning to the ocean. The beach was soaking wet, and a few trees had been knocked over. As far as we could tell, everything was safe. Jonah drifted us downward. We landed and looked around, not sure what had just happened.

Without warning Jonah was knocked down to the sand by a jet of water that slapped him in the back of the head. He groaned, and as Squeaks raced to check on him the pools of water she stood in turned to ice. Her feet were caught. Squeaks squawked and tried to pull free, but as hard as she tried to escape she just couldn't break the hold the ice had on her.

The ice was spreading. It was growing over Jonah and Squeaks' legs, their bodies. I tried to use my own Water magic to stop it, but it was far too strong. Whoever was controlling the element had more experience than I did. No matter how much I willed the ice to turn to water again, it just wouldn't obey my command.

Sophia raised her hand to shoot a jet of fire at the ice so it would melt and set Jonah free. But as she was doing so, I saw several small streams of water right from behind her. They formed into snow, then changed into daggers of ice, spinning in the air and shooting directly for Sophia's back.

"Look out!" I shouted, and I ran toward her. I was too far away, so I would never get to her before the knives did. But Sophia had good instincts, and she was able to spin around and duck before the daggers implanted themselves in her form.

I was already on my way, so I ended up tripping and knocking her down before she could free Jonah. Esis flew from her arm, landing a few feet away.

"Liam!" Sophia shouted in frustration. "I had it handled!"

"I just wanted to make sure you were safe," I shot back, but this was no time for arguing. Before our horrified gazes, Jonah and Squeaks were slowly being taken over by the ice. We rushed over. Sophia used her power to try and melt the ice, while I did my best to try and break it apart. Esis scratched at Squeaks with his little nails, but it was no use. Sophia's Fire wasn't powerful enough now. The ice had spread too far, had been given too much time.

I tapped on the ice with my knuckles. I could see Jonah inside, but he didn't move.

Oh, shit. He was dead.

I had helped to kill my best friend, now I knew. I was definitely cursed. Everyone who came around me met an untimely end. Maybe Haley was right and I was a burden to the tribe...

Suddenly, the ice turned to water and Jonah broke free, gasping for air. Squeaks crashed out of her icy prison and tumbled onto the ground. Esis made chattering sounds, looking her over and making sure she was all right.

"Jonah! Are you okay?" Sophia worried. He was coughing and gasping for breath.

"I used the pockets of air within the ice to survive, but there wasn't much in there," Jonah said. His skin was blue. Sophia lit a fire in her palms to warm him up, and he huddled close to it, shivering. Squeaks came up behind him and wrapped herself around his form, using her wings as a blanket.

"Well, I can hardly say I'm impressed," a voice behind us said. Baine was standing there, looking thoroughly disappointed and even more glum than usual.

"You did this?" I asked furiously. This was total bullshit.

"Yes, I did, Liam. And it's far from the worst you're going to experience out there during the tournament," Baine quipped back immediately. "If that was your best effort, none of you will make it past the first task."

"It wasn't our best," Sophia protested. "We were just unprepared."

"Do you think you're going to be prepared for what's coming?" Baine raised an eyebrow. "No one is going to hand you a list of what you're going to be put through, Sophia."

"Can't you just tell us what the tasks are?" Jonah whined, shivering under Squeaks' wings.

"Even if I would, I couldn't. The tasks change every year. This makes it so no one has an unfair advantage," Baine said.

Jonah groaned. Baine turned toward me with his hands in his pockets. "I'm surprised, Liam. I thought you trusted Sophia, but the way you acted made it seem like you don't think she has the ability to back you up."

"That's not true!" I snapped. "She's strong enough. Her magic's nothing to downplay."

Sophia's face was red. "No. You were too busy trying to *protect me*. If this had been real, Jonah would've died!" Sophia shouted.

I cringed. Yeah, that had been my fault. My first instinct had been to protect Sophia before anyone else. I told Jonah to get her out of the way of the wave before we made a cohesive plan to combat it together, and I messed her up when she was trying to save our friend. She saw the knives coming.

So why did I feel the need to interfere?

"The tribe as a unit is more important than any one person. You have to learn this, Liam," Baine said sharply. "There are no heroes or martyrs in the Elemental Cup. Only survivors and casualties."

My cheeks burned. Our first test as a group, and we'd horribly failed.

"Did you really have to put us through all that?" Jonah asked. He'd stopped shivering now and looked pissed.

"That's why I sprang on you. You need to learn to expect the unexpected," Baine said. "The tournament only gets harder each year. I will put you three through whatever I have to in order to make sure you survive."

You three? Baine didn't even notice one of our teammates was missing. I was going to start hitting my head against a tree in about two seconds.

"Get up," Baine told all of us roughly. "We've already wasted precious time."

Who's fault is that, since they showed up late? I thought bitterly. This guy was too much.

Jonah stumbled to his feet with the help of Squeaks. The rest of the morning was spent with Baine drilling us on our powers, doing so many summoning reps that it made my arms hurt. I sparred with Jonah and Sophia both, but none of us managed to get a hit on the other. I could've, seeing as how I was a Third Year and had sparring experience, but I already felt bad enough I'd hurt Jonah, so I left him alone, and Sophia...

I couldn't fight her, not even for practice. It just wasn't in me. She noticed, because her Fire kept getting more and more intense with every fireball she tossed at me. Fury burned in her eyes, but the angrier she got, the gentler I became. I just fizzled her fireballs out with my Water and tried not to look her in the eye. Esis watched us closely, his eyes darting back and forth with every bit of magic we flung at each other.

When it was time to break for lunch, Baine appeared even more disappointed than he was before. We headed back to the castle without him. Jonah mumbled that he had a headache and was going to lie down.

When we could no longer hear Squeaks tripping over things, I knew they were gone. I was going to head back to the Toaqua dorms, but I followed Sophia to the Koigni hall instead.

Before we got to the doors, she rounded on me. "You think I'm so weak I need to be escorted?"

"No. I just..." I hesitated. "I just wanted to hang out with you."

Her face softened a little, but my response wasn't enough to calm her down. "I already know that I'm the outcast here. But I thought you were the one person who believed I was capable of being your teammate. Now I know you just think I'm weak."

Damn Baine for putting words in my mouth. "It's not about being weak," I told her. My voice was calm and steady. "I just reacted today. That's all."

"If you react and don't think, we're all dead out there," she said harshly. Esis was at her feet, looking between us with droopy ears. He didn't like it when we fought.

"I just wanted to protect you." I leaned against the wall. "Is that so wrong?"

Sophia chewed her lip. "No. But you know how things go in the Elementai world. You have to be the strongest. Otherwise, people won't respect you. I may be new here, but I've learned that much. You can't protect me everywhere, Liam."

I was regretting so much of everything I'd told her when she got here. I wanted to take it all back and convince her things were different, but that would be a lie, because they weren't. "I think you're strong," I told her. "This was just the first training session. It's okay we made mistakes. We still have two more chances."

Sophia nodded. "I guess you're right." She put her hand on the Koigni door. "I would love to hang out, but I have to practice. See you later, Liam."

When she shut the door in my face, the sound of the door clicking was like a gunshot to my heart. I backed away from the door slowly, unsure of what I would do with myself. I'd been secretly hoping Sophia would come with me to town. Get some food, see stuff.

Not like a date, you know. Just friends.

I realized I really didn't want to spend another weekend hiding in my dorm like I had been. I decided to go look for Ez. Maybe he had nothing going on. I thought about hitting up Jonah, but he was in a rough way. He probably wouldn't get out of bed now until Monday.

I wracked my brain for other people to hit up, but I hadn't talked to most of them in... months.

Had I really pushed everyone in my life so far away?

As I walked back to the Toaqua dorms, Baine's words resonated in my head. I had to trust that Sophia was strong enough to stand on her own. It's not that I didn't believe in her or her powers.

I just didn't trust whatever the Elders had created to take us down.

I'd already lost Nashoma. I didn't want to lose her, too.

sophia

FOURTEEN

Exhaustion settled into my bones on Saturday morning. I lay in bed staring up at the ornate carvings in the shape of flames on the ceiling, thinking about yesterday. Baine's training session should've motivated me to train harder, but I couldn't seem to summon the energy to get out of bed. I just kept playing scenarios in my head of what obstacles we might face in the tournament and all the possible ways Liam would manage to screw it up— or save me. One of the two.

Thinking about Liam was always dangerous. Every time he crossed my mind, I thought about the pain he was in without Nashoma. I contemplated telling him about Esis so that Esis could heal him, but I also didn't want anyone knowing about Esis' power. It was the only way to protect him. And if I had to choose between a guy I might possibly be falling for and my Familiar— my literal soul— my Familiar would win out. Every. Single. Time.

I only wished I could find a way to protect them both.

Esis stretched from where he slept beside my head on the pillow. His weight shifted, and suddenly his big blue eyes were hovering over me. He placed a small palm on my cheek and made a chipper sound like a songbird.

I sighed. "I know it's time to get up, buddy, but I'm just not feeling it today."

I'd spent every weekend since I'd been summoned training with my magic so I wouldn't die in this stupid tournament, but all I really wanted was a break. And I didn't mean another study session in the library, either. Reading over the stats of previous years' tournaments was just depressing. There'd been more deaths in the tournament in the past few years than in the last century, and sometimes they didn't even find the bodies. The Elders were seriously stepping up their game so our generation had to work harder than any before to prove our place. I'd hoped the records would teach me something about what was to come, but I was starting to think that it didn't matter how much I trained or how much studying I did... I'd never be ready for this.

The only thing that would keep me alive was making sure my team was willing to work together. But I still hadn't heard from Imogen, and I wasn't sure Liam wanted to talk to me after the way I blew him off last night.

Which totally sucked because for some reason, all I wanted to do was hang out with him.

Esis patted my face again. When I turned my eyes to him, he stuck a thumb in his mouth and started sucking on it.

I couldn't help but smile. "Are you hungry, buddy?"

He nodded.

I forced myself to get up and stroked my hand through his fur. "Fine. We'll go grab breakfast after I take a quick shower."

Esis immediately jumped down from the bed and scurried across the room. My dorm was bigger than my room back home, with fancy decor that went beyond anything I could ever imagine. Deep red velvety sheets hung over the sides of my queen-sized bed. The bed frame was made from metal rods painted in gold, with a bed knob in the shape of a flame at the end of each post. The bed sat upon a large, ornate area rug, but the rest of the room had hardwood flooring. The walls were red to match my sheets. The long curtains in front of my window had various shades intertwining to create complicated patterns. Across the room stood a small brick fireplace with a plush red chair in front of it like the ones in the common room. Various other pieces of furniture were scattered around the room, including a vanity by the bathroom, a dresser near the walk-in closet, and a nightstand next to the bed. A candelabra chandelier hung from the high ceiling. The room was beautiful— I couldn't argue with that. But it seemed more like a place you'd spend the weekend than a place you'd call home.

Esis hurried into the open bathroom door. He jumped toward the towel rack, his tiny little fingers stretching high into the air. He chirped in victory when the towel came sliding down. It draped over top of him, but he burrowed his way out and dragged the towel into the bedroom behind him.

I stood, laughing. "Thank you, Esis. You're so helpful." I bent to pick up the towel and gave him a pat on the head.

He cooed in response.

Esis sat outside the bathroom while I showered and changed. At my dresser, he handed me my hairbrush and hair tie. He made sure to choose a green hair tie to match my shirt since he knew I didn't like to mix colors.

Esis perched atop my shoulder as we made our way to the dining hall for breakfast. The bright morning sunlight shone through the tall windows, casting rays across the red carpet in the Koigni hall. Like most Saturday mornings, the castle was quiet. When we reached the cafeteria it buzzed lightly with conversation, but most of the tables remained empty.

I grabbed two breakfast sandwiches from the takeout line and turned back to the main doors to head outside when I heard the sound of someone calling my name. I spun around and my eyes scanned the cafeteria. They landed upon Imogen in the corner, who was waving me over.

Relief flooded through me to see a familiar face, but it was quickly replaced with sickening doubt when I reminded myself what had recently happened between us. Then again, no Nivita Elders had shown up at my door to drag Esis away, so maybe there was still hope that Imogen hadn't abandoned me after what she saw.

I sighed and approached her, knowing I was going to have to face her sooner or later. Today she wore brightly-colored rainbow leggings with a rhinestone t-shirt. Her strawberry blonde hair was tied into a high ponytail with multi-colored strings mixed into the strands. Sassy's fluffy red tail poked out from beneath the table.

"I was starting to think I'd never see you again," I said lightheartedly as I slid into the seat across from Imogen. My heart felt anything but light.

She furrowed her brow. "Why wouldn't you see me again? I was sick, not dead."

I unwrapped the foil from one of the breakfast sandwiches and handed it to Esis. Suddenly, I didn't feel like eating. "Why'd you run away from us the other day? You weren't sick then, were you?"

"No... oh, my ancestors!" Imogen smacked her palm to her forehead. "You must've thought the worst of me! I'm so sorry. I should've got in touch with you sooner. It was just that inspiration struck, and I *had* to get home. Then my little brother got me sick, and it was just this whole thing." She waved her hands like it didn't really matter.

"So, we're still friends?" I asked cautiously.

"By the ancestors, of course we are!" Imogen placed a hand over her heart as if she was having a heart attack. "What did you *think* happened?"

I glanced around the cafeteria, but no one was close enough to hear us. I lowered my voice anyway. "I thought after what you saw, you might turn me and Esis in to the Nivita Elders." I dropped my gaze and bit my lower lip.

"What?" Imogen asked in disbelief. "I would never do that to you, Sophia."

I pulled Esis down from my shoulder and cradled him in my arms. "I'm just scared that if anyone knew what he could do, they might try to take him away from me. This kind of power isn't normal, right?"

Imogen took a bite of pancake and shook her head. "No, it's not. And it's probably best if you don't tell anyone else about it."

I gazed up at her, hopeful. "So, you'll keep our secret?"

"Girl, I'll take it to the grave." A moment later Imogen's eyes lit up, and she leaned forward to rest her elbows on the table. "Do you want to know what I've been doing the past few days?"

"Yes," I said, intrigued.

A smile spread across her face. "I've been researching Esis' origin. Do you want to come over to my house and see what I found?"

I couldn't contain my eagerness. "Absolutely!"

❧

AFTER WE FINISHED BREAKFAST, Imogen led me outside and through the gardens.

"My neighborhood is pretty far from the school," Imogen explained, "so we'll have to borrow a ride."

"Ooh," I said in excitement. My mood had drastically improved now that I knew Imogen and I were cool. "What kind of ride are we talking about? A peryton? A pegasus? A dragon?"

"No, no," she said, shaking her head. The strings in her hair swung from side to side. "I prefer to keep my feet on the ground. You know how to ride horseback, don't you?"

"Um... is it complicated?" My only experience riding a horse was at a petting zoo when I was six, but I wasn't sure that counted, considering the trainer held on to the reins the whole time and I only rode the horse for maybe five minutes.

Imogen shrugged, sending Sassy bouncing in her tote bag. "That's okay, the unicorns are very well trained and do most of the work anyway."

"I get to ride a unicorn?!" I exclaimed in excitement.

"Yeah," Imogen said, like it was no big deal. "Come on. We're almost there."

The trees opened to a large clearing with two huge red stables sitting side-by-side. Each of them had large sliding doors. I peered inside the first building to see a row of stalls on either side of the barn. I caught sight of several different creatures, including two perytons and a pegasus. Several guys milled around, tending to the animals.

"This way," Imogen said, gesturing me over to the second building.

A cool breeze rushed through the stables when we stepped inside. I didn't know why I was expecting to inhale a floral scent, as if the unicorns farted rainbows and pooped butterflies, but all that hit my nose was the scent of a barn— hay, wood shavings, leather and dust.

My eyes fell upon each unicorn as we passed. They had the body of a horse, with the same long nose, pointed ears, and large frame, but everything else about them looked as if they'd just stepped out of a fantasy painting. The first unicorn was completely white, with a mane that took the shape of cool blue water. It was as if a waterfall was flowing right out of its head, the water droplets disappearing into the air like magic. A shiny silver horn stretched a foot in length and twisted to a sharp point.

The next unicorn had brown fur, with hooves the texture of tree bark and a mane the color of grass. Its horn was like an expertly-carved branch growing out of its forehead with intricate carvings etched into it. I couldn't tell if the designs were natural or placed there deliberately, but given the magical beauty of these creatures, I guessed they were born that way.

In the next stall stood a black unicorn whose mane and tail flickered red and orange— like real flames. It was a wonder the stables hadn't burned down. Its horn looked as if it had been forged from a black matte metal, with subtle but elegant ridges traveling the length of it.

"Hey, Cade," Imogen greeted cheerfully as she strolled up to one of the guys scooping out an empty stall.

Cade shoveled a pile of used shavings into his wheelbarrow, then looked up at us. He wore a skin-tight cotton t-shirt that stretched across his broad shoulders and toned chest. His skin was naturally tan, but most of his Hawkei genes had been traded for Latin American features. He had short dark hair, and his brown eyes were soft and friendly.

Cade definitely had a sexy vibe going on, but looking at him in that way made me feel like I was cheating on Liam. Which was so totally weird, because we weren't together. I immediately pushed the thought from my mind.

Imogen, on the other hand, was eyeing Cade up and down like he was a god. I guessed he was Nivita, but he didn't have a Familiar at his side, so it was hard to tell.

"What can I do for you today?" he asked in a friendly tone as he wiped sweat from his brow.

"Is anyone up for a ride?" Imogen walked over to the nearest stall, the one with the Water unicorn inside, and patted her hand on the top of the door. "What do you say, Kiki? You wanna go for a ride today?"

"Kiki just got back from a ride last night," Cade said. "How about Daisy and Jack?" He gestured to the two unicorns in the stalls beside Kiki.

Imogen's eyes lit up, and she stepped toward the Earth unicorn. "I love Jack!"

Cade opened the door and coaxed Jack out of his stall. "You're not going to braid ribbons in his tail again, are you?"

Imogen swatted at him, and her cheeks grew bright red. "Shut up. He looked gorgeous."

Cade smirked playfully. "If I'm going to sign Jack out to you, you have to *promise* not to bring him back dyed purple or some crazy shit like that."

Imogen giggled like a little school girl. It was so unlike her. Esis threw his hands over his eyes and then slowly peeked out between them. He clearly couldn't watch their obvious flirting.

"I won't. I swear," Imogen promised.

Cade moved to the next stall to get the Fire unicorn. "Good."

"I'll bring him back blue," Imogen deadpanned.

"Imogen," he complained, but he didn't sound truly bothered.

"Fine," she relented. "I won't do anything weird. He's beautiful just the way he is. Aren't you, Jackie boy?"

Imogen rubbed Jack's head. He nuzzled into her arm, as if searching for treats.

"And here's Daisy," Cade said, patting her back.

Daisy stepped out of her stall until she was just a foot away from me. I reached up to stroke her soft black fur. It felt like velvet. Warily, I reached out for her fiery mane and was surprised when my fingers passed straight through it without feeling a thing. I glanced down at my hand, like I expected it to be blistered or something.

"She won't hurt you," Imogen said. "She's magical. Remember?"

Daisy pivoted on the spot until her middle was facing me.

"She likes you," Cade said. "She's inviting you to climb on her back."

I stroked her fur again, but hesitated. "Don't I need a saddle and reins?"

Cade laughed. "Not with unicorns. Would you like a boost?"

Before I could answer, Cade was helping me onto Daisy's back. I gave an involuntary yelp, and Imogen giggled. She didn't need any help hopping onto Jack's back. She jumped and swung her leg onto him, then sat there comfortably with Sassy secured safely in her bag. Sassy poked her head out and glanced around, looking positively at peace atop the unicorn's back.

I, on the other hand, clamped my hands around Daisy's neck, hoping I wouldn't topple off her back and be trampled. Esis chirped and hopped off my shoulder. He climbed up Daisy's head and wrapped a small hand around her horn. He stood there proudly, like a captain holding onto the mast of his ship. Daisy didn't seem to mind.

"Make sure to keep them both hydrated. Imogen knows the drill." Cade winked at her, and she went beet red.

"Thanks, Cade," Imogen said as Jack started leading her toward the open door.

Daisy followed. My hold on her tightened as I swayed from side to side with each step.

"Wait!" Cade called just as both of our unicorns stepped outside. "You forgot something."

Cade stopped beside Imogen and wiggled his fingers. Next to him, a green plant rose from the ground. Its thin stem twisted and grew until it stopped in front of Imogen's nose. A small purple flower bloomed at the end of it, confirming that Cade was Nivita.

Imogen smiled and plucked the flower from the long stem. She placed it in her hair behind her ear. "Thank you, Cade. You're the best. We'll see you later."

She waved. Cade returned to the stables while Imogen and I started down a nearby path. It wasn't as wide as the roads back home, but since no one used cars around here, I figured it must've been the main drag into town. Daisy and Jack walked beside each other at a brisk pace.

"So...?" I wiggled my eyebrows.

Imogen looked at me innocently. "Yeah?"

"Why haven't you ever mentioned him before?"

"Who? Cade?" Imogen's voice rose at least three pitches when she said his name. "He's just a guy I grew up with. He was my older brother's best friend. What's there to say about him?"

"How about the fact that you're totally crushing on him and never *once* mentioned it?"

"What?" Imogen squeaked. "I am not! Cade is just... Cade."

"Yes, sweet and handsome Cade," I agreed. "Who you have the hots for."

Imogen rolled her eyes and then stared straight down the road. "Girl, are you high or something?"

I laughed. "Okay, so you don't like him. But you *have* to know he likes you."

"Well, that answers that question. *Clearly* you're on drugs. No guy ever pays attention to me. I'm fat and weird."

"You're not fat," I countered. "And maybe he likes you *because* you're weird. I like your quirks."

Imogen pressed her lips together. She didn't look convinced.

I was starting to feel comfortable enough on Daisy's back that I loosened my grip on her mane. "He made sure you didn't leave without giving you a flower."

"So? He always does that."

I stared at her with raised eyebrows.

Imogen inhaled a deep breath. "Oh, my ancestors! I never knew. I totally friend-zoned him!" She threw her hands over her face and nearly fell off her unicorn in the process.

"Tell me about him," I said.

"I don't know what to say. We've known each other my whole life... we used to play in my treehouse when we were kids."

"So you're close?"

Imogen shrugged. "I guess you could say that. He was there when I bonded with Sassy almost a year ago." She dropped her head and bit her lip. "Anyway, that's not important. Cade and I can go weeks without talking, but we always pick right back up where we left off."

We reached town while she was recounting a story about how Cade and her brother had convinced her the forest was haunted. I listened to her story, but my eyes roamed the city. The only other time I'd seen it was when Liam and I had arrived, but that was only the smallest part of town. There was so much to see in the heart of the Hawkei village that I couldn't seem to take it all in.

We rode along the narrow streets of the Chinatown district. Paper lanterns hung above our heads, and the scent of fried rice and noodles filled my nose. From there, we passed into the Hawkei district. People milled along the streets and stopped at carts that sold things like potions and Hawkei food, such as corn roasted with butter and spices. I'd seen this part of town before, but it was like seeing it for the first time all over again. I barely had time to take it all in before Daisy turned and led us down a secluded street.

We left the buildings behind and traveled into the forest, where some of the largest trees I'd ever seen grew. They rose at least three-hundred feet into the sky. We hadn't made it far before my eyes fell on a large structure hanging high in the trees. I squinted, trying to make out its shape. Soon, more and more structures of similar size came into view.

Treehouses.

"Oh, my gosh!" I exclaimed. "When you said treehouses, I thought you meant a playhouse in your backyard. I didn't think you literally lived in a treehouse!"

Imogen laughed. "I'm Nivita. Where else would I live?"

I gazed upward in wonder. The treehouses were huge and suspended at least forty feet in the air. Each one was supported by at least three different trees. They all had wooden exteriors like log cabins, with wrap-around balconies, big windows, and slanted roofs, but each had its own unique charm. A network of bridges passed from house to house.

Daisy and Jack stopped below one of the bigger treehouses. I barely noticed we'd stopped. I was still trying to take in the sheer size of this neighborhood suspended in the trees. It went on farther than I could see.

Imogen slid off Jack's back and adjusted Sassy in her bag. Then she reached out to pat Jack's head. "You did so well, Jack! You deserve some carrots later. We'll be back soon, okay?"

I swung my leg over Daisy's back and landed softly on the ground. Esis chirped and scurried off Daisy's head and onto my shoulder. I glanced around, looking for any sign of steps or ladders to get up to the house.

"You look worried," Imogen said.

I turned back to her. "No. I was just wondering how we get up there. Are there stairs or something?"

"Yeah, but we're not going that way."

"Um... okay. How do we get up, then?"

"Oh, it's easy." She giggled. "Well, not for you."

"What does that mean?" I asked curiously. I wasn't going to have to learn how to climb the tree without footholds, was I?

Imogen smiled. "It means you'd burn this whole forest down if you tried my method. Here, stand over there."

Imogen took me by the shoulders and guided me away from the unicorns and to the base of the nearest tree.

"Don't try this at home," she warned. "Here we go."

Before I knew what was happening, something tickled my leg. I lifted my foot in surprise, but it grabbed ahold of me and wouldn't let me go. I looked down to see a thick tree root snaking up out of the ground and curling around my leg like the tentacles of an octopus. Several more roots crept out of the dirt and secured themselves around my legs, all the way up to my hips.

"Relax," Imogen said as another root wrapped itself around her. "I'm not going to hurt you."

I relaxed as she instructed and held tightly onto Esis so he wouldn't fall. The tree roots grew more and more until they were lifting us up into the sky. Although it should've freaked me out, I felt secure in the roots' hold, as if they were a safety harness keeping me from plummeting to the ground. We ascended skyward like an elevator. The roots arched over the railing and set us down on the bridge. Their hold on me loosened and they shrank away. I glanced over the top of the railing to see them retreating into the ground until they were completely gone. The dirt shifted to cover them, as if they'd never seen the light of day.

"That was really cool, Imogen," I said.

"Yeah, it's cool now," she replied. "Living in a treehouse wasn't so cool when you were a kid who had to walk *all* the way down fifteen houses to get to the stairs. You wouldn't believe it, but I could barely keep a weed alive. I didn't learn the shortcut until recently. Anyway, you wanna meet my parents?"

Imogen started down the bridge toward the nearest house, which rose two stories high and was supported by five massive trees. I hesitated as nerves settled in my gut. I knew Imogen didn't care that I was Koigni, but I wasn't sure her parents would like me. Like she said, I could literally burn this whole forest down. There was probably a reason they didn't have many entrances that other Elementai could enter through.

"What's wrong?" Imogen asked when she reached the front door.

I swallowed down the lump in my throat. "Will your parents be fine with having... a Koigni in their house?"

Imogen smiled. "Of course. Don't worry about it. My parents are a lot more... progressive than most. They think all the Houses should mix and that we should do away with most of our traditions."

My shoulders relaxed. "That's good to know."

Imogen turned and swung the door open. "Mom! Dad! I'm home! And I brought a friend!"

Two young boys raced in from the living room and body-slammed her with a group hug.

"I thought you were going back to school," the taller of them said, gazing up at her with a twinkle in his eye. He looked like he might be six, while the other boy looked around four. They both had Imogen's strawberry blonde hair, but they didn't have her sense of style. They dressed normally, both wearing jeans and a t-shirt.

Imogen bent to her knee. "I had to come back because Sassy missed you!"

On cue, Sassy leapt from her bag. She jumped playfully at the younger boy, who let out a gleeful laugh. Imogen stood, giggling as she watched her brothers tickle Sassy. Sassy rolled over like a dog and they scratched her belly.

I glanced around to take in the home. Everything was bathed in natural wood tones, from the hardwood floor and walls to the cupboards and the furniture. It was like something you'd see out of a travel magazine if you were looking for a quaint cabin getaway. A long wooden table with eight chairs around it sat to our left beside a pair of double glass doors that led onto the balcony. Beyond that sat a full kitchen. To our right was a living room with two long couches and a TV above a cute metal fireplace. A hallway behind the stairs stretched back into the house. The pile of dishes in the sink and toys scattered around the living room gave the home an obvious lived-in vibe.

"How old are your brothers?" I asked, trying to remember if she'd told me before.

"Oh, gosh," Imogen said with a sigh. "Levi is four, and Quentin is seven, then Roland is ten and Soren is fifteen."

"So, you're the oldest?" I asked.

"No. Well... yeah." Imogen dropped her head.

I laughed. "Well, which is it?"

"It's, um, complicated." Imogen didn't meet my gaze. "My older brother— the one who was friends with Cade— he's, uh, not around anymore."

My heart immediately sank. "Imogen, I'm so sorry. I shouldn't have asked."

"No, it's okay," she said, finally meeting my gaze. "You didn't know."

I bit my lower lip, wishing I had words for her. "Why didn't you mention anything?"

"I didn't want to scare you."

"Scare me?"

Imogen nodded. "Yeah. Because of how he died."

"Are you talking about Trace?" Quentin asked while still petting Sassy.

Levi stuck his bottom lip out. "I miss Trace."

"It's almost been a year, you know," Quentin told Levi.

"I know," Levi said, "but I can still remember him from when I was three. I can even remember from when I was two. Trace was the best brother ever... until he died in the tournament."

The breath left my chest. I suppose I couldn't blame Imogen for never mentioning him to me.

The conversation came to an abrupt halt as a blonde woman descended the stairs. She wore a pink polka-dotted scarf around her head and a blue dress that looked like it came straight out of the fifties. A pair of black cat-eye glasses famed her face. I could see where Imogen got her quirky fashion inspiration from.

The woman was followed by a type of canine I'd never seen before. It looked like a Pomeranian, but with longer ears. Its fur was completely white except for the rings of blue outlining its silver eyes and the matching tufts of blue on its ears. It wore a pink scarf around its neck that matched the one in the woman's hair.

"Hey, Mom," Imogen greeted. "Where's Dad and the boys? It's strangely quiet in here without them."

"Mushroom hunting," her mom answered.

"Yum... mushrooms." Imogen gestured to me. "This is Sophia, by the way. The girl I was telling you about."

Her mom's face lit up. "Oh, hello, Sophia!" She held her arms out as she made her way over to me. She drew me into a hug.

I squeezed her back awkwardly.

"I'm Gracie," she said, pulling away from me. "Imogen's told me all about you. Oh, who's this little guy?"

She smiled at Esis but didn't try to pet him. I was grateful for her respect of my Familiar.

"This is Esis," I introduced, scratching behind his ears. He responded with a purr and nuzzled into my fingers.

"He's so adorable!" Gracie clapped her hands together.

Gracie's dog barked once at Esis and then let his tongue hang from his mouth cheerfully. Esis jumped down from my shoulder and circled the dog. Gracie's Familiar nipped at Esis playfully as they chased each other around. Across the room, Sassy perked her ears up and quickly joined in on the game.

Imogen's brothers burst into a fit of laughter. I couldn't contain my own giggles. There was just too much cuteness in one room to handle all at once.

Gracie tore her eyes off our Familiars and turned her attention back to Imogen and me. "So, what are you girls up to?"

Imogen's eyes darted toward me but quickly returned to her

mother. "Um... we're working on something for Dragonology. We need to use the library."

Gracie's brows drew together. "You've already spent so much time in there the last few days. Your teachers are pushing you too hard. When I attended Orenda, we didn't have homework. And don't even get me started on the Elemental Cup. It's ludicrous how times have changed. Your father and I both—"

"Mom," Imogen cut her off. "Can we not do this again?"

Gracie looked at me, then back to Imogen. "You're right. Now's not the time. I'm sorry. You two go have fun. Can I bring you anything?"

"No, but thanks, Mom," Imogen answered before gesturing for me to follow her down the hall.

Sassy and Esis scurried behind us. We passed by two bedrooms and a bathroom before reaching the door at the end.

Imogen paused with her hand on the doorknob. "You like books, right?"

"Of course." I bounced on my toes, eager to see her family's library.

Imogen smiled. "Then you're going to love this."

The door swung open, and my jaw promptly dropped to the floor. When she hinted at a library in her home, I pictured a few shelves of books and a couch or something. This was much, much more than that.

The room was twice the size of the living room, with a vaulted ceiling and tall bookcases that covered every inch of the walls on my left and my right. There was even a short wooden ladder leaning against one of the bookcases so that you could reach the top shelf. The wall opposite the door was made entirely of glass and overlooked the beautiful green forest. Beneath the window, a plush couch stretched from wall to wall, providing the perfect reading nook. It was long enough that Imogen and I could easily stretch out on either side at the same time. A round table with two chairs sat in the middle of the room with several thick books stacked atop it. The same natural wood tones that covered the rest of the house were present in the library as well.

"Holy crap," I whispered breathlessly as I stepped into the room, taking it all in. "Your family really loves books."

Imogen just shrugged, as if it was normal for families to have their own home libraries. She pulled out a chair at the table and flipped open the book at the top of the stack. "Yeah, I guess you could call us bookworms. Most people just call us crazy."

"What?" I squeaked, sliding into the chair across from her. "Why would they say that?"

The truth was, I kind of understood. Imogen and her mom were a little... out there.

Esis hopped past me and jumped onto the couch. He fluffed one of the throw pillows before curling up on top of it. Sassy lay beside him. It was one of the first times I'd ever seen her sit still.

An unamused expression crossed Imogen's face. "Have you *met* my family? Anyway, no big deal. We might seem a little crazy, but being crazy has its perks."

"Like?" I prodded.

"Like the fact that our family is the only one brave enough to speak the truth."

I leaned my elbows on the table, intrigued. "The truth about what?"

"I don't know. Just things that no one else believes in. It's funny that we live with creatures of legend— unicorns and dragons and things like that— but none of the Hawkei actually believe in things they can't see with their own eyes. We have our own myths, you know. Gallyswanks, womgrombits, lillybats, you name it. They were all real once, yet most of the Hawkei refuse to believe it."

"Why wouldn't they believe it?" I asked.

Imogen shrugged. "After the war that killed the Anichi, certain species started dying off. I guess none of the Houses want to admit they were responsible for the mass extinction."

"How can you be sure these creatures existed?"

Imogen sat up straighter and pushed her open book toward me. "My ancestors made sure we wouldn't forget. Kimoko Kahnee was one of my great-great-great-grandfathers. Or something like that. Anyway, a lot of greats. In our native language, his name loosely translates to *brother of the beloved animals.* And he lived up to that name. He was very close with the magical creatures that roamed our valley. He recorded everything he saw. He discovered several new species, actually."

"That must be really cool," I said. "To be related to him, I mean."

"It is," Imogen agreed. "But he wasn't very well-known. My family has been pushing for years to get his journal published, but the Elders claim they can't authenticate it and don't want to be putting misinformation out to the masses."

My lips turned down. "That's unfair."

Imogen rolled her eyes. "Tell me about it. Anyway, the good news for you is that Kimoko wrote about the kurbles in his journal."

"Kurbles?" I asked with raised eyebrows.

"Yeah, that's what Esis is," Imogen said, in a dead serious tone.

I couldn't help it when I burst out laughing. "You're kidding."

"No." Imogen didn't even twitch.

"I'm sorry. I just don't think it fits Esis. It just sounds so..."

So what? Cute and cuddly? I glanced to Esis. His eyes were closed, and his chest rose and fell slowly. My heart filled with all kinds of positive vibes.

I turned back to Imogen. "Who am I kidding? Kurble totally fits him."

"Agreed. Anyway, I totally forgot I'd ever read about kurbles, until I saw Esis heal. There aren't many creatures who can do that, so when I saw it, I instantly knew I had to check out Kimoko's journal for confirmation. And it's right here." Imogen turned the book toward me and pointed to the left-hand page. "See? Kurbles."

The entry was entirely handwritten. At the top of the page was a surprisingly good sketch of a kurble, though it had black spots like a cow, unlike Esis' flawless white fur. Below the sketch was a list of words in a language I didn't recognize. Underneath that was the English translation in a different handwriting.

Size: Up to six pounds
Temperament: Good-natured and playful, but protective and territorial.
Fights when threatened.

Abilities: Healing
Notes: Eats a high-calorie diet, buries feces, and cleans self. Enjoys climbing and collecting shiny objects.

"That's it?" I asked in disbelief. There was nothing here I didn't already know, except the part about kurbles fighting. Though now the horns on Esis' head made sense. Somehow, I couldn't imagine Esis fighting anyone or anything.

"Unfortunately, yes, that's it," Imogen replied. "What else do you want to know?"

I turned the page, as if expecting more information on the next page, but it just led to another entry on something called wilmoths. "I don't know... maybe what he eats."

"He eats hamburgers," Imogen said simply. "Obviously."

I couldn't tell if she was being serious or trying to make me laugh. "Yeah, but they can't be healthy for him."

"Look at him." Imogen gestured to Esis on the pillow. "He's fine."

I chewed my lower lip while I watched Esis. His ear twitched while he slept. "Yeah, I suppose. I just... I wish I knew more about him."

Imogen sighed. "Maybe it's a good thing no one does, you know?"

"Yeah," I agreed after a brief silence. "No one else does know, do they? I mean, what about your parents or other relatives?" Worry filled my chest as I considered the possibility. What if someone recognized him for what he was? They could take him for his powers.

Imogen shook her head. "I don't think so. I searched through all of our books that might mention kurbles, and this was the only one it was in. I read these books cover-to-cover hundreds of times as a kid, and I barely remembered kurbles existed. I don't think anyone else knows. And I didn't tell my parents the truth of what I was researching, either."

Relief washed over me. "Good. So we can keep this between us, then?"

"Of course," Imogen agreed. "I wouldn't want anyone knowing if Sassy had unique magical powers like this, either. Your secret's safe with me, Sophia."

My shoulders completely relaxed. "Thank you, Imogen. You're a really great friend."

❦

WE SPENT the rest of the morning combing through the books in Imogen's family library. We didn't expect to find more on kurbles, but I couldn't let go of the hope that we would. I wanted to know all I could about them. What if Esis was allergic to something? How would I medicate him if he got sick? What if he had weird anatomy, like four stomachs or two hearts? How long did kurbles survive? And how old was Esis, anyway?

All of these questions assaulted me, but by mid-afternoon, I didn't have an answer to any of them. Esis had woken up and lay curled in my lap on the sofa while Sassy batted at him from the floor. Piles of books sat beside me on the adjacent cushion.

I rubbed behind his ears. "I'm sorry I couldn't learn more about you, buddy."

Esis snuggled into my belly, as if letting me know it wasn't my fault and that he forgave me.

"We should probably call it a day," Imogen suggested. "We need to get Daisy and Jack back to the stables, anyway."

Imogen had ducked out of the library earlier to give them a snack and water, but they needed a more substantial meal.

"Okay," I agreed. "You ready, Esis?"

He jumped out of my lap, trilling. Sassy chased after him toward the door.

"Whoa, girl," Imogen said with a laugh, following behind them. "Not so fast."

We made it down from the treehouse the same way we came and started the long journey back to the school.

"Hey!" Cade called cheerfully when we returned to the stables. He wore a clean blue shirt, so I figured he hadn't been in the stables all day. The way he looked at Imogen— and how she responded with flushed cheeks— I guessed that he came back just for the chance to see her again. "I was starting to think you got lost."

199

"Nah," Imogen said, patting her unicorn's back. "Jack would never lead me astray."

"Of course not," Cade said. He stepped up to Daisy and handed her a carrot, which she promptly gobbled out of his hand. "What are you girls up to tonight?"

"Oh, uh..." Imogen looked to me, as if begging me to say something. I'd never seen her look so flustered.

"Imogen's free," I blurted. "But I'm busy. She could use some company at dinner."

Imogen's eyes went wide, as if she didn't think I was doing her a favor. She'd thank me later. "Sophia, weren't you just saying—?"

"That I was going to grab takeout and meet up with Liam?" I cut in. "Yep."

What the heck, stupid mouth? Why was meeting up with Liam the first excuse I came up with?

"Ah, well, if you have plans, I'll let you get to them," Cade said while helping me down from Daisy's back.

Imogen just blinked at me, completely shocked. "I— I guess I'll help Cade with the unicorns and then... then we'll get dinner together?" She said it like a question, like she couldn't believe this was actually happening.

"It's a date," Cade said before turning a light shade of pink himself. "Well, not a date, but..."

"Oh, no," Imogen agreed immediately. "Not a date."

Imogen hopped down from Jack with ease and readjusted Sassy in her bag before leading Jack into his stall.

"Have fun on your *not-a-date*," I whispered to Imogen under my breath before raising my voice and waving to both of them. Esis waved from my shoulder. "See you later!"

Imogen shot me a huge, excited grin that Cade couldn't see. I turned away with a sense of victory filling me. I had successfully managed to get my best friend to go out with her very-obvious crush. Pride followed me all the way back to the castle and down the deserted hallway on my way to the cafeteria... until I heard the sound of my name.

I ducked behind the sprite statue next to Madame Doya's classroom when I realized the voices I'd heard were hers and Haley's. What the hell were those bitches saying about me?

"Yeah, I know," Haley said in a bored tone. "I've been following her, but honestly, the girl is a total bore. She's either sitting in her dorm or hanging out with her weird Nivita friend."

"She's started asking questions," Doya said, with almost no emotion. "It won't be long before she finds it. And when she does—"

"*I know*," Haley cut in. "I'll be right there to report back to you. Honestly, I don't know why you worry. Sophia's probably going to die in the the tournament anyway, especially with that useless fur ball of hers. I saw their first training session, and it was... laughable at best."

Anger pulsed through my veins. What the hell did Haley know? I urged to singe the sleek black hair off her head just to teach her some manners.

"Yes," Madame Doya responded coolly. "I'm well aware, but as I recall, your first session didn't go well either, did it, Haley?"

Oh, burn.

Haley went dead silent.

"That's it for now," Doya said. "I'll see you tomorrow after class for training. Let your team know."

"But we've already used up our allotted training sessions." Haley sounded confused.

"And?" I pictured Doya raising an eyebrow. "Who's counting? You let me worry about the rules. You just worry about your training, and keeping an eye on Sophia. Understand?"

My breath froze in my chest. I should've known Doya would cheat! But sending someone after me, to spy on me? That was crossing a line. Esis nearly jumped off my shoulder— to give Doya a piece of his mind, I presumed— but I held him back.

Haley's voice fell. "I understand."

The sound of footsteps met my ears, sending a wave of panic through me. I pressed myself to the wall, diving behind the statue so I wouldn't be seen.

Haley breezed out of the room and headed in the opposite direction of where I stood. Anwara flew behind her. My entire body remained tense until she was out of sight, and for at least another minute afterward.

When I was satisfied that Doya wasn't going to exit her room and that Haley was long gone, I stepped out of my hiding spot and bolted.

I raced toward the castle's main entrance, knowing there would be enough people there or in the courtyard that I could duck into the safety of the crowd. I didn't feel safe going back to my dorm, not when I knew there was a target on my back. In the deserted hallway, nerves rushed up and down my arms, making my whole body shake. It felt as if someone was watching me, even though I knew Haley and Doya hadn't known I was there. Still, I glanced behind myself just to make sure I wasn't being followed.

Just as I turned my eyes forward to round the corner, I smacked into something hard. I stumbled backward and caught Esis before he could tumble off my shoulder.

Whomever I'd run into cursed under their breath. When I gazed up, I saw the most beautiful pair of dark eyes staring back at me.

"Liam," I breathed. "Thank the ancestors!"

"What's wrong, Sophia?" he asked, immediate concern laced in his tone. He held onto both my arms. His eyes darted between mine as if searching for an answer in them.

"I— I heard Doya and Haley..." I swallowed deeply, still trying to catch my breath. "Liam, I need help."

Liam sighed and ran a hand over his face. He took a deep breath to collect himself. "What are you talking about, Sophia?"

"I overheard Madame Doya and Haley talking about me," I tried again, this time in a calmer tone. "Apparently, Haley's been following me. Liam, I'm literally being stalked."

Liam just stood there with worry in his expression, but he didn't say anything.

"Liam?" I prodded.

"I don't know what to say, Sophia," he replied. "You *just* told me you didn't want me to protect you. Now you're asking me to? You come to me all the time asking for help, then you push me away. Make up your mind."

"I—" I stared up at him, completely speechless. I mean, I couldn't say he was wrong.

Tears welled in my eyes. I tried to blink them away, but it only made them rise higher until the floodgates opened and a tear ran down my cheek.

"Shit," Liam muttered. "Please don't cry, Sophia."

"It's just— I'm just—" *A bawling mess.*

Slowly, Liam reached out and ran his thumb over my cheek, wiping away the tears. I sniffled and looked up at him. The most intense look of care filled his eyes. Without thinking, I threw myself forward into his arms. My hands flew around his neck, and my head rested just beneath his shoulder. Tears soaked into his t-shirt.

He tensed momentarily before relaxing and pulling his arms around me, squeezing me tight. Warmth tingled across my torso where he touched me. He smelled like a warm jacket and the rain-kissed needles of an ancient pine forest. I'd never felt as safe and protected as I did in Liam's arms. That only made me want to cry more, as if it was an invitation to let my emotions flow.

"It's okay, Sophia," he whispered, rubbing my back. "Haley's not worth it. Forget about her."

"How can I forget about her when she's stalking me?" I asked, burying my face deeper into his shoulder.

Liam sighed, like he didn't know what to say. He probably hated me right now. He didn't seem like the kind of guy who could handle crying girls. But I also couldn't bring myself to pull away. He was like a protective blanket hiding me from the monsters that lurked in the corners of the castle.

"How can I help, Sophia?" he asked softly.

I drew away from him and wiped my tears. "I don't know. I just... I guess I just needed to tell someone."

Liam nodded like he understood, then reached out and grabbed my hand. My breath caught, and my stomach did this whole flip-in-my-abdomen thing.

"I know what you need," Liam said as a light smile touched his lips. "Let's go have some fun."

Liam

FIFTEEN

Yeah, I knew what it looked like. Sophia Henley and Liam Mitoh, holding hands in the hall. Big whoop. Luckily, everyone was at dinner, so nobody saw us together. But I knew if they did, it would be a huge deal.

I knew what most guys in my situation would do. They'd take her back to the Toaqua dorms for a quickie in the pool.

But Sophia didn't need a quick bang. She needed to feel normal. And I really needed that, too. It'd been a long time since I'd felt any sense of normalcy.

We left the school grounds and headed into Kinpago. The village was pretty crowded this time of day, with everyone going home. I made sure to drop Sophia's hand the moment I sighted any people. She frowned, but the look in her eyes told me she got it. Esis chittered from her shoulder like he disapproved, but he could bug off.

"I'm starving," Sophia told me as the variety of delicious smells wafting through the square filled our noses. "What's good around here?"

"You pick. Any place you want, except that one, that one, and that one." I pointed out over half the restaurants in the square.

"You're picky." She giggled.

"I prefer traditional Hawkei dishes," I told her. "But I chose last time we ate, so I'm nice enough to let you choose this time."

"Such a gentleman." She scanned the square before her gaze settled on a tiny Italian place in the corner. "I want pizza."

"Of course you do." I smiled at her, because she was so utterly predictable.

"You don't? Who doesn't like pizza?" she said, astonished as we headed into the restaurant. I held the door open for her as we went in. It was empty in here, except for the waiter perched by the host station.

Sophia was still gaping at me and my hatred of pizza when we slid into a booth. Esis had an equally shocked expression, which didn't surprise me, because he was a garbage disposal. Anything you gave the little fur ball he sucked down in a manner of seconds.

"I really hate Americanized food. Like, buffalo burgers are fricken amazing, but it has to be not processed. I can literally taste the chemicals." I made a disgusted face. "Good thing the tribe grows and prepares most of our own food, because otherwise, I'd starve the way our food system in the US is."

"So you're not a fan of fast food?" Sophia asked. Esis jumped down from her shoulder and onto the table.

"Ew, don't even mention it. You're gonna make me puke."

She laughed. "I love drive-through chicken nuggets."

"Stop."

The waiter stopped at our table. I didn't know his name, but I knew he was from school, because I recognized him from my Survival Instincts class. He gave us a bit of a look— the Koigni girl and the Toaqua guy together— but I guessed he wanted a tip more, because he just dropped off the menus and said, "What can I get you to drink?"

"Water," both of us said at once, and we looked at each other.

The waiter walked off, and Sophia opened the menu. "What do you want?"

"Like I said, your choice." I crossed my arms and didn't even look at the menu. "This little outing is to make you feel better."

"Like you couldn't use it, too," she grumbled under her breath. Esis bared his little teeth at me, and guess what? I bared mine right back.

"How about we just share a pizza? Half and half?" she asked.

"Fine by me."

The waiter came back and placed the waters on our table. "What would you like to order?" he asked us, like this was the last place he wanted to be.

"We're going to share a medium— uh, I mean, large," Sophia stuttered as Esis screeched loudly. "On my half, I would like pepperoni, sausage, bacon, green pepper, onion, mushrooms, tomatoes, and pineapple."

By the ancestors, that sounded so gross. Esis clapped his hands happily and jumped down onto the table.

Sophia looked at me. I opened my mouth and said, "Just the crust, thanks. No cheese, no pepperoni, no sauce, nothing."

"Are you crazy? You can't just get the crust," Sophia said, shocked.

"Watch me." I stared back at her with a smirk on my face.

The waiter gave me a look like I was nuts, but wrote it down. "Anything else?"

"I think we're good," Sophia said. The waiter walked off, and Sophia laughed. "That's going to be one lopsided pizza. I don't even know how they're going to cook it right."

"Hopefully the little Fire critters in the back will figure it out." I shrugged.

She gave me a scathing look, one that I found quite adorable. "Is it your purpose to make life as difficult as you possibly can for everyone else?"

"Just the ones I find annoying."

"So... everyone," she said flatly.

I grinned. "Maybe."

This was ridiculous. The stupid grin hadn't left my face since we'd come here. I probably looked like one happy idiot. I hadn't smiled so much in months. It actually made my face hurt a bit. It was like my mouth had forgotten how to do it.

The sweet look fell from her face as something crossed her mind— I saw it in her eyes. "You never answered me earlier. About Haley. Do you think it's something I should be worried about, her spying on me?"

This again? I had hoped she wouldn't bring it up. The memory of her tears from earlier caused the grin to slide from my face. I didn't want her to start crying again. I hadn't known what to do, and

I felt like shit, like it'd been my fault she'd started crying. It'd been terrible.

"Don't worry about Haley. She might be stalking you, but so what? Everyone is watching us now. The tournament is only a few weeks away," I told her. "Doya probably told her to spy on you to get ahead in the tournament."

"I don't know," Sophia said slowly. "It sounded like whatever Haley was supposed to be watching me for, it was pretty specific."

"Doya could be sending Haley after you to get into your head," I said. "You can't let that happen."

"That could be true," Sophia mused. "Doya's team is cheating, by the way. They've had more than three practices."

"That's a big shock," I replied sarcastically. "What else is news, the sky is blue?"

"Shut up." Her cheeks turned pink, but she laughed. "I thought I should tell you, I finally got together with Imogen. She's been doing some research, and she found out that Esis is actually a rare animal called a kurble."

"A kurble," I repeated. "Sounds like something Imogen made up."

Esis let out a little growl. He put his head down and charged at me. He head-butted my arm with his stubby little horns, but I pushed him away.

Sophia didn't confirm or deny my claim, which made me think that whatever Imogen had found most likely had come from her head. But I was curious and felt like playing along, so I asked, "So, do kurbles have any special magic?"

"Uh..." Sophia glanced to Esis before shaking her head quickly. "Nope. No. None that we found."

"That's disappointing," I said. "We could've used some in the tournament."

Sophia nodded slowly. Sophia went on and on about kurbles, but most of everything she said was stuff we already knew about Esis just from being around him. I was hardly paying attention to what she was saying. I got that it was disrespectful, but I kept on getting sucked into her eyes.

While Sophia was gabbing, Esis did something weird. He waddled in front of me, puffed up his chest and fluffed his tail, expanding his ears and screaming.

"What the hell is he doing?" I asked, thinking he was gonna self-destruct.

"Oh, it's nothing," Sophia said, petting him. "It's just something kurbles do. I think it's a mating call, though I don't know why he'd be doing it now."

I swear to the ancestors Esis was wiggling his eyebrows at me at a very suggestive way. I was gonna kill this little shit. Next thing I knew, he was gonna start tossing roses and singing a serenade.

The server emerged from the kitchen and placed the pizza on our table, giving us a weird look. "Enjoy your uh... meal."

Our pizza looked so stupid. One half was literally nothing but bread, and the other half was loaded with every disgusting thing Sophia could bear to pile on it, including, ugh... pineapple.

But it was us, kind of. Sophia kept talking throughout the meal, but I stayed quiet. I wasn't much of a talker, and it was nice to hear her voice instead of the one inside my head.

By the end of the meal, I was pretty sure Esis had eaten more slices than either of us had. The server came back to an empty tray. He poorly hid his disgust as Esis burped happily and put down the bill.

Sophia reached out, but I snagged it before she could. "I got it," I told her. "I offered."

Her eyes glittered. We left the restaurant and looked around. By this time, it was dark. The crowds had thinned, and most of the adults had gone home. There were more students out this time of night, looking for places to hang out and something to do. We needed to go somewhere more private, before we ran into someone we knew.

"Come on," I told her. "I know a great place. Follow me."

Her eyebrow raised as we headed out of town. Usually by this point I'd be exhausted, but I was having a good day today. My body was actually cooperating for once, and I wanted to take full advantage of it... before I paid the price tomorrow.

I took her into the woods, but it was away from the castle instead of towards. Eventually, we reached a part of the forest that was so overgrown we had to stomp on the brush to clear a way through.

"Nashoma led me here a long time ago," I told her. "I didn't know why, or what for, but I'm pretty sure we were the only ones who knew about it."

I parted the foliage in front of us and let her step through. Her face brightened in wonder as she looked around, a wide smile spreading across her face.

Behind the overgrowth was a clearing, a small meadow of blooming white flowers called fairy lanterns spreading throughout the emerald grass. A stone beach nestled up against a deep pool, sapphire-colored and so clear you could see the bottom. A large waterfall poured down on the other side of the pool, the top cascading down from a mountain stream somewhere above us. Fall was mild here, so the trees didn't have a lot of color, but they made up for it by having magical butterflies as large as my face nesting in the trees, their wings glowing a crystalline blue. Grapevines twisted up the trees, and the moon shone through a hole in the top of the forest canopy, casting everything in a silver glow. The only sounds were the rushing of the water and the symphony of crickets in the bush.

Sophia looked brilliant. If I could make her smile like that every day, I'd never have to do anything for the rest of my life. That much would be enough.

"Liam, this is incredible," Sophia said. She put Esis down and spun in a circle around the clearing. "It's like a fairy tale."

I said nothing. I gently lifted my hand and turned it to the side. A wall of water rose from the pool, but it was soft and quiet. Within the water was a bunch of beautiful, colorful fish. They had broad and silky tails like betas, but had patterns on their bodies and heads like koi. They were neon and glowed in the dark underneath the color of the moon. I wrapped the wave around Sophia to give her an aquarium. Sophia laughed and reached out with her fingers, touching the wave.

When her fingers ran through the water, I gasped audibly, though she didn't hear it. To touch an Elementai's element was like touching their spirit— and she went right through whatever I still had. Despite her being across the clearing, her skimming the water felt like she was caressing my face.

Esis became alarmed and started batting at the water with his paws to try and reach the fish, but only ended up splashing himself. His touch was like an itch.

The fish in the water nibbled at Sophia's hand. She giggled, and I slowly brought the wave back. I returned the water and the fish to the pond and looked at her.

"Your element is so beautiful, Liam," Sophia said in a breathless way. "I wish I could do something like that."

"You'll be able to, one day." I walked over to a tree with large, twisting branches. I held my hand out and helped her climb it. We scaled upward until I pointed out a thick branch that I liked to sit on, one that would support our weight. As we climbed, the butterflies scattered and began dancing all around us, giving an elaborate show. Esis followed, climbing the limbs easily and squeaking.

I hadn't counted on the branch being so small. I'd only sat up here by myself, but it definitely wasn't big enough to hold two people. The end result was that Sophia was pretty much sitting on my lap.

"Oof. I'm sorry," Sophia said as her ass plopped down against my leg, and she blushed. "There really isn't a lot of room up here."

"Yeah." She was like, literally leaning against me and everything. I had nowhere to put my arms. They were above me, holding on to some branches when she sat down, but I couldn't hold them like that forever. I gave up and just put my arms around her, because, you know, it was more comfortable.

Yeah, sure. Whatever you say.

Sophia didn't seem to mind, but her magic gave her away. Her shoulder was pushing up against a tree branch, and it was starting to crackle.

"You're gonna burn the tree down," I told her.

"Sorry." I felt her temperature decline by a few degrees, and the tree stopped smoking. But that hardly helped, because now *I* was hot, and it definitely wasn't from her magic.

"Oh, wow," Sophia breathed, and I looked up. The butterflies had flown up against the sky and had changed their colors, their deep blue morphing to become the background of the starry night. You could see them as their wings beat against the darkness, making the constellations look like they were moving.

"They take on the background of whatever they're around, when they're threatened," I told Sophia. "It's a special sort of camouflage."

She nodded. Esis had totally disappeared. I had no idea where he went.

All around, tiny little yellow lights with wings of dragonflies started appearing. They buzzed around us, hovering up and down in a circle where they sat. I could hear their little melodic voices as they swarmed around our little spot.

Sophia gave an inquisitive look.

"Fortune Fairies. I told you about them earlier." I reached out and snatched one from the air. Carefully, I gave it to Sophia. She cupped it in her palms and moved her face close.

"They're like fireflies," Sophia whispered. The glow from the fairy lit up her face, and she looked up.

"Supposedly they only come to people with good luck. If they don't come near you, you're cursed." I snorted. "Someone didn't give them the memo about me."

She laughed before she opened her hand and let the fairy go. It floated away slowly, humming a pleasant tune. She leaned back and nestled against me, sinking her shoulders into my chest.

Alarm buzzers were going off in my head, but I took that alarm and smashed it against the wall, because, hell, I never liked being woken up anyway, and this was one damn good dream.

This was college. What was the big deal about a little bit of cuddling, anyhow?

My mind wandered. Surely there were people who screwed outside of House boundaries. Dating or marriage, no way, but hookups between Houses had to happen. One-night stands. Casual sex.

Bullshit. Your "casual sex" with Sophia would last a lifetime.

Hell yeah, it would. Sleep with her once, I'd never get over her.

I couldn't get over her now.

"Liam?" she asked, looking at me.

"Hm?"

"What are you thinking about?"

Inappropriate things that I shouldn't be. Things that are forbidden. "Nothing."

She seemed to sense that something was on my mind, because she said, "I know you wouldn't want anyone to see us like this."

"We aren't doing anything," I told her, which was a lie, because we'd already crossed so many boundaries.

"Right," she said, like she was trying to reassure herself. "We're just friends."

That was like a punch to the gut. It was almost a test, to see how quickly we could go to *just friends* to *something more.*

I wanted to say something that would confirm, but all that came out of my mouth was, "You ever had a boyfriend?"

What the hell was wrong with me right now?

She made a face like she didn't like to talk about it. "A few, but nothing serious."

"That sounds intriguing." And it did. She made the entire sentence seem ominous.

"I'm happy high school is over." She bounced her heel against the tree trunk. "It was nothing but a lot of drama. I had a bad falling out with a lot of my friends. By the time senior year hit, I was pretty much alone. I mean, I hung out with a few people, but I always felt like a third wheel."

"Oh. I'm sorry." High school had been okay for me. Just fine, nothing memorable. But Sophia made her four years sound awful.

"It wasn't your fault. I just went along with what was expected of me," she said. "It's one of the reasons I avoid conflict so much. There was always so much of it at school growing up. I had a tight-knit group for awhile, but I couldn't really connect with them. They were all interested in the arts, and I loved being outdoors. There wasn't anyone I could share that with."

"It was the Elementai in you. All of us love being in nature," I told her.

"I guess." She shrugged. "I always thought it was because I was a weirdo. That I was different."

That made me really sad. "I don't think you're weird."

213

"Thanks. Life was just... so boring." She sighed. "I miss my parents, but even after how hard it's been my first semester, I don't think I could go back now. This world is just so full of wonder and amazing things to see. I'd die if I went back there and did the same thing day in and day out."

"You never really answered me about the boyfriend thing." By the ancestors, why was I being so nosy?

"You first," she said. "Have you had any girlfriends?"

My stomach churned just thinking about it. "A couple, but there was one girl I really liked. She was a Toaqua girl named Mia. We got together because it was expected of us. Our parents basically hooked us up from the moment we were born. I was supposed to be chief, so I had my bride hand-picked for me."

"What happened?" Sophia asked.

My throat got kind of tight. "It just didn't work out, I guess."

"Liam," Sophia said, in a tone that suggested she wasn't buying my crap.

I sighed and said, "The truth is, I was into her way more than she was into me. She wanted to marry a chief, someone who could give her a good life, and I promised that. But then Nashoma died, and she told me she didn't want to be with me anymore. My dad let her out of the marriage contract, you know, because I didn't have a Familiar and I wasn't considered fit to marry."

"That's awful." She gave me a sad face. "Does that mean you can't marry ever?"

This was a tough conversation to talk about. It made my chest feel like there was a giant weight on it I couldn't lift off. "Not ever, but you'd have a hard time convincing a girl to marry someone like me."

I wasn't sure if I meant the Familiar-less part of me, the sick part, or both. Sophia didn't say anything, but looked thoughtful.

"I still see Mia around school from time to time, but we don't talk anymore," I said. "She's got another boyfriend now."

We really didn't talk, either. Mia always turned away whenever she saw me. I didn't blame her for breaking up with me, because it was what everyone thought she was going to do after Nashoma died, but I didn't think she would abandon me completely and act like I didn't even exist. At first, it really stung.

The funny thing was, I'd ceased to have any sort of feelings for Mia at all now that Sophia was around.

"That sucks. I'm sorry that happened to you," Sophia said kindly.

"Yeah, well. That's what you get for being stupid and wasting your virginity on someone who doesn't love you," I said, and I leaned back against the tree trunk.

"You had sex with her?" Sophia seemed shocked.

"Yeah. I guess I thought it would make her love me more. Or love me at all, really." I put an arm behind my head and looked up. "The shitty thing was, I found out she'd been screwing the guy she got with after me while we were still together."

"That really is terrible. I can see why you didn't want to talk about it," Sophia said.

"It's over with now," I said quickly. "Nashoma never really liked her. He always had a face whenever she came around."

Sophia laughed loudly. "I hope Nashoma would've liked me."

"I think he would've liked you very much." In fact, I didn't have to think about it. Deep down in my core, I just *knew* he would've loved her.

Sophia shivered, but I don't think it was because of the cold. "Okay. You told me yours, so I can tell you mine. I was friends with this guy in high school, and I really liked him, you know?"

I could see where this was going. "So, he turned you down, or..."

"It was prom night," she started. "I felt like I was so in love, and I wanted to try going all the way. We went together as friends, and I tried hitting on him, and he started flirting back. He was a complete gentleman until we got in the limo together. We started making out. We got to second base, but halfway through, I changed my mind."

This story was taking a way worse turn than I thought. The bones in my hands cracked. "And?"

"He reached up under my dress. I told him to stop but he got really mad. He told me I needed to finish what I started. He wouldn't stop groping me," she said. "I yelled for the driver to stop, then I got out of the car and walked the rest of the way home. When I got back to school the next week, he'd told everyone in my class I was a tease."

I was really far away from the pool, but the water down there was churning furiously. "Are you serious?"

"Yes. It kind of sucked." Her voice was choked up, but she cleared her throat. "It's over now. I'm over it."

She wasn't. I could tell by her voice. "I'm sorry I wasn't there. I would've beat that guy's ass."

She laughed again, and her expression cleared. "I bet you would've."

"I'm not kidding." If I could figure out who this guy was, I'd go looking for him and hunt his ass down.

Sophia seemed to notice I was serious. She turned around and touched my face. "Hey. It's all right."

I calmed down a little bit, but the possessiveness raging through me wasn't helping. Who the fuck did this guy think he was, assaulting Sophia like that? What gave him the right?

"Anyway, looks like we've both had really bad luck when it comes to love," she said, and her tone seemed lighter. "Hopefully the future will be better."

"Hopefully," I responded, though the answer came out more like a growl. I didn't like the thought of Sophia being with anyone who treated her like that. She was mine. *Mine.* My saucy little virgin.

Aw, fuck. I needed to take things down a notch. Fast.

There was a crackling noise by my ear, like little twigs snapping. I turned my head and saw that Esis had reappeared, dangling down from the trees. Sophia hadn't noticed him there. He had a small flower in his hands with a thin, twisty stem, and was holding it out to me.

He literally wanted me to give it to Sophia. This little shit was trying to play matchmaker! It was bad enough even the tree was trying to hook us up. That was *not* taking things down a notch.

"No," I told him softly. "That's not allowed."

His ears went back, and he hissed at me. Esis shoved the flower at me more insistently, this time poking me in the eye.

"Ow! All right!" I took the flower from him and he went scampering upward again. He was probably watching the whole thing from above, like it was his own personal daytime soap opera.

I was so nervous, but I handed the flower to her. My hand almost shook. "For you."

"Really? Thank you." She took it graciously. "Where'd you get it?"

"I don't know," I told her flatly. "It appeared like magic."

I heard humored chattering from the trees. If I got my hands on that little guy, he was going into the pool.

"That's so sweet." Sophia took the flower and wrapped it around one of the fingers on her left hand, tying a knot. She held it out happily. "It looks adorable. Thank you."

I felt a little more cheery. Okay, so the little guy had some moves. Maybe he was big with the kurble ladies.

Without warning, rain started pouring down from the sky. And I mean *pouring*. It was coming down in buckets. Sophia yelped and slid downward, off my lap and shimmying down the tree. I followed her, though not as fast.

"Hold on, I got it," I said when I reached the ground. I raised my hand. The raindrops falling down suspended in mid-air, frozen all around us. I thought of my intention, and the raindrops turned to crystal ice, resembling diamonds. I turned my wrist in a circular motion. The diamonds floated toward Sophia, nestling in her hair and giving her a shining headpiece, an ornate necklace and a shimmering dress.

Sophia's mouth opened wide and she gave a delighted sound of joy. Right then, she looked so beautiful, like a crystal princess. Nobody on earth had any idea how badly I wanted to kiss her. I hadn't kissed anyone in months, but Sophia made me want to again. I took a step toward her, because I wasn't a coward and I was going to do it.

But I was a coward, because I noticed some of the diamonds were sizzling against her skin. And I was reminded she was Koigni.

Almost as soon as the downpour started, it stopped. When I let the diamonds drop off of her and fall onto the grass, melting into the earth, the spell was broken, and it was like she woke up.

"Weird, huh?" Sophia said, looking skyward. "I've never seen a storm come and go so quickly before."

I said nothing. She didn't need to know it wasn't a storm at all, but how I felt.

"Do you...?" She started, then she waited a moment. "Do you think we could spend the night out here, just talking? I like being with you, Liam. It makes me feel better."

Talking with her was so easy. And it made me feel better, too. "Sure. Whatever you want, *pawee*."

We sat next to each other in the grass. Sophia talked about a lot of things— her old friends, her parents, Amelia, and especially Esis. He was up in the trees somewhere, cooing a song. Me, I just listened.

It was too late. There was no turning back now. I'd made my feelings for Sophia clear.

I just hoped that she felt the same.

I WOKE up the next morning curled against someone in the grass. At first, I thought it was Nashoma, and I was so happy that he was back. But then I realized my hand was tangled up in hair, not fur, and that Nashoma *didn't have boobs*.

I jolted awake with a start and skidded backward. Sophia had been curled up against me for ancestors knew how long. She was still asleep, breathing lightly with a smile on her face.

My body was pretty warm instead of the cool, usual Toaqua temperature it rested at, which meant I'd had my arms around her for quite some time now— possibly hours.

We'd literally picked opposite ends of the clearing to sleep on! How did we end up spooning randomly in our sleep? I looked around and saw Esis bathing in the pool, washing his fur with the water. He gave me a devious smile as he cleaned his fat cheeks.

He probably rolled us together in our sleep or something. He didn't look strong enough to do that, but I wouldn't put it past him.

I skirted away from her before she woke up. My movements didn't wake her, and I didn't want to touch her again to shake her awake, so I threw a twig, and when that still didn't wake her up, a small rock.

It bounced against her leg, and her eyes flew open. "Ow!" She sat up and rubbed her calf. "Did you really have to do that?"

"Yes. Now get up," I snapped. "We haven't got all day."

"Great. Mean Liam is back," she grumbled, pushing her hair out of her face. It'd fallen out of her ponytail and gotten all wild, which wasn't helping my *morning situation*.

"Mean Liam never left. Hurry up. I want breakfast," I told her.

"Breakfast is probably over." She yawned, and pointed at the sun. "It's almost noon."

Dammit. She was right. We'd way overslept. Hopefully nobody noticed that both of us had been gone from our dorms last night. "We need to get back," I told her, and I got to my feet. "Come on."

I went to head out of the clearing, but before I could, Sophia cried, "Wait!"

I turned around. She ran to the tree we'd climbed on last night and raised her hand. A small bit of fire appeared in her palm, and she moved it slowly over the tree trunk, burning an inscription into the wood.

"There." She stepped back, proud of her work. I looked at it. With her magic, she'd carved our initials into the tree: S and L.

"This is our place now," she said. "We've claimed it."

I couldn't decide if that was really cute or really annoying. "Come on, dork. Let's go."

Esis ran after Sophia, trilling and hopping on her back. We headed back to town, but this time, we didn't hold hands. We were acting like friends again now, instead of... whatever we'd been last night.

We were passing by Professor Baine's house. Baine lived closer to castle in Kinpago, instead of within the Water tribe's borders underwater, because it was a quicker walk to the school. He had a house on the beach, which I'm guessing he liked to be at whenever he wasn't bothering me.

I hoped Baine wasn't around, because he'd probably talk to us about the tournament and I wanted to keep thinking about Sophia's perfect everything. But whatever romantic daydreams I had for Sophia were completely smacked out of me by the sight that was waiting around the corner.

The air left my lungs, and Sophia gasped. It was November and chilly as fuck, but Baine was outside his damn house in a tight yellow Speedo, spread out on a lawn chair and sunbathing like it was the middle of July. As if anyone living wanted to see that much of him.

Today confirmed it. I had seen too much in my short life.

We tried to run away, but Baine heard our footsteps and lifted his head, waving. "Ah, Liam. Sophia! How are you this morning?"

He was talking to us and acting like this was completely normal. Ancestors have mercy. Even Esis was covering his eyes. He made no attempt to be shy about it.

"Um... we're good, thanks!" Sophia called back. "You?"

Of course Sophia would play along. Baine shrugged and said, "I have nothing to complain about. You all right, Liam?"

I grimaced and nodded, because I knew the minute I opened my mouth I'd be yelling at Baine to put some pants on.

"You have another training session tomorrow, by the way, seven o'clock in the evening," he told us. "Don't be late."

"We'll be there!" Sophia shouted back, and she grabbed on my arm to tug me away. I felt like screaming my head off, until Baine's house was out of sight and we were safely within the village limits.

Sophia was laughing. I'm pretty sure my skin had turned a nauseated green.

"I'm going to be scarred for life," I moaned, rubbing my face. Why did our tournament instructor, and my head of House, have to be so weird? Even worse, I had to claim him.

"Does Baine have a Familiar? I've never seen one," Sophia said.

"He does," I said. "She lives in the ocean."

"What is she?"

I smiled. "That would spoil the surprise, wouldn't it? I'm sure you'll see her during one of our sessions. She's incredible. It's bizarre something as beautiful and powerful as her would pick *Baine* to be her Elementai."

We passed by a little food cart selling one of my favorite things. My stomach rumbled and I pulled Sophia to a stop.

"What is it?" she asked as the vendor handed me three fluffy, fried pieces of heaven, round in shape and flat.

"Fry bread," I told her. "It's amazing. You'll love it."

I put venison, lettuce, tomatoes, sour cream and salsa on top of mine. I made a replica for Sophia before we started walking around again and eating. Esis had already sucked down his and was patting his stomach happily.

"Hey, Liam!" I heard Jonah cry out. He was walking ahead of us, Imogen by his side. Jonah was wearing a heavy flannel jacket, while Imogen was wearing overalls with bright pink galoshes and a magenta fuzzy jacket that looked like it'd once been a carpet. Her hair was up in pigtails, bows tying them together, and she was carrying a wicker basket. Sassy had an equally large bow tied into her tail. She rode on Squeaks' rear, who was making loud squeaking noises. Esis peeped as he saw them coming and jumped off Sophia's shoulder, chattering at Squeaks' hooves. The hippogriff lowered her head and clacked her beak at Esis like they were having a conversation.

"Hey, Imogen," Sophia said in a teasing way as they joined us. "How was your date with Cade?"

Imogen turned pink and said, "It wasn't a date."

I rolled my eyes. I don't know who Imogen was trying to fool. She was totally into Cade, and vice versa. They needed to stop avoiding their feelings and just get on with it.

That's the pot calling the kettle black.

"Anyway, how was your *date* with Liam?" Imogen jabbed, and she put her hand on her hip. She gave a smirk as she and Jonah made eye contact.

Sophia gaped like a fish, unsure of what to say. She'd told Imogen we were hanging out last night, before I even knew she was looking for me?

Sophia went to answer, but I subbed in for her, "It went great, thanks. What are you guys doing here?"

Sophia glanced at me. She was surprised I hadn't denied that we'd been on an actual date— even though, really, that wasn't what it was. It wasn't what it had started as, anyway.

"I met up with Imogen coming out of the gym. Somebody's gotta take care of these babies." Jonah flexed his muscles, kissing his biceps.

Behind him, Squeaks did a similar pose, sticking out her butt and trying to show off. Esis flexed his tiny arms and copied her.

"And I met up with Jonah while Sassy and I were looking for treats to catch burlangers," Imogen said cheerfully. "We decided to do some grocery shopping together." She lifted her basket.

"Yeah. Needed protein shakes. Gotta keep the machine well oiled," Jonah said in a very obnoxious way. "What were you guys doing? You look like you spent a night in the woods."

"We were, um..." How did I tell them we'd done just that?

"We just got lunch," Sophia finished. "We were heading back to school. We're going to hang out in the Commons and just chill."

The Commons was the only place in Orenda Academy where students from all Houses could hang out. Sophia had just read my mind.

"We'll come with you," Jonah offered. "We should probably get to talking about strategies for the tournament."

My stomach sank. Right. The tournament. I'd forgotten all about that.

We headed up the long pathway back to school, avoiding the crowds and maneuvering around the carts. The sun was starting to come out from behind the clouds, and Imogen sighed happily. "Oh, I've had such a nice morning."

"Lucky you. We just saw Baine in nothing but spandex," I mumbled.

"What?" Jonah laughed loudly. "How'd you manage that?"

"He was tanning outside his house in his swimsuit." Sophia giggled. "I thought Liam was going to have a heart attack when he saw."

"I wish. It would've ended my suffering." Now she had me thinking about it again, dammit.

"There are a lot of girls who think Baine is super hot, not just me," Imogen quipped. "People gossip about how sexy he is all the time."

"Not me." Sophia shuddered. "I always thought he looked like a dad. He's not hot at all."

"He's got a dad bod. Trust me, it's nothing to behold," I told them. "Those girls are nuts."

"My ancestors, Liam, you ruin everything," Imogen said.

"Yeah, you're such a sour grape," Jonah added. "Lighten up."

"I'm not a lamp," I grumbled. Of course, the entire conversation the way back to school was about if Baine was or was not hot. Sophia and I were on one side, while Imogen argued that she could see why some people would want to go out with him.

"I'd probably give it a chance, if I had the opportunity," Jonah said. "I'm not into old guys, but I'll try anything once, and I bet he has experience."

"Jonah, you'll fuck anything that walks," I told him. "Can we seriously stop talking about this? He's our tournament mentor. It's creeping me out."

Jonah went to argue back, but we were stopped by someone in the hallway. It was Professor Perot, and his peacock Familiar, Baxtor.

Perot had been really nice to me in class ever since I'd helped saved him. I skipped a few times and he still gave me credit, not to mention I know the last few tests I'd failed miserably and I'd still gotten top marks. He'd been acting weird, though, not talking to me much, just smiling a lot.

"Oh, Professor," I said. He stood in front of us awkwardly, wringing his hands. "You need something?"

Perot seemed to swallow, then gave a nervous smile. "I just wanted to thank the four of you again for saving my life. Baxtor and I are very grateful."

"It was really no problem." *Except I threw out my back dragging you out.*

"Well, yes." He flushed. "The thing is, I have been thinking on how to repay all of you for your bravery. And while I can't think of what I could do for you three"— he eyed Sophia, Jonah, and Imogen—, "I think there *is* something I can do for you, Liam."

"Oh," I started. "Okay."

There was an awkward moment of silence, and Perot gestured to us. "Follow me."

We hurried after him. He led us to his classroom, and then to his desk, where I noticed an assortment of papers and vials were scattered. Squeaks knocked over a couple of glasses on our way in, but Perot paid her no mind.

He sat down at his desk and said, "I've been looking into your case, Liam. I've heard about your illness, and think that with enough research and time, I'll be able to discover what ails you... maybe even cure it."

"You're serious?" My mouth dropped open. I felt like I was suffocating. My heart was practically beating out of my chest. This was too good to be true. Just a name would be a miracle, but a cure... that was unthinkable.

Then came the doubt. I shook my head. "No. No, I've been to the best medicine women and men in the tribe. Nobody knows what's wrong with me, or how to help me."

"I can't promise anything," Perot started, and Baxtor bobbed his head. "But I am a researcher, not a doctor, so I can look at your case from a different perspective. I think that a life for a life is the best way to repay my debt."

"Did you hear that, Liam?" Sophia said excitedly. "There might be a cure!"

Her expression was hopeful, but at the same time, I didn't want to believe it. I'd been through so much in the past few months. Hoping for anything, even just a diagnosis, seemed like a setup. It was easier to go on being miserable than to be let down again. That would really suck.

"Hold on," Jonah said. "I thought Liam was sick because Nashoma died."

I wanted to punch Jonah. He needed to mind his own business.

"It might be," Perot said. "But I have reason to believe that maybe Liam's condition isn't linked to Nashoma's death at all, but perhaps something that was dormant until that point. Grief can be a powerful trigger for chronic illnesses. We won't know for sure unless we do some testing."

"You are the only person who's ever survived the death of their Familiar, Liam," Imogen added. "Maybe this would be how to find out why."

"Some of the processes for investigating your illness would be...

invasive," Perot said slowly. "It wouldn't be a quick or easy process. But it'll be worth it in the end if we can determine exactly what's going on with you. Of course, it's your choice, Liam."

Everyone in the room looked at me, perched on my answer. I wasn't sure. I really didn't want to be put through anything else, being poked, prodded and questioned about something that was already deeply personal, not to mention a really sensitive subject. Half of me didn't care if I was suffering from something that was worsening, or even terminal. I just wanted to be left alone and enjoy the time that I had left, however much that was.

But then I saw the look on Sophia's face, and I knew what she wanted me to do. She didn't want me to give up. She wanted me to keep fighting.

Fine. If I had to be a guinea pig to get some answers, I'd be a guinea pig. "I guess I'm for it," I said. "What do you want me to do?"

"First, I'll need a sample of your blood, among other things," Perot said. He took out a few syringes with needles, and I swallowed. "I wouldn't need you back in until I'm done analyzing the results."

"I'm ready," I said. I wanted to get this over with. Hurry up and stick me like a pincushion.

I thought Perot would take me to a back room or something, you know, somewhere with a bit of seclusion, but he began sanitizing my arm and sticking me right in front of everybody. I didn't like needles, but I wasn't about to look like a wimp in front of my team. I expected the gang to turn their backs or something, but instead they kept on talking while Perot took his samples and set several vials of my blood aside. Imogen was blabbering about burlangers, while Jonah and Sophia happily subbed in.

Everyone was acting really natural, while here I was, looking like I belonged in a hospital. "Um," I started as they all kept gabbing on. This was awkward. A little privacy, please?

But then I realized something. They weren't staring at me like I was in a zoo. They kept carrying on like it was okay I was getting treated and experimented on. They were acting like me being sick was okay.

Yet they weren't acting at all. It was genuine. I didn't feel different.

I just... felt like everyone else.

"Oh, sorry." Sophia straightened up and looked down at the tons of needles shoved into my arms, as if she suddenly just realized they were there. "We can go."

I had to laugh. Sophia was totally clueless, and I loved it. "You're here now. Just stay."

A few minutes later, I was a little lightheaded. Perot had made it sound like he only needed a tiny bit of blood, but it'd felt like he took a gallon. Looking at all the vials on his desk made me want to throw up.

"You'll want to watch him," Perot said as he eyed me getting up from the chair woozily. "He's a little pale. He should be better by tomorrow."

"Lean on me, bro," Jonah said, and he flung an arm around my shoulders. "I got you."

Jonah was practically carrying me out the door. Sophia thanked Professor Perot and waved goodbye as she and Imogen followed us.

"Where to?" Imogen asked cheerfully. Squeaks snuck her head under my other arm and lifted me up so my toes were dragging on the ground, but I pushed her away. I didn't need to be carried like some wounded war hero, for ancestors' sake.

Sophia said nothing. She was watching me carefully out of the corner of her eye.

"The Commons sounds pretty good right now," I said. My voice was kind of slurred. "Those couches are like... so plushy."

Plushy? I was really out of it.

"Cookies, man," Jonah said wisely. "Just a shitload of cookies."

Jonah threw me on the couch when we got there. We got the good seats, the ones by the fireplace with the big TV. Imogen sat on the rug against Squeaks with Sassy in her arms, while Jonah took the big armchair. Sophia sat on the other side of the couch and flung her legs over mine. Jonah left for awhile and came back with literally three bags of cookies, which we all polished off while watching a movie. I'm pretty sure I slipped off one or two times, but I can't remember.

Sophia kept looking at me, and when she wasn't, Esis was, his eyes wide and unsure as he curled up on Sophia's lap.

He seemed... guilty. Though I'm not sure why.

That afternoon was pretty perfect. To people passing by, I'm sure we looked like a bunch of friends just hanging out.

But we were so much more than that. For the first time since Nashoma died, I felt like I wasn't a freak, and it was nice.

Maybe I could get used to these people.

sophia

SIXTEEN

"What's the deal with you and Liam?" Imogen asked.

We sat on the beach, staring out at the ocean. The November air was chilly, and the sky overcast. In the distance, snow was falling, covering the peaks of the mountains around us. I pulled the sleeves of my hoodie over my hands and wrapped my arms around me. I'd become used to the colder weather of Northern California these past few months, but I was starting to regret not packing a heavier coat. I called upon my Fire, raising it just to the surface of my skin to ward off the chill.

I shrugged, keeping my eyes on Esis. He was digging in the rocks and placing the shiniest ones into a pile at my feet. "Do we have to have this conversation again?"

It'd been a week since Liam took me to see the waterfall, and I still didn't know how to answer the question.

"Again?" Imogen repeated. She petted Sassy in her lap, who was batting at the lime green bows at the ends of Imogen's braids. "Sophia, you blow me off every time I ask about it. I think I deserve to know what's going on between my teammates. The tournament is only a few weeks away. Should I be concerned?"

"About me and Liam?" I laughed. "No. I'd be more concerned about Jonah's raging hormones."

Imogen covered her mouth with her hand to stifle her giggles. Our second training session went better than the first, but the moment Jonah spotted Renar passing by our obstacle course with a couple of friends, he lost all focus. He stumbled off the root bridge Imogen had built to get us over a pit of quicksand. Squeaks nearly got stuck trying to rescue him. All Jonah could talk about afterward was how appalled he was that Renar didn't even notice and try to help. Liam was furious with Jonah and totally erupted on him, though I thought he over-reacted.

Imogen rolled her eyes. "Men. But that still doesn't answer my question. You and Liam? What's going on?"

"I don't know." I absentmindedly rolled one of Esis' rocks around in my hand while I contemplated the question. What *was* going on between us? I liked Liam a lot— I knew that much for certain. After he told me the story about Mia, the girl who broke his heart, all I wanted to do was show him how much I cared about him. I sensed that after Mia, he didn't feel like he deserved to be loved.

And he was so, *so* wrong. I just wished my heart was enough to heal him. But I knew Liam would never accept it... though I hoped he would, one day.

"I told you about that magical night we had together," I said. "But we haven't really talked about what's happening between us."

"Oh, I see the problem," Imogen said. "You need to *define your relationship*."

I frowned at her. "Like you and Cade have?"

"This isn't about me and Cade. Besides, we're just friends."

I nodded slowly. "Sure you are."

"Why don't you just tell Liam how you feel?" she asked.

Nerves ignited in my chest just thinking about it. "I can't. What if he doesn't feel the same way? Things would be weird between us, and we can't have that before the tournament."

"So you'll tell him after the tournament?"

I dropped my gaze. "I don't know. I can't just come out and tell Liam that I'm falling head over heels for him."

"Why not?" Imogen asked. "I mean, if he feels the same way, what's the harm?"

I resisted the urge to bust out laughing. "We're just friends, Imogen. Like you and Cade. Liam doesn't feel that way about me."

It broke my heart and made it feel as if rocks had settled in my stomach. I wanted Liam to like me back. I'd run the scenario so many times through my head, what it would be like to tell him I liked him, for him to say it back. He'd reach down and brush the hair out of my eyes while I ran my fingers across his chest. I'd go breathless just being in his presence. Then he'd kiss me—a mind-blowing, passionate kiss I'd only ever dreamed about. He'd sweep me into his arms and carry me into the sunset, and we'd live happily ever after.

And then he opened his mouth in real life, shattering any hope of that fairytale coming true. I lived for the moments his fingers accidentally grazed across mine when we walked beside each other in the hall, the way his eyes lit up when we were together, and the smile that crept across his face every so often when I saw him staring out toward the ocean.

But that's all they would ever be. Moments. I couldn't have forever with Liam, even if I wanted to.

"Girl, you're blind," Imogen said, pulling me from my thoughts. "There's some serious sexual tension going on between you two. Can't you feel it?"

My eyebrows shot up. "Sexual tension? Oh, my God, Imogen. I must've missed the romance section in your library. You've been reading too much. I highly doubt Liam feels *anything* sexual toward me. I'm always in this baggy hoodie and jeans, with my hair tied into a ponytail and almost no makeup on. *No way* he finds that attractive. That one day I wore my hair down and that low-cut shirt like you told me to, he barely stole a glance at me."

Imogen rolled her eyes. "That's because he was trying to be subtle about it. Trust me, from my perspective, he was drooling."

Butterflies fluttered in my stomach at the possibility.

"Next time, wear a push-up bra," Imogen advised. "He'll have his face down your shirt in one-point-five seconds."

It sounded gross, but I wouldn't mind it. Liam could do whatever he wanted to my cleavage and more.

"Ugh, Imogen, can we—?"

"Oh, my ancestors!" Imogen hopped up to her knees and flapped her hands excitedly. Sassy rolled onto the ground, looking shocked. Esis paused with a rock in his hand and alarm in his eyes. "I know what you need!"

I leaned away a few inches as her hands nearly assaulted my face. "Um... what do I need?"

"You need a dress," she stated, like it was obvious.

"I don't wear dresses."

"For the *ball*," she emphasized. "You need to buy a smoking hot dress so Liam can't keep his eyes off you."

I bit my lower lip, considering her idea. At least it would be after the tournament. And it was a good excuse to dress up for him.

I sighed. "Okay. I might even wear a push-up bra."

Imogen jumped to her feet and bounced on her toes. "Yay! We can do your makeup and your hair and everything. You're going to look so hot he'll want to get nasty with you on the dance floor."

"Oh, my ancestors, Imogen." I turned beet-red as I stood. "Don't say stuff like that."

"What?" she asked innocently. "Nasty?"

I rolled my eyes. "Yes. That."

"Nasty, nasty, nasty," she teased. "It's not a bad word."

If possible, I flushed even redder. "No, but you're talking about me and Liam. If we... did it, it wouldn't be nasty."

Imogen wiggled her eyebrows. "What *would* it be like?"

"Imogen!" I shoved at her playfully while Esis scurried up my pant leg to crawl onto my shoulder.

Imogen only laughed. "Okay, fine. I'll stop. Let's go get you a dress that'll make Liam crazy."

❦

"No. Absolutely not." Imogen sat in a plush chair outside the dressing room of a little boutique shop in Kinpago called *Delilah's*, giving feedback on each dress I tried on.

I spun around to admire the dress in the mirror beside the dressing rooms. It was black, with a silk skirt that fell to the floor and a lacy top with three-quarter-length sleeves. "Why not? I think it's beautiful."

Esis clapped from the armrest of Imogen's chair.

"See?" I said. "Even Esis likes it."

Imogen frowned. "We're going for *kiss me now*, not *kiss me when I'm fifty*."

She'd had a similar response to the last three dresses I'd tried on.

"If you're such a fashion expert, what do you suggest?" I challenged.

"I'll be right back." Imogen smirked and rose from her chair. Sassy followed behind her.

I sighed and glanced around, my hands on my hips. The shop was packed with row upon row of colorful dresses, each one unique. A big window at the front gave a wide view of the street beyond, where people and their Familiars passed by. My eyes caught a creature that looked like a skunk, but had long tail feathers instead of fur.

I turned back to Esis. "She's going to come back with lingerie, isn't she?"

Esis just looked at me with his big eyes and shrugged.

"Here we go," Imogen said as she returned. She held up a long red dress with skinny straps and a neckline I already knew I was going to hate. She didn't miss the frown on my face. "It's for Liam, remember?"

I sighed and took the dress from her hands. "I'll try it on."

Imogen smiled. "Good. I'll go grab a few more for backup."

I returned to the dressing room, holding the door open a moment to let Esis jump inside behind me. Inside, I slipped off the black dress. My heart sank as I placed it back on its hanger. I loved it, but Imogen was right. It wasn't the type of dress that would stop Liam in his tracks. I stared at the red dress in uncertainty. It might do the trick, but it also might give him the wrong idea. Then again, Liam wasn't the *wham bam thank you ma'am* type of guy, was he?

"This dressing room is open," a woman said outside, making me jump. I'd been staring at the dress for far too long. "You let me know if you need anything." I heard the dressing room door beside mine close.

Shaking off my nervous jitters, I pulled the dress up over my hips, slipped my arms under the straps, and zipped the back. When my eyes fell on myself in the mirror, my insides did a weird summersault that was a mixture of both *hot damn* and *no thank you.*

Esis' brows shot up, and he whistled at me.

The hem of the dress touched the floor, but there was a slit that traveled all the way up to my hip. The front plunged to reveal more than I cared to ever show in public. If I did my hair up real nice, I'd be a knockout. But honestly, I'd spend more time worrying about a nipple slip than anything else.

"Come on," Imogen called when she returned. "Let's see it."

"I'd rather not," I replied.

"Please just indulge me, Sophia," Imogen begged.

"Fine," I agreed, "but I'm not buying it."

I quickly checked the price tag and nearly passed out. Unless it rained hundred-dollar bills from the sky, there was no way I was buying this dress. I'd barely brought that much money with me to Orenda in the first place. I wasn't about to blow all my cash on an outfit I'd wear for only a few hours— even if it did earn Liam's attention.

I took a deep breath and opened the door. Esis scurried out in front of me and sang a three-note tune as if he was announcing the arrival of a queen. Imogen's eyebrows shot up, while I crossed my arms over my chest.

"You look hot!" she sang with a wide smile.

I turned to the mirror, feeling incredibly self-conscious. "Do I?"

Imogen placed the dresses in her arms down on her chair and stepped forward to peer into the mirror behind me. "Maybe if you dropped your arms I could see the full dress."

Nervously, I let my arms fall to my side.

"Woop woop!" Imogen cat-called.

I quickly glanced over at two other patrons browsing the aisles, a mother and a daughter. They both looked up and caught my eye, but then continued flipping through dresses. Imogen didn't even notice.

"By the ancestors, Sophia Henley has boobs!"

"Shut up!" I swatted at Imogen with one hand and covered my cleavage with the other. "If you like it so much, you can wear it."

Disgust crossed Imogen's face. "Me in that? Can you imagine? I'm not buying a dress. I've been working on a homemade dress for the past year. It's going to be epic."

I heard the dressing room door beside mine click open, but I didn't think anything of it. "Maybe I'll have to make my own, too, because I'm not buying this one."

Someone scoffed from behind us. "Why would you?"

I whirled around to see Haley step out of the dressing room with her phoenix Familiar behind her. She wore a strapless black evening dress that was even more revealing than the one I had on. It was accented with golden beads that twisted around the bust in an elegant pattern. And damn it, she looked freaking perfect in it. *Bitch.*

"You'll never get a chance to wear it," Haley snarled. "You'll die in the tournament anyway."

My blood boiled, and my fists tightened. I held back my anger, only to keep the dress I was wearing from bursting into flames. Beside me, Esis bared his teeth and growled.

"What the hell's your problem?" The words slipped out before I could stop myself. It was better than losing control of my Fire and burning *Delilah's* down.

Haley just shrugged. "No problem. I'm just stating a fact."

"Well, you can shove your facts right up your pretty little ass. I'll see you at the ball."

My heart slammed against my rib cage. Holy crap. Had I just said that? Where the heck did those words come from?

Haley just stood there glaring at me. I held my breath, waiting for her to throw a fireball at my head or something. Instead, she just rolled her eyes and whirled around, slamming her dressing room door behind her.

My jaw dropped in disbelief as I turned to Imogen. I didn't make a sound, but my face said it all. I couldn't believe what I'd just done. Imogen let out a light squeal and threw her arms around me, squeezing me tightly.

"I'm so proud of you!" she whispered in my ear.

Just as we drew apart, Haley's door swung open again. She was dressed back in her normal clothes— tight black pants and a low-cut shirt that her boobs were spilling out of. The dress she'd been wearing hung over her arm. Her lips were tight. She didn't meet either of our eyes as she passed by, but she made it a point to step on the hem of my dress and slam her shoulder into mine. I rubbed my shoulder as Haley continued on her way, her Familiar in her wake. Then she turned back to me.

"Oh, Sophia?" she said, like she forgot to tell me something.

"What?" I snapped.

Haley held her head high and glanced down at my feet. "You might want to put that out."

I looked down to see flames singeing the corner of my dress. Imogen and I both immediately started stomping on it. By the time the flames were out and I glanced up, Haley had already left the store.

I gritted my teeth and turned to Imogen. "That wasn't me, you know. That was Haley. Now I have to buy the dress."

"Nah, it's fine," Imogen said. "We'll slip it into her dressing room and let her take the blame. It was her fault anyway."

I sighed. "Yeah, but—"

"Hot. Dayum." A female voice cut me off.

When I turned toward the voice, I couldn't believe my eyes. A woman with dark hair and a parrot sitting on her shoulder stared back at me. I must've been hallucinating or something.

"Amelia?!" I squeaked. I forgot all about Haley and rushed forward to throw my arms around my sister. Kiwi squawked. I squeezed her as tight as I could, letting all of my overwhelmed emotions flow into the embrace. "What are you doing here?" I cried as I drew away from her, still unable to believe it.

"I was headed to Orenda to see you, but then I saw you through the window and came in to say hi," Amelia explained.

"No, I mean, what are you doing here in Kinpago?" I was so excited that I pulled her into another hug.

Amelia laughed and squeezed me back. "That's what I was headed to Orenda to tell you about. I'm moving to town!"

"What?" I squealed, unable to contain my excitement. I missed her so much. "Why are you moving? Tell me all about it!"

I pulled her over to the sitting area, and we sank down next to each other. "This is Imogen, by the way, and her Familiar, Sassy."

Imogen smiled and reached out a hand to shake Amelia's before sitting down. Esis hopped onto Amelia's armrest and nuzzled his head into her hand, inviting her to pet him.

"And this is my Familiar, Esis," I said.

Amelia's expression softened, and she stared down at Esis with wide eyes. "Oh, my ancestors. He's adorable! Can I keep him?"

"Sorry, he's not for sale," I said with a laugh.

Amelia cradled him in her arms, and Kiwi squawked again. Apparently, he didn't like that.

"What are you doing here, Am?" I asked again. I wanted to hear all about her journey and how long she was going to stay.

Amelia took a deep breath. "Well, you know my job on the cruise ship?"

I nodded eagerly. "You could've told me it was a flying cruise ship, by the way."

Amelia laughed. "Yeah, well, you wouldn't have believed me, would you?"

I shook my head. "Probably not."

"Anyway, I got a promotion, which means I get more vacation days. I have a friend who's offered for me to crash in his guest room whenever I'm in town, until I find an apartment of my own. I'll be here for a few days before I leave again. Then I should be back at the end of December just in time for the Elemental Cup. I guess this means you'll be competing?" She glanced down at Esis.

"Yes. Oh, my gosh, Amelia. There's so much to tell you. Life has completely changed since I've been here. I wish I could've talked to you sooner. How are Mom and Dad?"

Amelia didn't look at me when she answered. "They were really upset at first, but they've come around. I visited them a few weeks ago and let them know I'd be coming into town soon to check on you. They won't be happy to hear you'll be in the tournament your first semester, but they'll be happy you've bonded."

"I wish they could come watch," I said sadly.

Amelia's expression fell. "They would if they could. Here. They asked me to give you this." Amelia pulled a thick envelope out of her purse and handed it to me.

"What is it?" I asked, taking it.

Amelia shrugged. "I didn't open it."

I peeled back the flap and peeked inside. My heart nearly stopped when I saw the wad of cash. With that kind of money, I'd actually be able to afford this dress— plus a new coat. A piece of paper was folded up inside. I pulled it out and began reading.

Sophia,

We miss you so much. We wish we could come to see you, but we fear it would cause more harm than good to visit you in Kinpago. We would not be welcome. We wish we could tell you all about it, but it's not something we can explain in a letter. We just wanted to tell you that we're sorry for how we acted. We never meant to push you away. We only wanted you to be safe. We wish we would've taken the chance to tell you goodbye before you left. We hope that everything is going well at Orenda Academy.

With Love,
Mom & Dad

P.S. We know the school takes care of everything for you, but we've enclosed some money in case you need anything in town.

Tears welled in my eyes. I could practically hear my parents' voices in my head saying the words directly to me. I didn't like that they were being distant, but right now, I hardly cared. My heart ached for home, to see them again. I quickly dashed the tears away.

Amelia leaned forward and placed a hand on my knee. "It's going to be okay." She eyed me up and down. "Is this the dress you're wearing to the ball?"

I shook my head and forced a smile. "No. I just tried it on for fun."

"Good," Amelia said. "It's awful and so *not* you."

"What?" Imogen asked in disbelief. "It's gorgeous."

"Yeah, if you're an escort," Amelia deadpanned.

Imogen threw her head back and laughed. "Fair enough. What *should* Sophia wear?"

A smile crept across Amelia's face. "I know just the one."

Curious, I stood and followed behind Amelia as she led us down an aisle and to the other end of the shop. She pointed to a mannequin in the window. My heart lifted when I saw the dress. It was an A-line sky blue dress with a tulle skirt, flowery lace petals above the waist, and a corset back. The neckline was cut just below the collarbone, with cap sleeves that looked modest and elegant. It had an antique style to it that I knew would suit me perfectly.

"I can't wear that," I said immediately, despite every muscle in my body itching to try it on.

"Why not?" Amelia asked.

"She's right," Imogen agreed, stepping forward. "It's not sexy enough. We're trying to impress a guy."

Amelia's gaze shot to mine, her eyebrows raised. "Ooh, a guy! Why didn't you say so?"

She beamed at me excitedly. Would her reaction be different if she knew the guy I was crushing on wasn't Koigni?

"No," I sighed. "It's not that. The dress is too... Toaqua. Everyone's going to expect me to arrive dressed in something like this." I gestured down to the red dress I wore.

Amelia pressed her lips together. "Maybe that's exactly why you *should* wear the blue dress."

My shoulders fell. I wanted *so* badly to wear it, but it would only draw attention. Everyone would think I was trying to cross House boundaries or something. I had no intention of drawing anyone's eye except for Liam's.

"I know you don't have Toaqua blood in you, Sophia," Amelia said, "but you have a Toaqua heart. You were, after all, raised by Mom and Dad."

"If that's the dress you want, then get it," Imogen encouraged. "Don't worry about what anyone will think. Go against the grain for once."

A shy smile spread across my face. Why was I so worried? I ignored the stares that followed every time I was with Imogen, and her

239

dress was bound to be wild enough to keep the eyes off of me. It was just a blue dress. It wasn't like I was publicly disavowing my Koigni heritage.

"Fine," I said. "I'll try it on."

After talking to the lady at the front desk, she helped us strip it off the mannequin. I returned to the dressing room and slipped it on.

Oh, my ancestors. It was perfect. Esis quickly picked his jaw up from the floor and chippered in approval.

"You like it, buddy?" I asked.

He nodded.

"Can you help?" I turned my back to him and sat on the dressing room bench. Esis' little hands tugged at the ribbon in the corset back, tightening it for me. "Thanks."

I stood and looked at myself in the mirror. It fit like a glove. I absolutely loved it.

"Hurry up," Imogen called. "Sassy's getting antsy. She wants to see it."

I took a deep breath and opened the door. Amelia and Imogen both went speechless, their eyes wide.

"It's gorgeous on you, Sophia," Amelia said once she found her voice. "He's going to love it."

I twirled around for them, mostly to hide the blush rising in my cheeks. "You think so?"

"Absolutely," Imogen said. "All you need now is to ask him to the ball."

I immediately stopped twirling. "I'm not asking him."

"Why not?" Amelia asked.

I didn't know the answer. "Um... isn't that his job?"

Imogen scoffed. "This isn't the Dark Ages, Sophia. Girls can ask guys to dances. If you want to go with him, you should ask him."

"Maybe..." I shrugged, enthralled by the idea but not sure I could go through with it. "I'll think about it."

"So, that's the one?" Amelia asked.

My heart fluttered. "It's the one."

"Cool. So, what are your plans for the rest of the day? I was hoping we could go out for lunch and catch up," Amelia said.

"That sounds like fun," I agreed. "Are you coming, Imogen?"

"Nah," she said with a wave of her hand. "I'll go find Cade and we'll hang out."

"In that case, have lots of fun," I told her. "Don't go too crazy."

Imogen rolled her eyes. "Girl, I'm way past crazy. But you already knew that. I'll see you later."

Imogen left the shop while I headed into the dressing room and put my normal clothes back on. Amelia, Esis, and Kiwi followed me up to the register, where I pulled out a few of the bills my parents had given me and handed them to the cashier. Luckily, the dress was far cheaper than the red one— and twenty-five percent off. I *loved* a good deal. I usually only bought things when they were on clearance, anyhow. The lady behind the counter placed the dress on a hanger and in a long plastic bag for me. I draped it over my arm as we left *Delilah's*.

"So, tell me what you've been up to," Amelia encouraged as we headed down the street toward the square.

"I don't know," I said with a sigh. "Mostly going to class, studying, training for the tournament. But we have more important things to talk about, don't we?"

Amelia plastered a look of innocence on her face. "No. I don't think so."

"Am..." I frowned. "You obviously know more about this prophecy and what happened with Mom and Dad than you're saying."

Amelia didn't meet my gaze. "What do *you* know about it?"

"Not much," I admitted. "The prophecy may or may not be a myth. If it's true, it apparently has something to do with me. According to Doya, Mom and Dad stole me as a baby. Oh, and I'm supposed to be looking for some magical object I know nothing about?"

Crap. I wasn't supposed to mention that... but this was Amelia. I could trust her.

Amelia whirled toward me, stopping in her tracks. "Listen to me, Sophia. You're wrong. About everything. Mom and Dad didn't kidnap you. They adopted you. Whatever it is you think you're looking for, you need to stop."

I gaped at her. "Am..."

"Doya's just trying to get in your head," she insisted. "Really. Just ignore this prophecy thing, and you'll be okay."

Amelia started down the street again, obviously unwilling to say more, but I couldn't bring my feet to move beneath me. I knew I could trust Amelia with my life, but something told me she wasn't being entirely honest with me.

Liam

SEVENTEEN

I felt like I was being a wimp, but the day of our last training session, I was nervous. We *had* to get this one right. If we messed up today, it would mean our performance in the tournament would be a disaster. Baine had already told us that students who failed the final evaluation before the Elemental Cup always lost at least one to three people in the tournament.

I didn't want to lose anybody. Which meant we had to do good today.

I stopped at the Koigni dorms an hour early to pick up Sophia. Usually I'd still be in bed, but I couldn't sleep last night. I kept having messed up dreams about Sophia. They started out good... really good... but then they always ended with her being crushed under a pile of rocks.

Obviously, I wasn't about that life, so I'd stayed up most of the night weaving baskets trying to calm myself down, and trying to talk myself out of sneaking into the Koigni dorms just to see if she was really okay.

"Esis wouldn't let anything happen to her," I muttered to myself. I didn't know what the little fur ball would do, or could do if Sophia got into trouble, but he cared about Sophia just as much and probably even more than I did, so it comforted me a little.

Finally, she walked out of the Koigni dorms in an oversized knitted sweater and thick jeans with hiking boots. Esis was bundled up in her arms, wearing a tiny wool hat and gloves. The sight of her safe and well killed my anxiety attack instantly.

I noticed she was wearing a bit of makeup today, which was weird. It was only going to run in the water. She'd never worn makeup a few months ago, but lately, it was everyday. I wondered why that was.

She bypassed a good morning and said, "I brought a wetsuit, like you said. I'm wearing it underneath my clothes." She paused. "Though why we're going swimming in early December, I have no idea."

"You'll be okay," I told her. "You have your Fire to keep you warm. But Jonah and Imogen don't, so it'll be up to you to regulate their temperature while we're out there."

"What about you?"

"Water doesn't bother me, no matter how cold it is. My body can withstand ice."

She looked doubtful. "Why do we have to go out into the ocean, anyway?"

"Baine," I answered simply. "He's going to be using his Familiar, and she has trouble walking on land, so we have to go to a platform on the ocean. You shouldn't be complaining. It'll be much harder for Haley to spy on us."

She nodded thoughtfully. "How are the others going to get there?"

"Imogen will make an earth bridge out of the bottom of the ocean, and Jonah will fly there using air. Your element is the only one that's useless for travel."

"Ha ha," Sophia said bluntly. "So, how are *we* going to get there? You'll take us by water?"

I smiled. "That would be too easy."

I led her outside the school, and we started strolling through the gardens. Secretly I'd been keeping something in the bushes near the greenhouses for ages, and today I was going to show Sophia.

"Cars aren't allowed, you know. And I'm betting bikes aren't, either." Sophia seemed to be reading my mind. "But you look like the type of guy who'd have one anyway."

"Bikes are for guys who have big egos and desperately want to impress people," I told her. "They're a huge sign of being insecure."

"So... guys like you?"

I smirked and didn't answer. I turned the corner, where I weaved my way through a bunch of brambles and hauled out an old motorbike. It was a bit rusty, but it ran good. I hadn't driven it in awhile. I hoped it still worked.

"I should have guessed." She crossed her arms. "You're so cliche, Liam."

"It was my dad's," I told her. "It'll be faster than taking perytons."

"How the hell is a bike going to get us into the middle of the sea?" she asked.

I rolled my eyes. "Just trust me, all right? Quit asking questions."

She sighed. "Well, what do you want me to do with Esis?" She held him up.

"Put him in this bag." I showed her a saddlebag attached to the side of the bike. "As long as he stays inside, he won't fall out."

"Do as you're told, Esis," she said to him as she slipped him inside the bag. She buttoned up the sides, leaving enough room for air. He peeked his little head up so his big eyes could see through the slit on the side of the bag.

"Once it starts, we have to get on, fast," I told her, and I slung my leg over the bike. "It's really loud."

I started it up. It was cold, so it took a few tries, but finally the engine roared to life. I looked expectantly at Sophia to get on. She stared at the bike like it was a bomb about to go off.

"Well, come on," I snapped. "I don't have cooties."

My tone snapped her out of it, and she sneered at me. "You're always so aggravated," she complained as she hopped on behind me.

"Well, maybe if you weren't so *aggravating*, I'd be in a better mood," I told her.

"Yeah, right. You've got a stick up your ass whether I'm around or not."

Couldn't argue with that. Sophia slipped on behind me, and her warm, soft body pressed against my back. It wasn't doing wonders for my vow of chastity.

Her arms were dangling downward. "You do have to hold on to me, you know," I told her. "Unless your pretty ass wants to go flying off."

She blushed before she stuck out her tongue at me. "Don't get too excited about it," she snapped. She wrapped her arms around my middle and squeezed tightly. Something in me stirred, and I told it to shut up. I revved the bike so that we took off flying.

Immediately, it felt like a vice was squeezing my middle. I gasped. Sophia was holding me so tight that it would cause bruising, her face pressed into my back in fright. I was sore enough on a daily basis. I tried to suck it up and pushed the bike faster, but it only made her crush me more.

Ancestors, she was choking me. I couldn't even expand my lungs. She was strong. I slowed down and stopped the bike on the side of the path. She let go, and I let in a thankful gasp. I turned around and looked at her. She seemed positively frazzled.

"Look," I said, "you don't need to hang onto me like it's life or death."

"I've never rode a bike, so sue me," Sophia shot back. "I know you don't like me touching you."

"That's not what I meant, Sophia."

Her comment bit into me. We were getting on each other's nerves this morning, and it was more than usual. For the past few weeks we'd been hanging out more often, but it was always with Jonah and Imogen around. We hadn't really been alone since we'd woken up in the clearing, but it was obvious something was different.

Nothing had progressed since that night by the waterfall, and it was bothering both of us. The tension was so bad I thought we were both about to burst.

I think Sophia wanted an answer on what we were. And I wasn't ready to give that yet, because I didn't know myself.

"I'm fine with you touching me anywhere— you know what I mean," I said when Sophia smirked. I could hear Esis' little chatters of delight from inside the bag. "What I mean to say is, it doesn't bother me. But I can't drive this thing if you make me pass out."

Sophia turned a little paler than before. "I'm just scared to fall off."

I gave her a look and lowered my voice. "Do you honestly think I would ever let you fall?"

Her expression cleared. She shook her head, and a few strands of hair fell into her face. "No."

"Good." I turned back around, and her arms encompassed me once again. "Then stop being a baby, and just trust me."

Sophia reluctantly put her arms back around my middle. This time she was holding on a little less tightly. I started off at a slow speed, then pushed the accelerator until the trees were racing by in a blur.

"Hold on," I yelled. "I'm going to speed up."

She didn't respond, so I kicked it into high gear. The bike's speed became faster and faster, until I really had to focus on where I was going in order to keep it steady. I took sharp turns and curves at a high speed, leaning into them. Sophia followed my movements easily instead of resisting against them, and for a moment, it was like we were one body.

There was a large hill that ended in a drop-off into the sea. The trees parted and disappeared as we raced up the hill. Sophia looked ahead and noticed there was nothing below but the ocean.

"Liam!" she screamed. I laughed and launched the bike off the hill and up into the air.

The bike was suspended for several moments. It was like everything was in slow motion. Sophia was screaming, and I felt more alive than I had in weeks.

We crashed down on the ocean, but instead of sinking into the water, we started riding on top of it. I barely had to think about it as the water rushed upward to support the bike. Sophia gasped in amazement, and I grinned wildly as I pushed the bike to its limit.

We had to be going a hundred and fifty miles an hour on the water. Water splayed out on both sides of the bike as I drove upon the ocean, and Sophia's screams turned to whoops of happiness. I could feel her racing heartbeat pounding through my back. Esis let out a exhilarated cheer from within the bag. I went breathless for a moment, loving riding my bike on the sea. Ancestors, I loved the water.

Dolphins jumped up beside the bike, and a whale in the distance smacked its tail down to say hello. I performed a few fancy maneuvers and did a wheelie to impress Sophia. The water was there to support the bike each time, putting it back in balance if I made a mismove. Sophia's fear had turned to joy. By the time the platform came into view, I actually heard her let out a little sound of disappointment.

The platform was nothing more than a wooden surface suspended in the middle of the ocean, almost a hundred yards long. I slowed down, and the water rose to make a ramp up to it for the bike to ride. I parked the bike, and we got off. Sophia's hair was a mess, and so was Esis'. He looked puffier than usual when she took him out of the bag.

"Wow, Liam. That was... it was incredible," she said, and her words were a little stuttered.

"Glad I pushed you now?" I asked. We walked toward the center, where Baine, Imogen, Jonah, Squeaks and Sassy were already waiting. I nudged her shoulder, and she nudged mine.

"It's nice of the two of you to show up," Baine started. He seemed in a sour mood, but I couldn't imagine why. It was killing my vibe. I was the only one allowed to be an asshole, after all.

"Sorry we're late, Professor," Sophia started. "It was my fault. I had something I needed to do before I came."

My curiosity peaked. What was Sophia doing before she met up with me?

"Miss Henley, I understand that you have a life, but from this moment on nothing is more important than this tournament," Baine said. "I hope you can understand that."

Sophia nodded meekly. Baine waved his hand and said, "Start practicing drills. We'll begin in a moment."

We separated. Sophia began practice by tossing fireballs around, while Imogen and Jonah started casting with both Earth and Air. I was more or less bored, just weaving water around. How was this going to help us survive, exactly? Baine needed to start teaching us what to do, instead of just barking at us. I felt completely unprepared for this.

"Hey, Liam, can I talk to you?" Jonah asked after a few minutes. He approached me like he had something important to say.

"Uh... sure, buddy," I started. What was this about? Jonah led me to the other side of the platform, away from everyone's earshot.

"I wanted to address the elephant in the room." Jonah seemed somber. What could this possibly mean?"

"Uh, okay," I said. I shrugged. "What's up?"

He sighed very dramatically. "I'm sorry, but I feel like I have to tell you this. You've been acting... different, lately, and I think I know why."

I couldn't breathe. This was an emergency. Did he figure out my secret? Had he put together that there was more between me and Sophia than I was willing to admit? My heart thudded against my ribcage. "Jonah, listen. It's not what it looks like."

"Don't try to deny it, Liam. I'm not blind," Jonah started. "You've been acting like a lovestruck puppy, and while it's cute, it's really desperate and kind of sad."

This was it. He was going to guess, and I couldn't deny it. If it was that obvious to him, how many other people had put it together?

"You can't tell anyone," I started. "People would freak out if they knew."

"Liam, baby, trust me. I'm not going to tell a soul," he said. "It would be *so embarrassing* if people knew you had a crush on me."

Had a crush on... then it hit me.

Oh. My. Ancestors. The buffoon actually thought that I was acting weird lately because I liked *him*, but in all reality, I'd been weird because I liked...

"That's not what it is." I shook my head. "Jonah, I'm not gay, I like—"

"Don't try to deny it, Liam. I know I'm hard to resist, even for a straight guy like you," Jonah said.

"Jonah, it's not—"

"Look, Liam, we've been friends since we were like, six. It's just gross," Jonah said. "You know I like Renar, and to be honest, you're too scrawny to be part of *this* package." He gestured to himself. "I'm just not that into you. I hope you understand."

My mouth dropped open. Jonah patted me on the shoulder and said, "There, there. I know I'm not easy to get over, but you'll find someone else."

I was too shocked to do anything. Jonah put his arms around me and gave me a really tight hug. "It's okay, bro. I know you're broken hearted, but we can still be friends."

He gave me a fucking *kiss on the cheek* before he ambled off to talk to Imogen. I was left standing on the platform with an open mouth.

What. The. Fuck? Was everyone going crazy around here?

Jonah should know I wasn't into him. I liked girls! It was clear I was into—

I stopped myself dead in my tracks. I wasn't going there. I promised myself weeks ago I'd stop.

Not that it was working, anyhow.

Sophia had made her way over, curious. "That looked really intense."

I shut my gaping mouth. I went to the other side of the platform to be by myself and, apparently, quit giving Jonah the wrong idea. Baine reached out and grabbed me by the arm.

"Liam, a moment please," he said, turning me around.

Oh, by the ancestors. Did he think I was in love with him, too? "What?" I snapped, in a tone more vicious than I intended.

Baine raised an eyebrow, and inwardly, I recoiled. Baine was still my head of House, and an Elder on the council, too. I needed to show him respect.

"Sorry," I said quickly. "What is it?"

Baine let go of my arm and stepped back. "It's the last training session before the tournament. It's only a few days away. There isn't any time left for me to deliberate. We need a Captain."

Inwardly, I groaned. I already knew where this was heading. "I don't want to be responsible for anybody. I'm no Captain."

"I don't think you have much of a choice. Imogen and Jonah aren't leaders; they're followers. You already know that."

"Why not choose Sophia?" I asked. "She's Koigni. They're born to do that type of shit."

"I *was* going to choose Sophia, but she isn't ready. The potential is there, but she's not in a place where she can back up a team, Liam. That means it's up to you. They need a Captain."

"I'm not a leader," I said, shaking my head and backing away.

"On the contrary. Nashoma wasn't any mere wolf. He was an Alpha. And he wouldn't have chosen anyone who wasn't his equal," Baine said firmly.

Did he really have to bring my Familiar into this? "Nashoma isn't here."

"But you are. And there has to be someone who leads the pack," Baine said. "Listen, Liam. I know you don't want it to be all up to you, but if there's no chain of command and no one for them to follow, it's going to lead to disorganization. Then you're all going to die out there."

He really knew how to sell it to a guy. "Fine," I said, rather salty. "I'll be the damn Captain. Just don't expect them to listen to me."

Baine ignored me. He led me back to the center of the platform where the rest of the group was waiting.

"Liam's the boss," Baine announced to the group. "He'll be serving as your Captain. You'll be taking orders from him during the Elemental Cup."

"What?" The gust of wind Jonah had been blowing around died instantly. "But Sophia—"

"Needs more time. Time we don't have," Baine said strictly. "Does anyone have a problem with it?"

Jonah opened his mouth, but before he could say anything, Baine answered, "Good. Then let's move on."

Jonah shut his trap and gave me a look that obviously said he thought we were all going to die. Imogen seemed nervous. Did these people really think I was that incompetent?

I couldn't blame them, really. I didn't believe in myself either.

Sophia didn't seem bothered she wasn't Captain. In fact, she looked relieved.

"Gather around," Baine announced. We stood in a circle around him, and he said, "The first thing we should do is test your weaknesses and see where you stand."

He snapped his fingers and pointed at Imogen. "You. You're the shortest. I've noticed you've had trouble summoning your element."

"Yes, sir," Imogen said. She looked around, unsure of where this was going.

"Earth Elementai are supposed to be strong— the strongest of all the elements. We need to know you can carry your weight... and be able to move mountains."

Baine fixed his glasses, thinking. He pointed to Jonah. "Your team-mates might get injured during the tournament, and it'll be critical that you can get them to safety. I want you to try and carry Jonah for me, please."

I nearly choked. He had to be kidding. I'm pretty sure Jonah's one arm weighed more than Imogen's entire body. She was barely five feet. She hardly came up to his waist.

Jonah, of course, was more than willing for an opportunity to play actor. Jonah laid down on the platform and pretended to be dead, squinting through one eye to peer at her.

"Well, come on," Jonah said. "I'm bleeding out, here."

Imogen gulped. We were in the middle of the ocean, so unless she shifted the ocean floor, which was already wet and unstable, she wouldn't be able to move Jonah. She instead tried the old-fashioned way and swung his limp arm over her shoulder before wiggling under his back to carry him on her back.

Imogen tried to lift Jonah, but all it resulted in was Imogen falling over.

"Come on, Imogen. You can do this," Baine encouraged.

This guy was asking for the moon. Imogen eventually managed to get Jonah onto her back, before she huffed and puffed for a few moments and tumbled over sideways again. Sassy tried to help her by putting Jonah's leg on her back, but it flattened the poor fox to the ground.

"I've seen what I needed to," Baine said, waving his hand. "Please stop."

Imogen was breathing like she had just lost a marathon. Jonah gave her a look and said, "You've killed me. Way to go."

"Jonah," Baine said abruptly. "It's your turn. I want you to cross the platform— without making a sound. Sneaking around and staying silent will be crucial for your success during the tournament, and your size already puts you at a disadvantage."

Jonah straightened up. He swallowed nervously before nodding. He crunched into a sneaking position. His crouch was still about the height of an average person.

I had the immediate thought that Jonah should take off his gigantic boots, but Jonah was dumb, and I couldn't help him. Every step he took across the platform sounded like it was coming from a giant.

Squeaks didn't help. Her hooves tip-toeing across the wooden platform resembled a tap dance. Before they reached the end, she tripped, and she sprawled into Jonah head over hooves. The two of them made a crashing sound as they rolled off the platform and into the water.

Baine seethed as Squeaks and Jonah pulled themselves out of the ocean. He was getting agitated. "Very well."

He turned around and looked at me. "Liam, we already know your weakness is going to be endurance. But there's no way to test that with the amount of time we have, and there will be little rest during the tournament, so you're going to have to find a way," Baine said simply.

"Gee, thanks," I grumbled, and I crossed my arms. He didn't need to remind me that I'd already be slowing the team down out there. But coming in last place was better than not making it there at all.

"Sophia!" Baine said abruptly, and she started. "I want you to create fire-rain and shelter the rest of us from it."

"Like... right now?" she asked meekly.

"You have to be able to control and sustain fire at a moment's notice, without thinking about it. By now it should be second nature to you," Baine said. "There's no telling what kind of firepower you'll have to fight against during the tournament. You need to learn to expect what's coming."

Baine looked at her expectantly, and so did everyone else. I glanced away to try and take the pressure off her, but I think she took it as a sign I didn't believe in her, because her face became more panicked.

She raised her hands, palms facing the open sky. Her arms shook as she tried to make fireballs rain down from the heavens, but all she managed to do was make a few embers trickle down through the air.

I didn't like fire, obviously. Hated it, in fact. But I still felt bad for Sophia for being unable to control her element. This was advanced Koigni stuff— things that older students would know, not freshmen.

But it didn't matter. There were people of all ages in the Elemental Cup. She had to be just as good as the others if we were going to make it through this.

"Come on, Sophia," Baine growled. He pushed her, bunching his hand into a fist to shake it at her encouragingly. "You can do this! You have the potential!"

"I'm sorry!" she yelled. Her face scrunched intensely. "Just... give me a few moments to get angry!"

Sophia, you haven't learned anything. She thought firepower was about being pissed off all the time, and that wasn't it at all.

Course, that was probably my fault. I'd been the one how to teach her to access her element, after all.

Sophia gave a gasp and doubled over. A few fireballs came down from the sky, but they were small and sizzled out quickly in the ocean. All that was left was a few lingering flames flickering around her fingers.

When she looked at me again, the fire in her hands blazed out of control. Baine had to bring up water out of the ocean to put it out.

"Boo!" Jonah shouted, giving a thumbs down. Squeaks copied him and gave a hiss. Sophia blushed and quickly put her Fire away.

I felt so bad for her. She'd just been introduced to this world, and already, she was trying to do magic that I wouldn't expect seniors to be able to do on a whim.

"This isn't getting anywhere." Baine sighed and rubbed his eyebrows. "All right. I've had enough. I'm just going to throw you into it."

Baine walked toward the edge of the platform. He knelt down by the water and whispered something to it before he stood. He was watching the waves closely, eyes narrowed.

I could feel her beneath us, moving through the water. The ripples she created washed over my skin, even though I was standing here dry on the platform. She wasn't but a few feet below us. A long shadow loomed underneath the platform, and the water trembled as a low croon emitted from the ocean.

"What's that?" Sophia said in fear. She backed up a few steps, looking around. Esis was doing the same, glancing this way and that from Squeaks' back. Sassy danced nervously, waiting.

I smiled. "Thalassa's coming."

"Who?"

It soon grew too loud to answer. The swelling of waves crashed upon the sea, and the clouds parted as the shadow grew closer to the surface, the sun blazing down on a magnificent creature that crashed out of the water.

She was bigger than any Familiar I'd ever seen— even bigger than Alric's Familiar, Valda, or Costas' Familiar, Hera. Her scales were a dark cerulean blue, and they shone as she broke through the water and leapt over the platform, performing an elaborate jump. Sophia's jaw dropped as she watched Thalassa soar over us and dive back down on the other side, causing a huge wave to rise up and come crashing back down. Thalassa broke the surface again, splashing her beautifully fanned tail behind her.

The sea serpent had kind eyes that glimmered like sapphires, long lashes in the designs of coral donning her eyelids. She held her massive webbed paws in front of her body and looked down at us from high above. Thalassa was so big, she nearly blocked out the sun. What little light that did burst through hit her blue scales and bounced off in a million different directions, creating rainbows. There were wings on her back, enabling her to glide if needed, but they functioned more as fins than for flight. Thin spines lined along her back, and two pointed horns accented the top of her head, thin whiskers drooping down from her lips. She smiled slightly, revealing sharp and pointed teeth.

Baine's face brightened in joy, and he laughed, spreading his arms out wide. Thalassa lowered her head so that it was at Baine's level, and he wrapped his arms around it (what he could, anyway). Her skull was larger than Baine's entire body. Her eyes closed in happiness, and she let out a contented note that was high-pitched and shook the platform.

"*That's* Baine's Familiar?" Sophia squeaked.

"Not what you were expecting, is she?" I asked smugly.

"She's so beautiful," Imogen whispered in awe, and she held tighter onto Sassy.

Baine let go of Thalassa and motioned her downward. She lay her head on the platform. He climbed on and sat in the nook where her head ended and her neck began. He held on to her horns as he rose back up.

"Your task for the day will be to subdue Thalassa and me," Baine called from above. "If you can get us to submit, you'll have passed the final session and be ready for the tournament."

"But... she's a Water creature. What about my Fire?" Sophia asked reluctantly.

"You won't hurt her. Trust me," Baine said. "Not even your Fire will be enough to damage her— not at Year One level. What I'm asking is for you to get her to surrender."

"Believe me, Sophia. All your Fire could do to her is tickle," I told her.

"I'll give you five minutes to strategize before I make my attack." Baine hung on as Thalassa dove downward and swam away.

I turned to the group and tried to think. This was going to be a challenge. Thalassa was practically a mile long, and she was a goddess of the water. Pinning her down was going to be near impossible.

"First things first," I told the group. "We need to get changed."

"I'm always down to strip," Jonah said. Thankfully, everybody was wearing their wetsuits underneath their clothes, so I wasn't subjected to that. I paced by the waterway and tried to come up with a solution.

"Well?" Jonah asked me. "What's the plan, big guy? We've got like, two minutes left."

"Give me a minute," I muttered. I had to play to Thalassa's weaknesses, but as far as I knew, she didn't have any.

"Sophia, Imogen, get onto Squeaks," Jonah told them. "She's not big enough to carry me, but she can handle you two."

Imogen and Sophia did just that, and Esis joined Sassy on the platform. Who was leader, here? "Jonah will be able to fly around. I'll handle being on the water," I told them. "We'll take Thalassa and Baine on from all sides."

"What's our strategy?" Imogen asked me.

I didn't know. Taking on Baine alone during the first training session had been hard enough. I didn't know how we were going to beat him and Thalassa.

"I might be able to pin her down in the ocean. Make the currents strong enough so she can't move. If you guys distract her, I'll make it so she won't know what's coming."

"Will it work?" Imogen asked.

I shrugged. "It's a long shot."

Jonah looked up, and his face paled. "Well, it's what we got, because she's coming this way!"

Thalassa was sailing toward us full speed, carrying Baine, who had summoned a large wave behind him. Squeaks took off with Sophia and Imogen, and I leapt into the water. It swelled around my middle and carried me throughout the ocean, safely out of the way. Jonah jumped off the platform. The air carried him upward so that he was floating far above Thalassa. Esis and Sassy stayed on the platform and ducked, getting soaked by Baine's wave.

"Now, guys!" I shouted. I summoned deep waters from below and surged them over Thalassa's body, trying to make her stay still, but controlling her fins was like holding back a propeller on the *Hozho*. She was strong.

Our attack was disorganized. Instead of working together as a unit, we all seemed to be doing our own thing. Jonah, Sophia and Imogen all focused on a different place on her body to attack instead of one spot, shooting their elements at her with everything they had. Thalassa shook as if brushing off flies and yawned.

Sassy and Esis were still on the platform. They ran back and forth, throwing little pebbles and coral that had washed up on the wood at Thalassa to get her attention. Obviously, she gave them none.

Esis got tired of being ignored. He jumped off the platform and onto Thalassa's tail, running up her back and avoiding the little spines. He wove this way and that, avoiding Baine as he reached her head and beat his tiny little fists into Thalassa's temple.

"Esis!" Sophia shouted. "Get back here!"

He didn't listen to her and kept ramming her on the forehead. Thalassa's eyes crossed to look at him, as if he was an annoyance.

The brave little fucker. I was honestly impressed. "Sophia, get Esis back to you!" I shouted. "This is it!"

Squeaks flew close to Thalassa, and Esis leapt from Thalassa's head and into Sophia's arms. They soared out of the way just as Thalassa clamped her jaws over the air they'd been soaring through a moment before.

There was no coddling at Orenda Academy, obviously. Baine didn't mind breaking our bodies if it meant we'd be prepared for the competition.

Esis had given me an idea, though I wasn't quite sure what it was yet. I broke my concentration and scanned over my teammates. Despite Sophia shooting out fireballs, Imogen tossing large sections of sand over Thalassa's back to weigh her down, and Jonah doing his best to create a windstorm that kept her in place, Thalassa acted like she was out for a morning swim. She paddled around, almost bored and opened her mouth to roar at us. It sent Squeaks into a spiral she only recovered from last minute.

Baine wasn't bothered, either. He was easily holding on to Thalassa with one hand and keeping my magic at bay with the other. I was at war with Baine, and though I found I could keep up with him, which was encouraging, I couldn't surpass him.

The plan wasn't working. Thalassa was too big to control, and Baine had too much power over the water. We couldn't beat them in a show of brute strength. We were going to have to improvise.

My mind worked furiously. This session was all about weaknesses, but it seemed like neither one of them had any.

One of Sophia's fireballs went rogue and went ricocheting toward Baine. It was already fizzling out, but Thalassa turned quickly and brought her tail fin up to block Baine from the hailing embers.

I was confused. The fireball wouldn't have even hurt Baine if it did hit him, but Thalassa protected him anyway.

Then it clicked. Thalassa *did* have a weakness. It was Baine.

"Guys!" I shouted. "Get in front of Thalassa! Keep her eyes ahead!"

"Are you crazy?" Jonah screeched. "That's right in the line of fire!"

"It's only for a few moments!" My tone seemed to convince them, because Sophia steered Squeaks in front of Thalassa and started shooting. Her fireballs smacked at Thalassa's snout, while Imogen's mud-pies splattered in the serpent's eyes. Jonah blasted an assault of wind at Thalassa, causing her to be unable to go forward. Sassy stood on the platform, yipping as loud as she could.

Thalassa shook her head and closed her eyes, trying to stop the assault so she could see again. Baine was forced to grab on with both hands in order to keep himself balanced, and his magic instantly halted.

"There's the opening," I whispered. But instead of trying to subdue Thalassa, I went for Baine. I lashed out a hand and a stream of water raced upward and wrapped itself around Baine's torso, pinning his arms so he couldn't use his element. I yanked it downward, and Baine was dragged underneath the ocean on a trip to the bottom.

Thalassa screeched. She splashed around, kicking her large flippers in search of Baine, and causing a tidal wave.

When she didn't find him, she twirled around and looked at me.

"Give up, Thalassa," I told her calmly. "It's over."

Thalassa lowered her head calmly and bowed to me. Only then did I bring Baine splashing to the surface. The four of us returned to the platform. Thalassa brought Baine back up to us with her tail, placing him gently beside us.

"Well done!" Baine coughed and wiped water away from his eyes. "Well done, children!"

"Did we pass?" Imogen asked, squeezing Sassy.

"With flying colors. I daresay you're ready for the Elemental Cup to begin." Baine swept his hair out of his eyes.

What a relief. I felt a little better, before I realized that this was it — there were no more training sessions. Next time, it'd be the real deal.

"I applaud your innovation, Liam," Baine congratulated me. "Sometimes you've got to outsmart what's in front of you instead of beating it down."

I nodded. I felt a little bad we'd won by manipulation, but hey, this was life or death. "Thanks, Professor."

"I suggest all of you rest up as much as you can before the tournament, and train sparingly, as to not reach your peak before its time," Baine said. "You'll do well. All of you."

His opinion of us had drastically changed in a short time. Taking that as a dismissal, I headed toward my bike, which was now waterlogged, by the way. I motioned for Sophia. She slid off of Squeaks and joined me.

I successfully drained all the water out of my bike and was able to get it started again, but it ran like shit. Like, shittier than before. Despite being Toaqua-proof, this thing was seeing the end of its days. I got back on and Sophia slid behind me. Esis scurried across the platform and jumped into the saddlebag. We took off before Baine could hold us back.

I drove slow on the way back to Orenda. I hid the bike back in the bushes before I leaned against the stone wall, looking at Sophia. She seemed like she... disapproved of something. Esis sat at her feet, looking up at her.

"Shouldn't we have stuck around to talk more about the tournament?" she asked.

My stomach clenched nervously. "I didn't want to stand around and talk about the inevitable," I told her. "I hate discussing variables and what-ifs. I'll just take life as it happens."

"It's not just about you," she said. "Jonah and Imogen are nervous, too. Especially Imogen." Sophia sighed. "She's worried she's going to end up like... well."

Yeah, I'd heard what had happened to Imogen's brother last year. It'd been brutal.

"It's just going to make us more anxious," I said. "We need to focus on the now."

"You mean enjoying the time we have left."

Her tone was so direct. I put my hands in my pockets. "Yes."

Her expression didn't change. I knew what she was thinking. She thought I was running— like I wanted to run from my sickness, from a possible diagnosis, from everything.

So what if I was? I wanted to keep running. Just a little while longer.

"Why would you do that to Professor Baine, drag him under like that?" Sophia asked. "He could've died."

"It's pretty hard to drown a Toaqua," I told her. "We can hold our breath longer than others. Baine was never in any danger."

She pushed her hair away from her eyes. "It seemed cruel."

"We did what we had to do. Like we'll have to do out there," I insisted. "We don't have a choice."

"What if we do?"

"Sophia, we've been over this," I said firmly. "Elementai society doesn't work that way."

She huffed before she changed the subject. "I can see why Baine keeps Thalassa in the ocean instead of with him," Sophia said. Her tone was lighter, and she was trying to smile.

"Right. Can you imagine fitting her in the castle? Insane." I gave her a weak grimace back. Fuck, I was tired. I didn't realize it until now, but my entire body was aching. Fighting Baine today had wreaked havoc on me, and he wasn't even the worst we'd face out there. To make things worse, I could feel a cold coming on. My chest was congested and my head throbbing. It'd come out of nowhere, no warning.

We were in trouble. I had to get better before the tournament, otherwise, Imogen would be dragging *me* around instead of Jonah. Right now, all I wanted to do was crawl back to my dorm, take a long bath, and go to sleep.

"Hey, Sophia," I said, and I pushed off the wall. "I don't really feel well. Talk to you later?"

"Okay." She frowned, seemingly sad to see me go. I went to walk off, but before I could, she called out, "Liam?"

My heart throbbed. I turned back around. "Yes?"

She hesitated before she cautiously said, "I was thinking... about the Elemental Ball... would you like to go with me?"

My cold was temporarily forgotten. It felt like I was rushing through the ocean a million miles an hour. Sophia was asking *me* to the dance?

I knew what the rules were, that I should say no, but I wanted to say yes. Really badly. I opened my mouth, torn between the two answers, but the only stupid thing that came out was, "But... aren't I supposed to ask you?"

She gaped at me for a moment, unsure of what to say before her face turned red. "How dare you!" She stomped forward, and Esis covered his eyes. "These... these aren't the *Dark Ages*, you know! Independent, strong women can ask men out to dances whenever they like!"

"Um," I started, having no idea what she was talking about.

Her expression changed. It went from really pissed to really, really depressed.

"Never mind," Sophia said. "It was a stupid idea. I just thought—"

"No." I caught her wrist as she turned away, and she looked back up at me. "No, Sophia, I— I would really like that. I'd love to go to the ball with you."

Her eyes brightened. "Are you serious?"

"Yeah." I let go of her wrist and nodded. "It'd be cool."

It'd be cool. Really fucking smooth, Liam. I'm pretty sure at our feet, Esis did another facepalm.

"Oh." It wasn't the reaction she'd been looking for, but what did she expect? For me to grab her and sweep her off into the sunset? Did girls still want those types of things? Hell, I didn't know.

"Is that okay?" I asked. By the ancestors, I was going to puke. She was going to take it back, because I couldn't even say yes the right way.

"Of course." She smiled. "I guess it's a date."

She slayed me. A fucking date. "Awesome." I backed away. "I can't wait to go to the ball with you."

"Me either." She held her breath. "That is, if we make it through the tournament."

"We'll make it," I said instantly. "No problem."

"Your attitude sure has changed." She grinned.

"I want to go to that ball, and I want you there with me," I said. "Trust me. We'll be partying as full Elementai by the end of the tournament."

Her expression brightened like the fire she cast. She waved goodbye, and Esis copied her movement. I raised a hand in farewell before I headed into the castle. I was practically skipping up the steps.

Shit, a dance. I needed a suit. And better shoes. I hated dances. What was wrong with me?

My mind whirled with questions of why Sophia would pick me to be her date for the ball. Maybe it was a way for Sophia to redo her prom and have a better one with me.

Me. She asked *me.* Who was acting like the girl now?

As I walked up the steps to the dorms, the cold came rampaging back, and I felt awful, but I hardly cared. I was going on an official date with Sophia Henley. *To the Elemental Ball.*

Things had changed now. I was determined to survive this fucking tournament, come hell or high water. All to put on a monkey suit and dance with the girl of my dreams.

Some women were just worth walking through firestorms for.

sophia
EIGHTEEN

I t was finally here. The day of the tournament.

And I was freaking. The eff. Out.

"We haven't practiced enough. We should've trained longer. What are we going to do without Baine out there with us?" I paced back and forth in mine and Imogen's changing room, my hands shaking. My Fire raged just on the surface, begging to escape. "Oh God, Imogen! What if someone gets hurt and Esis has to heal them? Liam will kill me when he finds out I never told him—"

Imogen's palm cracked against the side of my face. "Pull yourself together, woman!"

I froze in place, completely shocked. Did Imogen just *slap* me? What the hell?

"Seriously, Sophia. You can't go out there like this." Imogen acted tough, but I could see the worry in her eyes. She crossed the room and sank into one of the chairs in front of the big mirrors lined with bright lights.

Our morning had started with a big celebratory breakfast for the contestants, followed by a speech from Head Dean Alric. It was supposed to prep us for the tournament and get us motivated, but afterward, I only felt more clueless and hopeless than ever.

After Alric's big speech, our teams had been ushered into carriages pulled by unicorns and led away from the castle. Liam gave us a pep talk in the carriage, but it sounded forced and nervous, like he was only doing it because he was team Captain.

When the carriages stopped, we entered a huge stone building at least five stories tall. The arena. Through the trees, I couldn't even see either end of it. The exterior looked a lot like a mini version of the castle, but the inside was more modern. We followed everyone else down a long hall with doors that had our names on them. The rooms were the size of my dorm, with two sets of uniforms hanging from the hooks on the wall to our right and loads of makeup sitting on the counter in front of the dressing mirrors on our left. There were chocolates set out for us, but I didn't have the appetite to eat them. As soon as Imogen and I were safely inside our shared room, I promptly started to freak out.

"Let's just take it one step at a time," Imogen suggested, taking a deep breath.

"Okay," I agreed, but I couldn't keep the worry from my tone. "First step?"

"First step is to get dressed before our makeup artist arrives."

"Makeup artist?" I asked, glancing to all the hair and makeup supplies in front of us. "Isn't that kind of... pointless?"

"We have to look nice for the opening ceremony," Imogen said, like it was obvious. She grabbed a blush brush and began tickling the end of Sassy's nose with it. Esis jumped out of my arms and joined Sassy on the counter, waiting patiently for his makeover.

"Why does anyone care?" I asked. "Our makeup will be a mess after the first trial."

Imogen shrugged. "I don't know. They just want us to make a good impression. We want to look good on TV, and it'll help us win bets."

I gaped at her. "This thing is *televised*?!"

She nodded. "On our local station."

"And no one bothered to tell me?" I started pacing again.

"I didn't realize you didn't know," she said innocently.

"And what's this about bets?" I demanded.

"Oh," she said, like it was no big deal. "It's mostly to raise money for the school, since they get a portion. But it gets everyone in Kinpago involved and excited."

My eyes went wide. "They're excited to watch their own children die?"

Imogen's face fell, and she turned away from me. Shit. I'd gone a step too far. I really did need to pull myself together, or I was going to tear my team apart.

"I'm sorry, Imogen," I said softly, taking a step toward her. "I didn't mean—"

"No, you're right," she cut me off. "It's sick. Really, it is. I never said I agreed with it. Let's just get ready, okay?"

I nodded and turned to the uniform marked *Sophia* on the wall. The shirt was a form-fitting, sweat-wicking t-shirt. It was completely black, except for the white cap sleeves. On the back was a red emblem in the shape of a flame. I slipped off my lucky jeans and pulled the uniform pants on. They were made of a soft black fabric and hung loose and comfortable on my hips. They had tons of pockets on them. Finally, I put on a pair of high-top hiking boots, also black. Everything fit perfectly. Imogen's uniform was the same as mine, except with a green leaf on her back for Nivita.

It wasn't long before our makeup artist showed up with a tiny chameleon-like Familiar at her side. The woman's name was Coco, a shortened version of a Hawkei name I couldn't pronounce. She was thin and tall, with legs that went on for miles and sleek black hair that fell to her waist. She had long eyelashes that were probably fake and perfectly manicured eyebrows. Her eyeliner was flawless.

"Hello, ladies," Coco greeted with a smile. "Are you ready to get beautified?"

Coco was nice enough, but I got the sense that she didn't like me and Imogen. At first, I declined makeup at all. I wasn't trying to impress anyone. But Imogen insisted I go with at least a subtle amount of makeup for the cameras.

"Okay, but I'm not coloring in my brows or using lipstick," I compromised.

"Please," Coco begged. "You'll look beautiful. I promise." Clearly she was hoping to showcase her best skills for us.

"I'd rather not," I said, actually proud of myself for not caving in. "But I'll let you curl my hair."

Coco looked pleased with that, but frowned when I promptly pulled my fresh curls into a high ponytail. Imogen let her go all-out on the makeup, but when Coco insisted on taking the green bows out of her high pigtails, Imogen protested.

"Sorry, but no can do," Imogen said. "The bows and the pigtails are here to stay."

"If that's what you want." Coco tried to hide her disappointment, but I could hear it in her voice.

"Are you ready?" Imogen asked as soon as Coco left. She took a long, nervous breath.

"I guess so," I answered, glancing at my bag in front of me on the counter. "I just wish I would've had a chance this morning to talk to Amelia."

A knock came at the door, and someone stuck their head inside. "What about me?"

I leapt up from my chair and threw my arms around Amelia's neck. "Am! I'm so glad you're here."

Amelia slipped inside the room, followed by Kiwi. "I had to sneak in, but it was worth it. I wanted to wish you good luck out there."

"Thank you," I said. "So... how bad is it? The tournament."

Amelia frowned. "I'm not going to lie. It's tough, but if you stick with your team and work together, there's no reason you shouldn't make it."

I could think of about a thousand reasons.

"I placed a bet on you, so you better make it," Amelia said with a laugh.

"I will," I promised, even though I knew now wasn't the time to be making promises I couldn't keep. "We all will."

I sniffled involuntarily and turned to my bag to pull out a small envelope.

"I wanted to give this to you, Am... to give to Mom and Dad." I handed her the envelope and wiped my eyes. "It's not much, just stupid stuff like how much I love them and that no matter what happened when I was a baby, I still love them and—"

Amelia's body crashed into mine, halting my babbling in its tracks.

She squeezed me tightly, which only made me more emotional. A tear slid down my cheek.

"It'll be okay, Sophia," she said, her voice cracking.

"Great," Imogen said lightly. "Now I'm going to cry."

I gestured to her, and she joined us in a group hug. Esis hopped off the counter and onto Imogen's shoulder, wrapping his tiny arms around my neck. Sassy rubbed her fur against our ankles.

Amelia drew away when a whistle sounded from down the hall. "That's your five-minute warning. I better leave before they line you up. I'll be in the stands cheering you on, okay?"

I nodded.

"Here." Imogen shoved a tissue in my face, and I gladly took it. I had already ruined my makeup. I knew it was stupid to put it on.

"Bye." Amelia waved as she left the room. It felt like my insides were caving as I watched her go.

I cradled Esis in my arms, and we waved back. Before the door swung shut, Jonah stuck his head inside.

"You two beauty queens ready?" he asked. "It's time to line up."

Imogen scooped up Sassy, and we followed Jonah out into the hall. It was crowded with contestants, all wearing the same uniform except with different colored sleeves and symbols for their Houses. Jonah and Liam both had white sleeves to match mine and Imogen's uniforms. Baine stood there with his hands crossed in front of him, looking proud. Squeaks followed beside them. I tried to catch Liam's gaze, but he just stared ahead down the hall with a hard look on his face.

Hiding his emotions once again, I see.

A guy with a goatee who didn't look much older than me held a clipboard in his hand and was directing everyone to where they needed to go. "This way and to the right," he called. "Make way for Familiars. Line up in this order: white, purple, pink, blue, yellow..."

Nobody really paid attention beyond his first instructions. We all started down the hall and to the right.

"Of course we're first," Liam mumbled.

I glanced between Imogen and Jonah. "Is that a bad thing?"

I mean, I didn't want to go first, but Liam made it sound like it had some sort of hidden meaning.

Imogen leaned over and whispered to me. "They save the best for last."

"Oh," I said flatly. Which meant everyone expected the least from us. We really were the reject team. "They must've placed us in the wrong spot." I only said it to uplift my team, but I could see it on their faces that they all knew I was bluffing.

We entered a large corridor wider than the Koigni common room, with a high ceiling fit for a dragon to pass through. I wasn't surprised when I saw a red dragon at the end of the hall. TVs lined the wall opposite us. They all played the same thing, but it was too loud in the corridor to hear what was happening on the TV.

"White Team, you're first," the guy with the goatee repeated. It was difficult to hear him over all the chatter.

"Come on," Jonah said glumly, gesturing to the front of the line. "Wouldn't want someone taking our spot."

"Don't let this get you down," Baine said. "You're ready for this."

"Losers!" a Koigni guy called as we passed him.

Liam whirled around, but Jonah caught him. "Save your energy for the course," Jonah warned, pushing him along.

Reluctantly, Liam gave in. We stopped at the end of the hall beside a pair of huge doors that looked like they belonged in an aircraft hangar.

"Let's come up with a motto," Imogen suggested. "We're seriously lacking some team spirit."

"How about *Let's not fucking die?*" Liam offered, crossing his arms.

I was preoccupied, my attention locked down the hall. I was trying to get a good look at which team they were saving for last. My eyes caught Haley's at the back of the line. She smirked, sending my blood pressure skyrocketing. She stood next to Doya, but thank God Doya didn't notice my eyes on them. Beside them was a Koigni guy with tree trunks for arms, who was petting the dragon I'd seen earlier. Haley and him weren't on the same team, as evidenced by their mismatched sleeve colors— hers red and his metallic silver— but they were definitely both top picks.

I glanced around for other members of the Red Team. I spotted a huge Nivita guy who had to be half-giant. He stood beside a creature that looked like a lion carved from marble, though it moved with ease.

The Yapluma member of their team was a girl with short black hair spiked in the front. She had at least three piercings, two in her lip and one in her nose. Her eyes were ringed in thick black eyeliner. She looked like the kind of girl who thought she was a vampire and would suck your blood just to prove it. Beside her sat a huge black cat similar to a jaguar, but with leathery wings attached to its back and sharp teeth that curled over its lip as if in warning.

The Toaqua girl beside them didn't have a Familiar, which I could only guess meant it was an insanely powerful sea creature like Thalassa.

I looked between Esis, Squeaks, and Sassy, then to Liam's empty side. It was pretty clear why we were going first. And damn it, I didn't want Liam to be right.

I guess we're just going to have to prove everyone wrong.

Baine stood at the front of our group and adjusted his glasses. "You have nothing to fear. The contestant pool is small this year, so the other teams shouldn't get in your way. You're prepared for whatever else you might find out there. Just trust each other, and I will see you soon."

Liam rolled his eyes and muttered, "Great pep talk."

Baine shot him a pointed expression. "Did I perhaps make a mistake in choosing the team Captain?"

Liam hesitated, then stood up straight. "No, sir."

Baine nodded approvingly. "Good. I wish you all the best of luck."

Goatee Guy rushed in front of us. "White Team, you're up in less than thirty seconds."

"Smile," Baine encouraged. "You're on TV."

Esis slapped his cheeks three times and then grinned. Nerves knotted in my gut, but I forced a smile to my face as the massive doors slid open. The intense sound of thousands of hands clapping spilled into the wide corridor. Sunlight assaulted my eyes, and I had to cover them to see properly.

"First up, we have the White Team!" an announcer's voice boomed through the speakers.

I blinked a few times before I could finally make out the scene beyond the doors. A huge stage spanned out in front of us, bigger than the concert stage at the huge music festival Amelia took me to when I was in high school. Rows upon rows of seating stretched far beyond the stage, rising high in the back of the stadium. There must've been at least ten thousand people here, if not more. It looked like most of Kinpago had come to celebrate the Elemental Cup. My heart pounded so hard that I didn't hear what Goatee Guy said. I only saw him waving us forward.

Liam led us out onto the stage, where Alric stood in front of a microphone. We stepped out into pleasant air and clear skies. I assumed this was one of those times when Elementai were allowed to control the weather. The roar of applause quickly turned to sounds of criticism. People booed us and yelled obscenities at our team. I caught a guy in the front row yelling, "Get off the stage!"

"Well, folks," the invisible announcer said with a light laugh. "It appears the White Team is *not* a fan favorite, though that's not a shocker if you've been paying attention to the board."

Liam walked across the stage rigidly, but Jonah and Imogen didn't let the comments bother them. They smiled and waved, looking excited like they were supposed to.

All I wanted to do was run back the way I came and find a place to hide in the woods or something. The tournament couldn't be any worse than what it felt like to walk across that stage. I thought I might puke right there in front of everyone.

My eyes scanned the stadium walls, keeping my gaze above everyone's head so I wouldn't have to look at the faces of my fellow Hawkei who were basically cheering for my death. My gaze fell upon a pair of huge screens. The first was an image of my team walking across the stage, reflecting this exact moment. I saw the surprise cross my expression when the camera angle switched to a close-up of my face.

Uncomfortable didn't even begin to cut it.

Beside that screen was another that showed the team colors in rows, with stats alongside them. Underneath the bets column, I saw that only three bets had been placed for our team.

Probably Amelia, Baine, and Imogen's parents. The Red Team was up to over six thousand bets.

"I think I'm going to be sick," I whispered to Imogen, but she didn't hear me over the roar of the crowd.

We stopped next to Alric at centerstage. He guided us to stand on small stickers stuck to the stage floor while the announcer continued his spiel.

"First up, we have Imogen Ahnild, Nivita, with her Familiar Sassy, a red fox!" The announcer made it all sound exciting, but the crowd didn't look pleased in the slightest. Still, Imogen beamed and waved to them despite the booing.

"Next up, Jonah Chanee, Yapluma, with his Familiar Squeaks, a hippogriff!" a second announcer said.

My heart raced, and my mouth went dry. I knew they were coming to me next, and I feared what they might say about me... about Esis.

"Beside Chanee, Sophia Henley, Koigni, with her Familiar... oh dear ancestors, what is that thing?" The first announcer let out a deep belly laugh as the cameras zoomed in on Esis.

I pulled him close to my chest. The entire stadium broke out into laughter, but he didn't notice. Esis just waved at them as if he was the star of the tournament.

"I think that may be a rabbit of sorts, Louis," the second announcer cut in.

"You think so, Eli?" the first announcer said.

"Maybe a chinchilla?" Eli guessed.

"That is certainly what it looks like," Louis said with a laugh. "Either way, I don't think it's going to help them in the tournament."

"I think you're right, Louis." Eli chuckled. "Let's move on to our final contestant on the White Team. Ladies and gentlemen, put your hands together for Liam Mitoh, Toaqua, with his Familiar—"

Eli cut off mid-sentence, and my blood ran cold. The camera's focused on Liam's face. His jaw was tense, and his skin had gone pale. One by one, the audience members began to fall silent until only whispers passed over the stadium. It was agonizing.

Eli cleared his throat into the microphone. "Liam Mitoh, Toaqua. Familiar deceased."

A gasp spread across the audience, but I had the feeling they weren't surprised at all about Nashoma's death. It was more like they were shocked Liam was showing his face and still going through with this.

Liam rolled his eyes straight at the camera and turned to Alric. "Can we get this over with or what?"

Alric's blank expression turned into a forced grin, and he leaned into his microphone. "Ladies and gentlemen, I present to you, the White Team!"

Nobody clapped for us except Imogen, Jonah, and Esis.

"Before we welcome our next team, is there anything your team would like to say?" Worry touched the corners of Alric's eyes.

Liam stepped forward, but Imogen slipped in front of the microphone before he could reach it.

"I think I speak for my entire team when I say we're really excited to be here," Imogen said in an excited voice I could tell was fake. "I won't let you down, Mom and Dad." She blew a kiss to the crowd before turning on her heel and gesturing for us to follow her to the other side of the stage where rows of chairs were set up for the contestants.

"What was that for?" Liam growled when we took our seats.

Imogen shrugged as they called the next team on stage. "I didn't trust you. You'd probably flip off the whole tribe on TV."

Liam looked momentarily shocked, but it quickly turned into a smirk.

"Translation," Jonah leaned over and whispered to me, "he was totally planning it."

Liam frowned. "I was not. Shut up and watch the ceremony."

It felt like hours before all the teams made it across the stage. Any hope I had of making it through this tournament gradually waned as they presented more and more powerful Familiars.

By the time Haley's group made it on stage, I was feeling completely hopeless.

"Red Team," Alric said. "Is there anything you'd like to say?"

Haley was the first at the microphone. Anwara fluffed her feathers, looking proud on camera. "We're so grateful for everyone's support," she said in a sickly sweet tone.

Ugh. Gag. She was so fake.

"We can't imagine how we'd *ever* make it through this tournament if you didn't believe in us." Haley shot a smirking glance my way.

I didn't let my emotions show since we were on camera, but inside, I was fuming. She was using her speech to insult us! *Bitch, our three people believe in us more than your six thousand put together!*

"You can rest assured that the Red Team will make it back to the finish line first," Haley concluded. "May the ancestors bless you!" Haley waved at the cameras, a big fake smile plastered on her face.

Alric stepped to the microphone as Haley's team headed for their seats. "As you all know, it is now time to send the contestants on their way. We will be coming to you live as soon as they hit the course. Ladies and gentlemen, one last round of applause for the contestants of this year's Elemental Cup!"

The crowd went wild. All around us, the contestants stood and cheered. I quickly got to my feet to join them, but I merely clapped for show.

Soon we were ushered backstage and outside, where the covered carriages we rode in were waiting for us. This time, however, they weren't being pulled by anything.

"Everybody in," Goatee Guy shouted. "Larger Familiars will follow behind you. All you need to remember is to head for the flag. Good luck!"

Our team climbed into our carriage. Squeaks got in last, squeezing herself between the facing benches so that her feathers brushed our legs. It was a tight fit.

"What do you think our first task will be?" Imogen asked.

"I don't know," Liam replied flatly. "That's kind of the idea, isn't it? To surprise us. That's what Baine's been training us for."

I sighed and stared out the window. "I hate surprises."

Jonah smirked. "Sweetheart, you'd better get used to them."

Just as he said it, the carriage lurched into the air like an elevator. I immediately went tense and gripped the side of my seat.

"It's just Yapluma," Jonah said lightheartedly. "Same way they move the cruise ship around."

I breathed a sigh. "Oh."

"Okay, so our team motto?" Imogen said as our carriage rose into the sky. "What was your suggestion, Liam? *Let's not fucking die?*"

Liam's expression was a strange cross between amusement and anger. "You betcha."

Imogen nodded. "Okay. I like it. No matter what, I've got your back."

"Me, too," I agreed.

"Me, three," Jonah said.

Liam sighed. "If I have to..."

"Yes," Imogen insisted, sticking her hand in the middle of the carriage above Squeaks' back. "*Let's not fucking die* on one, two, three?"

I stuck my hand on top of hers, and Jonah followed. Liam didn't do anything, until Jonah punched him in the arm. Liam sighed and stuck his hand out.

"One... two... three..." Imogen said.

We cheered the team motto, but it was anything but in unison. Everyone said it at a different time. Imogen and I laughed. Even Liam cracked a nervous smile. I glanced back out the window to see we were high above the ground now and headed out over the ocean.

"Is everyone feeling all right?" I asked.

"As good as I'll ever be," Liam answered.

"Good," I said, pointing. "Because I think our first task is Water."

Everyone glanced out the windows to the vast ocean below us. Sassy peeked out the window beside Imogen.

"There's an island!" Imogen shouted, pointing.

Jonah groaned. "And the flag for the finish line is way over there on the mainland."

I glanced to where he pointed and saw a huge orange flag flapping above the trees near the horizon. There were miles upon miles between us and the finish line. We had to make it across the ocean, over a mountain and through a large part of the woods before even coming close. I couldn't even see Kinpago or the castle from here.

"Crossing the ocean shouldn't be hard," I said. "I mean, Liam can control the water. Squeaks can take me and Imogen over, and Jonah can fly."

Jonah's eyebrows shot up. "You've really never watched one of these things before."

I shook my head. I mean, that much was obvious.

"You're delusional if you think the only thing we have to do is cross the ocean," Jonah said. "Princess, there's going to be a thousand things that will knock you on your ass before you make it back to the mainland."

I held my breath. How bad could it be?

"We don't have any more time to strategize," Imogen said as our carriage descended.

We landed softly on the sandy beach of a small island miles off the coast. The other teams began piling out of their carriages, glancing around and keeping an eye out for the first obstacle— whatever it was. I reached for the carriage door.

"Wait," Imogen said, placing her hand on mine to stop me. "Whatever happens out there, I want you guys to know I love you."

Imogen had no idea how comforting that was.

"I love you guys, too," I said, glancing between each of them. My cheeks went beet-red when my eyes connected with Liam's. I quickly averted my gaze and climbed over Squeaks to duck out of the carriage just as Jonah was professing his love for us, "but not in that way."

Once all contestants were on solid ground, the line of carriages rose into the air and headed back toward the mainland. Two dragons and a pegasus circled above us, each with a person on their back. They didn't wear the contestant uniforms, so I had to guess they were the camera crew.

I glanced to the other teams, but everyone looked just as clueless as we were. The Pink Team was already working on an earth bridge, while the guy with the dragon was ushering his team onto his Familiar's back. Haley just stood there with her hands on her hips, staring out into the ocean. She looked positively relaxed, like she knew what was coming and already had a plan of attack.

"Who wants to bet Doya was cheating beyond holding extra practices?" I muttered.

"There's a reason Doya's team is always one of the top picks," Imogen sneered.

"Team motto, guys," Liam snapped. "We're not here to beat the other teams. Let's just focus on getting to the finish line in one piece."

"Agreed—" I started to say, but a high-pitched scream across the beach cut me off. Several people gasped around us as the sky turned an almost immediate dark gray.

"Incoming!" Jonah yelled.

I followed his gaze, and terror spiked through my body. We didn't have time to discuss our plan.

A tidal wave was headed straight for us.

NINETEEN

S ophia and the rest of the group were looking at the massive wave coming toward us like it was their doom.

I knew better. I could feel the water moving the moment we were put on this island. There wasn't just one giant tidal wave coming toward us.

There were *four*.

On all sides. And I could feel the people controlling them. They were Elders. I couldn't stop them, not even if I tried. I turned on the spot. Sure enough, three other waves equal in size to the first were barreling toward us. Such a thing shouldn't be possible— most Toaqua would find something like that impossible to pull off, as it went against the rules of nature— but apparently the tribe was pulling out all the stops for this tournament.

Everyone else on my team had realized what I'd known minutes before. They started screaming as the waves rushed toward us at a high speed.

I had to get us off this island. If I didn't, I'd hopefully survive, but the rest of my team would certainly drown.

The majority of the other teams were already off the island. The Pink Team was running down the earth bridge they'd made while their Toaqua member made a shield around them with water to push back the tidal wave. The wave simply moved around the blockade and kept going. The Silver Team was flying over the ocean on a dragon, safe far above the waves, and the Green Team had created a boat out of water. They sailed over the tidal waves a little less successfully, though no one fell out as far as I could see. The Orange Toaqua member had taken her team underwater and was trying to pull them through the inside of the wave by a bubble she'd created, but that was risky. Even from this distance, I could tell she was at risk of losing control.

Purple had decided to tag-team the challenge, with their Yapluma member flying two people above the ocean and the Toaqua teammate skirting himself and another partner overtop of the waves.

The Blue Team had created a chamber of ice and was skating across the water, though it wasn't working very well. The water pressed down on the ice tunnel, making it crack under the pressure of the wave, and people were slipping inside trying to get away from the raging water.

Yellow wasn't doing much better. They'd gotten off the island, but their Toaqua was a First Year. It was all he could do to keep his team's heads above water as the ocean battered them this way and that. Their Familiars, a unicorn, a chimera, a gargoyle and a manatee, pushed their Elementai onto their backs and tried to paddle through the violent waves, though the approaching tidal wave soon swallowed them all.

Haley, as always, was prepared. She and her team were calmly riding on the back of a liopleurodon, who assassinated the waves. The giant marine reptile handled the waves like they were nothing while Dina, the Toaqua team member I knew, kept the rest of them dry as her Familiar did all the work of getting them to the mainland.

"Liam!" Sophia screamed at me. "What do we do?"

I realized we were still the only team left without a game-plan, and froze. My mind calculated our options. We didn't have many.

"Put the Familiars on Squeak's back, and send them away," I ordered. "They won't be any use out here. Jonah, send Squeaks to shore to wait for us."

"Do what he says!" Jonah shouted at Squeaks, waving his hand.

She hesitated and stomped her hooves, looking scared at the prospect of leaving Jonah.

Sophia was crying as she put Esis onto Squeaks' back. Esis grabbed hold of Squeaks' feathers and tilted his head, like he didn't understand. Imogen was upset, but she at least seemed somber as she put Sassy onto Squeaks' haunches.

"Sophia, we'll see them soon, I promise," I told her, and she nodded.

The waves were growing closer. I pointedly looked at Jonah, and he smacked Squeaks on the hindquarters, shouting, "Squeaks, go!"

Squeaks took off. She soared into the sky, taking Esis and Sassy away to safety. The three of them looked at me, seeming even more lost now that their Familiars were gone.

"What now?" Imogen asked weakly.

I knew this was my task, but ancestors, did I have to do *everything*? "Hold on!" I told them. I created a spinning waterspout that reached out and grabbed the three of them by the waists. They screamed, and I concentrated on making the waterspout larger, growing it above the approaching tidal waves. Soon, they were high above me, appearing like tiny dots in the sky, though I could still hear them screaming their heads off. I trusted Jonah to regulate the air for the girls so they'd be able to breathe as I increased the height of the waterspout.

Any time I had left to get myself off the island was wasted. Sound was drowned out by the roar of the waves. They blocked out all light, darkening the island and creating shadows. Each wave had to be fifteen-hundred feet tall. They'd crush me when they came down.

I barely got my teammates above the approaching tsunami before it crashed down upon me. I managed to create a small shield of water around my form that took most of the blow and made it so the water wouldn't break my bones, but that singular act of pushing back the waves completely shattered my magic and made me weak. My shield broke, and I was caught up in the undercurrent. I held my breath just before the waves dragged me under.

The average person could hold their breath for up to two minutes underwater. I could go for six. People like Baine could withstand ten, but I wasn't going to push my luck. I tried figuring out which way was up, but the waves spun me around so much I lost all sense of direction. I was quickly pulled a hundred feet below the surface. I couldn't swim. I couldn't do anything but let the ocean do as it wanted with me.

My poor mother was probably watching the TV right now and wailing in grief. It would be really embarrassing for my tribe that the Toaqua chief's son had been killed by his own element, but with how my year was going, I really shouldn't have expected anything else. I bet when Haley won, she'd go back home and rewind the moment of my death over and over, laughing harder and harder each time she saw it. A Toaqua drowning. Hilarious.

Even so, in the back of my mind, I made sure that Jonah, Imogen and Sophia were safe and far out of the tsunami's reach.

The waves spun me around. I was at the mercy of them— until I realized that I was born to be in water, that it was time to act and stop being stupid. If I died, my magic would stop working and my team would end up just like me.

I wasn't about to let that happen. I was the firstborn son of the Water Chief, dammit. I could die in this tournament, but later. Not now.

It took everything, but I used my powers to put myself upright in the churning ocean and stop the spinning. I was running out of air, fast. I couldn't tell how long I'd been under, but I was starting to see stars, and my vision was growing dark.

I put what I had left into pushing myself upward. I worked with the wave instead of against it, summoning my magic so the upwelling surrounded me and rushed me back to the surface. My head broke, and I took a deep gasp of air.

My waterspout was still spinning, but it was smaller now. The island was gone, engulfed by water. The tsunami was no longer there, yet the ocean was churned in its place.

Where there once had been light, now there was only darkness. Huge black clouds covered the sky, and rain was falling down torrentially. The wind picked up. The sky looked like glass as dozens of lightning bolts shot across it.

They were using Yapluma Elders to create storms and Koigni to make lightning, as if we didn't have enough to worry about. I looked upward to where the waterspout still was. My team was dangerously close to the storm.

Sophia was a First Year. She couldn't handle lightning.

With my right hand held up out of the water, I started to bring them back down. But before I could, a colossal roar got my attention.

The Green Team's water boat had a large tentacle wrapped around it. The team members scattered as the tentacle cracked down on the boat, and a giant squid rose up out of the water.

A fucking kraken. To make things worse, the Elders were sending their damn Familiars after us!

The Pink Team was running on their earth bridge from a megalodon that swam beside it. The oversized shark chased after them and blocked the way, preventing them from creating another bridge and forcing them to reevaluate.

Out of the corner of my eye I saw that a few other teams, though I couldn't be sure which ones, were trying to defend themselves against a gargantuan blue crab and a killer whale.

Haley's team was fighting off a leviathan from the back of the liopleurodon, and though they'd been making fast progress, I could tell the creature was giving them a hard time and blocking the way to the beach.

Nothing had gone after us yet, which meant we were lucky. We needed to move.

I lost track of who was on whose team as bodies started flying around. People were thrown out of the air and tossed into the ocean, either by the storm or whatever creatures they were fighting. Somehow, the red dragon from the Silver Team was knocked out of the sky and sent crashing into the sea. I lowered my team back to the ocean's surface while directing the rest of my power downward. The churning ocean split, and we were carried downward until our feet hit the ocean floor and I was holding up two separate walls of water on either side of us.

The shore was at least another mile off. My arms were starting to wobble under the effort of holding the ocean apart.

"Liam?" Sophia turned and looked at me.

"Don't dick around," I gasped. "This is hard."

I had to keep the ocean parted so we could get back to shore. My team started to run. They raced toward the beach while I walked forward steadily, my arms held out in front of me.

It felt like I was bench pressing the Pacific. My entire body screamed. It was incredibly painful, but I was used to pain, and I was fucking stubborn. The whole damn ocean was going to have to kick my ass before I'd let my team die.

Then a spasm wracked through my back, and I let out a gasp of agony. I fell to my knees, unable to control my body's reaction to the sheer effort of holding up my magic. The walls still held, but water was starting to splash over the sides and onto the sand.

I could do this if Nashoma was here. But he was gone. I couldn't pull from his strength. Just another reminder that I was doing this alone.

"Guys, Liam needs help!" Sophia shouted. She'd noticed I'd fallen. She, Imogen and Jonah came rushing back, instead of pressing ahead like I wanted them to.

No, don't come back for me, I wanted to scream, but even talking took too much effort. I gritted my teeth as my upper body started to go numb. Water was pouring in over the sides of the walls now.

"We're not going to abandon you!" Sophia said. She and the others stood around me, their faces pale with fear, but also set in a determined way that told me they wouldn't leave me behind no matter what.

I couldn't do it. The two walls came hurtling back down, and as the water started rushing in I screamed, "Everyone grab onto me!"

They didn't fucking hesitate. Jonah, Imogen and Sophia latched onto my arms, and as we were submerged underwater I used my magic to propel us forward like a bullet.

I rocketed us toward shore. And damn, it wasn't easy, the fatasses. We were easily going hundreds of miles an hour. We'd reach the beach in less than a minute, but already, I could feel Sophia's grip on my arm start to loosen. I glanced to the left and saw that her eyes were half-closed. She was Koigni. She couldn't last as long in water as Imogen and Jonah. I had to go faster.

It hurt, but I urged my element to give me just a little bit more. The beach was in sight— but then I ran out. There was just no more magic left.

We started to slow down. I tossed Sophia upward, and Imogen and Jonah let go. We broke the surface. The two of them started paddling to shore.

Sophia was sinking. She was about to pass out. I swam up behind her and put my arms under hers, grabbing her shoulders so both of us were tilted upward. I swam backward until I was able to pull her onto the beach. She came to, coughing up water once we hit the sand. I let her go and rolled onto my back as the earth rocked like the waves.

Everything hurt. I'd pushed my limits far past what I knew I had the ability to do, and I was paying for it. Little needles were pricking me all over my body, while a steamroller mashed my insides. It was so painful I really wanted to cry.

But we were probably still on TV, so I sucked it up and forced myself into an upward position, even though it made my eyes water.

I took a shuddering breath. We were safe. For now.

Squeaks raced up the beach with Esis and Sassy on her back, giving a happy squawk as she head-butted Jonah.

Well, at least someone was having a good time.

"Esis!" Sophia scrambled up and got Esis from off of Squeaks' back, while Imogen held Sassy. I was too weak to dry everyone, so we stayed wet.

I looked back at the ocean. What about the people who had been behind us? What was their fate?

The Yellow Team had to be gone. There was no way. They were in the water when the tsunami had crashed onto shore, and the Toaqua freshman had been struggling before then. I'd barely made it out alive, and I was a Third Year.

The rest of them had no chance.

A deep cavern of dread started eating my insides. That had only been the *first* challenge. What kind of hell did we have still waiting for us?

"What do we do now, Liam?" Imogen asked weakly. The team looked at me, expecting an answer.

Shit. What *did* we do now? I wasn't sure. I was supposed to be Captain. What did Baine say?

Protect the pack. Protect the pack. Right. "We have to get a sense of direction," I told them. "Then we can start heading toward the flag. We're sure to run into the other tasks along the way."

We couldn't see the sun. Clouds blocked them out, no doubt an effort from the Elders to prevent us from figuring out which way was north.

"I can do that," Imogen suggested, kneeling down to the ground. "I can feel the earth's magnetic poles."

"Me too," Jonah said. "I can sense which way the wind is blowing and use the currents to judge where we are."

"Fantastic." I lay back down on the shore and closed my eyes. I needed to rest. Just for a minute.

Sophia walked over to me, then knelt on the ground. Esis chattered in her arms. "Liam? You okay?"

"Peachy, *pawee.*" *It hurts to literally exist right now.*

Esis made a mewling sound and put a tiny paw on my arm. For some reason, once the little guy touched me, I felt a little bit stronger. Everything went from being unbearably agonizing to mildly tolerable. I was able to sit up easier this time.

"The flag's this way," Imogen said, walking toward us with Jonah by her side, pointing north. "Though it's really, really far away."

I got to my feet. "Good. Let's get moving. We'll walk until nightfall." I tried not to wince, but it was hard, and I was pretty sure the team noticed.

"Liam, get on Squeaks," Jonah suggested.

"No way." A rolling, sharp pain went through my gut. I involuntary clutched at it, bending over. This sucked.

"Liam." Sophia stared at me. "You have to."

"You'll slow us down," Imogen said gently. I know she meant it to be kind, but it stung.

"There's no way I'm hitching a ride when the rest of the team is walking," I told them sharply.

"Liam, just do it," Jonah said. "You saved our asses back there.

Quit nursing your pride, or I'm carrying your ass. And I'll make sure it looks as gay as possible for the cameras."

I figured we'd all have to take turns riding on Squeaks sooner or later, so I just gave up. "Fine." I climbed on Squeaks, though it was no easy effort, and held on to her feathers as we headed into the forest.

Sassy and Esis led the way, chattering. I think I fell asleep on Squeaks' back, because I closed my eyes and everything went numb.

By the time I opened them again, it'd gotten dark and we were in a clearing. I felt a little better, but where the pain once was, now there was soreness.

"We just stopped," Sophia told me quietly. "We haven't run into anything so far."

"Glad I didn't miss any action." I slid off of Squeaks' back. Imogen and Jonah both looked exhausted. Esis' eyes were drooping.

"We have to find drinking water," I told the team. Right then, I couldn't draw up a droplet out of the ground if I wanted to.

"There's a freshwater spring nearby that we passed," Jonah said. "We can drink from that."

"Okay, good," I said. "We also need shelter."

"Imogen can do that," Sophia offered before Imogen said anything. "She's good with roots and things."

I looked expectantly at Imogen. She blinked, then nodded. She raised her hands. A few roots popped out of the ground, but it was nothing monumental. Sassy played with them before looking at Imogen and giving a bark.

"Come on, Imogen," I said in frustration. "This should be easy for you." I'd seen her do harder things at home.

Imogen grimaced, then a large collection of roots rose up out of the earth. I stepped forward and started weaving them together. The rest of the team followed suit, bending the roots into something that would shield us from the elements, creating a dome that would encompass the four of us fully.

Imogen looked embarrassed. I wasn't sure what was coming tomorrow, but I was pretty sure Earth was next. I worried Imogen wouldn't be up to the task.

287

"You're not weaving it tight enough. It looks sloppy," I said to them. Imogen and Jonah glanced up at me, but didn't say anything.

"Liam, it doesn't need to be perfect," Sophia shot back. I went to open my mouth, but found myself too tired to argue.

Sophia moved her way over to me on the other side of the shelter. "Liam, you're being hypercritical," she whispered to me. "You have to stop."

I noticed that both Jonah and Imogen looked a little down. "I just... I want everyone to make it out of here," I told her. Some Captain I was, demoralizing the team.

"I get it, but you don't have to be that hard on them," Sophia said. "They're doing the best they can."

Sophia brushed my hand before going back to twisting the roots. Esis gave me a little pat on my leg.

About an hour later we had a shelter made, but it was obvious we were all starving. Squeaks' stomach was making rumbling noises, while Sassy had her nose to the ground, sniffing. Esis rubbed his belly and stuck out his lip.

"I'm going to look for something edible," I said. "You guys stay here."

It took another hour, but I managed to scrounge up a few cattails, conifer bark, and acorns for us to eat. It wasn't much, but we had to consume something. I passed it around. Jonah took it with a wrinkled nose, but the girls didn't complain. We sat in a circle outside the makeshift shelter and ate in silence around a campfire Sophia had made.

Squeaks ate a majority of the acorns. Esis sniffed at the conifer bark I offered him and turned his nose up at it.

Jonah sighed as he chewed on his bark. "This blows," he complained. "What I'd do for a burger right now."

"If you talk about food, I'm going to kill you," Imogen said. Sassy put her ears back and hissed at Jonah.

"Come on, people. Our ancestors lived like this every day for thousands of years. We can suck it up for a few nights," I told them.

"Uh, wrong," Jonah said. "Our ancestors lived like this, but they didn't have giant monsters chasing after them, or other Elementai out there literally trying to kill them."

I flipped Jonah off, because he ruined everything.

"That guy with the dragon is probably at the finish line by now," Sophia said glumly as she munched on a cattail.

"There are rules against flying," I told them. "You can fly through one of the challenges, but for the rest, you have to walk, to make it fair. Otherwise people with flying Familiars would just race to the ending, fly over all the challenges and win easily."

I shivered. I suddenly realized it had gotten very cold. Small white flakes began descending from the sky. It was snowing, and we didn't have much in terms of clothing.

"Snow," Jonah said, looking upward.

"It doesn't snow in this part of California, except for the mountains," Imogen protested.

"During the Elemental Cup it does," I replied. "Everyone, get inside."

We huddled inside the shelter, but it was still fricking cold. The light snowfall outside was quickly turning into a blizzard.

"Sophia, we need warmth. Before we freeze to death." I told her.

She nodded. She reached outside to gather the firewood we'd harvested while I poked a hole in the roof through the roots. She lit a fire and we gathered around it, arms wrapped around our forms.

Even with the roaring fire inside, it was still really cold, and we didn't have blankets or coats. It looked like the Water part of the challenge wasn't over yet.

"Can you regulate the temperature any more, Sophia?" I asked. My teeth were almost chattering. I was pretty sure I was turning blue. The cold couldn't hurt me in Water form, at least, but the temperature certainly could.

"I'm trying. I've never been met with this much... resistance before." Sophia shivered. "It's almost like someone's blocking my powers."

Damn Elders again. On the ground, Esis waddled up to Squeaks. He nestled against her feathers like a pillow before pulling Sassy to

289

him, using her tail as a blanket. Esis sighed happily, totally cozy. The rest of the Familiars huddled up together, unbothered by the chill.

"Hey, Esis has the right idea," Jonah started. "Let's cuddle."

"No," I said flatly. Ancestors, this tournament was pushing every button I had.

"We're supposed to survive, and that means not becoming an icicle," Jonah shot back. "But if you're opposed to the cuddling part, there are other ways to keep warm." Jonah winked.

"I'm gonna hit you," I growled.

"Jonah's just playing around," Sophia said. "Besides, it's not like these outfits are exactly sexy." Sophia pulled at her suit.

"Baby, unisex still has the word *sex* in it," Jonah said.

I was getting real tired of Jonah's shit.

"Jonah's right," Imogen said. "Not about the orgy thing, but we *will* stay warm if we share body heat."

"Nothing shares body heat like a big love-pile," Jonah added. "What do you say, Liam?"

I shivered again, and Imogen said, "Well, I'm not waiting around for *your* approval."

She lay on the ground next to Squeaks, and Jonah followed her. He reached out and grabbed Imogen, crushing her to his giant chest. She giggled. Sophia was usually shy, but it must've been so freaking cold she didn't care, because she lay next to Imogen and scooted against her.

"Come on, Liam." Sophia raised her eyebrows. "Your turn."

"Uh-uh." I shook my head. "Nowhere in the rulebook did it say in order to make it through this, I have to spoon my teammates."

"You can be little spoon." Jonah wiggled his eyebrows.

"Hell to the no." I really was cold. My body was giving in.

Sophia looked really concerned about me. She and Esis were mirrors, both big eyes that were adorable and sucked me in.

Fine. If I was cuddling with anyone, it was going to be Sophia. Because we'd already done it once, and to be honest, I kind of liked it. Though having Imogen and Jonah here was really killing the mood.

I got down on the ground and slid my body against Sophia's, so that my head was resting on one of Squeaks' legs. I shivered when she put her arm around me, though it wasn't because of the chill.

"This doesn't leave the hut. *Ever*," I said. I was glad the cameras couldn't see us inside the hut, because this was taking things a step too far.

"This is like a porn I watched once," Jonah spoke up.

Ancestors help me. I was going to murder these people.

"Relax, Liam." Imogen spoke up. "We're all friends here."

"Reluctantly."

Sophia giggled against my back. I smiled. It was warmer, at least. And I was glad Jonah was on the other side of the hut, because I didn't trust him not to make it weirder than it already was.

"Goodnight, everyone," Imogen said pleasantly. "I hope we all have sweet dreams."

Never mind. Imogen made it weird, anyway.

"Goodnight, my lovelies," Jonah said. I immediately heard a large snore afterward. The bastard had already slipped off.

"Goodnight," Sophia said, and she sighed, sinking her head between my shoulder blades. That little touch sent fireworks skyrocketing through my skin.

Squeaks, Esis, and Sassy all sounded off with their own farewells. There was silence, and Imogen said, "Liam... you didn't say goodnight."

I sighed. "Goodnight. Now everyone shut the hell up!"

THE NEXT MORNING, the fire had burnt out, but I noticed that when I woke up it wasn't cold anymore. The snow outside was gone, which meant the weather was back to normal— for now.

I wondered if anything was waiting for us out there. It didn't occur to me that we should've posted someone to keep watch, but we were all so tired last night I doubt that it would've done much good anyway.

I closed my eyes again, wanting to rest for just a few more minutes. I got woken up when something furry and bloody got shoved in my face.

"Ugh!" I shouted. I sat up. In my lap fell a dead rabbit, its throat ripped out. Sassy looked up at me proudly, swishing her tail.

"What is it?" Jonah replied sleepily. The others sat up, woken by my yell.

I rubbed my eyes. At Sassy's feet was a collection of six rabbits, freshly hunted. I could hardly believe my eyes. Her snout was bloody and she grinned with pride.

"Sassy!" Imogen squealed. She hugged her fox enthusiastically. "Good girl!"

"Finally, something substantial to eat," Jonah said.

Sophia looked at me. "Do we have time? Or should we hit the road?"

I hesitated. Cooking the rabbits would slow us down, but we weren't trying to win. It was more important to stay alive. We needed energy.

"I can skin and butcher them," I said. "You guys can cook them up."

"All right, *Mom*," Jonah said. I sneered at him.

Sophia stayed on the other side of camp while I did the dirty work. This kind of stuff didn't bother me, because I grew up doing it with my dad, but Sophia turned green when she saw me sharpen a rock to a point to use as a knife. She was fine with cooking them, though. Soon we were gathered around the fire with full stomachs again, though I knew what little protein the rabbits had wouldn't last long. I hoped Sassy would keep hunting.

Squeaks consumed two rabbits herself, raw. Sassy didn't eat, so I supposed she'd already fed herself. I noticed that Esis ate a few bites of the rabbit, but not much. Still, he didn't seem to be fatigued. Was Esis a kind of animal that could go a few days without a meal, and live off fat stores? It would explain why he ate so much when there was food to go around.

We were on the road again before late morning. We'd been walking for two hours and hadn't run into anything. I'd gotten nervous.

The mountains were looming in the distance. Imogen pointed to them. "We need to get over those. That's the biggest hurdle to getting to the flag."

Sophia stopped in her tracks. "I don't know, guys," she started. "I think we should go the other way." She pointed deep into the forest.

"But that's in the other direction, and it's overgrown," Jonah said. "Why would you want to go there?"

Sophia shrugged. She seemed anxious. "I don't know. I just... have a feeling."

I raised an eyebrow. "We need more than feelings, Soph."

Sophia chewed on her lip. She didn't want to speak up. "Well... a straight shot to the flag is the obvious way to go, which means everyone will be going that way, and through there, we'll meet the biggest obstacles. Going around might take longer, but it reduces our chances of getting hurt."

She had a good point, but Jonah shook his head and stepped in. "No way. It doesn't matter which way we go, there will be obstacles everywhere. The hike up the mountains won't be easy, but it'll be quick. We should go that way."

"I agree," Imogen said. "Do we want to get this over with, or not?"

"You're Captain," Jonah said, poking me. "You decide."

Way to put me on the spot. I looked between my friends. For some reason, I had a feeling that climbing up the mountains was a bad idea, too. I wanted to do what Sophia said.

But on the other hand, Jonah and Imogen had an actual plan. If we went any deeper into the forest, there was a chance we'd get lost. It was pointless to aimlessly wander around when we only had so much energy to spare.

"Let's just try the mountains, for now," I said, and Sophia's face fell. "If it doesn't work, we can turn around."

Sophia didn't say anything when we left the forest. I didn't want her to be mad at me, but I was just trying to save everyone's life.

The closer we got to the mountains, the more we saw signs of the other teams. We found footprints, remnants of food, and abandoned campsites. By my estimate, all the other teams... the ones that were still around, anyway... were way ahead of us.

Who cared? We still had everyone. Couldn't say the same for—

My blood ran cold as I saw a body lying on the ground with red sleeves. It was the Toaqua from Haley's team, the one with the liopleurodon. She was lying in front of a stone house that looked like a Nivita had constructed. Sophia gasped, and the other two halted in their tracks. I walked up to the body and knelt to the ground to inspect it.

Her eyes were still spread open. She'd frozen to death last night in the cold. Her fingernails were bloody, and there were marks on the door— like she'd been trying to claw her way in.

I couldn't believe it. Haley used her to get off the island, then just... disposed of her. And her teammates had let her do it.

Sick bitch.

I got up. "She's gone, guys. Been dead for hours."

"Shouldn't we bury the body?" Sophia asked.

I shook my head. "The officials will come to get her shortly. We need to keep moving." I hated leaving a fellow Toaqua there like that, but what could I do? She was dead. There was no bringing her back.

I heard sniffling behind me. Sophia was crying. She put a hand on her mouth, trying to suppress the sobs that were coming out.

"Hey," I said. I reached out and pulled Sophia into a hug. "There's nothing we could do."

Sophia sniffed. When I let her go, Esis jumped onto her shoulder and gave her a kiss on the cheek.

Imogen and Jonah were stone-faced. They'd grown up in this society. They knew that not everyone made it out of the tournament alive, though it was different seeing it in real life instead of on screen.

"Let's go." I gestured to my teammates, and they followed. The Toaqua girl's blue eyes were burrowed into my conscience as we continued onward. Haley wouldn't be blamed for murder. The Elders would say that the girl should've been smart enough to survive on her own. That's what this tournament was all about, anyway.

About a mile up ahead, we ran into the mountainside— and more bodies. I assessed the situation. Two Elementai, one from the Silver Team and one from the Blue. Their Familiars lay beside them, expressions gaping and legs positioned like they were still running.

"Looks like they were crushed," I mused. I was distracted, thinking about where the other teams were. Maybe if we could figure out what they ran into, we could avoid it ourselves.

Esis was acting crazy. He was running in a circle around us, making loud screeches at the top of his lungs and trying to get our attention.

"Esis, what's wrong?" Sophia said. She tried to pick him up, but he wouldn't let her. He pushed her away and kept dancing around, pointing at the mountains.

"Esis, what—?"

Sophia got my attention when she cut her sentence off. Imogen and Jonah both had large, gaping mouths. I slowly turned to stare at what they were looking at. The reason why the Elders had made it snow so much last night socked me in the gut. Large boulders barreled down the side of the mountain, picking up speed, along with a torrent of snow.

I figured out what the other teams had met. It'd been a landslide, and another one was coming our way.

sophia
TWENTY

"**L**iam!" I cried as I stared up at the landslide barreling toward us, my heart slamming against my chest. I scooped Esis into my arms and held him tightly. "What do we do?"

He froze, eyes locked on the incoming landslide. It was like he was someplace else entirely.

"Liam!" I shouted to get his attention.

He hesitated for a second before shouting, "Run!"

The four of us took off sprinting in different directions. Sassy was cradled in Imogen's arms as she started in the opposite direction of Liam and me. Squeaks ran alongside Jonah directly away from the landslide, as if they could outrun it. It was total chaos.

"This way!" Liam shouted, catching their attention.

Imogen and Jonah quickly joined us as we raced parallel to the mountain. I glanced up, and fear rocked my body. The landslide must've been half a mile across, and it was coming in fast. There was no way we could outrun it. We had to think of something. Quick.

"Can't you... stop it... Imogen?" I asked through labored breaths.

"Could you stop a freaking *fire tornado*?" she shot back in a distressed tone.

I'll take that as a no.

"Jonah!" I called as I ran. "Can Squeaks get us above it?"

"Not all of us. We have to stick together," he answered.

"Imogen," Liam snapped. "We need shelter, *now*. As strong as you can."

"Do you have any idea what you're asking me to do?" Imogen fired back.

"Yes!" Liam roared. "It's do or die out here! You have less than thirty seconds to decide what you want it to be!"

Imogen skidded to an abrupt halt and bent to the ground to bury her fingers in the earth. The landslide must've been two hundred yards from us now. It'd land on us any second and squash us. I hadn't been counting on dying in this tournament, but now it seemed like a reality.

Imogen shot to her feet and pointed. "Straight ahead and around that boulder!"

Nobody questioned her. There wasn't time. We raced around a boulder jutting out from the mountainside and found ourselves in front of a tall rock face. I noticed a small opening that sank far back into the rock, but it was only big enough to fit an arm in.

Imogen shoved Sassy into Liam's arms. "There's a small cavern here. I just..."

She raised her hands and pointed them at the rock. Her eyebrows constricted, and her jaw tightened.

I stole another glance at the incoming rock and squeezed Esis tighter. *Come on, Imogen!*

The rock surrounding the hole tumbled to the ground, widening the hole until it was three feet across. It stretched back at least fifteen feet. Liam rushed forward and tossed Sassy inside.

"Everyone in!" he shouted. I could barely hear him over the roar of tumbling rock above us.

Imogen scurried into the tunnel behind Sassy, and Esis and I quickly climbed in after her.

"No way!" Jonah protested, eyeing the small tunnel with a knitted brow.

Liam stomped forward and shoved a fist into Jonah's shirt. "Get in there now, or so help the ancestors. I'm not going to watch you die! Squeaks, get in!"

Squeaks dove in behind me. Her body was so large that she barely fit and blocked all the light behind us. The earth rumbled above us, but I pushed forward despite my trembling limbs.

The shaking of the earth intensified. Somewhere beyond the deafening sound of tumbling boulders above our heads, a shriek echoed throughout the tunnel.

"What happened?" Imogen shouted, but I barely heard her.

I tried to glance back to see what was wrong, but Squeaks' beak poked my butt, and she nudged me forward. Worst case scenarios ran through my head. Had Liam been crushed? Did Jonah make it into the tunnel?

The rumbling passed over us, and I held my breath, waiting to hear if everyone was okay.

"Sophia!" Liam called. Jonah sobbed beside him.

Relief flooded through me.

"We need some light!" Liam demanded.

I was so relieved I could cry. My voice cracked. "I— I can't. Squeaks is in the way."

"Come this way," Imogen said in front of me. It sounded like her voice was bouncing off the walls of a cavern much bigger than the the tunnel I was crawling through.

I heard Esis scurry forward and followed behind him. I produced a small flame in my palm to see that the cavern was twice the size of my dorm room, with a ceiling tall enough to stand in. Small tunnels broke off in various directions, but nothing that was wide enough to fit through, unless we sent Sassy or Esis. My light cast shadows across Imogen's face, which was etched in worry.

"We need that light sooner than later!" Liam yelled.

"Squeaks!" I cried. I ducked back inside the tunnel and pulled at her front leg. She wouldn't budge.

Jonah groaned in pain, and I felt Squeaks tense in response. "My leg!" Jonah cried. "I'm hurt!"

"I know you want to help, Squeaks," I said, "but none of us can help Jonah if you don't move."

That got her attention. She crawled forward and pulled herself out of the tunnel, nearly getting her butt stuck in the process. I relit my flame and held it into the tunnel opening.

"What happened?" I asked in a rushed breath.

"I don't know," Liam shot back. "Jonah, can you crawl?"

Jonah was just a lump in the tunnel. All I saw was his bun wiggle as he shifted his head, but I wasn't sure if it was supposed to be an answer. Beyond him was nothing but blackness. The layers of earth from the landslide had buried the entrance.

I tried not to think about running out of oxygen or starving to death. All I cared about right now was whether or not Jonah was okay.

Esis jumped into the tunnel and hopped over Liam. He grabbed Jonah's arm and started tugging, as if he could help drag him.

Jonah groaned and rolled over. His face was bright red, and he was breathing hard. "I'll make it. Just give me a minute."

Liam waited until Jonah pushed himself to his elbows and began dragging himself along army-style before crawling forward. I took Liam's hand in mine— the one that wasn't flaming— to help him out of the tunnel.

Imogen and Liam helped Jonah out of the tunnel, with Squeaks right beside them keeping a close watch. Jonah stood on one foot but held his other up, taking in long, deep breaths.

"Sit down," Liam instructed, guiding Jonah to the ground.

Squeaks dropped to her belly behind Jonah, allowing him to lean against her for comfort. We all hovered around him. Imogen rubbed his shoulder, and I held my flame close so everyone could see.

"A falling rock hit my foot while I was climbing into the tunnel," Jonah explained.

"Let me look." Liam reached for the hem of Jonah's pants, but Jonah swatted him away.

"Dude," Jonah snapped. "Don't touch it."

"Do you think it's broken?" Imogen asked in a shaky voice.

Jonah stared at her with a pointed expression. "Do I look like a doctor to you? All I know is that it hurts like a mofo."

Liam stood. "You're alive, and that's what matters."

Esis inched forward and reached his tiny paws for Jonah's shoe. My hand instinctively shot out for him, holding him back as worry ran through me. I couldn't let him show his power now. Liam would hate me. I knew I had to tell him... eventually. But during the middle of the tournament was not the time. This kind of secret could tear our entire group apart, which could get us all killed. As much as my gut twisted watching Jonah huff in pain, I'd rather we deal with a broken ankle than with a teammate's death.

Imogen caught my eye when I pulled Esis away. I shook my head at her. I couldn't tell them yet. Imogen turned away, but didn't say anything. She looked visibly paler than normal, and her pigtails were in disarray. Her arms shook as she cradled Sassy.

"Okay, Imogen," Liam said. "You're up."

Imogen glanced up at him with a blank expression. "What?"

"The landslide is over," Liam said, like it was obvious. "You can unblock the entrance."

Imogen's eyes nearly bulged out of her skull. "Are you serious? Liam, you know that—"

"What other choice do we have?" Liam cut her off. "Do you want to send Esis down one of these tunnels to see if there's a way out? It would take him ten years to dig us out with those little paws."

Esis crossed his arms, offended.

"Are you even going to try?" Liam challenged.

Imogen hesitated, then set Sassy down. She sighed and walked over to the wall of the cave and placed a flat palm to the rock. She closed her eyes and took a deep breath.

When she opened them, her face fell. "The smaller tunnels go on forever. And there's almost fifteen feet of dirt the way we came. That's more than what my brother had—"

"I don't care what trial he faced," Liam said, his hands tightening into fists. "He's not here right now. Right now, we have you, and you're our only way out of here."

Liam was growing visibly distressed by the second. Jonah was starting to rock back and forth, muttering something under his breath like a prayer. Imogen's eyes brimmed with tears. I was feeling exhausted, hungry, and useless. Had our team already reached its breaking point?

"My Water and Jonah's Air is useless down here," Liam said. "And all Sophia's power is good for is sucking up oxygen."

My eyes widened, and I instantly reduced my flame. Jonah gasped through the darkness.

After a moment of silence, Imogen spoke. "I— I can try..."

"Good," Liam said flatly. "Let's get on it."

Imogen's hands ran across the rock as she lowered herself back into the tunnel.

"Liam," I said.

"What?" he snapped in a harsh tone. As soon as the word left his mouth, he took a breath and spoke softly. "Shit. Sophia..."

"You need to calm down," I told him. I tried to keep my voice steady, but inside, my heart was racing. "If Imogen is going to get us out of here, she needs to concentrate. Sometimes you can be a bit harsh."

Liam scoffed. "Yeah, well, I'm team Captain. If we want to survive, I have to push you guys."

"No, Liam," I insisted. "You don't have to be like that all the time."

He just shrugged.

"The landslide is past," I said. "Why are you still freaking out?"

Liam took a long breath, then let it out in a *whoosh*. "Because I'm an asshole."

I couldn't help but giggle. "That's not true. You always have a reason."

Liam dropped his gaze, his expression suddenly shifting. There was a sad look in his eyes when they met mine again. He spoke softly. "This is... this is a lot like how Nashoma died."

My heart fell. He wasn't just scared for us... there was something darker in his eyes, like he was reliving Nashoma's death and trying to keep it all together at the same time.

I reached out a hand. My fingers grazed against the skin on his arm, sending electric tingles up my hand. My fingers trailed down to his, and I felt his hand tremble beneath my touch.

"I'm sorry," I whispered.

A stretch of silence passed between us. Time seemed to slow as I stared at the shadows flickering across his face. I only snapped out of it when I heard Imogen shift in the tunnel next to us. I didn't know why I was still touching him, so I pulled away.

Liam cleared his throat. "How's it coming, Imogen?"

Imogen sniffled. "I... I can't do it. It's too much at once."

"Take it layer by layer," Liam suggested, irritation entering his tone.

"It doesn't work like that," Imogen called back down the tunnel. "There's a limit to my powers— a range. Any earth between me and the end of that range acts as a barrier. I'd have to move it from the inside out, or all at once."

"Come on back, Imogen," he said.

As soon as she emerged from the tunnel, Liam ducked inside.

"What does he think he's doing?" Imogen asked under her breath.

"Just let him go," I said. "He needs something to do."

"He's wasting his energy," Imogen said, her voice cracking. "There's no way out. We're going to die down here."

Imogen broke into quiet sobs and stomped over to the other side of the tunnel. My light barely reached her. She curled up in a ball beside Sassy in the corner, while Jonah had his eyes squeezed tightly shut and was chewing fiercely on his lower lip.

I turned to Imogen, but as I approached her, she buried her head into her knees and turned away from me.

"Go away," she mumbled.

My stomach sank, and tension formed in my head. "I just want to help," I whispered, squatting down next to her.

"You can't help me," she sobbed without looking up. "Go help Jonah."

I backed away from her slowly, feeling like the worst member of the team right now. I was useless.

"Hey, Jonah," I said softly as I approached him.

His eyes were still closed, and his breathing was ragged. Guilt consumed me. I wanted to offer Esis to heal him, but I couldn't bring myself to do it. Not yet, anyway.

I sat beside Jonah, holding Esis in my lap with one hand and a flame in my other. "How bad is it? Your foot?"

He shook his head without looking at me. "That's not what's bothering me."

I breathed a sigh of relief.

"It's this damn cave," he muttered. "I don't do small spaces. I'm totally claustrophobic. There's hardly any air down here. I can't use my element."

"Oh," I said flatly. How was I supposed to help with *that*? "Would you rather I put my flame out? Then you wouldn't know the difference."

Jonah slowly peeled his eyes open, but quickly shut them again. He nodded.

I closed my hand, and the cave went dark. I could still hear Imogen in the corner and Liam shuffling around in the tunnel. Jonah reached out in the darkness to take my hand. He squeezed it so hard that I thought he might crush my fingers, but I bit my lower lip to keep from crying out. As long as I was helping *someone*, that was all that mattered.

"You know, Jonah," I said. "When I'm scared, I like to sing a song."

"I'm not scared," he said, though I could hear the fear in his voice. "I'm just... uncomfortable is all. But... you can sing me a song anyway."

I hesitated. I was in choir in high school, but only so I could goof off with my friends. I'd never considered myself a good singer. But I opened my mouth to sing anyway. The truth was, I was a little scared myself, and I knew it would help. I went with the first thing that came to mind, a lullaby my mom used to sing to me when I was a kid, one I'd nearly forgotten until now.

> *"Earth, Water, Fire, and Air*
> *Gifted to us by the breath of a prayer*
> *Separated these powers shall be*
> *Until reunited in sweet harmony."*

My voice drifted away on the last note. I'd never really paid attention to the words until now. Maybe my parents hadn't hidden *everything* from me...

"What are you doing, Sophia?" Jonah asked.

"Huh? Um... singing?"

"You're butchering the song," he accused.

I laughed lightly. "I never said I was a good singer."

"Your voice is fine," Jonah said. "But the lyrics are all wrong."

"What? No, they're not. My mom used to sing it to me all the time when I was a kid."

"Yeah, well, your mom must've changed the lyrics," Jonah said with amusement in his tone. At least I was cheering him up.

"Okay, so how does it really go?" I challenged. I only did it to indulge him, even though I knew I was singing it right— *my* version, at least.

Jonah began singing, taking on the same tune I'd used, though he sang horribly off key.

"Earth, Water, Fire, and Air
Powers almighty for children to share
Those in the clouds will forever be
The perfect balance of harmony."

I raised my eyebrows, though he couldn't see me. *"Those in the clouds?* It sounds like you think very highly of yourself, Yapluma," I teased.

"You're *both* singing it wrong," Imogen said from her corner, though she was being anything but playful. "The original song didn't have any lyrics. It's the tune the ancestors played when they gifted us our powers. Each House took the tune and turned it into something else. So if you want to be accurate, you wouldn't use lyrics."

It sounded like something she must've read in one of her books. She didn't sound interested in it. It was more like she was stating fact.

"Let's hum it, then," I suggested.

Jonah and I began humming the tune, though the last line was a little shaky, since we couldn't quite agree on the rhythm. Eventually, we compromised until Jonah began drifting off. He slumped against Squeaks like she was a pillow and began snoring.

I sat there for another hour in the dark, trying to not make any noise so that Jonah could rest. But I couldn't take the sounds of Liam clinking rocks together in the tunnel. It didn't matter how determined he was. He wasn't going to dig his way out of here. I could hear his breathing becoming more and more labored with each passing minute. He needed a serious reality check.

"Liam," I whispered, bending down to the tunnel opening with a flame in my hand. All I could see were the soles of his shoes, since rocks and dirt were piled up around the rest of his body. When he didn't acknowledge me, I repeated his name.

"What?" he snapped, turning his head back to me. His forehead was covered in sweat, so much that long strands of hair stuck to the sides of his face.

"You need to rest," I said.

"No," he protested. "I need to get us out of here."

"We'll get out," I assured him, though I couldn't know that for sure. "But maybe we can take turns. You're working yourself too hard, and you need a break."

"I'm fine," he lied. "You can save the lecture for when we get out of here."

"Liam," I said firmly. "You need to stop."

He glanced back at me. "I'm making progress."

"You're making yourself sick," I countered, taking note of the faraway look in his eyes.

"Trust me," he said, "I've handled worse."

"Yeah, well, I haven't," I snapped back. "What am I supposed to do when you pass out? We have no resources down here. You're no use to us unconscious. Please, just take a break."

Liam clenched his teeth before letting out a sigh. "Sophia, I—"

"No excuses, Liam. Lie down and rest."

I wasn't going to put up with this. He didn't get a choice. I climbed into the cave and reached for his ankle.

"Ancestors, *pawee*." He jerked away. "Fine. I'll take a short break."

"Good," I said, satisfied.

I backed up to let him out. Liam stood straight and wiped the back of his hand across his forehead. His knees visibly shook, and he looked two minutes from passing out.

I pointed to a level spot near the edge of the cave. "Lie down. I'll start digging."

"You don't have to do that, Sophia."

"Why not?" I raised an eyebrow at him. "Because I'm a girl?"

Liam shook his head. "No, but..."

"But what?" I asked. I knew digging would be useless, but Liam didn't seem like the kind of guy who could rest if nothing was being done. Only one person could dig at a time, so at least he wouldn't feel the need to jump right back into it.

Liam shrugged. "I don't know. It's... it's cold down here, don't you think?"

It sounded like he was just making small talk, but I wasn't really in the mood for that. Instead, I stomped up to him and grabbed his arm, dragging him over to where I'd pointed. He seemed curious and didn't speak.

I sat down and patted the spot next to me. "Come on."

Liam did as he was told, though it seemed to take him forever to lower himself to the ground, as if he had the body of an eighty-year-old. Which I could tell through his skin-tight shirt was *definitely* not the case.

I lay on my side facing him, and my arms curled in front of me and pressed against his chest. His breath rushed across my face, and I caught the scent of a pine forest after a fresh rain. He hesitated a moment before draping an arm across my body. Esis scurried up next to me and snuggled into the small space between us. I called upon my Fire just enough to warm the surface of my skin. Liam's body felt so cold on mine, like the chill from the ocean, but I barely noticed.

Instead, I was focusing on the nervous pounding of my heart and the voice in my head screaming. *When the hell did you grow a pair of balls, Sophia?* Seriously, where did the courage to yell at and then cuddle a guy I wasn't even dating come from?

My body trembled against his. I only hoped he didn't notice. Fantasies of what I'd like to do with Liam— *to* Liam— here in the dark ran through my mind. I couldn't control it. I should *not* be thinking things like that at a time like this. Besides, it wasn't like anything was going to happen between us.

Which might've been a lie. *Something* was definitely going on. I could feel it. Liam shifted his hips until I could no longer feel *him* against me.

"Better?" I asked, my voice shaking.

Liam's shoulders relaxed. "Better," he whispered.

❦

IT FELT like hours had passed when I finally woke. I didn't have the sun to judge by, but I guessed it was already morning. Jonah and Liam were still asleep, but Imogen sat staring at the tunnel with a blank expression on her face. I wiggled out from under Liam's arm. Esis stirred but didn't wake. He shifted just enough so that his head curled down by Liam's chest and his butt stuck up in his face.

"Hey, Imogen," I said softly as I made my way over to her. A small flame in my hand lit up her face. Sassy lay curled up in her lap. I took a deep breath, but it didn't feel like I was getting enough air.

"Hey," she said flatly without meeting my eyes.

I sat beside her and spoke in a whisper so I wouldn't wake anyone. "Are you ready to talk about it?"

Imogen shook her head.

I bit my lower lip, unsure of what to say to her. I settled for the truth. "We need you, Imogen. Liam may think he can dig his way out of here, but he's just being stubborn. We need a Nivita. We need *you*."

"I'm sure that's what Trace's team said to him, too," Imogen mumbled.

"Is this... is this how your brother died?" I asked. I wished there was a way to tiptoe around the subject, but there wasn't. We had to face this head-on if we hoped to make it out of here.

Imogen nodded. "Trace failed his trial. His team wanted to take a shortcut through the mountain. They thought that by going through a cave they could bypass the trials and make it to the finish line first. But you can't outrun the trials in these mountains. The cave collapsed, separating their team. The Koigni girl and Yapluma guy on their team said Trace and the Toaqua girl were far enough ahead that the cave-in wouldn't have crushed them. Which can only mean one thing... Trace failed. He couldn't get them out. The half of his team that survived had to backtrack to the cave entrance and face the rest of the trials alone. They were the last team to make it back."

"Imogen," I whispered. "I'm so sorry."

"Can you imagine?" she asked rhetorically, like she hadn't heard me. "I found out about my brother's death while watching TV in my living room. His teammates walked out of that cave without him, and I just..."

She broke into sobs again, her shoulders shaking. I wrapped an arm around her but didn't say anything. It took Imogen a few minutes to compose herself again.

"It's funny," she said. "The day I lost my brother, I found my soul." She stroked Sassy's fur.

"That's when you bonded?" I asked.

She nodded sheepishly. "As soon as I saw Trace didn't make it, I ran out of the house and into the forest. Cade was there because his family was watching the tournament with us. I didn't want him to see me cry, so I ran. He followed, calling my name. I kept going until I tripped over a rock. I remember just lying there with my face in the dirt, letting my tears soak into the earth while I thought about how I'd never see my big brother again. I heard Cade's footsteps behind me. He bent down and ran his hand through my hair and down my back. He told me it was going to be okay, that I'd see Trace again one day. I told him I didn't want to wait until death to see him, that he should've made it out of the tournament alive. Trace had promised me he would.

"And then— I remember it so vividly— Cade went rigid, and the whole forest went silent. It was like time had stopped. He whispered my name and told me to look. When I lifted my head, there Sassy was, staring at me through the underbrush. I still remember every detail of our bonding. The color of the trees seemed brighter, and I heard the sounds of a flute in the distance. It smelled like the pages of an old book and tasted like honey. It was enough to give me a sliver of hope. Sassy walked toward me until her whiskers were tickling my face... and then she licked me."

Imogen let out a light laugh, but her face quickly fell again. "It just doesn't seem fair."

"No," I replied sadly. "It doesn't. But Imogen, this isn't the same thing."

"It's exactly the same," she argued.

"No, it's not. That rock out there? Those aren't the same rocks your brother had to move. And you? You're Imogen, not Trace. You have different strengths."

Imogen sighed. "If we have any chance of making it out of here, I have to move more rock than I ever have before. I know I'm Nivita, but I'm not good with dirt and rocks. I'm better with plants."

"Okay... well, that's a strength."

Imogen glared at me. "It's not exactly going to help us, is it?"

My mind raced a million miles per hour. What could I possibly say to her to convince her to give it another shot? An idea suddenly struck me.

"Yes!" I cried. "Maybe it will."

Imogen's eyebrows drew together.

"I saw this documentary once," I explained. "It showed a time-lapse video of roots growing through concrete until the concrete broke. Imogen, your power is *strong*. What if you used the roots to get through the dirt and rocks?"

Imogen's eyes lit up, and I could see the gears turning in her head. "You think that will work?"

I honestly didn't know. "All I know is that we can't give up yet. I believe in you, Imogen."

Imogen visibly blushed. "I guess it's worth a shot."

Yes!

"But Sophia," Imogen said in warning, "if this doesn't work, I'm sorry."

I refused to accept her apology. "It will work, Imogen. Trust me."

A hint of a smile touched the corner of her lips. "I do."

"Then let's get going," I encouraged.

Jonah stirred. "Hey, what's going on?"

"We're strategizing," I said vaguely as Imogen and I stood. I didn't want to tell him and put too much pressure on Imogen.

"Oh, okay," Jonah said in a groggy voice. "Let me know when we're out of the woods."

Imogen scoffed. "Sweetheart, if this works, I'll carry you out of the woods myself."

"Deal," Jonah agreed.

Imogen just rolled her eyes and started for the tunnel. Sassy climbed in behind her. I squatted at the entrance to offer my light. Imogen crawled over the loose rocks Liam had left behind and to the end of the tunnel where a pile of dirt blocked the path. She placed her palms flat to the rock and took a deep breath.

I waited. And waited.

Finally, she dropped her hands and twisted back to me. "There are roots all around me. I can get to them, but I'm going to need some time to figure out exactly what I'm doing. I don't want to risk caving in the tunnel."

"That's all right," I told her. "Take all the time you need."

"We don't have forever."

My head snapped in Liam's direction. He'd woken up. He pushed himself to a sitting position, disturbing Esis. When Esis realized I was all the way across the cave, he quickly rushed to my side.

"We'll eventually run out of air," Liam said.

"Stop it, Liam," I groaned. I glanced into the tunnel to make sure Imogen hadn't heard him. She was in her own little world, focusing on the earth.

He shrugged. "I'm only stating fact."

"You're being a pessimist," I told him. "We won't get anywhere with that kind of attitude. Just let Imogen do her thing."

Liam held up his hands in surrender. "You know, for a girl who didn't want to be team Captain, you're doing an awful lot of lecturing."

I shrugged. "Yeah, well, someone has to keep you in line."

Amusement touched the corner of his lips. "Of course that'd be your job, *pawee*."

"And I take that job seriously," I said. "Sit back and relax while Imogen works her magic."

It took another fifteen minutes until I saw the ends of the first roots snake through the dirt.

"Don't get too excited just yet," Imogen warned. "Plants can be kind of touchy. It might take a while."

Slowly, the roots began to carve out the dirt until the sunlight peeked through and touched our little cave. I let out a sigh of relief.

"Almost there!" Imogen yelled back.

The path she'd created widened more and more, until the sunlight flooded through the long dirt tunnel and onto the rocks Imogen lay on. Thick layers of root outlined the dirt, pushing back against the hard earth and providing structure to the new length of tunnel.

"Imogen, you did it!" I cried.

She shot me back a shy smile, then raised her voice to yell, "Time to go!"

Sassy and Imogen crawled forward, while I turned back to Jonah. He was struggling to get to his feet and stumbled when he tried to put weight on his bad ankle.

"Do you need help?" I asked.

"Nah," he said with a wave of his hand. "I've got this."

He tried another step, but his ankle twisted under him. Squeaks was there in under a second to steady him. Liam rushed to his other side and grabbed Jonah's arm to drape it over his shoulder.

"Can you crawl?" Liam asked him.

Jonah nodded. "I think so."

"Good," Liam replied before turning to me. "Go ahead, Sophia. I've got him."

I hesitated. Liam's knees shook under Jonah's weight. He didn't look like he was doing well. I wanted to go last to make sure they both made it out all right.

"He may need help at the end," Liam said. "Imogen can't pull him out on her own."

He had a point.

"Okay," I agreed. "I'm right in front of you if you need anything, Jonah."

I turned and crawled through the tunnel behind Esis. The sunlight was blinding when I emerged, but it felt good on my skin. I barely recognized the landscape around me. Where there was greenery yesterday was only mounds of dirt and rock today. Trees had been plowed over, and I couldn't even see the boulder we'd run around the day before.

Imogen took in the devastation, her eyes traveling far down the mountain through the path of the landslide. "It's a shame the Elders had to kill so many trees. I hope they restore this area when the tournament is finished."

"Hopefully they will," I agreed.

Jonah moved slowly through the tunnel, but eventually, he reached the end. His hands searched the opening for something to grab onto and pull himself out. Imogen and I each offered a hand to help. It was like trying to drag out a full-sized tree. It took all my strength. The guy was huge. Squeaks pushed from the other side of him, and we managed to yank Jonah out. He lay in the dirt to catch his breath.

As soon as Squeaks squeezed out of the tunnel, I turned back to it to offer my hand to Liam. His palm was clammy and slipped in mine, but he took it anyway.

"Good job, Imogen," Liam said through heavy breaths. He sat beside Jonah and wiped at the sweat on his brow. Dark circles had formed under his eyes.

"Are you going to be okay, Liam?" I asked.

He nodded. "I'm more worried about Jonah. Should we take a look at that ankle?"

Jonah sighed. "I guess we're going to have to."

Liam reached for Jonah's shoe and began untying the laces. Gently, he pulled Jonah's shoe off and then peeled back his sock. Everyone leaned in to take a look. Honestly, it didn't look that bad. There was only a slight bruise and swelling on the back of his foot.

Liam scoffed. "Seriously, Jonah? This is it?"

"You think I'm lying?" Jonah shot back. "It's in a *very sensitive* area. Besides, broken bones don't always look bad from the surface."

Liam's eyebrows shot up. "You think you broke something?"

"Well, um..." Jonah hesitated. "I don't know. I might've..."

Liam sighed, then glanced up to the peak of the mountain. We had a long trek ahead of us. As my gaze followed Liam's, I noticed a creature circling above us. It was smaller than a dragon but bigger than a bird, and looked as if someone was flying on its back. I squinted at it and realized it was a winged lion. Another member of the camera crew, I was sure. Everyone in Kinpago was probably laughing at us. We had to be at least half a day behind the other teams.

Liam's jaw tensed. "Can you at least *try* walking?"

"I don't know," Jonah snapped. "Can you *try* showing a little compassion?"

"We can try wrapping it," I suggested quickly, before they bit each other's heads off. "Like in our Medical Care of Familiars class."

"We don't have a first-aid kit," Liam pointed out.

"I'm sure we can find something," I said. "Like some sort of vine."

"Forget about it," Jonah insisted. "Squeaks can carry me."

"You up for it, girl?" Imogen asked as she stroked Squeaks' feathers.

Squeaks nodded and straightened her back, eagerly waiting for Jonah to climb on. Imogen and I each took one of Jonah's arms and helped him up.

As soon as he was on Squeaks' back and she started forward, her front foot caught on a rock, and she stumbled. Jonah's hands flew out to catch himself, but he landed on his bad ankle. He let out of a cry of pain as his leg crumpled beneath him. He rolled down the mountain-side a good fifteen feet until coming to a stop.

"Oh my God!" I screamed the same time Imogen and Liam cursed the ancestors.

The three of us raced over to him. From up the mountain, Squeaks hung her head in shame. Jonah slammed his fist against the dirt to keep from screaming. My gut twisted. I couldn't watch this.

"Esis, come here." I gestured to him.

Imogen's eyes met mine, and then she glanced to Liam, though he didn't notice. "I have an idea," she blurted.

Esis hopped into my lap. I pulled him close but paused to listen to her.

"I can... I can carry Jonah," Imogen said.

Liam scoffed. "We all know how that worked out last time."

"That's because I wasn't thinking about it like an Elementai," Imogen pointed out. "I'll use the trees to carry him. Just watch."

I held my breath. Nothing happened for several seconds, but then the ends of tree roots rose up from the ground.

Jonah drew in a surprised breath when the roots lifted him. His body hovered just inches above the ground and glided along from one group of roots to the next, as if riding a conveyor belt. Imogen was careful with his foot, making sure to keep it elevated without letting the roots touch the tender spot.

Jonah glanced around to see he was off the ground. "Well, this is... kinda cool. It's like a little massage."

Liam stood and crossed his arms. "Do you think you can keep that up, Imogen?"

She nodded. "Once we reach those trees, I'll use the branches to hold him up."

Liam looked skeptical, but Jonah just raised his arms into the air and made a rock-and-roll sign with his hands.

"Crowd surfing, baby!" Jonah teased.

Liam just shook his head and frowned. "Fine. Whatever works. Let's get going."

HOURS PASSED as we climbed the mountain. Though we'd stopped for lunch to cook up the two chipmunks and a squirrel Squeaks had caught for us, we were all starting to slow down. It wasn't a very substantial meal, and the incline was killing my legs. I was certain everyone else felt the same. The higher we climbed, the thinner the trees became. The clouds darkened, blocking the sun, and the air cooled. I could see it in Imogen's tired eyes that she was straining to stretch her magic by moving Jonah from tree branch to tree branch.

Jonah had passed out, snoring as the trees grew around his form, cradling him and passing him from one tree to the next like a bucket brigade.

Liam looked the worst of all. His hands shook, and his hair was in disarray around his face. His lips were dry and cracked, and his face paler than normal. His eyes glazed over, but he kept them locked on the mountain peak— like that was the only thing pushing him forward. He shivered, but when I'd offered to share some of my warmth, he declined.

"I think we need to take a break," I suggested.

"We're almost to the top," Liam said without slowing his step.

MEGAN LINSKI & ALICIA RADES

"The trees are thinning, and we need to figure out something else for Jonah," I pointed out. "Maybe he can try riding Squeaks again."

Liam whirled around, almost stumbling over the rocks at his feet. "Or maybe he can try walking like the rest of us."

"Liam, he's hurt—" I started, but he promptly cut me off.

"Please," he scoffed, gesturing to Jonah hanging in the trees. "He's living in luxury there. The dude's taking a fucking *nap* while the rest of us are climbing Mount Fucking Everest."

I stopped in my tracks, completely taken off guard by Liam's tone. Imogen came to a halt behind me. Jonah's snoring and the sound of heavy winds were all I heard.

I blinked several times, trying to find the words. But what was I supposed to say to *that*? Liam obviously wasn't looking for comfort.

Imogen stepped in for me, though her tone was anything but comforting. She was beyond irritated. "I'm sorry, Liam," she snapped. "Were you looking for a free ride to the top? I mean, did you want to break an ankle? At least you can *walk!*"

"Yeah," Liam bit back sarcastically. "I have so much to be thankful for. Thanks for the reminder. Never mind the fact that—"

He cut off abruptly.

"What?" Imogen demanded.

Liam turned away from her and fixed his eyes on the mountain peak again. "Nothing," he mumbled.

"No." Imogen stomped up to him and stood on her toes so he couldn't avoid her gaze. "I want to know. What were you going to say?"

A muscle popped in Liam's jaw. "It doesn't matter."

Imogen crossed her arms. "It does. If you have something to say, say it."

He spoke through clenched teeth. "Sophia's right. We need a break. Besides, I know a plant in this area that might help relieve some of the lumberjack's pain."

Liam shoved Jonah's shoe he still held into Imogen's hands. Then he whirled around and started down the mountain.

"Liam!" I called, but he ignored me. I turned to Imogen. "He's being ridiculous."

"I know," she agreed. "But it's Liam. He needs to cool off."

I nodded. "Thank you, by the way. For carrying Jonah to keep our secret."

Imogen shrugged like it wasn't a big deal. "We don't need to piss Liam off more than he already is."

"Agreed," I said. "I plan on telling him... but after the tournament. We don't need him abandoning us in the middle of it. He's coming back, right?"

Imogen glanced to his retreating form. "Yeah. He's coming back."

Imogen lowered Jonah to the ground beside us. He stirred, and his whole body shivered.

"I don't know how we're going to get him over the peak of the mountain," Imogen said.

I bit my lower lip, staring down at him. "I think we need to heal him."

"Liam will know something's up," Imogen protested.

"He already thinks Jonah's faking it," I argued. "Right now, Jonah is worse off than Liam. We need to help him."

Imogen hesitated. "Fine. But Jonah can't tell Liam. Not until we make it out of here. Liam will freak."

"I know. Esis, come on buddy."

Esis hopped down from Squeaks' back and scurried over to where Jonah lay.

I knelt down beside them. "Do you think you can help him? The same way you helped Aisha?"

Esis nodded eagerly, then placed his tiny little hands on Jonah's skin just above his sock. I didn't get to witness his miraculous recovery since the injury was internal, but watching Jonah's energy return was magical enough on its own. Slowly, color returned to his face, and his eyes fluttered open as the bruise faded.

"How are you feeling?" Imogen asked.

Confusion settled over his face, and he wiggled his foot. "Surprisingly well. How long was I—?"

Jonah cut off when he saw Esis at his feet, his tiny hands on him and his eyes closed. Realization crossed Jonah's face.

"Holy shit!" Jonah cursed as he shot upright to a sitting position. "Esis can *heal*?!"

"Yes," I confirmed in a nervous tone. "But it's a secret."

"Why didn't you say anything sooner?" Jonah demanded. "He could heal Liam!"

"Shh," I cried, slapping a hand over his mouth. He promptly stuck his tongue out to lick me. "Ew! Jonah, really?"

"Don't put your hand on my mouth," Jonah snapped back. "But... seriously, Sophia? How could you not tell Liam? He could finally get better!"

"I know. And I want him to. But can you imagine his reaction?" I pleaded.

Jonah contemplated it for a moment. "He still has a right to know. If Esis healed him, we could make it back faster."

"I know, I know," I insisted. "But what if it tears our group apart? If Liam feels betrayed... if he feels like he can't trust us..."

"We can't deal with that right now," Imogen finished for me.

Jonah still looked skeptical. "How long have you known?"

"A few weeks," I said, dropping my gaze. "We kept it secret to protect Esis. I don't want anyone taking him from me."

"You could've trusted us," he said.

"What would you do if Squeaks had unique magical abilities?" I asked. "You'd do whatever you had to in order to protect her, wouldn't you?"

Jonah glanced to Squeaks, who was nipping playfully at Sassy on her back. "Yeah. I guess I would."

"Please don't tell Liam," I begged. "I need to protect Esis. We need to protect our team."

"Liam's my *best friend*," Jonah said harshly. "You want me to keep it a secret that the cure for whatever he's suffering from is right there in front of him?"

"Yes. Because we have no choice," I said firmly.

Jonah hesitated. "Fine. But you better tell him after we make it out of here. Not telling him... it's cruel."

I flinched. "I will," I promised.

"I'll let him ride Squeaks to the top," Jonah said. "He's lighter than me, so she should be able to take it."

"If she doesn't trip over her own feet," Imogen mumbled.

Squeaks shot her a death glare.

"Sorry, Squeaks." Imogen shrugged. "You're kind of a klutz."

Liam's loud footsteps and mumbling reached my ears. He was already on his way back. I could see him trudging through the thin trees.

"This forest is fucking useless!" he shouted.

"Ancestors," Imogen muttered. "He's like an emotional hurricane. I thought Toaqua were supposed to be gentle."

Jonah just rolled his eyes. "Can I have my shoe?"

Liam stomped out of the trees and toward us. "Excellent. You're up. Looks like you don't need that painkiller after all."

Jonah forced a painfully fake yawn. "Nah, dude. That nap really helped. My ankle's feeling better. I think I can walk from here."

Liam huffed and started back up the mountain. He muttered under his breath loud enough for us to hear. "Unbelievable. Yet no one listened when I said you were being a baby."

"Hey," Jonah called as Liam distanced himself from us. "You wanna ride Squeaks?"

"And fall down the mountain when she trips?" Liam yelled back. "No thanks. My own two feet are pretty reliable."

Which I could tell was a total lie, because he was struggling to walk. Why was he so stubborn?

"Are you coming or not?" Liam asked.

We all hurried behind him. Nobody spoke as we continued our trek, finally cresting the mountain and starting down the other side. Hours passed until the sky began to darken into evening.

"We need to stop," Jonah finally broke the silence.

"We still have some daylight left," Liam replied. "It won't take long to make a shelter now that we know what we're doing."

"I don't mean stopping for the night," Jonah said. "The pressure in the air just shifted. I think a storm is going to reach us soon."

Liam glanced to the darkening sky above us. The clouds rushed by, swirling into indistinct shapes that warned of danger. The wind around us picked up almost instantly, and thunder rumbled in the distance.

"How soon?" Liam asked.

"Um, now!" Imogen shouted, pointing above us.

I followed her gaze, only for my stomach to instantly bottom out. A funnel cloud was forming in the clouds above.

And it was going to land right on top of us.

Liam

TWENTY-ONE

As if we didn't have enough to deal with. We'd just gotten over being buried alive, and we hadn't even gotten a good night's rest before a fucking twister decided to fuck up the party.

This monster was no joke. It hadn't reached the ground yet, but I could see that the funnel cloud was a quarter of a mile across and had huge power. The roar of it was so loud that it was hurting my ears. Once it reached earth, it would send us flying all the way across the country.

I quickly analyzed the area. There were no ditches to lay down in, and outrunning the twister wouldn't work.

"Imogen, can you get us underground?" I asked at the top of my lungs as the tornado drew closer. I could barely hear myself. I didn't know how the others would.

"I don't have enough time!" Imogen shouted. "It would take a few minutes, at least!"

That was it, then. We only had one option.

"Jonah, you're up!" I shouted. "This is your task!"

Unlike Imogen yesterday, Jonah looked completely determined. His face was completely calm as he shouted, "Imogen, use the tree roots to hold everyone down! I'm gonna end this big bastard!"

Imogen did as she was told. She wrapped the surrounding trees roots around our legs and ankles, securing me, Sophia, Sassy, Esis, and herself down. For extra precaution, I drew up water from the ground and froze it around our feet and between the roots so that we were firmly held in place. The ice crept up Esis' body until only his head was sticking out. He gave me a scathing look I ignored.

Jonah didn't need to be held down. He forced the air around him and Squeaks to calm, making an invisible shield that the tornado couldn't penetrate. But he could only protect himself, not us.

Squeaks remained outside with Jonah, taking a wide stance and screeching at the tornado, like it was a challenger that had encroached on her territory. Jonah wasted no time and threw his hands out in front of him, shooting out a strong gust of wind that was meant to break the twister's rotation.

The twister seemed to slow, but it didn't stop its descent. The moment the twister touched down about fifty feet away, things really started going to hell. Rocks and debris were picked up and thrown around as projectiles, and smaller trees began getting uprooted.

"Look out!" I shouted. Imogen and Sophia ducked as a sapling was hurtled toward us full-speed. It was hard to move around against the strength of the storm.

Jonah kept increasing his power, trying to break the funnel of the twister, but it wasn't working. No matter how hard he tried to get the tornado to break and the winds to go in a different direction, it only seemed like the twister gained intensity. Squeaks kept her wings pinned to her sides and concentrated, giving what power she could to Jonah.

Even from a distance, I could tell Jonah was working really hard. The twister was more powerful than he was. A majority of his magic went to keeping himself anchored. But he couldn't be tangled up in the roots like us, because he still needed to move around in order to use his element. He was stuck.

I heard large breaking noises as trunks behind us were shattered by the force of wind. The larger trees were coming up, too. There had to be four or five Elementai behind this twister, controlling it. I couldn't imagine how the Elders expected us to survive this. I could feel the ice starting to crack around our heels, and the roots were starting to break, too. It wouldn't be long before the twister pulled us up.

"Squeaks, I need help!" Jonah screamed.

Squeaks ruffled her feathers and shook her head. There was a fierce glint in her eye. She drew a deep breath and then opened her mouth, screaming at the top of her lungs at the twister.

The very ground shook, and it wasn't because of the twister. Squeaks' shout caused the twister to waver, rocketing back and forth at the force of her cry. Jonah's Air gathered around her and pushed the tornado backward. Squeaks walked forward, still braying, and the tornado started to head in the other direction. It was backing off!

Holy shit! Squeaks is powerful.

I thought that Squeaks was going to have it handled, but then she coughed and staggered to her knees. She got back up, but when she shouted again her scream wasn't as strong as it had been before.

The twister buckled at her shout, but remained, then started spinning toward us again. Squeaks' scream had weakened the tornado, but it hadn't broken it.

"I can't control it!" Jonah yelled. "But I have an idea. Everyone, let go!"

"*What?*" the three of us shouted in unison.

"Are you crazy?" Sophia yelled.

"Just trust me!" he cried back. "Imogen, let go of the roots! Everyone make a chain!"

There wasn't time to argue. I melted the ice around Sassy and Esis first. Esis dragged himself toward Sophia and held onto her leg while Sassy launched herself at Imogen, clinging to the front of her shirt. We all held hands, me grabbing onto Sophia's and Imogen's as the last of the ice melted. Imogen began to release the roots, and we started to lift into the air.

"I hope you know what you're doing!" I yelled at Jonah as he grabbed Imogen's hand. Squeaks unfurled her wings. She was immediately carried off, swirling around the edge of the twister.

I realized Jonah's plan the second before it happened.

"Everybody hold on!" Jonah screamed, and the roots broke loose.

We were instantly carried off into the air. The twister sucked us up, and all sound drowned out as we entered into the eye of the storm. The tornado spiraled us around violently. I felt like my arms were going to be ripped off as I held on to Imogen and Sophia's hands. My stomach churned as we were sent spiraling around. I was going to throw up.

Though I couldn't hear anything, I could see the horrified looks on everyone's faces and I knew they were yelling. Imogen was crying, Sophia had her eyes closed, and Esis' chubby cheeks were getting blown back by the wind. Sassy dug her nails into Imogen's chest, holding on for dear life.

The only one who wasn't screaming his head off was Jonah. Though we were in the middle of the tornado, his eyes were narrowed in concentration. He was completely calm, like he was born to be up here.

Using his element, Jonah ricocheted us away from the tornado. We went flying hundreds of feet above ground at a high speed, but it was away from the twister.

Once we were out of the reach of the vortex, we started falling. Fast. While we were all screaming our heads off, Jonah shut his eyes. Calm air gently came up beneath us to support our weight like a parachute. We drifted toward ground at a leisurely speed until our feet hit the grass softly.

Squeaks was already there waiting for us, peeping happily. The mountains were far in the distance now. We had landed in a valley on the edge of the forest.

I collapsed when my feet hit the ground, and so did Sophia and Imogen. Jonah was the only one still walking. He had his hands on his hips and was looking very full of himself. "There. Safe and sound."

I gagged. Sophia held her head like she had a headache. Imogen lay spread out on the ground with Sassy, who had all four feet above her so it looked like she was dead. Esis rubbed Sophia's temple until she rose to a sitting position.

Jonah raised an eyebrow. "Hey, you guys okay?"

"Are we fucking okay." I closed my eyes and tried to make the earth stop moving.

"I hate heights." Imogen shivered. She sat up, and Jonah helped her to stand. "I like keeping my feet on the ground."

"Well, let's hope that we never have to do that again." Jonah clapped Imogen on the shoulder.

After a few moments, I managed to push myself to my feet. The ground was still moving, but it wasn't like that hadn't been happening for me for the past two days now, anyway, so I forced myself to rise. I needed to tough it out. "Let's hope so. That was some pretty spectacular stuff, Jonah."

"Wasn't it?" Jonah threw an arm over Squeaks. "But it was nothing me and my girl couldn't handle."

Squeaks chortled and nipped at Jonah's hair. His bun had come loose in the chaos, and now his hair was down around his face. It was a mess.

Imogen's lips quivered. "You know, Jonah, with your hair down like that you look like a sexy Viking."

"Yeah." Sophia giggled nervously. "Like Thor."

"More like Tarzan." He brushed back his messy hair with one hand. "Though if you ladies want to play Jane, I'm sorry to disappoint. I'm looking for a wild man myself."

Imogen and Sophia burst out laughing. It was the kind of laugh people made when they were on the edge and just needed to loosen the tension. Jonah joined in, and I shook my head. This tournament was making us lose it.

We walked for awhile, until we reached the trees again. "We should rest," I said. "We barely slept in that cave."

The group nodded in agreement. Imogen began building her root house again, and Sophia and Esis started looking for firewood. Jonah dragged over two large logs for us to sit on. I sat down, and Sophia put her kindling in the middle before starting a fire.

I wanted to help the group, but I just couldn't. I didn't have anything left. I managed to draw up a small well of water we could use to drink before I put my head in my hands and sank it between my knees. I. Felt. Awful.

Sometime, I started coughing. Hard. Jonah kept looking at me, but

I ignored him. I struggled to take deep breaths and concentrated on just breathing.

I didn't know how long I sat there, but after awhile, I could smell rabbit cooking. Sophia offered me a leg, but I shook my head. Just looking at it made me queasy.

"Liam, you have to eat," she said, shoving it toward me again. I took it and forced down a few bites, though my stomach churned and cramped with each swallow.

After a couple of minutes, I stood up. "Hey, guys, I'm going to scout ahead really quick," I told them. "See where we should go in the morning."

Nobody questioned me. I took off into the woods, far enough away so nobody would hear, and threw up the few bits of rabbit Sophia had forced me to take.

I felt clammy. I pressed a hand to my forehead and flinched at how hot it was. I was running a fever.

I coughed again, and quickly covered my mouth with my hand. I slowly drew it away. When I did, I noticed my fingers were covered in blood.

The grim reality set in. I was dying. I knew that already. I'd been hiding that from my team since we'd gotten buried in that mountain. It'd taken everything I had to get us this far.

I knew I wasn't going to make it through this tournament. I'd never see my family again, that much I was sure of. My only goal now was to get my team as far as I could, before the end. They didn't realize why I was pushing them so hard, because they thought we had no time limit.

Oh, we had a time limit, all right. It was me. And my clock was ticking, fast. It wouldn't be long now before my time would be up.

I knew I'd been a bigger asshole than usual during this tournament. I didn't mean to. I'd been trying to control my temper, but I wasn't a superhero.

They didn't realize how hard this was. They all had their Familiars to lean on for support. I had no one. When I fell, I had to catch myself. Doing this tournament with a Familiar was difficult, but without one... it was fucking impossible.

I wiped the blood off my face and hand before I headed back to the fire.

"That was quick," Jonah remarked suspiciously. His eyes followed me as I sat down.

He was on to me. Whatever. I shrugged, and Imogen commented, "Hey, guys... do you realize that there's only one more task left?"

"Yeah," Jonah said, clarity dawning on his face. "We're almost done. We might get to go home tomorrow."

I thought about it. We *did* only have one more task. This awful tournament wasn't going to go on forever. There was just one more trial we needed to pass. Maybe I'd last that long.

I coughed violently again, and didn't let myself get my hopes up. I had a day left, if that.

Sophia didn't say anything. She stared into the fire with Esis curled up in her lap, looking haunted.

Fire was the only thing left. That meant it was up to Sophia. I didn't know if she believed in herself enough to do it.

That frightened me. We didn't come all this way just to die tomorrow, did we?

Well, I did. I just didn't want that to happen to everyone else.

"Hey, Imogen," I said, and she looked up. "I'm sorry I was such an ass back there in the cave. I didn't want to hurt your feelings. I just knew you could do it."

Imogen didn't say anything, but Sassy climbed up on my lap and licked my cheek a few times. Her tail swished back and forth happily, and I knew Imogen had forgiven me.

"That goes for all of you," I said, looking at Jonah and Sophia. "I know I've been kinda rough on you guys so far. But I know you can make it through this thing. If I push you, it's because I want you to succeed. Sorry if it comes off in a shitty way. I can be over the top sometimes."

"Sometimes?" Jonah asked, and Sophia smirked. Everyone laughed— including me.

I cleared my throat. "Anyway, what I'm trying to say is... I believe in you guys. And I'm sorry for constantly freaking out on you."

"Aw," Imogen said, and Sassy let out a happy bark. Esis clapped, and Sophia smiled.

"Group hug!" Jonah announced, and he got off his seat.

"No, this isn't that kind of—"

Nobody heard me. Imogen, Jonah, and Sophia rushed toward me and gave me the biggest, most sappy hug that has ever happened in all of existence. Sassy twirled herself around my legs, and Squeaks threw out her wings to encompass us fully. I could even feel Esis on the top of my head, squeezing me tight.

"All right, all right," I said, and I pushed everyone off of me. "That's enough of that. This isn't the Bleeding Hearts Club."

I yanked Esis off of my head and handed him back to Sophia. Her eyes... they were sparkling.

"We're totally going to do this, guys," Jonah said. "We're going to get through the tournament, and it's going to be together!"

Imogen and Sophia cheered, but I only plastered on a fake smile. I knew they'd have to make it to the finish line without me.

Imogen and Jonah went to bed before Sophia and I did. They took Sassy and Squeaks inside the root hut, and soon it was just the three of us gathered around the fire. Esis sat by the flames and rubbed his little paws together to keep warm.

Sophia crossed her arms and held them tightly against her body. "I'm worried, Liam. What if I can't do it?"

"You can," I told her. I was starting to shake, but it wasn't because of the cold. I tried to force myself to stay steady so she wouldn't notice.

"I don't know." She threw a stick into the fire. "We don't know what's coming. I'm not prepared. I'm not ready. I'm—"

She dropped her head, and Esis put a paw on her calf for comfort.

I'd go over to her, but I was having trouble moving at all at the moment. "Come here," I said. I opened up an arm, and Sophia got up. She left her log to sit next to me. I pulled her close and laid my head on top of hers as we stared at the fire. Her just pressing against me was enough to make me feel a tiny bit better.

My pants were practically doing the happy dance. Despite the fact that my body was shutting down, my dick was working just fine. I couldn't seem to help the fact that I got a boner every time I got within three feet of Sophia. Though we were in a life-or-death situation, all I wanted to do was lie down for another long cuddle and... something else.

Last wish, maybe?

She sighed. "I don't think I can do this."

"You don't have a choice," I told her softly.

"You don't understand, Liam. I'm not strong enough. I'm going to fail."

"No, Sophia." I grabbed her shoulders and shook them. "You have to pass that task tomorrow and get Jonah and Imogen through this, you hear me? *Whatever it takes.*"

She stared at me. "I notice you didn't mention yourself."

I stayed silent, and she added, "It seems like you're saying if something happens, to go on without you."

My heartbeat sped up. "I didn't say that."

"Sounds like it."

She pressed further into my chest. "That was really sweet, apologizing to Imogen and Jonah," Sophia said quietly.

"I'm not above apologizing," I told her. "Ancestors know I'm the biggest fuck-up on this team. I know how to ask for forgiveness."

"You're not a fuck-up, Liam. You're the best person I know," Sophia said.

"You've met a lot of shitty people, then." I laughed under my breath, but secretly, I felt like flying. I can't believe she thought so highly of me. I didn't deserve that.

"I really do mean it." Her voice became heavy. "But I can't help but wonder if that was really an apology, or a goodbye."

My insides rolled, and I shuddered. "What do you think, Sophia?"

"I think you're the one who cares the most, but you don't like people getting too close, so you push them all away," Sophia said. "This isn't goodbye, Liam. We cross that finish line together, or not at all."

It was awesome she didn't want to give up on me, but I was a lost cause. "Sure. I promise, *pawee.*"

She seemed a little less nervous now. "I'm glad you're here, Liam. I want you to be there with me when we finally reach the end."

I just wrapped my arms tighter around her for an answer. I wanted to be there more than anything. But the truth was, I wouldn't be able to. My body wouldn't let me.

The hardest part of this tournament wasn't going to be losing my life. It was going to be leaving Sophia.

❧

"WELL, well, well, what do we have here?"

A huge figure blocked out the sun. It was Jonah, looking down on us with a smug smile on his face. Squeaks was nearby, her head tilted in curiosity.

Sophia untangled herself from my limbs and stretched. I slowly pieced together what was going on.

Aw, fuck. We'd fallen asleep by the fire, while Imogen and Jonah had spent the night inside the hut. I damn well hope the cameras hadn't caught that.

Imogen was nearby, and she had the most satisfactory smile on her face. "Ha. I knew it."

"Shut up, Im." Sophia sat up and yawned. She rubbed her eyes and brushed her hair out of her face.

Though my body felt like it'd been pummeled by a ton of bricks, I rolled onto my stomach and forced myself onto my feet. I was sweating all over, and though it was cool out, I felt like it was a hundred degrees. My fever had gotten worse overnight. My throat was dry, and it hurt to speak, but I knew my team needed a final pep talk. It'd probably be the last one they'd get from me.

"Okay, team. We're tired, gross, and hungry, but we're almost there," I said. "Let's finish this."

It felt like I had concrete on my feet. But we only had a few miles left to go, maybe a little less. I forced myself forward, and my team followed.

As we walked through the forest, I noticed the team separated. The girls were up ahead, talking lowly. I'd bet money Imogen was interrogating Sophia about us. Nothing got the team moving quite like gossip.

"Hey, what's up between you and Sophia?" Jonah asked me without so much as a *good morning*. "Are you two together?"

Like I said. Screw food and a shower. The latest on my sex life was enough to sustain Jonah for days. "Enough, Jonah." I sighed.

"Did you guys *do it*?" Jonah whispered. "I want all the deets."

Squeaks widened her eyes and squawked.

"No, Jonah," I said in irritation. "Besides, there's not exactly a convenience store around here to swing by and pick up condoms."

"Hey, when nature calls," Jonah offered.

"If you really think Sophia and I are gonna bone when we're in the middle of—"

I stopped mid-way through my sentence to take several short, quick gasps. I literally couldn't breathe. It felt like there was an elephant sitting on my chest. I tried gasping for air again, but hardly any came through. My mind whirled, and the earth started spinning. It felt like I was underwater and there was no way up. Jonah's playful expression changed to concern.

"Liam," Jonah said, and he stepped in front of me. He grabbed my shoulders and looked me in the eye. "You need to breathe, brother. There's hardly any air getting through your windpipe. I can feel it."

My gasping had gotten the attention of the girls up ahead. They turned to look at me while Jonah took one hand off my shoulder and started making back-and-forth motions with it.

He was literally pushing air through my lungs. Imogen held her breath, while Sophia squeezed Esis. Esis had little tears welling up in his eyes, but I couldn't be sure why. Why was the little bugger so upset?

"I'm... fine," I said as I got my breath back. My throat was open now, and I could feel air filling up my lungs. I didn't have to struggle. Things righted themselves for a minute before I coughed, hard.

This time there was no hiding it from the team. A huge globule of blood came out of my mouth and nose, and I struggled to catch it. I stumbled forward before Jonah caught me. The girls gasped when they noticed the blood, and Jonah's eyes narrowed.

Jonah put a hand on my forehead before I could push him away. "He's running a fever," Jonah said viciously. He was pissed.

"You didn't notice how hot he was?" Imogen turned toward Sophia, surprised.

"I... I thought it was just because I'm naturally warm," Sophia said. "I couldn't tell."

I coughed again, and more blood came up. I wiped it away with my sleeve, but that didn't stop the looks my team was giving me. Even Sassy and Squeaks' mouths were open.

"Liam..." Sophia spoke softly, like she couldn't believe it. Like this was her worst nightmare, happening right in front of her.

"Liam, this is bullshit. Why didn't you tell us you were this sick?" Jonah asked. His hands were bunched into fists.

I opened my mouth, unsure of what to say. How could I tell them this was it for me?

But I didn't get a chance to answer, because right then a fireball whizzed by my head.

I jumped backward. The fireball whirled by my face and smashed against a nearby tree, singeing it.

At first I thought it was the trial, but then I noticed we weren't alone. Haley was standing across the clearing from us, along with Anwara, her two teammates and their Familiars.

At the start of the competition, Haley had looked confident. Now she was a mess. Her outfit was stained and torn, and her hair was in tangles around her face. She and her teammates were sporting various scrapes and bruises. Anwara was missing feathers, while the stone-lion had chunks of it that were gone and the winged jaguar was carrying a hurt paw. They looked like they hadn't rested in days.

"Haley," Sophia started, and she put herself in front of me. "What are you doing here?"

Haley didn't answer. Her face contorted into a snarl, and she yelled, "Attack!"

Fire, Air and Earth started coming at us from all sides. We had no choice but to react. Imogen immediately brought up a wall of dirt that we ducked behind. Sophia started tossing fireballs back at Haley, while Jonah blew a gust of air at his fellow Yapluma, trying to push her back. Imogen was in a battle with the Nivita guy. Her plants acted like whips, breaking apart the stone boulders that he tried to chuck at us.

This crazy bitch was literally trying to kill us! All for a damn trophy. Had she lost her mind?

I heard loud squeaks and snarls, and I dared to look over the wall. Squeaks was in a tussle with the stone-lion, while Esis and Sassy both were taking on the winged jaguar. The jaguar was bigger and more threatening, but Sassy and Esis were small and quick. The cat couldn't get a firm grip on them. They bit and scratched at the jaguar, taking turns distracting it. The stone-lion was too heavy for Squeaks to move, but Squeaks wasn't exactly tiny herself, so she used her bulk to throw the other Familiar around while her hooves chipped at the lion's rock-hard skin.

Anwara was flying above us. She opened her mouth to breathe a jet of flame, but I summoned my element and water came splashing upward into her mouth. I used what power I had to keep the phoenix subdued, dousing her in as much water as I could summon from the ground. Anwara was soaking wet, but she continued to try and light us up, all with desperate glances back at Haley. Haley grew more furious with her Familiar every time she failed to hurt one of us.

Teams sometimes tried to sabotage each other on their way to win during the Cup, but a full-on war between two teams had never happened before. This was absolutely ridiculous. I bet the fans back home were loving this drama.

"Haley, we're outnumbered!" the Nivita guy shouted. "We should go!"

"No! We're not going to lose to a bunch of freaks!" Haley screamed. She increased her firepower, but she was the only one who did. The Yapluma girl was starting to back off Jonah, and the Nivita guy hesitated in throwing more boulders, unsure of what he should do.

But the Yapluma girl had made up her mind. She dropped her hands and stopped summoning her element, causing Jonah to halt his attack. Her winged jaguar batted Sassy and Esis away, returning to his Elementai's side.

"I don't want to do this anymore, Haley!" she screamed. The Yapluma girl backed away against a tree. "We shouldn't be attacking our own people, even if they are our competition! It's fucked up!"

"Shut up!" Haley screeched.

"It's just a stupid Cup! I'm leaving!" The Yapluma girl turned her back on Haley and stomped away. Her Familiar followed her, trotting to his Elementai loyally.

Haley gritted her teeth. "Nobody turns their back on me."

Haley screamed, and the sound that came from her mouth was so primal... it was almost evil. At her command, the trees around her Yapluma teammate lit up in flames. Branches crashed to the ground, and a large one cracked and fell downward, landing on the Yapluma girl and her Familiar. I could hear their agonized screams as they started burning to death.

"Haley! Stop!" Sophia screamed in horror, but Haley only increased the size and heat of the flames.

Haley grinned widely as her teammate cried for help, and her right eye twitched. The Yapluma girl tried to escape by pushing outward with her element, but the Air she provided only fueled Haley's Fire.

"Stop it!" Sophia had enough. She ran forward and pushed Haley down. Sophia used the power of her element to suppress Haley's and make the fire smaller. I snapped out of it and brought water coursing up from the ground.

I tried to put it out as quickly as I could, but it was no use. The Yapluma girl and her Familiar were already dead. There was nothing left but their blackened corpses.

Haley laughed. It was twisted and sick. It wasn't even human. Sophia's entire body was shaking as she backed away from the charred bodies.

Haley only had herself and her Nivita teammate left. She had to make sure both of them survived in order to pass the tournament.

The Nivita boy was pale. He reached out to steady himself on his stone-lion, staring at the blackened husk of the person that had been there just moments before.

Haley took off running. It was only a few seconds before the Nivita boy and his stone-lion followed. Anwara soared after, but her sharp eyes lingered on the fallen tree and the ashes that remained.

Sophia heaved for air next to me. Her face was red, eyes absolutely burning. Her expression was furious, and her whole body shook in rage.

"*Haley!*" Sophia screamed. She started forward and chased after her housemate. Esis tried to stop her by yanking on her pant leg, but she shook him off and continued to pursue Haley.

"Sophia, don't!" I yelled, but it was too late. Sophia had already taken off. Imogen, Jonah and I raced after her, trying to catch up. Haley was drawing us to the one place we didn't want to go.

The final task.

sophia
TWENTY-TWO

vil! She's pure evil!

ERage rocketed through me as I raced through the woods behind Haley. Flames begged to escape through my closed fists. My hands burned until I couldn't take it anymore and fire shot between my fingers. I didn't know what I was going to do to Haley when I reached her. All I knew was that somebody needed to teach her a lesson.

Haley and her teammate dodged around thick trees and jumped over fallen logs, their Familiars close on their heels. She shot a glance back over her shoulder. A satisfied smirk touched her lips when she saw how far behind I was. Her laughter echoed through the forest.

My legs burned as they moved beneath me, and my head spun. I hadn't eaten much the last few days, and it was starting to show. The way Haley moved so quickly and agile, she'd probably shoved some energy bars in her pockets before the opening ceremony.

"Sophia!"

I heard someone's voice behind me, but I barely registered it. All my attention was focused on Haley. She was headed straight for a sharp decline in the forest, an area that looked as if a river had once flowed through it. In a last-ditch effort, I drew my arm back and hurled a fireball at the back of her head.

She jumped before my fireball made it to her. Her body dropped out of view as she slid down the ravine.

I pushed past the heat climbing up my legs and raced faster. I reached the ravine and braced myself. My feet dug into the dirt to slow my fall down the hill, but I managed to keep my footing. My eyes darted from one side to the other, but Haley was nowhere in sight. She was gone.

Sassy jumped into the ravine behind me, Squeaks and Esis closely following. Squeaks tripped over a rock on the hillside and tumbled the rest of the way down. She landed with her wings spread out beneath her and her legs straight up in the air. She quickly righted herself and shook her head. Esis scurried up my pant leg and onto my shoulder.

Imogen almost lost her footing as she raced after me, but a loose rock jumped upward on her way down the hill. She stepped on it to steady herself before stopping beside me. Jonah and Liam made it to us a few seconds later. Liam gritted his teeth and breathed heavier than I'd ever seen him breathe before.

"Sophia, stop!" Imogen demanded.

I barely heard her. "I think she went this way."

I took a step to my right, but Liam's hand shot out and grabbed mine. He instantly pulled away as if my skin had burned him.

"Sophia," he said, concern etched in his features. "We can't waste our energy fighting against other teams."

"She *killed* her teammate," I growled, unable to control the anger coursing through me. I couldn't remember the last time I'd felt so out of control— probably never. "She *murdered* someone."

"I know," Liam said with a sigh. "But we can worry about Haley later. We're almost to the final trial, and—"

Jonah's scream cut through the air. He ducked just as a fireball at least a foot across whizzed by his head. It landed in a pile of dead leaves that instantly burst into flames.

My eyes darted in the direction it came from, only to see that another dozen fireballs were headed our way, each one bigger than the last.

We all took off running in the same direction down the length of the ravine. Beside me, Liam tripped, but I caught him before he could face-plant. His body slumped against mine. He was so weak now that he could barely walk.

"Duck!" I shouted as another incoming fireball headed our way. I couldn't even tell where they were coming from.

Above us, trees lit up in flames. Jonah and Imogen, along with their Familiars, hesitated ahead of us to make sure we were coming.

"We have to get out of here!" I cried.

Jonah climbed the steep side of the ravine. He reached out a hand and helped Imogen up in a single swift motion.

I supported Liam's weight and helped him over to Jonah. Jonah grabbed Liam's hand and heaved him upward. Liam tried to stand, but by now, his legs were pretty much useless. Squeaks pushed on Liam's butt with her head to help him up. Esis tugged on my hair just in time for me to see another fireball flying in my direction. It flew so close to me that it singed the hair on my left arm and ignited the leaves on the ground only a foot away from me. Heart hammering, I reached out for Jonah and hurried to my feet beside them.

Sheer hopelessness slammed into my gut when I finally got a good view of the landscape above the ravine. Ahead of us, the entire forest was engulfed in flames as far as the eye could see. A sharp pain assaulted my nostrils as I inhaled thick smoke. It felt as if a cinder block had been dropped on my chest as heavy air settled in my lungs. The heat radiating off the nearby flames was almost unbearable.

This was *bad*. My team couldn't take as much heat as I could. I had to get them out of here now.

"This way!" I shouted. I guided them through a maze of flames, following the path of fresh underbrush. Fire was closing in on the greenery quickly, narrowing our way out.

Flames completely overtook the path ahead of us. I whirled around, searching for an alternate route, but I couldn't see one... couldn't *feel* one. I stopped in my tracks in a small circle of untouched earth. It was barely ten feet across and shrinking by the second.

Imogen's eyes darted around the forest as if calculating our options. "It's your trial!" Imogen cried to me over the crackling sounds of burning wood. "What do we do, Sophia?"

I didn't really have time to think about it, but I also didn't know the answer. When I tried to access the fire to test its power, it was too much. Rage and prejudice hung thick in the magical flames. I could literally feel the hatred of the Elders as they pressed their Fire toward us. They *wanted* us to die, the misfits we were. We didn't belong in this society, and they wanted to make sure we knew it— or they were testing me, seeing if I was the prophesied child they'd been waiting for. But prophecy or not, there was no way I could calm the Elders' Fire on my own.

Instinct told me to do the exact opposite.

"I have to make them bigger." I aimed my hands at the closest flames that were creeping across the forest floor toward us.

"No!" Liam wheezed. His body was half-draped over Squeaks' back. He barely got the words out. "You have to calm the flames."

"Agreed," Imogen said, looking worried. "You need to clear a path."

I hesitated. The Fire inside of me begged to escape, as if it was trying to tell me something. But my teammates were right. Calming the flames made the most sense. They were more experienced at this Elementai stuff than I was, so I was just going to have to trust them.

It wasn't going to be easy. Putting out Doya's flames in class was hard enough. I didn't know how I was going to calm *myself* first, not while I was still fuming over Haley— and while my teammates were dangerously close to cooking to death.

I stared at the flames in front of me, willing them to shrink. They were almost as tall as I was, and growing.

From beside me, Jonah started humming the melody to the tune we sang in the cave. Imogen joined in. My anger and worry slowly began to wane at the comforting sound of their voices. I did my best to ignore the heat and the heavy smoke.

Slowly, the flames in front of us shrank enough that we could trample over the embers. I started forward, attacking the next flames as I went. Sweat dripped from my brow, and my knees shook. I could feel my energy draining with each passing second.

I glanced ahead of us and saw nothing but burning forest. Behind us, I could see where the fire ended at a clearing only fifty yards away.

My gut twisted at the thought of turning back, but I'd rather keep my team alive than rush to the finish line.

"I don't know how long I can keep this up!" I told my team. "We should turn back."

Nobody had a chance to agree or disagree. Just as I said it, a wall of fire surged in front of us. It was at least twenty feet tall and so unexpected that I leapt backward, nearly tripping over Sassy. Esis teetered on my shoulder but quickly righted himself.

The flames' power surged through me. I had less than a split second to decide my next move. Against my better judgement, I acted on instinct. I took hold of that power and threw my anger back at the wall of flames.

The flames shot high into the air, touching the tree tops and burning the leaves above our heads. When they calmed a second later, they were barely higher than my knee. It was better, but not enough to walk through.

"Soph—" Liam tried to speak but started coughing uncontrollably instead. Blood shot from his mouth and sprayed on the ground below him.

Guilt shook my body. How had I not noticed how sick he was getting before? Liam could barely hold himself up. There was no way we were making it to the end of this fire labyrinth with him conscious.

I rushed forward and guided his arm over my shoulder. "We're going back. We'll find another way once Liam's feeling better."

He'll feel better soon, I told myself with each step I took. *Once we make it to the clearing, Esis will heal him. Liam's temper be damned. I can't keep it a secret any longer.*

"Let me"—Jonah coughed through the smoke— "help."

He reached out for Liam's other arm, but before he could grab it, a fireball flew down from the sky and whizzed between them. Jonah jumped back next to Imogen and both of their Familiars.

"Let's get out of here!" I shouted.

My words were drowned out by the wind picking up around us. Air rushed by my face, throwing my ponytail in every direction. The flames died down for a moment in the wind, but quickly came back in full force as soon as the energy pulled back. Flames rose high above our heads, and sweat dripped down my skin. I willed the flames to shrink just long enough that we could make it out of the wildfire and into the clearing up ahead.

I started forward, but Imogen's scream caught my attention. I whirled around just in time to see a swirl of fire cutting through the space between us. Sassy jumped backward and *yipped*, letting me know she'd been burned.

Esis gasped and jumped off my shoulder. He leapt through the underbrush, straight for the wall of flames separating us from the rest of the group.

"Esis!" I cried.

He disappeared into the flames, sending my stomach plummeting downward.

"Imogen! Jonah!" I screamed. The flames were so high that I couldn't see them.

"Go ahead of us!" Imogen called back. I could barely hear her over the angry roar of the fire.

"No!" I yelled. "I'll get you out!"

"I'll manage it!" Jonah screamed back. "Save Liam!"

I hesitated, but I didn't have the luxury of thinking it through. Liam coughed and doubled over, stumbling out of my grasp. He caught himself by landing directly on a flame burning a sapling beneath him. He jerked his hand away, but the damage had already been done. His palm was red and blistered. He stared down at it with a blank expression, like he barely knew what was going on. If I didn't get him out of here *now*, the thick smoke was going to kill him. But...

"Esis!" I cried. I held my hand up in front of my face, shielding my eyes from the burn of the flames. I didn't hear if anyone replied.

My Familiar was gone. I had no idea where he went, or if he was even still alive.

Liam sputtered again and rolled onto his side. I didn't want to leave everyone else behind, but I had to help Liam. Jonah and Imogen at least had a fighting chance. Liam only had me.

My hands shook as I reached for Liam, to help him to his feet. His arm draped limply around my shoulder while mine wrapped around his waist. He was seriously heavy and was dragging his feet, but I forced myself to hold on to him and put one foot in front of the other.

"Earth, Water, Fire, and Air..." I began singing, knowing that the distraction was the only thing that would get us through the flames. My voice cracked, and tears began to slide down my cheeks. I could barely see the clearing anymore, but every few seconds, it revealed itself through the flickering flames.

Almost there...

"Gifted to us by the breath of a prayer..." I continued.

Sobs broke out in my chest as Liam's head lolled to the side, resting against mine. "Please, Liam," I whispered. "Stay with me."

He coughed again, but it sounded more like wheezing.

The flames ahead of us were dying down, but they weren't going away completely. Behind us the flames grew higher and higher, licking into the sky like a beacon to the ancestors. The underbrush around us had almost been completely consumed. I didn't have a choice but to head forward into the smaller flames.

My boots stomped out most of the flames as I dragged Liam forward, but there was a wall of fire beside us that made it increasingly harder to breathe. Liam's arm was starting to slip from my grasp as sweat coated our skin, drenching us both.

"Not that much farther," I said, though I had no idea if he was still conscious. "We can do this!"

My knees wobbled beneath me. I could barely hold Liam up. I thought I might collapse right there for the wildfire to consume us. At least it'd be a quick death...

And then, just like that, we broke through the flames. Cool air rushed around us, and I inhaled a deep breath. I dragged Liam farther away from the flaming trees until the heat was barely a tingle across my skin. When I glanced back I saw that the flames were no longer advancing on us. They stopped abruptly at the edge of what looked like an invisible wall, as if the Elders were keeping them contained for a purpose. Above us, dark clouds swirled, as though a thunderstorm was rolling in to make the last task even worse.

I dropped to my knees and gently laid Liam down on the earth beside me. His eyes were closed, and his face expressionless. His arm flopped to the ground when it slid off my neck.

"Liam! Liam!" I pressed my hands to the sides of his face, smacking him lightly in hopes of startling him awake. "Open your eyes! Please, ancestors! Liam!"

Tears streamed down my face and fell onto his shirt. I inhaled a deep breath to steady my trembling fingers, then dipped my head down to his. I intended to give him mouth-to-mouth to breathe some clean air into his lungs, but before my lips connected with his a noise bubbled up from his throat.

I pulled back and stared down at him. "Liam?"

He cleared his throat and forced his eyes open. It looked like he was trying to lift bricks with his eyelids. "I'm fine, *pawee*."

I sniffled. "You're not fine. Not in the slightest."

"Leave me," he said in a dry, scratchy tone.

"No." I shook my head.

Liam coughed so hard that it took him a good ten seconds to get over it. When he could finally speak again, he asked, "Where's Esis?"

Concern knotted in my gut. "He— he went after Sassy."

"Go," Liam begged. His eyes finally opened enough that he met my gaze. "Believe me, you don't want to lose him. You don't want to live like this." It sounded like it took all his strength to tell me that.

"I can't just leave you!" I protested, wiping my runny nose.

"You have to, *pawee*," he insisted. "I'm dead weight... literally."

"Don't say that," I sobbed. "You—"

Liam reached out to me. His rough fingers ran over the skin on the back of my hand. His bottom lip trembled, and his eyes glistened as he gazed up at me. "I was never going to make it back alive, Sophia. We all knew it from the start. I got you all this far, but you're going to have to get everyone else to the end."

"Liam, please..." Tears flowed from my eyes like a river.

"Stop acting like you have a choice, Sophia," he said softly. "You can't save me."

"I could have. I still can." My head dipped so low in guilt that I rested the side of my face on him.

The rise and fall of his chest was so comforting. I couldn't let him go. I knew it was selfish, but I would miss him too much. He was the first thing at Orenda Academy that made it feel like home. I'd never truly thought we wouldn't make it to the finish line together.

Liam raised his hand and laid it on my head, brushing away my flyaway hairs. "Sophia, please go. The team needs you. Esis needs you. There isn't time."

I lifted my head and blinked away the tears. He was right. I didn't have the luxury of lying to myself, of convincing myself he would make it. It was a miracle he'd made it this far. It tore my insides into a million tiny little pieces that could never be put back together, but I had no choice.

Liam's heavy eyelids fell shut. "It's okay, Sophia. I've had my extra time. I'm ready to go."

"Liam," I squeaked in a small voice.

"What, *pawee?*" he asked in a labored tone.

"I— I—" I couldn't bring myself to tell him how I felt about him. I would never be able to leave his side if I did.

Instead, I brushed the hair out of his face and bent to press my lips to his forehead. "Please tell Nashoma about me."

He sighed heavily. "I will," he whispered.

That was the last thing either of us said before I rose to my feet and raced back into the flaming forest.

THE SMOKE WAS THICKER than ever. I coughed uncontrollably and squinted my eyes. I could hardly see anything as I walked back through the flames.

"Esis!" I shrieked. "Imogen! Jonah!"

No answer.

A terrifying thought occurred. What if the rest of my teammates were gone? What if I was the only one left?

"Ancestors, no!" I cried aloud. "Please, please, please..."

In front of me, four figures swooped down from the sky. I took a step back, startled. I didn't recognize the Familiars at first... not until they shifted, their coloring washing across the landscape like a watercolor painting. Two men and two women stood in front of me, gazing at me with proud looks upon their faces. It was like the fire didn't bother them one bit. Why would it? They were only spirits... my ancestors.

I remembered them from the night Liam took me up to the mountain to meet them. It was the same four: the warrior in a headdress, the guy in a cowboy hat, the redhead in a ballgown, and the woman with long black hair.

They'd been watching over me, and they'd come to answer my prayers.

I cleared my throat. "Please, ancestors. I've lost my Familiar. I need to get to him."

None of them spoke. They simply turned in unison and pointed to my right.

"Thank you!" I exclaimed. I wished I could stay around and get to know them more, but now, there wasn't time.

They each offered a sweet smile and took a bow. I bowed back. When I lifted my head, they were gone.

Without hesitation, I sprinted in the direction they'd pointed. I ran maybe thirty yards before my eyes fell upon a small white figure moving through the trees. Relief and panic swept through me all at once.

Esis scurried around on the surface of a large rock. Flames engulfed the earth on all sides of him. He glanced upward, as if calculating whether or not he could reach the branches above him, but those too were on fire. Fear glistened in his big blue eyes, and he let out a tiny scream of horror. He was searching for a way out that he was never going to find.

"Esis!" I screamed across the space between us.

His ears perked up at the sound of my voice, and his eyes scanned the forest until they landed on me. He stood on his toes and reached his tiny little arms upward for me.

"I'm coming!" I called.

I concentrated on the flames between us, forcing them to die down. My concentration broke when a tree branch snapped from behind me and slammed to the ground. It landed with a thundering *thump*. The crackling sound of burning trees surrounded us. I was completely out of time. If I waited for my power to control this fire any longer, we'd both be pinned beneath falling branches.

So I did the only thing I could. I raced into the flames.

I managed to keep the ones around me lower than my hips, but they licked up from the ground and seared the skin on my legs. My pants caught fire just as I reached the rock and lifted myself up onto it. I immediately grabbed Esis and wrapped him in my arms.

But I barely had a second to enjoy the relief flooding through me. The fire covering my pants burned my skin. I knew I was Koigni and could hold fire in the palm of my hand, but facing someone else's Fire was unbearable. If it was normal fire, I'd be fine, but this was magical, powerful. Pain radiated up my leg as I tried to smother it by clapping my hands against my pant leg. The slapping motion made it even worse.

What was I doing? I couldn't fight a Koigni's power with this *stop, drop, and roll* shit. As Esis snuggled into my shoulder I held my hand just above the flames scalding my skin. I pulled against their power, fighting to kill the flames.

To my relief, they disappeared before my eyes, and all the Fire in the immediate area died down, leaving nothing but blackened trees and ashes. There was a huge hole in my pants, and my skin was blistered, but I was still conscious. I could still find the others.

Esis hopped down from my shoulder and onto the rock, then placed his tiny little hands on my leg. *Of course! Why didn't I think of that to begin with?* The burning pain crawling up my leg eased. Right in front of my eyes, the blisters shrank, and the red burns faded until there was nothing left but smooth, untouched skin.

I scooped Esis up in my arms and hugged him close. "Thank you! I'm so glad you're okay."

Esis chippered and glanced around nervously.

"Right." I rose to my feet, glancing around our rock in search of an exit. Truth be told, one way wasn't any better than the other. "Which way did the rest of them go, buddy?"

Esis' eyes widened at the question. He lifted a hand to point one way, but hesitated and pointed in another before pulling his hand back and shaking his head.

He doesn't know.

Unease swept through me. Imogen and Jonah could be anywhere... they could be dead. I had three-hundred-and-sixty degrees of burning forest to search through. I'd never find them. The best I could hope for was that Jonah had been able to get them out.

Esis jumped out of my arms and looked around. His little nose twitched as he rose up on his hind legs and his ears perked up. He gave a long, lonely call, but nobody answered.

He glanced back at me, unsure. In the pit of my stomach, I knew.

Esis was looking for Liam.

"He's gone, Esis," I said. I forced the words past the lump in my throat. "I had to leave him behind."

Esis' blue eyes swam. He couldn't speak, but I knew what he was saying. *But you love him.*

I forced back a sob. "It doesn't matter. He's already dead. He told me to go. He's not going to make it. He was never going to."

Esis stared at me like what I said was a lie. I tried wiping my face, but the tears kept on coming. I didn't want to live a life without Liam. It was impossible to think about. Everything I knew about being an Elementai, about this world, he taught me.

Everything I wanted, he was.

I put my head in my hands and cried. "I don't know what to do." I didn't know what direction my friends were in, or how I could help them if I did find them. I'd left the man I loved to suffer a painful death. I wasn't an Elementai. I was just a stupid girl from Utah. I didn't feel like I could do anything.

I heard the sound of chimes on the wind, and a low drum accompanied by a slight breeze. I looked up. My ancestors had returned. They gathered around Esis and me in a circle. Three of them— the warrior, the cowboy, and the woman with black hair— started to dance, twirling and circling to the beat of the drum.

The red-headed woman in the ballgown approached me slowly and reached out.

My hand was shaking, but I allowed her to touch me. I couldn't feel her skin against mine, but I could see it. The red-haired woman took my hand and smiled at me gently. She didn't speak, but when she squeezed my hand, powerful emotion flooded through me. It was small and warm, spreading throughout my body slowly and making me feel happy and safe all over. It was love, and the love my ancestors gave me swept away any doubts or insecurities I had about not being good enough to finish this tournament, not being good enough to be an Elementai... not being good enough to save Liam. That kind of love stopped my tears and made everything seem like it was right again.

It was the same thing I felt every time I thought of Liam.

In that moment, I knew what I had to do. Liam Mitoh might be ready to leave me, but I sure as hell wasn't ready to leave him. I was going to save his life, then we'd go and find Imogen and Jonah together.

Even if I failed, I was going to be there with him as he died. So he wouldn't be alone— and so I could finally tell him what I felt for him was real.

"Thank you," I whispered to the red-haired woman. She smiled at me again, then slowly vanished as the breeze swept by.

My ancestors gradually faded away, their colors bleeding into the wind. But I knew they weren't truly gone. Though I could no longer see them, I knew that they'd always be by my side to guide me.

Esis chittered at my feet. He tilted his head to the side and looked up.

"How good is your healing ability, Esis?" I asked.

He gazed up at me with those big blue eyes and shrugged.

"Well, we're about to find out. We're going back for Liam."

liam

TWENTY-THREE

This was the last way I wanted to die.

I lay flat on my back on the ground and looked up at the sky. It took all my energy just to breathe, and every breath got harder. The pain had mostly gone away, and my body had gone numb. Though parts of me were burned, I could feel myself growing cold as each breath grew more and more shallow. For a second I thought my heartbeat had stopped, until I realized just the sound was growing fainter in my ears, beating lighter against my chest.

To make things worse, it'd started raining. And it wasn't a little drizzle, either. The rain was coming down so hard and in such big droplets that it made it hard to move my limbs. The wind was whipping against my face, and the fires raging in the distance still filled the air with smoke, so it was even harder for me to breathe. Dark clouds gathered above, and lightning crackled throughout the sky while thunder shook the earth. I was absolutely soaked in a matter of seconds. The dirt quickly became thick mud underneath me, and my clothes absorbed the mess. I tried to make the rain stop, but my element was like the rest of my body. It just wasn't working.

Have you ever felt yourself actively dying? It's like, the worst thing ever. You can feel your organs shutting down and everything getting weaker. The smallest task takes a tremendous amount of effort. It's like your entire body's giving up, but at the same time, you've never wanted to live more than in that very moment. Your intention is to cling to life, but the vessel you're riding in says no.

I hoped that during the tournament I would get taken out quickly by one of the tasks, but my luck wasn't that good. I was dying, but it was slowly. This could take hours.

I didn't know how I was going to say goodbye to this world. I wouldn't get a goodbye with my family. Sophia had been all I had, and fuck, that nearly did me in. I didn't want her to leave me. More than anything, I wanted her to stay by my side so I wouldn't have to be alone.

But at the same time, I didn't want her to see me die, and I knew Jonah and Imogen needed her more. So I let her go.

But that's what you did for people you loved. You sacrificed your life so they could go on. That's what love *was*. Anyone who didn't agree, who said that love was just chemicals in your brain or selfish fulfillment or whatever, was just fucking stupid.

And ancestors, I loved her. My heart was so full for her it was about ready to break.

Being on my back was putting a lot of pressure on my lungs, so I forced myself to roll over onto my stomach. I didn't know where I harnessed the energy, but I somehow managed to force my weak limbs into doing what I asked. I ended up flat on my face in the mud. The dirt actually felt like a pillow against my head. I wanted to close my eyes, but I knew the minute I did, that would be it, so I forced them to stay open.

I had wished to die for months, but now that the time was here, I wanted to stay. I had been so foolish. I'd wasted so much time longing for the end I didn't realize what a gift I had when I had it. I wished I could go back and see Sophia smile one last time, or make Jonah laugh again, or just hang out with my brother. Instead, I'd squandered away my time hiding away in my room and being too scared to face the world.

I let out another breath. They were getting really shallow now. Maybe it wouldn't be as long as I thought. It sucked it had to be on TV.

A pair of black paws appeared in front of me. Yep, definitely not as long as I thought, if Nashoma was already here.

"Hey, buddy," I rasped. "You here to take me home?"

I couldn't see anything but his paws and the end of his tail. I was too weak to lift my head up. Nashoma didn't bend his head down to lick me or anything, just stood there. *Get up.*

I would've died of shock if I wasn't already there. "What?"

Get up.

"Are you fucking serious?" I had to struggle to get the words out. "Nashoma, it's over. It's time to go home."

Get up. He was stubborn. His paws didn't move.

"Didn't you hear me?" My mouth twisted in a snarl that was half-agony, half-rage. "I'm ready to die!"

GET UP.

Apparently, he didn't think I was. "This is crap," I muttered, but it was more of a wheezing gasp. I tried to push myself upwards, but my arms shook, and I failed. I only ended up face-planting in the mud again.

Get up, Liam. Get up! His paws started to dance in front of my face. At his insistence, I reached out with both hands and pulled myself through the mud. He moved out of the way, walking beside me and shouting, *Get up, get up!*

Other people's Familiars probably greeted them with hugs and kisses on the other side. My jackass Familiar had to make me prove I was worthy. Crawling on my hands and knees would've been faster, but I couldn't manage that, so I more or less slid my body along the mud. Nashoma started to bark, and I managed to move a little faster. My hand that was burnt all to hell was throbbing, but I ignored the sharp pain jolting through it and continued on to ancestors knew what.

A cave came into view, only about ten or so steps away. I realized Nashoma's plan. In the cave, the cameras wouldn't be able to see me and I could die in peace. It wouldn't be televised for the entire tribe to see.

I wanted to die with whatever dignity I had left. So I forced myself to crawl on my stomach toward the cave. I could hear Nashoma's steps beside me as the mud turned to solid rock.

I reached the cave wall. Somehow, I forced myself upright and into a sitting position. It was easier to breathe that way. I lay back against the rock and heaved for air. At least I was out of the rain.

"Out of the sight of the cameras," I breathed, and I reached out a hand to graze Nashoma's fur. "Good idea, buddy."

My hand brushed nothing but air. He was already gone.

I tried to roll my eyes. Even that was too much effort. Whatever. I'd see him again in a minute, anyway.

Colors were starting to muddle together and become fuzzy shapes. I think I saw a group of people gathering around me, though honestly, I was so delirious I couldn't be sure. In a tree outside the cave an eagle looked down and cocked his head, giving a sharp cry.

"Grandpa?" I gasped. It was the last thing I had the strength to say. My head lolled to the side. I saw someone running toward me, a fuzzy white shape at their feet, before I slipped away.

§

I CAME TO SLOWLY. I wondered if I had melded with Nashoma yet and what that would feel like, but then I realized that I was very much still in my own body and still hurting, though not as bad as before.

And I was *still in this fucking cave.*

But it was all right, because Sophia was there. She kneeled next to me on her knees, her beautiful face studying me carefully. Her thin eyebrows were scrunched together as if she was watching something take place.

"Sophia?" I whispered. I pushed myself upward off the wall, before I realized I shouldn't have the energy to do that. I started, and Esis gurgled unpleasantly. He was on my lap and looking pleased with himself.

"Liam!" Sophia flung her arms around me and squeezed me tight. I hugged her back, but I was still kind of in shock. What was going on here?

"Sophia, let go. I can't breathe," I gasped. She was crushing me. Poor Esis was getting squished between our chests.

"Oh, sorry." She backed away nervously, and Esis plopped out between us. Esis massaged his head and grumbled at her.

"You always give the tightest hugs," I said, and I rubbed my ribs. "Not a bad thing," I added when she opened her mouth.

"Liam," Sophia said, and she pointed. "Look."

I did. My hand... it was okay. The blisters and burn wounds were gone. It was like the skin was brand-new. I brought it in front of my face and turned it around. Not a mark on it. In fact, all the scratches and bruises I'd sustained from the tournament were also gone. I was no longer sore, and my lungs felt clear instead of full of blood. The only thing that still remained was the constant inflammation pulsating through my muscles that I usually felt on a daily basis. I hardly even registered it. I even felt hungry... starving, in fact. That was a miracle in itself.

"I'm... I'm not fucking dead," I said, stunned.

"No, you're not," Sophia said. She looked even more relieved than I felt.

"What the hell happened to me?" I asked. "I was pretty much dead, and now I feel fine. Well, not fine." I shifted uncomfortably. "I still hurt. But it's like I was at the start of the tournament. I can breathe fine and everything now."

Sophia hesitated. "I... I don't know what happened," Sophia stuttered. "I just came back to find you, and when you weren't where I left you... oh, God, Liam."

She put a hand over her mouth and tried not to cry. "I thought you were already dead and that the officials had come and got you, but Esis made me follow him, and I found you here. You were all healed up when I arrived."

"This cave must be super magical," I said, looking around. "It's the only way to explain why I healed so fast. Maybe it's one of the original sites of the tribe, or a place where the ancestors commune."

Sophia made an *em-hm* noise and said, "Yeah, that must be it."

Esis let out a trilling noise. Inside, I was hollow. Nashoma hadn't come to take me to the ancestors. His only job had been to get me to the cave, to heal me.

I felt tremendously grateful and horribly bereaved all at once.

"Liam, I was wondering. How... how do you feel?" she asked cautiously.

I rolled my shoulders back. "I don't know. Not one-hundred percent, but I can walk and stuff."

"Oh." She seemed disappointed.

"Yeah, I guess it would be too much to hope that the cave would cure me completely, right?" I asked cheerfully. But I sure as hell wasn't complaining. Being disabled was a big step up from being dead, so I was going to take it and be grateful. "Did you find Imogen and Jonah?"

She shook her head. "I just found Esis. He pretty much convinced me I had to come back for you."

"Did he really?" I scratched Esis between the ears. "You miss me, little guy?"

Esis gave me a sneaky grin and wagged his tail.

I looked at his Elementai. "Sophia, why did you come back?" I asked lowly. "I didn't want you to stay. I wanted you to be safe."

Her brown eyes were heavy with all sorts of unsaid things. "Liam, I think you know why," she whispered back quietly.

She leaned forward. I didn't realize it was to kiss me until she had done it.

You ever just stand in the ocean and let a wave crash over you, but it's a lot more powerful than you thought and it ends up knocking you off your feet? That's what it felt like when Sophia kissed me, except ten times stronger. If her existing was the wave, kissing her was like the whole damn ocean. Her lips were warm against my cold ones and felt really soft. She smelled like crushed autumn leaves, and smoke, and even like the ocean at midnight. She put so much emotion into the kiss I could feel it, and I allowed the strength of her feelings to wash over me as she brushed my face.

Without thinking, I reached upward and caressed her hair back, running my fingers through her hair until my fingers were entwined in her locks and holding the back of her neck. Sophia moved forward. Her lips didn't part from mine as she sat on my lap and hooked her legs around my hips. I wrapped my free arm around her waist and held her tightly to me as she deepened the kiss even more, drinking from me as if I was her life.

She parted her mouth a little, and I let my tongue slip in. Sophia moaned and moved against me, biting sharply on my bottom lip before pushing her tongue into my mouth in response. Ancestors, this was fucking amazing. Like, the best kiss of my life. I squeezed her even tighter and gave an involuntary thrust up. She responded by rolling against me and I. Nearly. Died.

"Liam," she groaned.

I took her mouth against mine again before she could say more. I had to keep kissing her, because if she said my name like that again, I'd lose all self control.

It got to me how incredible we were together. Months of repressed emotion and want came boiling over as her hands ravaged my hair, her fingertips rippling down my chest. My eyes were closed, but the way she made me feel took away any need I had to see. It was almost too much to handle. My entire body felt like it was riding a huge wave that could see over the entire world, only to come spiraling back down before it rose to the top again.

I thought that she'd stop kissing me, that she'd get tired of it, but she didn't. She kept loving me like she didn't realize I was just broken parts. I always thought that when you kissed someone new, you had to get used to the way they did it, but not us— we kissed each other like we'd been doing it for ages.

We didn't even have to think about it. We just let it be. It was like we were made to exist together.

I knew right then. She could kiss me forever and it wouldn't be enough.

Why did Sophia come back for me? I knew why. It was because she loved me.

When she finally pulled back, I'm pretty sure it was only because both of us had to breathe. Esis gave a low whistle. Sophia blushed. I grinned and pushed him over. Ancestors, I was literally seeing stars.

That had made me lightheaded. How long had we been making out? Was it just minutes? Because it felt like days.

That kiss had been everything I'd secretly dreamed of and hoped for since I walked into her living room back in Utah. I only wish I'd been the one to kiss her first.

Sophia stared back at me. She was slightly panting. "Liam... what are we?"

I didn't know what to say. How could she ask me something like that when my hormones were raging and all I wanted to do was tackle her and make love to her on this cave floor, even with Esis watching?

But then something registered in my brain, and the question made me run cold. What *were* we? Obviously more than friends. Were we boyfriend and girlfriend? I hated the word *lovers* because it creeped me out and made it seem like what we were doing was dirty and wrong.

We were in love with each other. Obviously. Neither of us could deny it anymore. But what did that mean? There were still rules we had to follow. Toaquas and Koignis couldn't be together. Our world wouldn't allow it.

I wanted to say, *I love you and let's run away together,* but what came out was, "We should probably talk about that when our lives aren't in danger and when we know our friends are okay."

She nodded. "Right." She clambered off my lap and nearly fell over. It made me laugh under my breath. I got up and reached out a hand to pull her to her feet. When her hand was in mine, I didn't want to let go. Sophia gave my fingers a reassuring squeeze before she finally pulled away. It was hard to look at each other, because we'd just acknowledged the elephant in the room that we'd been avoiding for months.

And damn, it was taking up the whole cave.

"Where should we go?" I asked, just to break the tension and move on from that bomb kiss that I desperately wanted to go back to.

Sophia put a hand to her chin and said, "I have a feeling we should see where this cave leads. Back there is just a bunch of smoke and fire. Maybe Imogen and Jonah are already ahead of us."

"I'm following you."

Esis led the way, his little nails clicking on the stone as Sophia moved forward. I stayed behind and tried (and kinda failed) to not watch her ass.

I was alive, dammit. I was making the most of it.

Unlike the cave we'd gotten stuck in the other day, this one was well-lit, with multiple holes in the top and walls that were made of black stone with small silver flecks. It was more like a cavern. It looked like the rain had cleared up and the sun was out again, from the sunlight that was bursting through the top of the cave. From what I could tell, it was around dusk, from the orange light gleaming in through the crevices in the ceiling.

My steps were really bouncy. I felt like I was on top of the world.

"You seem like you're in a good mood," Sophia said, and she smiled.

"Fucking giddy." And I meant it. That'd been a close call back there. Not to mention my not-dying prize had been kissing Sophia Henley, because that had been pretty rad.

"I bet that kiss had something to do with it," Sophia said coyly. "Something else is pretty happy, too."

"You mind your business, *pawee*," I told her. "There's still some things I have to teach you, and believe me, I'm gonna have fun doing it."

Sophia blushed. The pink in her cheeks got me excited. I couldn't wait until I could put my lips all over those cheeks, and her hair, and about a million other things...

I needed to stop. We were still at risk out here. All that fun stuff would come later.

Sophia and I went quiet, both lost in our own heads. Eventually, we came to a place where the cave split. Esis went to the right side and started hopping up and down, pointing down the long pathway.

"I think he wants us to follow him," Sophia said, turning to me.

"That little guy has good instincts, and so do you, Sophia," I said, pointing at her. "I think if we had listened to you all along we wouldn't have gotten so turned around in this tournament."

Sophia had a determined look on her face. "I don't know. But I am sure that I'm never going to make the mistake of second-guessing myself ever again."

I was happy about that. Sophia had come to school so unconfident and unsure. She'd even been too scared to confront Haley. Now she had faith in herself. It was enough to make me proud.

The tunnel ended and widened into a huge opening, where the cave opened up to the great sky. Here, I could see that the sun really was setting. It bathed the entire cavern in a blood-red glow. A tiny waterfall trickled down from an unknown source into a silver pool that was only about as deep as our ankles. But that wasn't the strangest thing about the cave.

It was a totem— at least, that's what I could describe it as. It looked as if it was carved from white bone, and had all five House symbols on it— Koigni, Toaqua, Nivita, Yapluma, and Anichi at the very top. It was only about as big as my palm, and could fit in my hand. It was floating— literally floating— over the middle of the silver pool, and was bathed in a soft ray of white light that seemed to emit from the totem itself.

A soft music hummed in the background. Chimes, drums, and the whispering of the wind. I'm certain I heard the ancestors' voices in there somewhere.

My element wavered within me, signaling something was up. The closer I got to the totem, the more my Water wanted to freak out. Whatever that totem was, it was insanely magical.

Esis stood by the edge of the pool and looked intently at Sophia. It was like he was asking her to grab it.

Sophia was transfixed by the totem. Her face glowed, and she had a strange expression on her face, like all she could look at was the floating talisman. She started walking toward it slowly, her feet entering the pool as she approached.

"Sophia, don't touch it," I said, wary. "We don't know what it is, or what it does."

"It won't hurt me, Liam," she said. Her voice was far-away, enchanted... it was like she was under a spell. "I just... I know it's meant for me."

Like that made a whole lot of fucking sense. I opened my mouth to say something, but found myself absent of words as Sophia reached out and grasped the totem in her hands.

I had to duck as a blast of air shot backward from the totem. It blew Sophia's hair back and created a whirlwind as the sun was swept out. The room was bathed in colors of silver, blue, and white shadows. Dark figures of creatures I didn't know the names of ran along the stone walls, creating an ancient dance that had long been forgotten. Sophia held the totem tighter in her hand and blue fire lit up her form, creating a raging inferno that she was completely immersed in. But the blue fire didn't hurt her— it just made her more beautiful. It grew and intensified, shooting up to the ceiling in a spectacular show. Sophia looked up at the dazzling display, stunned by the show of magic she was creating. Esis' blue eyes widened and he cheered loudly, like his Elementai had finally accomplished what she'd been destined for.

I about fell to my knees. I had to force myself to stay standing as I watched Sophia bring the totem close to her heart. She was like a goddess, invincible and unreachable. When I saw her like that, holding the totem with that blue fire blazing all around her, I didn't need to ask if she was the one the prophecy was talking about.

I knew she was.

The prophecy was real. Sophia was the one who was to bring glory to Koigni. Everything... *everything* the Fire House had talked about for hundreds of years... had been about her.

The rumors were true. The end times for the Hawkei were here. Koigni House was going to take over and rule over everyone.

And Sophia would be the one to end all things for the Elementai.

The blue fire eventually died down. The shadows fled, along with the dark creatures. The sunlight came back to the room again. Sophia looked over her shoulder at me, her chestnut hair settling around her shoulders.

This was crazy. Sophia was strong, stronger than I ever imagined. She was only a First Year, but give her enough time and her magic would make fools out of us all. She was so powerful she could rule the entire tribe. I bet she could even take it over by herself, if she wanted.

And I was in love with her. If I thought things couldn't get more complicated, I was a damn liar.

Sophia moved toward me. I took a few steps back, and she paused.

"Liam, what's wrong? You look like you've seen a ghost." She seemed puzzled.

I had a hard time responding. It hit me. I was afraid of her.

I snapped myself out of it and said, "Hey. Are you okay?"

"I think so." She made a face. "What was all that?"

Poor *pawee*. She was always so behind. Guess that was a good thing in this circumstance, though. "I'm not sure," I lied. "But I think you should put that totem back."

"Put it back? No!" she said, and Esis hissed loudly. "I'm not doing that. Besides, where do you want me to put it? It was floating in mid-air!"

Good point. I was really glad the cameras hadn't caught what had happened, because I didn't know if Sophia was ready to face all of that.

I wasn't sure if I was, either.

She opened her hand and looked at the totem. Beneath each House were various inscriptions. It was ancient Hawkei, but it was some sort of code I couldn't read. "What do you think it means?"

"I have no clue." I tried to study it, but I was spooked. All looking at that totem did was make me nervous, but I no longer thought it was the totem that was all-powerful. That was Sophia herself. Whatever that thing was, it was just a tool that she used to channel her power. She didn't realize that.

"Should we tell Imogen and Jonah about this?" She held the totem out for me to take.

I shook my head and folded her fingers over the totem, gently pushing it back toward her. "No. I think this should stay between us."

Sophia nodded and pocketed the totem in one of her pant pockets, securing it with a button. "Okay. Our little secret."

We sure were coming out of this cave with a lot of secrets. This was like the Tunnel of Love slash Tunnel of Stuff-I-Didn't-Want-To-Get-Involved-In.

I grabbed her hand and tugged on it. I was almost scared to touch her, like I would get shocked, but that was stupid and I told myself to stop being a dumbass. "Come on, Sophia. Let's get out of here."

Sophia lingered a moment longer in the cave, like she didn't want to leave it, before she finally relented to me tugging on her arm. We walked out of the cavern and into the cool forest air just as the sun was going down over the horizon. Sophia lit up a tiny fire so we could see as we hiked through the woods, looking for Imogen and Jonah.

After a few minutes, Sophia spoke. "Liam," Sophia said cautiously. "You're acting different."

I shook my head. "I'm fine, *pawee*. This tournament has just been really something."

Esis chattered in agreement, and Sophia nodded. I felt guilty. I didn't want to treat her different. She was still my sweet Sophia, wasn't she? I couldn't imagine her hurting a fly. She was too nice and innocent. She was still a virgin, for crying out loud. I didn't think she could kill anyone, or be a dictator over an entire tribe.

But that's not what the prophecy said. And judging by what I just saw, Sophia could slaughter anyone with her powers in the blink of an eye.

Maybe I was getting ahead of myself. The prophecy only said that she would bring Koigni glory. Maybe it wasn't as doom-and-gloom as the Toaquas made it sound. What if instead of taking over the tribe, Sophia helped the Koignis learn how to get along with the rest of us?

Doubtful, Liam. You know how Koignis are.

No. Not Sophia. She wasn't that way. Not all Koignis were like that.

Sophia was incredible. She was a wonderful person... and her element was soon going to be unchallenged.

If the wrong Koignis got their hands on her... they could turn her bad. They would try, anyway. I didn't think Sophia would turn— not unless something awful happened to make her that way.

My eyes wandered toward Esis. There were Koignis alive who would hurt him to get Sophia to do what they wanted, I was sure.

It was all the more reason for me to stay close to her.

You can't protect her forever, Liam.

I could fucking try. I'd give my fucking life to defend her now, I knew that. I'd do everything I could to keep the Koigni Elders from getting their filthy hands on her. Anyway, if Sophia did end up going crazy and taking over the tribe, she probably wouldn't kill me if I was her sugar baby. And I'd still be in love with her anyway, so it was a win-win.

I heard branches snapping in the trees ahead of us. I held out an arm to hold Sophia back. "Wait," I said lowly.

She paused. We proceeded with caution toward the noise, peeking out through the branches.

Thank the ancestors, it was Jonah and Imogen! They were alive, huddled up against Squeaks for warmth, Sassy in Imogen's lap. They didn't look hurt or injured. They were awake, but on the verge of nodding off.

I went to go say hi, but Sophia held me back, a mischievous smile on her face. She crept through the bushes until she was right in front of them.

"Boo!" Sophia yelled loudly. Jonah and Imogen both screamed. They toppled over as Squeaks got up and ran for cover. Sassy nearly jumped out of her fur.

Sophia laughed. "Surprise!" she cried. "It's us!"

Jonah's eyes widened in shock, and Imogen's face spread into a wide grin. Sassy gave a happy *yip* as she rushed to greet Esis. Squeaks was so excited to see us, she started doing a dance.

"You assholes!" Jonah roared. "Do you realize how glad we are to see you?!"

Jonah stormed forward and picked both Sophia and me up at the same time, raising us off the ground and hugging us tight. When he dropped us, Imogen latched on to Sophia and clung to her best friend like she was all she had in the world.

"You guys stuck around? Why didn't you go forward?" I asked, baffled.

"We couldn't move on without you guys," Imogen insisted. "We weren't gonna leave you behind until we were sure we had no other choice."

My cold, dead heart was about full of all the affection I could take today, but Imogen's words made it melt a little faster. "Thanks, Imogen."

Jonah pumped his fist in the air. "You have no idea— wait." Jonah paused. His eyes widened as he looked me over. "What happened to you? You look... better."

"It's a long story," I started. "I went into this cave, and I passed out. When I woke up, I was completely fine." I shrugged. "Weird, huh? It must've been magic."

Jonah and Imogen looked at each other. "Yeah. Weird," Jonah said.

"We're almost at the finish line," I continued. "We still have each other. We can still do this. Sophia?"

I looked at her. She seemed so much more sure of herself than she did last night. She stepped forward and said, "I wasn't ready before, but I am now. I can handle my task, guys. It was really rough before, but I have an idea on how we can get through the flames."

Her hand fell over the pocket that held the totem.

"You've got this, Soph," I said finitely. "I trust that you can handle this alone."

"But she doesn't have to," Imogen said, realization dawning on her face.

"We'll work together," Jonah suggested, and his words sped up as he got excited. "I'll send away the smoke so we can breathe, Liam and Imogen can use their elements to try and douse the flames, and Sophia can control it. If we all lend a hand, we can get through the final task together."

Sophia's face glimmered. "You guys mean that?"

"Of course!" Imogen flung her arms around Sophia's and Jonah's shoulders. "What are friends for?"

Squeaks squawked in approval. From her back, Sassy and Esis cuddled up against each other and gave noises of agreement.

"All right," I said, satisfied I didn't have to come up with the plan for once. "If we feel like we can take this, let's get this over with."

The team cheered, and we started walking toward the finish line again. The final task was only a short walk away, but I didn't feel terrified of it anymore. We'd already been through hell and back. We'd seen the worst and come out stronger. Nothing could break our team now. I was sure of it.

"So, Liam..." Jonah said as a really bad way to start off a conversation, and I suppressed a groan of irritation. He held me back, away from the girls as we headed forward. "I can't help but notice something's changed between you and Sophia."

"And how'd you gather that, Jonah?" I asked tiredly. I hadn't even touched her since we got back.

"I sense the sexual tension in the air," Jonah said, and he waggled his eyebrows. "What exactly happened when you guys were separated from us?"

I decided to cut out all the sad stuff and get straight to the point. "We might have kissed."

Jonah gave a girly squeal. "You guys *kissed*? No way."

"Keep your voice down! Yeah, so we kissed, big deal," I snapped back under my breath. "It's not like we banged or anything."

Up ahead, the girls had their heads together and were giggling. I bet anything Sophia was up there telling Imogen every minuscule detail of our make-out session.

I hoped I was impressive. She'd impressed me. I prayed Sophia didn't think I drooled or anything, or worse, that I sucked at kissing. How embarrassing would *that* be? I thought I was pretty good.

"This is just the start," Jonah said, rambling on. "Before you know it, you guys will be making *the cutest* babies. I'll get to be Uncle Jonah."

Jonah's stupid words brought up all sorts of emotions. Part of me was like, *Hell yeah! I hope she lets me put a baby in her!*

But a bigger part was like, *Yeah, never gonna happen.*

"It was just a kiss, dude. Let it go." I sighed.

"Oh, my ancestors. Liam, are you in love?" Jonah's jaw dropped.

"Shut up," I growled.

"You are!" Jonah jumped up and down and clapped his hands. "I'd never thought I'd see the day! My little boy, all grown up!"

"I'm older than you, jackass."

"Aw." Jonah reached out to pinch my cheeks, and I slapped his hand away. He craned his head around. "Hey, girls! Liam's got a crush!"

"Okay, that's it. Team meeting!" I shouted loudly, and everyone turned to look at me. I slashed my hand through the air to get their attention and said, "Newsflash, and as *I'm sure everyone has heard*"— I shot a look at Imogen, and she giggled— "me and Sophia made out in the cave. So what? Can we please move forward and end this thing? I really want to go home."

Jonah smiled like it was his birthday. Imogen was giggling, and Sophia was beet red. I caught her eyes, and we both grinned and looked away.

"Like Liam said, it was *just a kiss*," Jonah said, mocking me. "And... a lot more than that." He scrambled the words together quickly. "But, he's right. We need to get home. We have a ball to get to!"

Imogen *whooped* happily. She jumped on Jonah's back and he piggy-backed her ahead, letting out a victory cry.

Sophia and I stole a glance at each other. She was still pretty red. "Liam Mitoh's got a crush, huh?"

"Yeah I do," I whispered, and I dared to reach out and brush my fingers through hers for a few seconds. I was really fucking glad the cameras only caught visuals and couldn't record audio from so high up, because what we were saying was so incriminating. There'd been talk of hooking the contestants up with microphones a few years ago until the tribe decided it was too expensive. Thank the ancestors they didn't go through with that plan.

The mood got somber as we approached the site of the final task. All jokes fell to the wayside as everyone got serious. We really screwed up last time. It wasn't just Sophia's fault. And we needed to rely on each other to reach the end.

We finally reached it. We stood in a line, watching as flames sprang up out of nowhere before us. They didn't approach, but they didn't move, either. The flag was on top of the mountain just on the other side of them. They were even hotter and angrier than they were before. I could feel the heat from here.

Sophia swallowed. She stepped forward and said, "Let's do this, guys. Together."

Sophia led the way. Her powers pushed against the flames, protecting us as we headed back into the inferno. The rest of us got right to it. Jonah redirected the smoke away from us and manipulated the oxygen so it didn't empower the flames any more than it already was. Imogen piled dirt on top of the fire. The Familiars walked behind, calling encouragement as we continued at a steady pace.

I summoned as much water as I could from the earth and used it to put out as many of the flames as I could, though they basically sprang back up the minute I got rid of them. But with our combined efforts, it was easier than before. It was still hot, but we slowly made progress. The flames were pressing inward and getting closer, but none of us panicked. We just continued calmly as a unit.

We didn't have to say anything, but it was decided between all of us that if one of us didn't get out, none of us got out. We were in this together or not at all. We'd survive as one or die as one. There was no other option.

Mid-way through the flames, Sophia turned and locked eyes with me. Passion ignited between us, hotter than the flames closing in, and it was like I could see the change in her. Something behind her gaze clicked, and I saw her face clear. She knew what to do.

"Guys!" Sophia said. "Pull back your elements! I can do this!"

"Are you sure?" Jonah cried back. "We're doing pretty good as it is!"

Sophia gave a broad smile. "I can handle this. I know I can."

Imogen and Jonah seemed nervous, but I wasn't. I had complete faith in my girl. "She's got it, guys!" I shouted. "Trust her!"

At the same time Jonah, Imogen and I stopped casting, the fires roared to life beside us and rushed in to devour us alive.

But instead of making the flames smaller, Sophia made them bigger.

Imogen, Jonah and I ducked. But we shouldn't have. The flames ricocheted backward and rocketed toward the sky. Yet we didn't feel the heat. The air around us was cool, the temperature regulated. Although there were twenty-foot walls of fire raging around us, it felt like we were walking through a freezer. The flames were so close I could reach out and touch them, but even so, I didn't think they would burn me even if my hand was stuck in the middle of them. Sophia had them under her command.

The sight of Sophia's magic, what she could do... it was nothing less than fucking incredible.

"Stay close to me," Sophia instructed. Her face blazed like the flames she controlled. "We're going home."

Sophia proceeded forward. Esis jumped off of Squeaks and ran to be on Sophia's shoulder, where he belonged. I looked up at the massive fire walls, hardly able to believe what was happening. Was this really real?

Everything felt like it was in slow motion. We must've looked like total badasses for the cameras, walking through the flames with Sophia in the lead like they were nothing to handle. Even I could feel the rage of the Elders as they tried to break through Sophia's magic. But it didn't work. She sustained her protective shield around us with no more than a bat of an eyelash.

This was impossible. A Koigni couldn't do this.

An *Elder* couldn't do this.

But Sophia could. I worried her secret about being the prophesied child wouldn't stay secret for long.

We finally reached the end. Sophia shut her eyes, and as she did, the fires behind her went out completely. My. Jaw. Dropped.

When she opened her eyes again, she smiled. "That's it. The final task is done."

I felt so relieved. I wanted to fall on my ass and cry. Imogen and Jonah jumped up and down, holding onto each other. "We did it, we did it!" they cheered.

I could see the orange flag. It was literally right up there, only thirty feet or so above us. All we had to do was climb. "There's the finish line, guys!" I shouted. "Let's go!"

Squeaks trotted up the mountain like it was nothing. Sassy nipped at Imogen's heels cheerfully, while Imogen and Jonah sang the elements song, off-key and loudly. I started up the mountain at Sophia's side. My body screamed in protest at the hint of climbing one more mountain, but I blew it off and told it to behave, just this once. Nothing could ruin this moment. Not today.

"Sophia, you did great back there," I said as she hiked beside me. "I knew you had it in you all along."

She cleared her throat. "I realized something, Liam," Sophia said. "All this time, I thought anger was the key to Fire. But it's not. When I saw all you guys helping me, I felt such strong emotion for you all, and the ability to handle the flames just came on its own. Passion and love is the key to sustaining a flame. What I feel for you helped me gain control of my powers."

When she said that, I wanted to kiss her again. But we were back on camera, so I just said, "I'm glad, Soph. Really."

The last bit was kind of hard. The rocks were so jagged and craggy that it was almost impossible for anyone to climb them alone.

But we didn't have to do it alone. We helped each other climb, giving a boost and taking turns pulling each other up the mountain. The Familiars helped where they could, giving an extra push or lift when we needed it. It was like we were one long chain, and we got the system down, each of us doing our part to make sure everyone made it to the end. When we got to the summit, Imogen and Jonah reached down and grabbed me by the arms, yanking me to the embankment.

I reached down for Sophia's hand. She wrapped her fingers around my forearm, and I pulled her to the top. The flag waved in front of us in the wind.

We were here. All of us had made it. I gave everyone a look, and said, "On the count of three. One, two, three!"

All four of us grabbed onto the flagpole. From far away, I could hear the drums being played in the arena as a signal that a team had made it to the finish line. A floating carriage instantly came down from the sky, and I felt myself shaking in relief.

Food. A shower. A bed. It was only a short ride away.

We scrambled to get inside the carriage as soon as possible. I didn't even care that I was crushed against Squeaks' ass. Everyone was smiling. I wasn't sure if it was from delirium or happiness, but I didn't care.

You did good, Liam, I told myself, and I realized with a start that I'd done it. I'd kept my team alive for the entire tournament, even myself. Sure, I kinda cheated a little with the magic cave, but specifics.

The carriage floated down into the arena and landed on stage. I looked out the window and noticed that the arena was completely sold out again, full of people looking to welcome the teams home. As the doors opened, we all tumbled out of the carriage and landed on our faces. A graceful exit, as what we were known for.

We clumsily got to our feet. Squeaks shook her feathers, and we could hear it. The entire arena was completely silent. A single raindrop could've fallen and we would've heard it. Every face in the stadium stared back at us with an open mouth, like they couldn't believe it.

Aw, shit. Had we arrived so far behind the other teams that the whole tribe was stunned about how slow we were? When had the other teams showed up? Days ago?

Head Dean Alric hurried onstage. At least he'd stuck around to welcome us. I felt sorry for wasting his time. He was a nice guy.

Alric cleared his throat and spoke into the microphone. "Please welcome this year's winners of the Elemental Cup, the White Team!"

The stadium absolutely erupted. It sounded like the walls were about to come down, the crowd was so loud. The stage shook with the weight of the applause. My legs wavered beneath me, but I don't think it was from the cheering.

"Looks like the White Team went from being the least-favorite team to being adored by the fans." The announcer's voice, Eli, echoed over the stadium. You could barely hear him over the crowd.

"Everyone loves an underdog, Eli," Louis replied. "And this team definitely came from behind to win."

Wait. Winners?!

It took me a minute to realize what was going on. Jonah and Imogen were freaking out. Jonah was blowing kisses to the crowd, Squeaks copying him. Imogen was holding onto Sassy and crying tears of joy. I bet she hoped her brother could see her now.

Sophia had a smug look on her face. She turned to look at me and said, "Told you."

This was too good to be true. We'd won the Cup? I didn't know how we'd beaten the other teams back, but I didn't care. We'd gotten every member of our team through the tournament alive, and we'd *won*. That was practically unheard of.

Baine was hurrying onstage. He was wearing this really outrageous pinstripe suit that was bright turquoise with a blue carnation pinned to the front. He looked like a proud dad. He was carrying a golden trophy that was as big as my torso and had the symbols of all four Houses engraved on it.

"Congratulations," he said as he passed it to me and Sophia. Each of us took a handle. "I told you there was something special about this team."

Sophia and I looked at each other. Simultaneously, we lifted the Cup up to the crowd in victory. The stadium exploded again. I'm pretty sure the sound could be heard from here to San Francisco.

I caught sight of my family in the stands. My brothers and sisters were high-fiving each other, and my mother was weeping. Dad puffed out his chest and nodded to me, giving a thumbs up.

"We won," I said. It was almost like we were in a dream. "We really fucking won."

The reality of everything I'd been through in the past couple of days hit me like a tidal wave, and I wasn't ready for it. I had turned to smile at Sophia, but the Cup had already slipped out of my grasp, and my eyes were rolling in the back of my head. My knees buckled beneath me. I didn't realize I had collapsed until I hit the ground.

I heard Sophia calling my name, and the crowd screaming.

And then, nothing.

sophia

TWENTY-FOUR

Liam Mitoh was perfection in every sense of the word. I didn't care that he could barely walk a half mile most days and breathed as if an elephant was sitting on his chest. He'd just been dealt a bad hand in life. It was what was in his mind and heart that mattered. It was the way he called me *pawee*, as if it meant something more. It was the night he took me up to the mountain to meet my ancestors and dance with them. It was the red-hot passion in the cave when I kissed him. Those were the things that truly mattered.

Which was why when I watched him collapse on that stage, my heart shattered into a million pieces.

I'm so sorry, Liam. I'm sorry I couldn't save you.

I'd cradled him in my arms as Esis placed a tender paw on his forehead. Tears rolled down my cheeks. I didn't even worry that the cameras were watching. Even a week later, guilt settled into my stomach like a heavy rock.

"I can't do this, Imogen," I said nervously, turning away from the mirror.

Imogen's dorm room was smaller than mine, and the decor was almost the complete opposite. Whereas my room assaulted you with shades of red, her room was bathed in lighter, natural tones that had a more welcoming feel. The walls were a wooden texture like the hardwood floors, and her twin bed sat low to the ground, as if to keep her closer to the earth. Various plants were scattered throughout the room, including ivy that framed the window. Late December sunlight spilled into the room, bouncing off the bright white furniture. I wasn't really supposed to be in the Nivita dorms, but Imogen wanted to get ready for the ball together. And now I wasn't even sure I wanted to go — not if Liam wouldn't be there.

"Yes, you can, Sophia." She dusted blush across her cheeks in the bathroom.

Across the room, Esis and Sassy played together, chasing a piece of yarn Imogen had tied phoenix feathers to.

I plopped down on Imogen's bed, taking in shallow breaths, and not just because she tied my dress too tight. "It doesn't feel right without Liam."

"He'll be fine," she said with a wave of her hand. "He'll be out of the hospital in a few days."

Ugh. I didn't need the reminder about how long it'd be before I got to talk to him again. I wasn't allowed to visit him since I wasn't family, so I hadn't seen him since the medics carried him off stage.

"Everyone's going to want to congratulate us for winning," I pointed out. "It doesn't seem fair that he won't be there. He's the one who got us through."

Imogen peered through the bathroom door and frowned at me. "It was a team effort. You know we couldn't have done it without you."

"I know." I sighed. "But I never could've gotten us through the last task if it wasn't for Liam."

"What do you mean?" Imogen asked, turning back to the mirror to apply her makeup. "Was it the kiss?"

My heart lifted in my chest at the thought. That kiss with Liam was everything a first kiss was supposed to be, and more. If I thought Orenda Academy was magical when I arrived, it was nothing compared to Liam's kiss in the cave. That was beyond the realms of magic.

I knotted my hands in my lap. "I... I don't know. I guess something just happened in the cave that helped me realize how to control the fire."

Imogen raised an eyebrow toward the mirror. "What all

374

happened? I thought you guys just kissed." She drew in a sharp breath. "Should I be expecting little Toaqua babies running around here soon? Oh, ancestors. I hope they have Liam's eyes!"

"Imogen!"

She laughed.

The truth was, I hadn't told her about the totem Liam and I had found, though I didn't think that had anything to do with making it through the last task. Still, I didn't feel like I should mention it. It was like the ancestors *wanted* me to find it, but they didn't want me telling anyone I had it. I'd secured a string around it and usually wore it around my neck, tucked under my shirt, but I'd left it in my room for the ball.

"I already told you what happened," I said. "We kissed. That was it."

My stomach sank. Was that really it? Was that all it would ever be? I wanted so much more with Liam, but even if we officially got together, we'd always have to keep it a secret. *Koignis and Toaquas couldn't be together.* It totally sucked.

"What about when Esis healed him?" Imogen asked. "You never really told me about that."

I shrugged. "What's there to tell? Liam was almost dying. Now he's back to normal. Well... almost. Once he gets out of the hospital."

"And when he does, will you finally tell him about Esis?"

My mouth went dry. I wasn't ready to think about that yet. "I... I don't know. I was ready to tell him all about it in the cave, after Esis had healed him. But when he told me he was still in pain, I couldn't bring myself to do it. I don't want him to resent us... because Esis can't cure him completely."

"You have to tell him," Imogen insisted.

I glanced over to Esis, who was tugging at Sassy's tail. "I know. But I want to test it more first and see what Esis' limits are. I don't want Liam to get his hopes up."

"Okay..." She sounded uncertain, but she set her makeup down and stepped out of the bathroom wearing a plush robe. "We can worry about that later. Are you ready to see my dress?"

I sat up straighter. "I'd love to!"

"Okay, but you have to close your eyes."

I placed my hands in front of my face, careful to not mess up my makeup Imogen had spent the last hour applying for me. I heard Imogen's closet door open and the sound of fabric rustling.

She spoke while she changed. "You probably already know this, but everyone likes to represent their House when they go to the ball. Usually, people just dress in their House colors: red, orange, or black for Koigni, green or brown for Nivita, blue or silver for Toaqua, and purple for Yapluma. Well, I wanted to do a little more to represent my House... and the others. So... what do you think?"

I pulled my hands away from my eyes and opened them. My jaw dropped when Imogen twirled. The top half of her dress was made from twigs, as if it were a whicker corset. The skirt was layered in fern leaves so thick that it bulged out at least three feet in all directions. Flowers of all different colors were woven between the leaves, creating intricate colorful patterns. It reminded me of the mural on the wall in the dining hall, with red flowers for Koigni swirling into blue for Toaqua and purple for Yapluma.

"Oh, Imogen," I said breathlessly. "It's beautiful."

"Oh, wait." She turned to her dresser and pulled open the top drawer. When she turned around, she lifted a flower crown to her strawberry-blonde hair. "What do you think?"

I stood and walked over to her. I couldn't take my eyes off her dress. "I love it!"

Even Esis stared up at her in awe.

"Really?" she asked nervously, twirling around for me again. "It's been really hard keeping everything alive."

"Yes, really," I said. "I adore it."

Imogen smiled. "Thanks. So... um... since neither of us have dates, I kind of invited Jonah to escort us to the ball. I hope that's okay."

Just another reminder that Liam wouldn't be there, but if I had to go with anyone, I was glad it was these two.

I forced a smile. "Yeah, it'll be fun."

"Good," Imogen said. "Because he'll be here like... now."

On cue, a knock sounded at the door.

I drew in a mock breath of disapproval. "Imogen. A guy in your dorm room? Such a rebel!"

She swatted a hand at me before crossing the room to open the door. Jonah stood in the hallway with a proud smile on his face. He wore a black suit with a purple tie and a matching calla lily on his lapel. His hair was down from his usual bun, and it hung loose around his shoulders. His beard had been trimmed up nicely. Hot damn. He looked like Aquaman or something. I didn't know why other dudes weren't lining up to take *him* to the ball.

"Ladies, your ride is here." He stepped aside and gestured to Squeaks, who was wearing a purple vest that matched his tie. She was attached to the cutest little pony carriage. I absolutely adored it, but there was no way both Imogen and I would fit, especially with Imogen's dress.

"Just a second," Imogen said. She hurried over to her closet and pulled out a pair of high heels that looked like they'd been carved from wood. She slipped them on. "Okay, ready."

Jonah extended a hand and helped Imogen and me into the carriage. Imogen's dress draped over my legs, but I was surprised to find that we both fit.

"Esis, come on." I gestured to him.

He smoothed down his fur and straightened his blue bowtie, taking one last glance in the mirror before bounding over to me and hopping on my lap. Sassy wore a flowery collar and jumped on Squeaks' back for the ride.

Jonah shut Imogen's door and then turned to us. He folded his hands formally. "Ladies, as winners of the Elemental Cup and now the owners of a *very large* sum of money, which regrettably, I had to split between you, I would like to inform you that you are now officially Elementai Princesses... at least for tonight, that is."

Imogen leaned over to me and whispered, "He talks like we're rich. Does he realize how much my parents and your sister got from betting on us? Talk about *money!*"

Jonah continued like he hadn't heard her. "Fortunately for you, you have breasts." He gestured to Imogen's generous cleavage and wiggled his eyebrows. "Which means guys will be fawning over you two all night long. But unfortunately for you"— he adjusted his tie and held his head up high— "I call dibs."

I burst into a fit of laughter while Imogen plucked a petal from her dress and tossed it at him. He used his Air power to blow it away.

"Oh, shut up," Imogen laughed. "Take us to the ball before I turn into a pumpkin!"

Jonah cleared his throat and turned to Squeaks. "As you wish."

Squeaks pulled us down the hall of the Nivita dorms and past the common room, where a thick tree big enough to have reading nooks cut out in it grew up through the ceiling. The wheels on our little cart squeaked down the hall and filled the quiet air. The castle was pretty much deserted by now, since everyone was attending the ball and we were running a little late. Jonah led us down three different hallways before we reached the third-floor balcony that looked over the grand entrance. I held on tight to the side of the cart and pulled Esis close to my belly when we reached the stairs, half expecting us to tumble down them. But Jonah used his Air power to keep our cart floating while Squeaks trotted down the steps. We took a second flight all the way to the first level, and our wheels touched ground again.

The main entrance buzzed with conversation that spilled out from the ballroom. A few people milled around beneath the elaborate chandelier, and others were looking down on us from high up in the fourth and fifth floor balconies. A couple of people noticed us pull up in our little cart and were staring, but it didn't really bother me. They were probably just looking at Imogen's dress. Or maybe we drew eyes because we were the winners. Whatever. I was used to it by now.

Jonah led Squeaks to the ballroom doors before pulling on the reins. Inside, the sound of soft music played, and I could see a large crowd of people and their Familiars spinning around the dance floor.

"Ladies," Jonah said formally. "Thank you for riding the Hippogriff Express. We do take tips, but we unfortunately cannot provide services at the end of the night if you are feeling a little tipsy, seeing as your host himself will be too drunk to drive." He gestured to himself before extending a hand to help me out of the cart.

Imogen hopped out by herself and snorted at him. "Apparently if we need anything, we know exactly where to find him."

Jonah smirked. "I'll be at the bar, chatting up hot guys and making Renar jealous."

Imogen scanned the dance floor like she hadn't heard him. The ballroom was gorgeous and bigger than any banquet hall I'd ever seen. At least twenty huge golden chandeliers hung from the high ceiling. Various shades of velvety curtains framed long windows, some of which were open to different patios. A string quartet played at one end of the room next to an empty DJ stand, while a bar ran the length of the other. Tables were set up near the bar, where people sipped their drinks and chatted amongst themselves. The setting sun cast a dull glow across the room but reflected off glittering surfaces, from the polished marble floor to the jewelry hanging from girls' necks, bringing the whole room to life.

"Looking for Cade?" I asked.

Imogen twisted her hands together. "Yeah. He never asked me to the ball, but I was hoping he'd at least want to dance with me."

"I'm sure he will. And I think I see him over there." I pointed to a guy in a green tie talking to a girl with a unicorn Familiar beside her.

Imogen's eyes lit up. "Oh, good. I'm going to say hi to him."

She hurried off with Sassy at her heels, and I turned to Jonah. He was struggling with the pony cart, trying to unhook it from Squeaks' hips.

"Um... do you need help?" I asked.

"Nah," Jonah replied. "I've got this. You go ahead."

I hesitated. I didn't really want to interrupt Imogen and Cade, and I had no one else to talk to. But Jonah seemed a little embarrassed that he got the cart stuck, so I turned into the ballroom to give him space.

My eyes scanned the thick crowd. I saw a few people I recognized from my classes. I even noticed Haley sulking near one of the patio entrances. She was wearing the revealing dress I'd seen her in at *Delilah's*, but had her arms crossed and a tight look on her face. Anwara sat on her shoulders, swaying back and forth slightly to the music until Haley swatted at her to stop.

I turned my gaze from Haley and looked to the other side of the ballroom. I knew it was useless, but I was hoping to spot Liam in the crowd. For obvious reasons, I didn't.

My eyes fell upon at least one friendly face, though. *Baine.* He was actually put together today, with his hair slicked back and his stubble freshly shaven. He wore a light blue vest beneath his black suit. I guess when he cleaned up I could kind of see where Imogen crushed on him a little, but he was so *old.*

I was just about to make my way over to him, just so I had someone to talk to, when the sound of my name caught me off guard. I turned to see Madame Doya coming my way. She wore a long, silky dress that matched her fiery red hair. Her makeup was immaculate, and her nails freshly done. She held a glass of champagne that was nearly gone.

I forced a friendly smile, only because I didn't think anyone would appreciate me singeing the ends of her curls. I was so glad I was done with her class, though I had no idea if I would have her again. I hoped not.

"Madame Doya," I greeted pleasantly.

Esis growled from my arms, but I squeezed him lightly until he stopped. I glanced around for Naomi and saw her prowling around by the entrance with a golden headpiece, looking my way every so often with that heavy gaze that reminded me so much of Doya.

"Sophia," Madame Doya said coolly. "Congratulations."

My whole body tensed. There was no way I heard her correctly. "Um... thanks?"

"I must speak to you about something." Doya grabbed my elbow and started leading me to the corner of the ballroom before I could protest.

I followed, only because I was curious about what she had to say. Would she finally apologize for the way she treated me in her class?

Doya glanced around the room and lowered her voice. "You need to know what winning the Elemental Cup means."

"Uh... okay." I had no idea where she was going with this.

"The Elders weren't sure before if you were truly the prophesied one. Now that you've won the Cup, they will be keeping a very close eye on you. Don't screw it up." Her eyes narrowed.

My jaw went slack. It almost sounded like she expected me to fail.

I fixed her with a challenging gaze. "Screw up how? What does the prophecy mean, exactly? What am I supposed to do?"

Doya sighed and pulled me tighter into the corner. "I, along with the other Koigni Elders, believe there is a war coming between the Houses. Koigni House has more... political sense than the others. But the other Houses are unwilling to work with us. If we had full power, we could bring order to all of Kinpago, but the other Houses won't allow it. If a war breaks out, our numbers could be cut in half. Thousands of Koigni could die, and our House would be shamed to the highest degree. It's up to you, Sophia, to save us."

Oh, shit. Doya wasn't playing around. The thought of thousands of people dying because of me churned my stomach. My House was truly counting on me.

I swallowed, but my throat felt like sandpaper. "What do I have to do?"

Madame Doya's expression hardened. "The prophecy is unclear. I once believed all would be revealed when you arrived, but that's clearly not the case. I now believe that the prophecy is longer than expected, and the Houses are hiding pieces of it from one another. The magical artifact you will have to find... that's something Koigni never shared with anyone. The other Houses have been keeping secrets as well. You, Sophia, will need to uncover those secrets to discover how to fulfill the prophecy and prevent total Elementai annihilation."

Her words echoed through my head. *Total Elementai annihilation.* My knees shook. I nearly forgot I was standing in a room full of people. She couldn't truly believe that if I failed, this entire magical society would fall, could she?

My eyes met hers, and I witnessed a fire behind them that told me everything I needed to know. She totally and thoroughly believed every word she said. Sure, this place had its issues, but there were thousands of people living in Kinpago, not to mention the magical creatures. I couldn't let this magical place be destroyed, the place that Liam, Imogen, and Jonah called home... and the place I thought was home as well.

But... Doya was jumping from one impossible task to another. There was no way I could do what she was asking of me.

"I'm not really cut out for this," I said. "I barely know anything about Hawkei history. I'm only a First Year."

Doya held her head high. "I will train you."

Wait... what? This lady was talking crazy talk.

My brow furrowed. "Um... okay. Why didn't you offer earlier?"

Doya pursed her lips. "You had yet to prove yourself on your own. I was trying to protect you."

The crease between my eyebrows deepened. "Protect me from what?" I demanded. I couldn't help it when the words burst out of me. Doya made no sense, and it was enough to make my Fire rise to the surface. I pushed it down before we both lit up in flames. "You spent the entire semester pushing me away and making me feel like a failure. Now you claim it was for my own protection?"

Doya cleared her throat and glanced around, as if making sure I hadn't caught anyone's attention. I didn't care if I did. I just wanted Doya to tell me the truth.

She returned her gaze to mine and lifted her chin. "I can't reveal everything at this time. Just remember, Sophia, the Elders are watching. You must be cautious. And you must not tell anyone what I've just told you. Do you understand?"

The pointed expression she gave me was almost enough to burn a hole straight through me— and it may have, if I weren't Koigni. It was clear that I didn't have a choice. I had to find the missing pieces of the prophecy and fulfill it. Either she or the Elders would make sure I would.

"I'll be careful." I purposely didn't answer her question directly.

"Good," she said in a clipped tone. "Enjoy your night. It may be one of the last you have before everything changes."

Doya turned from me and started toward Naomi by the doors, leaving me completely frozen in place and shocked by her words. Esis growled at her, pulling me back to attention.

"Relax, buddy," I told him while I stroked the fur around his nubby horns. "She doesn't mean it. She's just got a stick up her ass, and she has to say stuff like that to make herself feel better."

I was a liar, and there was no doubt in my mind that Esis knew it. Doya didn't joke around... ever.

My gaze scanned the ballroom nervously. I worried that everyone could see my arms shaking and the sweat breaking out across my brow. Then my eyes fell upon a champagne glass in a Toaqua girl's hand.

Alcohol. I needed some.

Pulling Esis closer to my chest, I navigated through the crowd and to the bar. I'd never had alcohol before, unless you counted that sip of beer I had at my friend Emily's when we were sixteen. I didn't even swallow it because it tasted like piss. But maybe champagne would taste better. At least it would take the edge off.

"Hey, Sophia!" Jonah called from where he sat at the bar.

I squeezed between a group of people and stopped next to him. "I need a drink."

Jonah eyed me curiously and raised his glass to his lips. "What's wrong?"

"What?" I asked innocently, brushing hair out of my eyes. "Nothing's wrong? Why would you think that?"

Esis poked my arm, as if calling me out as a liar. *Yeah, yeah.*

"I didn't take you as a drinker is all," Jonah replied with a shrug.

"Yeah, well, it's to celebrate," I told him. "We won. I think I deserve a drink."

Jonah nodded his approval. "What can I get you?"

I thought about it for a moment, but Jonah was right. I wasn't a drinker and didn't have the faintest clue of what to get. "Um... something that doesn't taste like piss?"

Jonah let out a deep-belly laugh. "That doesn't leave many options."

I swore my face went pale, which only made him laugh harder.

"I'm kidding. How about I surprise you?" he asked.

"Okay," I agreed.

While Jonah waved down the bartender, somebody reached past me to place a tip on the counter. The bar was so crowded that his body pressed against mine. Heat radiated across my skin as his shirt brushed across my shoulder and his breath ran across the side of my cheek. Somehow, without even looking, I *knew* it was him. It was like my body was in tune to his. It had to be, considering the way my heart fluttered and my head spun just from the close proximity.

I whirled around, beaming. "Liam!"

Esis leapt from my arms onto Liam's shoulder. I flung my arms around his neck, squeezing them both tightly. His pine forest scent filled my nose. Liam gasped, and I quickly pulled away. Esis stayed put on his shoulder, pulling at strands of his long black hair.

Liam's eyes were bright, and a smile stretched wide across his face. He looked so amazing that I could almost believe he wasn't sick anymore. Liam looked me up and down, and desire flickered across his eyes. He totally loved my dress.

I liked his outfit, too. He wore black slacks and a white collared shirt, with the sleeves rolled up to his elbows. Hot damn. Why were forearms so sexy? A red tie hung around his neck. I'd never seen him wear the color before. Dare I say it actually looked really good on him?

"I thought you weren't coming," I said, still trying to get over the initial shock of seeing him here. It was like a dream.

Liam shrugged and pulled his hair out of Esis' grasp. "I snuck out."

My heart sank. "Oh. So they didn't discharge you? How are you feeling?"

Liam wrinkled his nose, but that radiance about him never faded. "I'm fine."

I rolled my eyes. "Which is code for, *I feel terrible and don't want anyone knowing.*"

Liam hesitated, then dropped his shoulders. "Maybe. I'm the same as always, I guess. I'll survive."

Jonah stood and held out a hand toward Liam. He took it, and they did that weird guy handshake-hug thing.

"We're so glad you made it, man," Jonah said before sitting back down at his stool. "And you wore the tie."

Liam smoothed out the red fabric and avoided my gaze. "Yeah... I, uh, it was all I could find on short notice."

"Obviously," Jonah said. I didn't miss the wink he shot Liam's way, as if they shared some secret I wasn't a part of.

"I'm so glad you're here to celebrate with us." I resisted the urge to throw my arms around his neck again. With Liam here, I didn't need the alcohol to take the edge off. Just his very presence made me forget all about the bad in the world. "I still can't believe we won."

Liam scoffed. "Yeah, well, it's easier when you're not trying to kill off your teammates."

Jonah took another sip of his drink. "Thanks, by the way, guys. You know, for not killing me."

I swatted at him playfully. "Stop it! We would never do that." I lowered my voice and hissed, "We're not Haley."

"I need to tell you something about that." Liam glanced around to make sure no one was listening and leaned in. Even if someone was eavesdropping, there was no way they could hear over the chatter around us. "All of Haley's teammates are dead."

I drew in a sharp breath. "But that Nivita guy—"

"Didn't make it," Liam interrupted. "Haley only passed because she got him to the finish line alive. But only barely. He was in the hospital with me. He passed away a few days after the tournament."

My hand shot over my mouth. "That's horrible."

Liam and Jonah nodded in unison. Meanwhile, my eyes scanned the crowd for Haley. She was no longer standing by the patio, and I didn't see her anywhere else.

"Sophia." Liam pulled my attention to him. "Don't go looking for trouble. Second place is still a highly honorable position. Haley has proven herself to the tribe and will become Chieftess of Koigni after her mother steps down. It wouldn't look good for you to pick a fight with her."

I gaped at him. "I wasn't going to..."

Okay, yeah. Maybe I was. I just wanted to see her show some remorse.

But Haley could wait for another time. I wasn't going to let her ruin the magic of this night.

I reached for Liam's hand and started toward the dance floor, but he remained firmly rooted in place. "Come on." I tugged at him. "Let's dance."

Liam stumbled a step but quickly righted himself. "No, Sophia. We can't."

My bottom lip jutted out. "Why not?"

Liam lowered his voice. "Don't you notice something about the couples?"

I looked toward the dance floor and didn't see anything out of the ordinary at first... until I realized it was all color coordinated. "So they're all dancing with members of their own House. Who cares? We were on the same team. We deserve to celebrate together."

Liam bit the inside of his lower lip.

I crossed my arms. "Well, if you're not going to dance with me, I want to dance with Esis. And seeing as he's not going to leave your shoulder, you'll have to dance with me, too."

Esis peeked out from a curtain of Liam's hair.

Liam sighed, and smiled a little. "I guess I can't really say no to that."

I pulled Liam out onto the dance floor. His left hand came up to meet my right, and his other hand settled high on my back. Electric tingles spread up and down my spine. Oh, ancestors. How was I supposed to dance with my heart going haywire? Seriously. The damn thing was trying to beat its way out of my chest. Surely Liam could feel my blood raging through my veins. He was Toaqua and sensitive to all the water in my body. He had to feel the shift in energy.

His hand dropped further down my back as we started to spin, and I gasped. Oh, what I wouldn't give to let those hands roam over me.

Liam gazed down at me with soft eyes, and I stared back into his. The whole ballroom seemed to fade away around us. It felt like I was in a fairytale, floating across the room like a princess who'd found her prince. If I could just lean in and kiss him again, the way we did in the cave—

"Ow!" I cried as Liam's feet stumbled over my toes.

He hopped backward. "Sorry. I'm so sorry."

I giggled as Esis leaned over Liam's shoulder to get a good look at my feet. "It's okay. I'll be fine."

Except my toe was throbbing. It seemed as if *I'm fine* was starting to become a code word between us.

"Good," Liam said, "because people are staring."

As much as I didn't want to take my eyes off him, I did. People were, indeed, staring. I even saw one Koigni girl pointing our way.

"Seriously?" I asked with an eye roll. "You barely stepped on me. We can't be dancing *that* bad."

Liam's lips tightened. "It's not that. What we're doing, Sophia... it's kind of an act of rebellion."

"An act of rebellion?" I asked. "By dancing together?"

Liam shrugged but continued twirling me around the dance floor. "We're wearing each other's House colors *and* dancing together. It kind of looks like... something."

"Well, it is something, isn't it?" I asked. "I mean, *shouldn't* we challenge House boundaries? How else are we going to be together?"

Liam's entire body tensed, but he didn't stop dancing. "Do you... uh... want to get out of here for a second? Away from all these prying eyes?"

What was he suggesting? Every instinct told me to answer with a *hell, yes!*

Instead, I just said, "I guess so." All the while, my heart was beating ferociously. *Liam Mitoh wants to get me alone!*

Liam led me off the dance floor. We passed through the patio doors and out into the gardens. It was cold outside, but not chilly enough to cover up. Either I was too hot from my Fire rising to the surface under Liam's touch, or the Elders had allowed a small weather change for the event. Either way, I found the evening air peaceful.

There weren't many people out in the gardens. The farther we walked from the doors, the fewer people there were.

"Where are you taking me, Liam?" I was partially worried and partially excited. He was walking too fast for a leisurely night stroll, so he either wanted to break some bad news or break some more rules.

Liam stopped me behind a big bush sculpture of a pegasus. The wide wings and the darkening sky helped conceal us from the people back in the ballroom. Esis jumped off Liam's shoulder and climbed up the pegasus sculpture's wings, then hopped from the end of it to the next sculpture of a horned bear.

Liam took my hands in his. "Sophia, what you just said about us being together... I don't think you understand."

MEGAN LINSKI & ALICIA RADES

My brow furrowed. "What's there to understand, Liam? It's against the rules. So we'll change the rules. No big deal."

"*No big deal?*" Liam hissed. "Sophia, this is the way it's been for hundreds of years. These rules aren't just about controlling us. It's to keep our powers stronger so that no other House dies out after Anichi."

I shrugged. "So we just don't have kids. Simple."

Holy crap. Were we seriously talking about having kids? We'd only kissed once! But damn it, that was all we needed. It didn't matter what Liam said about the House rules. There was no turning back from the line we'd already crossed.

Liam raked his fingers through his hair. God, he looked sexy when he did that. I wanted to run *my* hands through his hair... and down his forearms... and in other places I probably shouldn't be thinking about. Which could definitely lead to kids someday.

"It's not that simple, though," Liam said. "The Elders would never allow it. This isn't just about us, Sophia. If we started dating, then so would other people."

"So what? Is there actually any evidence that children from two Houses are weaker?"

Liam opened his mouth, but hesitated.

I raised an eyebrow. "Liam, I don't care about the rules. I want to be with you."

"Ancestors, Sophia. You can't talk like that."

"Why not? It's the truth."

"Because..." Liam sighed and glanced toward the castle. No one was close enough to hear. "Because if you say things like that, it just might come true."

"I know. I wouldn't say it if I didn't want it to happen, Liam."

He stared down at me, his expression hard to read. He looked conflicted— like he wanted to agree with me but argue at the same time.

A thought suddenly occurred, and I drew away from him. "Do you... do you not want to be with me?"

Liam looked hurt by the question. "Of course I do. But we don't have a choice."

I relaxed slightly. "You always have a choice, Liam."

His hands balled into fists, and his lips tightened until he couldn't hold it in any longer. "Aw, fuck, Sophia."

Liam growled. He honest to God growled. And then like a wolf trapping his prey, he pounced on me. One second he was standing a few feet away from me, and the next he'd swept me into his arms and claimed my lips for his own.

The world spun around me so quickly that I could no longer feel the stone path beneath my feet. Liam held me tightly to his chest. One hand tangled in the hair at the base of my neck while the other settled on my hip. His lips parted, and I took the invitation to deepen the kiss. My hands ran up his back until they climbed so high they reached the side of his face. I pulled him in even closer until every possible inch of our bodies were touching. My hands moved to his hair, tangling into the strands like he did with mine. He inhaled a sharp breath in response.

Heat exploded through my chest like fireworks. I didn't even care if my Fire surfaced and burned my dress off of me. Liam would like that, I was sure. And damn it, so would I. But my Fire didn't escape. It hung out just below the surface, just enough to feel amazing and to warm Liam's cool skin.

Kissing Liam was like witnessing a fire tornado colliding with a hurricane. We stood in the calm eye of the storm while the elements combined and raged around us. The fire stood no chance against the rain, but the rain couldn't put out the fire. It burned brighter when the rain touched it until the two elements matched each other's rhythm and swirled together to become one. The way Liam made me feel was breathtaking and... impossible. Yet here we were, Fire and Water. We shouldn't mix, but we did. We *so* did.

Liam's tongue grazed my bottom lip, and I moaned. Which only made him wrap his arms tighter around me. His hand hesitated on my hip, as if he wanted to touch me in other places but wasn't sure he was allowed. I didn't know what I was doing until I did it. I untangled my fingers from his hair and guided his hand to my backside. It surprised me considering I didn't know until that very moment how comfortable I'd become with him. I knew Liam would never hurt me, and there was so much I wanted to share with him. My heart... my soul... my body. He just sort of rested his hand there, like he didn't know how far to take this.

Read my signals, Liam! I want more!

I wrapped my hand around the collar of his shirt until I had a fistful of tie, and I tugged him even closer— if that were possible. Liam gasped.

Squeeze my ass, damn it!

Message received. Liam's hand tightened on my butt as my tongue slid deeper into his mouth. Heat traveled down my chest and settled between my thighs. Being with Liam like this was unlike anything else. It was so overwhelmingly amazing that I thought I might cry. Feeling this way should be illegal—

No sooner did the thought cross my mind did it hit me that that was exactly what this *was*. It was illegal. Liam and I were breaking the law by kissing like this... by kissing at all.

Elders be damned. Breaking the law was great. If I knew it'd feel like this, I would've rebelled sooner.

Esis chittered, pulling me out of the spell Liam had put on me. We both jumped away from each other. Esis was sitting on the bear statue's head, staring at us with interest.

After a moment, Esis put his hands together and began a slow clap, then rose to his feet and cheered for us. My face went beet red, as did Liam's.

"Esis," I scolded. "Calm down. It's not a big deal."

I apparently lied a lot.

Esis hopped down from the bear bush and scurried over to me. I bent and scooped him into my arms.

"We should... probably get back..." Liam sounded out of breath.

"Yeah," I agreed in the same shaky tone. "We probably should."

Liam gestured to my hair. "You should probably..."

I smoothed down the strands. "Yeah. You too."

Liam ran his fingers through his hair and started toward the ballroom. If he thought that was the end of this, he had another thing coming.

"So... what was that, Liam? Was it a farewell kiss?"

He didn't meet my gaze. "I— I don't know."

"Well, will it happen again?"

Shut up, Sophia. You're ruining it.

Liam stopped and turned toward me. He gazed down at my hands, but we were where people could see us again, so he didn't take them. "It's up to you, Sophia. I'll never be able to resist you."

My heart swooned at his words. "I guess you'll just have to wait and see what happens, then." I smirked. "Let's get back inside before Imogen and Jonah start accusing us of things."

Liam laughed. "They wouldn't exactly be wrong, would they?"

"No. Definitely not."

We walked past a group of Koigni in the gardens. The guy from the Silver Team, the one with the big dragon familiar, shot us a look of disgust. I'd heard he came in third place and lost one of his teammates. I bet he wasn't too happy we won.

I entwined my fingers in Liam's hand and breezed right by him. Liam squeezed my fingers back, but dropped them as soon as we entered the ballroom. I spotted Imogen and Jonah by the bar, Sassy and Squeaks nearby. We started making our way over to them.

Before we reached them, Haley stepped in front of us. Anwara ruffled her feathers, and Haley crossed her arms.

"Congratulations, *White Team*." Haley didn't sound the least bit genuine, but I'd already made it a point not to let her ruin my night.

"Thank you," I said kindly.

Haley blinked a few times, like she didn't think she'd heard me right. "I wasn't actually complimenting you, you wolpertinger. Do you know how embarrassing it's been to lose to a bunch of misfits?"

"Haley, do we have to do this?" Liam protested.

I shrugged, but inside, my Fire raged. "That must be the worst. You know, right after killing all your teammates."

Haley's face twisted in anger. "Anything's fair game out there. I did what I had to do to win."

"And you still didn't," I snapped.

Haley's eyebrows shot up, and a fireball formed in her hand. She was going to use it.

Liam quickly pulled water from six champagne glasses in people's hands around us and doused the flames. Water splashed up on Haley's dress, and she shrieked. All around us, people were starting to stare. A few took in sharp breaths, but the ballroom was big enough and plenty was going on that our little confrontation barely stirred the crowd.

Haley held out her other hand, but before she could conjure flame my hand shot out and clamped around hers. I pushed back against her heat, stopping her Fire in its tracks. To anyone else, it looked like a mere handshake, as if I were apologizing for the mishap, but I made sure to put as much strength and hostility into my grip as I could. I even added a bit of my own heat for good measure— only as a warning. Then I leaned in close enough for only Haley and Liam to hear.

"This isn't the Elemental Cup anymore," I hissed. "You can't just do whatever you want. But should you decide to, I will be there to extinguish your flame. Every. Single. Time. I know you're watching me, Haley, and I'm not afraid of you. Be careful, or you just might get burned."

And then I swept past her with Liam at my heels, leaving her standing there wet and dumbstruck. Esis clapped from where he was cradled in the crook of my elbow.

"Holy ancestors, Sophia," Liam whispered. "That was hot."

I smirked. There was surprisingly a lot more where that came from.

Imogen rushed away from Jonah and squealed when she reached us. "Tell me I just saw what I think I saw!"

Jonah was close behind her. "Did you just tell Haley off?"

I beamed, still riding the high of Liam's kiss and standing up to Haley. "Yeah... I think I did."

"That's my girl," Jonah said, clapping me on the back.

"Just as long as, you know, you don't start shooting fireballs at each other across the dance floor," Imogen teased.

"I won't be throwing anything at Haley," I promised, "but I can't say I won't be setting the dance floor on fire. It looks like the DJ is about to take over." I pointed toward the guy tinkering with a computer behind a pair of huge speakers.

"Yes!" Imogen gushed. "We should've choreographed something."

"Aw, man," I said. "That would've been fun."

"If you're all going to dance, I'm going to need a drink," Liam announced before turning to me. "Can I get you anything, *pawee*?"

Imogen's eyes went wide beside him.

"Yeah... uh, surprise me?" I suggested.

"Sure." Liam headed toward the bar.

Imogen and Jonah watched him go, then whirled back toward me in unison.

"Oh, my ancestors, Sophia," Imogen raved. "He called you *pawee*. That is so sweet!"

I glanced between the two of them, feeling like I was missing something. "Yeah, so? He calls me that because I'm so inexperienced— like a child, he said."

"But that's not the only meaning," Jonah pointed out.

"It isn't?" I asked, uncertain. Whatever the second meaning was was probably horrible. They seemed too shocked for it to be anything else. "What's the other meaning?"

Imogen exchanged a glance with Jonah before she finally spoke. "*Cherished one.*"

"He's basically calling you his soulmate," Jonah whispered. "It's like, the most beloved word a Hawkei can use to describe someone."

My heart tumbled around in my chest as I stared at Liam, who was leaning against the bar. No way did he mean it like that. *No way.*

But then he lifted his gaze and smiled at me, and I knew. Whether Liam admitted it or not, he was in love with me.

Come hell or high water, we would be together. This society couldn't stop us. Even the prophecy couldn't stand in our way. Sure, my knees buckled just thinking about what was to come— about the prophecy, and the people who might die because of it. But more than anything, I didn't want to see Liam hurt. We were in this together, now until the end.

No matter what the Elders did to keep us apart, I would watch this society burn before I ever found myself separated from Liam Mitoh. It didn't matter if we were *allowed* to be together.

I would forever be his *pawee*.

Liam

TWENTY-FIVE

I was tired. My muscles were sore, and it took a lot of effort just to move around. Every now and again the room would spin a little.

Yeah, I felt like shit. But I felt like shit everyday, so that wasn't new. This was one of the most amazing nights of my life, and I wasn't about to miss this. Not for the world.

My doctors were gonna flip when they found out I'd not only snuck out, but also had been drinking, but I won the damn Elemental Cup for crying out loud. I deserved a beer.

I snuck another glance at Sophia out of the corner of my eye. I'd been staring at her all night, but I couldn't keep my eyes off her. Her chestnut hair was in large curls, and she wore sparkling eyeshadow that brought out her chocolate eyes.

Her dress was phenomenal. I was *so* into the fact she was wearing blue. Turned me on. And I think she liked that I was wearing red, too. I was really glad Jonah had told me to wear a red tie, though I didn't get why at the time. He and Imogen must've set this up. Wearing Koigni red when I was Toaqua was huge— just like Sophia wearing blue wouldn't go missed.

Not to mention we couldn't seem to part from each other for a second. We were basically wearing signs that screamed we were together.

I took a shot for courage. Whatever. I didn't want to think about that right now. I just wanted to enjoy the rest of the night.

I took the beer and the mixed drink the bartender handed me and walked back to Sophia. I noticed there was something different about her. She was looking at me... a bit weird. Like she'd just found out some big secret or something. Were those *tears*?

Fuck, I must've done something wrong. I held out the drink for her to take. I was so nervous I ended up spilling part of her drink on her dress.

"Oh, shit, sorry," I said hastily. I grabbed a napkin off a table and started dotting her midriff, trying to clean up the mess. I hoped it didn't stain.

Sophia actually laughed instead of yelling at me for ruining her gown. "Don't worry about it." She took a small taste of her drink, and her face lit up. Her earlier weirdness was forgotten.

"I hope you like it," I said. Ancestors, I was embarrassed. I threw the soaked napkin on the table.

"What is it?" she asked, taking a sip.

"Sex on the Beach," I rattled off mindlessly, and Sophia gave me a grin. I reddened a bit and said, "Don't take it like that. It's fruity and girly. Something I thought you'd like."

"It's something I'd like, all right," she said coyly, chewing on her straw. She was eyeing me provocatively.

"Down, virgin," I told her. "You don't even know what you're asking for."

She blushed a little, but then added, "I thought virgins were supposed to be hot to guys."

It was *totally* hot, but I didn't need to encourage us. We were already bad enough. "Come on, *pawee*." I laughed and took her arm, guiding her to the table where Imogen and Jonah were.

Her smile got even broader when I called her my little pet name. Had someone told her something?

Imogen and Jonah were at the table, drinking and chatting. Sassy and Esis were both on top of the table, and it looked like they were having a drinking contest.

"Chug, chug, chug," Jonah chanted, pounding the table. Sassy gurgled and fell over, spilling her mug of ale, but Esis managed to finish his and let out a loud burp, patting his stomach happily.

Cade had joined them at the table, along with my brother. Ezra had a girl on either side of him, both of whom I was pretty sure were his dates. Player.

Cade had his arm around Imogen's waist at the table. She leaned against him, looking super happy. Were they a thing yet, or...?

A Nivita girl in a green gown came up to the table and put her hand on Cade's shoulder. "Hi, Cade," she said, batting her eyelashes. She totally ignored that Imogen was all over him. "Would you like to dance?"

"He's kind of busy at the moment," Jonah snapped at her. The girl's eyes narrowed at him.

"No, it's okay." Imogen pulled away from Cade and looked down. "You can go if you want, Cade."

Cade seemed puzzled— like he didn't know what to do. If I could read his mind, I would've sworn he thought Imogen was sending him away. "Oh... okay." He got up and walked away with the girl, and Imogen frowned sadly.

Ugh, Imogen, get it together. You practically just let him walk away!

"You look really beautiful tonight, Im," I said, to try and bolster her confidence. "Your dress is great."

"Oh, thanks." Imogen smoothed out a flower on it bashfully. "I guess. Maybe I should've worn something more traditional."

"Bitch, please," Jonah said, and he flipped his hair over his shoulder. "You're the prettiest slut in this room."

Imogen forced a smile for him, but I couldn't help but notice her eyes followed Cade as he half-heartedly danced with the Nivita girl. If I didn't know any better, I would figure Cade wanted to ask Imogen to dance... he was just scared that she was so shy, she'd say no.

I looked at Sophia, and she shrugged sadly, in a way that said we couldn't help Imogen if she wasn't ready.

Ezra gave me a sly grin as I pulled my chair closer to Sophia. "How *you* two doing?"

"We're fine, Ezra," I said, putting emphasis on the words so he wouldn't ask questions.

But Ezra was a pain in my ass, so he kept prodding. "You two were gone for a while."

"Yep, just slipped out for a minute," I told him sharply, and he snickered. Sophia gave me side-eye, asking questions with her gaze.

I'd told Ezra about the kiss Sophia and I shared during the tournament. I didn't mean to, it'd just slipped out when I was still kind of out of it and doped up in the hospital. I was lucky he was the only family member around at the time, though he hadn't stopped teasing me about it since.

Still, I trusted him to keep his mouth shut. So that brought the total number of people who knew to... three.

That was a dangerous number. Luckily, the two Toaqua girls were too busy fawning over my brother to read too much into what we were saying.

Ezra stood up. "Ladies." He offered an arm to each girl, and they took it as they swaggered toward the dance floor. Three more Toaqua girls materialized around my brother, and I swear all of them were fine taking turns dancing with him.

Jonah leaned in once Ezra was gone. "Dude, does he know?" he asked, thumbing at Ezra.

"Yes," I said lowly, before I grimaced and glanced at my girlfrie— I mean, Sophia. "Sorry, Soph."

"I don't care," she said, and she waved her hand. "I'm fine with your brother knowing."

Of course she didn't mind, because she didn't know what that meant. "The more people who know about... us... the more we're at risk," I told her.

"Is there an *us*?" Imogen asked curiously, her happiness back. She and Jonah leaned forward like they couldn't wait to hear all the juicy details.

"Who are you guys, the Hawkei tabloid reporters?" I asked. "You two know because there was no keeping it from you during the tournament, but now that we're back home you need to mind your own business."

Thankfully, that was the moment the music changed from classical to modern, and the lights darkened, giving the ballroom a club-like atmosphere. Jonah jumped up from his seat like he'd been electrocuted, gossip about my love life forgotten.

"This is my song!" he squealed, and ran onto the dance floor. Squeaks followed, racing after her Elementai almost deliriously.

Imogen jumped up from the table and grabbed Sophia's hand. "Come on!" The two girls raced off after Jonah. Esis and Sassy scampered to follow. I got up to lean against a pillar and watch them from afar.

Imogen and Sophia didn't hold back at all. The girls bounced up and down to the music, grinding against each other like we were at a strip club. They pounded their fists into the air, did a waltz, and then the tango. At one point Imogen got down and did the worm, rising up on all fours to shake her butt. Sophia slapped it, and they almost fell over laughing. They were fun to watch. It's like they didn't care about what people thought of them, only having fun.

Jonah was worse than the both of them. He was twerking in the middle of the dance floor, shaking his ass so hard I'm surprised it didn't fall off. Squeaks copied him, wiggling her hindquarters until the music increased in tempo and she did her best moonwalk.

It didn't help that Jonah was requesting the filthiest songs he could think of. The DJ made faces, but since Jonah was a Cup Champion, he couldn't protest. Some other gay dude in a purple suit, with eye glitter and false eyelashes, sauntered onto the floor with his griffin Familiar. He did some crazy sick moves, gliding along the floor like he had choreographed steps for each song. Jonah copied him until half the dance floor stood back to watch them in complete awe.

I was pretty sure Jonah had spent the last few months practicing his moves more than preparing for the cup. It pissed me off a little, but the tournament was over now, so whatever. He could have his fun.

People were watching on the sidelines, whispering to each other and laughing under their breath at my team's ridiculous dance moves. But fuck them. They were having the time of their lives out there.

"Hey, you were on their team. Do you think Sophia Henley and Imogen Ahnild are lesbians?" a dude I didn't even know leaned over and asked me when Sophia and Imogen started doing some sort of sexy dance against each other. His friend was next to him, watching me carefully for a response.

"Um, no fucking way," I said, irritated. "They're just friends."

"I swear that Sophia girl is bisexual," the other bro said, nodding his head as if that sealed the deal.

Couldn't confirm that for sure, but at least I knew she liked dick. I mean... I *couldn't* say for certain, because I hadn't shown that part of me to her yet and didn't know that she wouldn't run off screaming, but I was pretty sure she was into dudes. The way she was dirty dancing with Imogen, though, even made me wonder.

Imogen knelt down on the floor. She pulled a small box from her dress and presented it to Sophia, opening it like it contained a wedding ring. There was a small bracelet inside, one it looked like Imogen had made, with Koigni and Nivita charms attached. Sophia squealed and pretended to accept the fake proposal tearfully. It made me chuckle how close they were.

"See. Total lesbians," the bro added.

Great. The way this school was, half the student body would be utterly convinced the girls were engaged and getting married next summer. People were so stupid. They were just girls being girls.

Though if the Elders did suspect they were engaged lesbians from different Houses (which, if it did happen, I was leaving this whole society) at least it wouldn't be as severe... because they couldn't reproduce together. They'd probably just end up with some jail time and a fine.

It was different with us. I could get her pregnant. And that's what the Elders feared the most.

"Sophia *is* cute, though," the bro said, interrupting my thoughts. "Too bad she's from Koigni."

"For sure. What I'd give to get my hands on that body. Sucks she's not Nivita," the other dude groaned.

"Hey, back off," I growled. The guys stared at me with open mouths, and I stomped off before my big mouth could get me into more trouble. I couldn't be protective or jealous. Not in public.

And it sucked. I had noticed that half the guys in here were eyeing

Sophia, especially the Koigni guys who knew they actually had a chance.

But maybe they didn't have a chance, because her heart belonged to me.

Watching her out there, enjoying herself with Imogen and Jonah, made me think back to our second kiss in the garden and how perfect it'd been. In the moment, I couldn't control myself. After a week of not feeling those lips against mine, I just had to kiss her. When she'd practically forced me to grab her ass, I nearly came right then and there. Sophia had the *most perfect* ass. It was better than even my dreams had been. I was scared to touch her, because I worried she'd get triggered because of what that creep had done to her on prom night.

But she didn't. She wanted me just as badly as I wanted her. Which boggled my mind. How could someone as incredible as her, love me?

Sophia gestured for me to join her and Imogen. I shook my head, and she frowned. She seemed hurt.

Sophia didn't understand. She thought I didn't want to be with her. That wasn't it at all. She wasn't taking this seriously. If people found out about us, we could be banished or imprisoned. Worse, we could be executed.

She would be separated from Esis. I didn't have anything to lose in this game, but I wouldn't do that to her.

Still... her words gave me hope. Maybe there was a way we could change the rules. Maybe the tribe would make an exception for us.

It was doubtful.

Sophia kept glancing at me. It made me feel bad. She really wanted me out there with her.

Fuck it. I went to the bar, ordered another shot, and took it before I strolled onto the dance floor.

At this point, Sophia and Imogen did some sort of coordinated dance— though I was pretty sure Imogen had made it up off the top of her head and that Sophia was just following along. Esis and Sassy copied them, trying to duplicate the moves their Elementai were making. Jonah had joined in, and with Squeaks as backup, they looked like a horribly uncoordinated boy band.

Sophia saw me coming. She reached out and grabbed my hand, pulling me in.

I was a terrible dancer. I couldn't keep up with the rest of them, but I still tried to follow Imogen's movements, trying to play along. People moved off the dance floor and gave us room as we started tripping over each other, then getting down the rhythm of the dance. At the end of the song, we pretty much fell against each other laughing. I was breathless, and Sophia gasped for air. Her eyes sparkled, like she wished this night would never end.

If I was a sap, I'd say something nauseating, like I believed in that moment the four of us would be friends forever.

The lights came up again. Dinner was ready. We staggered off the dance floor and returned to our table. Baine was sitting there waiting for us. As our tournament mentor, he was supposed to eat with us.

"People were staring at Imogen and me when we were dancing," Sophia said before we sat down. "Like we were freaks."

"They're just jealous they don't have the courage to dance like that," I told her gently. "Don't let them bother you. Their opinions don't matter."

We sat down, and Baine grinned at us. "Enjoying the ball?"

"Yes," we all responded in unison. Servers started bringing us plates of roast corn, ground cake, buffalo steak, a sweet berry mixture, and a bowl of mutton stew.

Oh, thank the ancestors. I hadn't had such a good meal in like, weeks. The hospital food wasn't bad, but it was nothing like the school's cooking.

Baine immediately dug in. He wasn't as bad of an eater as I was, but he ate loudly and had to constantly use his napkin to smear away the juices on his face. I couldn't understand this obsession women had over him.

"By the way... how did we win, Professor? I thought for sure we'd come in last," I asked before taking a bite. I tried to eat more politely this time, seeing as we were at a ball after all.

"You mean you didn't watch the recaps?" Baine's eyes widened.

I glanced at my teammates, and we all shared the same expression.

I didn't have to ask. None of us wanted to watch the replay of our Cup win. We probably would, someday. Right now, it was just too fresh.

"Well, let's see." Baine raised his fingers and started ticking off names. "The Yellow Team failed at the first task. None of them made it out of the ocean alive."

A pit sank in my stomach. That's what I'd been afraid of.

Baine continued, as if he wasn't talking about college kids dying and just making polite dinner conversation.

"The Silver Team came in third, but lost one of its members in the avalanche. The Blue Team was fourth, but only had two members left by the time they made it to the end. Two died, one from the avalanche and and one from dehydration," Baine noted. "Purple and Orange were both next, but they decided to unify their teams instead of fighting, and they made it to the end together, although there were only six of them left by that point."

Baine cleared his throat and eyed Sophia. I could tell he was thinking about how our team and Haley's had fought against each other. Nobody had brought it up, because it wasn't polite and anything was legal during the Elemental Cup. But it was still shocking, because it hadn't been done before. As far as I knew, no one in the history of the Cup had ever *murdered* their teammates.

"What about the rest?" Jonah asked, clearly to steer the conversation away from Haley's insanity.

Baine shrugged. "The Green Team tried to avoid the mountains, but got lost in the woods and had to backtrack, which cost them a few days. And, well, the Red Team... I'm sure you've heard what happened with them."

Baine made a unfortunate expression. Out of the corner of the room, Madame Doya came into view, Naomi prowling proudly at her side.

Every move that she made was elegant and poised. She was a gorgeous lady, and beautiful to watch, even if she was the most evil woman in the world... though I was pretty sure Haley had booted her to second place in the past few weeks.

It had to be an embarrassment for Doya to only have Haley

survive, even if she did get second place. Her behavior... or rather, her murders... had been filmed on live TV for all to see.

Those families weren't going to be happy with the Koigni tribe. They'd blame every Fire person alive for their kids' deaths, not just Doya and Haley. Despite nearly winning the Cup, Haley had shamed her tribe. And I was sure Sophia's incredible display during the Fire challenge didn't do much for any of the other tribes but make them all nervous.

It seemed like we *were* heading toward a war. And since I was pretty sure Sophia would be at the center of it, that scared the hell out of me.

"The Pink Team came in last, but they took their time and made sure they were prepared before they went into any challenges." Baine slurped the last of his soup. "Besides the Pink Team, you were the only other team that had all four members survive."

That was a humbling statement. "It sounded like we just got lucky," I said.

"Way to ruin everything," Sophia said, and she elbowed me.

"You won because you paced yourself well and worked together. None of the other teams took care of each other like you four did," Baine said. "Not to mention that instead of doing things the conventional way, all of you did things in a way that worked best for you."

We all looked at each other with soft smiles. Baine was right. We had each other's backs. Now and always.

Baine rambled on and on about the rest of the teams and how they had performed during the tournament, which was fine, because it gave the rest of us time to eat. I had my meal down in seconds, though Imogen and Sophia took forever. I'm pretty sure Jonah drank more than he ate.

As Baine went on about how the other contestants had died... falls, cave-ins, or lost within the region... I got a little confused. As far as I could remember, there were deaths every year, but the death toll had been steadily going up every year since I'd attended Orenda. Were the Elders making the contest harder or something?

I'd noticed Baine's eyes had hardly left Madame Doya's form the minute she strolled into the room. He rose to his feet and bowed to us.

"Well, at any rate, I'm glad you four did so well," he said, rather hurriedly. "I hope you enjoy the rest of your night."

Baine went to the center of the room and held out a hand to Madame Doya. Naomi growled, but after a moment, Doya took it, and soon they were turning on the dance floor. Baine's awkward and stiff dad-moves looked very strange next to Doya's intricate twirling.

Baine and Doya danced in a very proper way together. It more or less looked polite. I figured it was expected of them to dance together, since they were both the top two mentors this year.

"I wish the Hawkei didn't celebrate death," Sophia said, and she whooshed out a breath. "I don't understand how they can watch their children die and be happy about it. This Cup is so cruel. I wish there was a different way."

"Well, no one's really happy," Jonah explained. "It's just what's done."

Imogen pursed her lips like she didn't agree, but didn't say anything. Sophia looked sad.

"This is how our society is, Sophia," I told her quietly. "People don't really consider it barbaric. Just how things are."

She bounced her foot. "Well, maybe someday the rules will be changed, and the Cup won't require sacrifices."

There she went again with changing the rules. She didn't get it. No one could change anything, not even if they wanted to.

The servers brought out peach crumble for dessert, and the invitation of sugar was at least enough to get Sophia talking about more pleasant things.

"Are you sticking around during the break?" Sophia asked me. She fed Esis a bit of peach crumble off her fork, and he nearly fell over with how delicious it was.

"I, uh, won't be around much," I said regrettably. "After Christmas I usually travel with my Dad on the *Hozho* to Europe. Water tribe stuff."

"Aw." She seemed disappointed. "But isn't Ezra supposed to handle that stuff from now on?"

I shrugged. "Yeah, but Dad still wants my help, I guess."

Which was hopeful. Maybe if I couldn't be chief, Dad could still give me a place in the tribe. Not something as entitled as Elder, but at least some position where I could be useful.

"Hm. Well, I'll miss you," she said.

"I'll miss you too, *pawee*."

Imogen and Jonah gave each other another cutesy glance when I called Sophia that, and I sent them a death glare. Imogen and Jonah totally knew what I was calling her, and I bet they'd told her, the little shits.

"What are you doing over break, Jonah?" Sophia asked. She gave her fork to Esis, and he used it to suck down the rest of her dessert.

"I'm going to every rave this side of California!" Jonah practically yelled. "Squeaks and I are going to hit all the Hawkei nightclubs, won't we, girl?"

Squeaks squeaked excitedly, thrilled at the prospect of partying with Jonah over New Year's.

I made an obnoxious sound. Jonah was going to come back next semester with a month-long hangover— Squeaks, too.

"Are you spending Christmas with your fam—?" Sophia started, but I quickly shook my head *no* at her. She went quiet. Luckily, Jonah hadn't heard her.

"Jonah's spending Christmas with my family," I told Sophia quickly. "He usually does."

"Oh." Sophia said quietly. "Are his parents here to celebrate our Cup win?"

Unfortunately, Jonah had heard that. "They couldn't be here. They were, uh, busy," Jonah said quickly. Then, after a few seconds, he hurriedly added, "But I'm sure they're proud of me."

Sophia had the good sense not to ask any more questions. Personally, I was glad Jonah's asshole parents weren't here, along with his snobby older sister and her stuck-up girlfriend. Jonah's family was awful. Though it looked like he still wasn't over sticking up for them, which broke my heart. I'd hoped he'd finally seen the light, but I guess not yet.

Imogen changed the subject, thank the ancestors. "We're spending a quiet Christmas at home before we go exploring the Mayan ruins in Guatemala."

"I don't know where I'm going to go," Sophia said glumly. "I'm sure Doya won't let me go back home."

"You can stay with me," Imogen offered cheerfully. "Mom would love to have you. We always need extra help exploring."

"Thanks, Im." The girls smiled brightly at each other.

"Will Cade be there?" I teased. I knew his family usually vacationed in South America this time every year.

Imogen blushed. "I don't know."

Jonah and Sophia teased Imogen about Cade for a few minutes while we finished our desserts. Esis was practically rolling by now, and Sassy had peach crumble smeared all over her whiskers. We went back to the dance floor, because as I'd learned in the past hour, Sophia couldn't be contained if there was good music on.

"Hey, losers," a dude called out as we passed. "Congratulations on getting lucky!"

I knew him. He was Kent, from the Blue Team. I noticed that he was wearing sunglasses at night, which was a totally douchey thing to do. His friends, people from Silver and Green, snickered.

I'd noticed that since we'd been crowned Champions, some people had been trying to suck up to us, to increase their status in society. Not everyone was like that, though. It didn't matter that we'd won the Cup. To some people, we would always be outsiders.

I went to say something back, but Jonah beat me to it. He threw his shoulders back and swaggered toward Kent like he had something to say.

"Uh, no," Jonah said in a very sassy way. He moved forward, swaying his hips with attitude. He snatched the sunglasses off the guy's face and put them on his own. "We're not losers. That's not our name. For your information, we're the Reject Team, *bitch*."

Jonah strolled out of there in style, his hands waving above his head. Sassy strutted after him like a peacock. Sophia laughed, and Esis gave Kent the finger on both hands. Imogen scuttled off to the bar with Sassy, giggling. I couldn't stop grinning as we joined Jonah on the dance floor, who was currently dropping it so low I'm surprised he didn't fall over.

"Reject Team, huh?" I asked as Jonah bumped against me.

"Don't blame me, you came up with the name," Jonah replied.

"I think it's perfect for us," Sophia said. She was absolutely glowing.

Imogen had come back. She was carrying four glasses of champagne, which she distributed to each of us. "Here's one for the Reject Team!" Imogen cheered, and she raised her glass.

Sophia and Jonah raised their glasses to meet hers. I wasn't about to be the asshole who ruined the moment, so I raised my glass too and clinked it against the group's. I downed it in one go.

I felt like I was gonna ride the high of this night for the rest of my life. We were tournament winners, and we were freaking awesome. Fuck everyone else.

Jonah and the two girls resumed their crazy dancing. I more or less did that fist-bump thing guys do when they don't know how to dance, because, well, I didn't, and I didn't want to stand there looking like a jackass.

I noticed Professor Perot was there at one of the tables, Baxtor hopping on his lap. He winked when he saw me. He'd visited me a few times in the hospital. I'd had to sign a waiver so the doctors could give him my medical results for his research. As far as I knew, he hadn't made any progress on what was wrong with me. It was a bit frustrating, but since I'd squeaked by death more than once in the past week, I decided to let it go.

As the night wore on, Jonah got less and less in control of himself, and more and more drunk. He slammed drinks like they were going out of style, and impressed the girls with his flexibility.

"Jonah's... out of control," Sophia said, though I wasn't sure that was the right word for it as we watched him tumble, doing a breakdance.

"Nobody can quite drop it to the floor like Jonah," I said, rolling my eyes. He had every gay dude at Orenda's eye on him. Even some straight dudes in here were checking him out.

Except for one. I noticed Renar had hardly glanced his way all night. Jonah was too drunk to notice.

Oh— shit. Maybe that *was* the reason he'd been drinking so much.

I shook my head. Jonah deserved so much better than that piece of shit.

The crazy music became slow, changing into a song I hadn't heard since high school. Jonah grabbed the gay Yapluma guy and was turning drunkenly around the room with him, casting desperate glances at Renar. Squeaks' eyes seemed to frown, and she turned away from her Elementai.

I noticed Imogen had disappeared. Where had she gone off to? Sassy was still here, on her hind legs and swaying back and forth while Esis held her up in his version of a slow dance. He seemed refined and cool, like he'd done this before. Show-off.

Sophia stared at me expectantly. This was different than the dance we had earlier to the string quartet. It was more intimate. I knew we shouldn't, but I didn't want to tell her no.

She raised an eyebrow. "Aren't you supposed to ask me to dance?"

There was that Koigni attitude. I chuckled and took her into my arms, wrapping my arm around her waist and taking her free hand while she put the other one on my shoulder.

It became very obvious very quickly that she wanted to do this dance her way. She pulled me around like this was her job and not mine.

"I'm the man, I'm supposed to lead," I protested as she dragged me in the other direction. We were totally uncoordinated.

"Then act like it," she leaned forward and whispered in my ear, giving me a smirk.

Oh, *that* was a challenge. She wasn't just talking about dancing, either.

"Maybe you need to learn to *listen* to me," I hissed sharply. I pressed my hand onto her lower back, yanking her to my body.

She gasped, and I made sure that *I* led this time as we continued to waltz around the room. As the song went on, we pressed together even closer, until we hardly moved at all and were more or less just swaying against each other. She let her head rest on my shoulder, and I allowed mine to fall so that it lay against her head. I wrapped her tightly in my arms and squeezed her, hoping I would never let her go. Snowflakes began to fall from the ceiling, something extra the Toaqua teachers added for ambiance. People were watching, but I didn't care.

I wanted to be this close to her all the time. It wasn't fair that couldn't happen.

Change the rules.

I wanted to. So badly.

The song ended. I hated prying myself away from her, so I didn't let go, more or less just pulled away a little.

"You should kiss me right now," Sophia said lowly. Her tone made me want to do it, but I knew what would happen if I dared.

I wrinkled my nose. "*You* need to behave."

I pinched her ass, quickly so nobody else saw. She jumped and made an adorable squealing noise.

People were staring at us, whispering to each other behind their hands. Screw them. To them, we were just teammates celebrating our Cup win.

I finally untangled myself from her. We headed off the dance floor without even holding hands. Sassy and Esis followed us, dizzy from their slow dance. I noticed Sophia was pouting.

"This sucks," she complained. "A dance like that and I didn't even get a little kiss at the end."

"If you're a good girl, you'll get it later," I said, under my breath so only she heard.

I sent her a smoldering look that told her to do as I said. Sophia turned pink and went quiet, and I felt a grim note of satisfaction.

Oh, she was going to be fun to tame. My mate.

Agh! I had to stop doing that! There were consequences to this shit!

Now that the slow stuff was over, Imogen was back. Her eyes were kinda red. She looked like she'd been crying.

It was probably over Cade. But I didn't want to ask and make her more upset.

Jonah stumbled toward us, and I grabbed on to him so he didn't fall onto the floor. "Let's take a picture, guys!" he slurred. "So we can remember this night forever!"

He fished in his pocket. I nearly fell over when I saw that he had a smartphone in his hand.

"How'd you sneak a phone in here, Jonah?" I marveled.

"I have ways," he said wisely. "Quick, let's take one before the teachers see. Ready?"

He turned the phone around to take a selfie, focusing in on all of us. "One, two, three!"

Sophia gave a squeal and jumped into my arms. I caught her and managed to smile just as Jonah took the photo.

We looked at the picture. Jonah was front and center. Imogen was on the right side, beaming a bright smile, Sassy squirming out of her arms. I held onto Sophia on the left, and Esis was on top of my head, cheering. Squeaks was in the back, giving the camera a sultry look. Jonah hastily shoved the phone back in his pocket.

I told the others I had to piss, and went to the bathroom. When I came back Jonah, Imogen and Sophia were huddled together. Their expressions looked serious, like they were talking about something important. I only got the last fringes of the conversation as I approached.

"I just need more time. He's not ready," Sophia said anxiously, and she squeezed Esis to her.

Jonah gave her a look I couldn't read. "That's not fair, Sophia. You need to tell him."

"Tell me what?" I asked as I sauntered up to the group. Everyone's faces went kind of pale, especially Sophia's. She wore a panicked expression.

Were they talking about me?

"Uh... nothing important," Sophia said quickly. "It doesn't matter."

Imogen fiddled with her dress. Jonah had a disapproving look on his face, but I chalked it up to his drink being gone. Sophia stuttered to explain, but I pulled her to my side before she could answer.

"Hey, you don't have to tell me everything. I trust you," I told her.

Sophia turned a little pink, and Esis crossed his arms. I was curious and wanted to ask more, but at the same time, I figured it wasn't anything major. As much as I doubted the team at the start of the semester, I fully trusted each of them now. They were my friends, and Sophia was amazing. We'd all survived the tournament together.

My friends wouldn't hide anything from me.

Imogen left the ball shortly after that with Sassy, saying she was tired... but I figured it was more to look for Cade. Sophia, Esis and I danced to a few more songs, though none of them were slow and Sophia and I didn't get intimate again— which was a good and bad thing.

Jonah. Was. Drunk. He was on top of the bar, singing shrilly and shaking his chest like he had boobs. Squeaks was just about as plastered as he was, and was knocking over stools as her eyelids lolled. The three crates of beer bottles she'd gone through were scattered all over the floor.

"Get off!" The bartender started slapping Jonah with a towel. Jonah slowly clambered down from the bar and ended up falling on his face.

Everyone else had more or less gone home. There were a few stragglers on the dance floor, but for the most part, the ballroom was empty.

"All right, bud, here you go," I said as I pulled Jonah to his feet. He hung onto me, barely able to keep his balance. "I think it's time we took you to bed."

"I'd say," Jonah drawled. "Somebody has to."

"Not like that." I started guiding him toward the door, and Sophia followed. His hippogriff moaned on the floor.

"Sorry, Squeaks," I told her. "You'll have to walk. Can't carry you."

Esis patted her head, and Squeaks was able to stand. Incredibly, she walked in a straight line. How was Squeaks less clumsy when she was drunk versus being sober?

As we dragged Jonah into the hallway I noticed Ezra was leaning against the wall, kissing the girls we saw from earlier. Yes, both of them. He would make out with one girl for a few seconds before he'd turn his head and make out with the other. The girls watched with wide and adoring eyes, as if they loved watching him kiss another girl just as much as they liked being kissed by him.

Ez was really milking the college life. What exactly was this magical effect he had on people, especially women? He got away with everything.

Ezra opened his eyes and pulled his mouth away from the one girl as we dragged Jonah by. "Hey, Liam," he said. "Dad's walking around. He's looking for you. You'd better be careful."

"Thanks, Ez," I told him, giving him a nod. We took Jonah around the corner. Fuck, he was so heavy, but luckily the Yapluma dorms weren't far from here.

"What does your dad want?" Sophia asked. Jonah gagged, and I tried not to recoil from him. If Jonah threw up on me, I was going to lose it.

"Ancestors only know. Probably to yell at me for sneaking out of the hospital," I told her. That was all I needed, my dad following me around to babysit.

We finally got to the Yapluma dorms. I let go of Jonah, and he leaned on Squeaks. He was able to walk on his own a little better now, so I hoped he made it to his bed. Or, at least, a couch.

"Why'd you guys make me leave?" Jonah asked. I doubted he would remember this in the morning. "I was having so much fun!"

"You're wasted, Jonah. You need to get some sleep," Sophia said kindly.

"Yeah, sure," Jonah slurred. "You guys just want to get rid of me so you can do this."

Jonah turned his back, put his arms around himself and made movements like he was making out. I pushed him, and he fell over again. He barely managed to pull himself up by Squeaks' legs.

"Take care of yourself, brother," I said as I pushed the door open for him. Jonah and Squeaks stumbled inside, and I heard the sound of him puking just as the door closed.

Poor guy. He was gonna wish he was dead in the morning.

Sophia turned toward me. "So... now what?" Her face was slightly worried, but also, anticipatory.

"What do you mean? It's time for bed," I said blankly.

Sophia stared at me before she burst out laughing. Esis put his head in his hand and sighed.

"No, I mean..." Her expression cleared up, and the humor left.

"Are we going somewhere?"

I had no clue what she was talking about, until Esis did that mating-call thing again he'd done when we'd gone out for pizza. She was talking about... wow. I felt like an idiot.

"I don't think we're ready for that," I said. I reached out and put my arm around her waist as we walked back to the Koigni dorms. This time of night, no one was in the hallways, so I wasn't worried about being seen too much. Plus, right now, I just wanted to touch her, because I knew I wouldn't be able to for the entire break.

If ever again.

"I just thought you would expect something, you know. Because it's the night of the ball, and this is college, after all." She talked quickly, like she was trying to explain herself.

"I don't expect anything," I said, amazed. How many shitty guys had Sophia met in her lifetime?

"You're such a gentleman." She smiled softly. Esis skittered up her dress and sat on her shoulder. He was eyeing me, as if expecting me to respond a certain way.

"I just... think it's too early to talk about sex," I said quickly. "Especially when we don't know what we are."

Esis glanced back to Sophia's face, which had fallen. "Right," she said.

I was pretty sure that was the best answer. I didn't think Sophia wanted to sleep with me tonight, anyway. She seemed like she wanted more from me before that happened... if it ever did... though I wasn't sure what that would be.

We stopped in front of the Koigni dorms, and Esis slid down the front of her dress and to her feet. We had to make this quick, as her dorms were the most restrictive and there was no telling when we could be found out. Saying goodbye in front of them was dangerous, but I didn't feel safe letting her wander back to them alone at night, even if we were at Orenda Academy, the safest place in the world.

"So what about my reward for behaving?" Sophia asked, putting her hands on her hips.

"Reward? I didn't say you'd get a reward," I teased.

"That's not fair." She pouted her bottom lip out like a little kid, like the *pawee* I'd come to love so much and want to claim as my own. Seeing her like that, it was hard to come to terms with the fact that she was far more powerful than I was... more powerful than all of us.

And one day, she was going to determine the fate of this tribe. Thinking about it made my legs want to become water.

I laughed lowly and forced myself to calm down. "Well, I suppose you *have* been good, haven't you?"

Her face brightened, before she paused to ask something. "About... what you call me. *Pawee.* Jonah and Imogen said you were calling me your soulmate," she whispered. "Is that true?"

I knew they had told her. But that was okay. I raised my hand and brushed back the curls from her face. "You shouldn't have to ask, *pawee.*"

Then we were kissing again. Fuck, it's like everytime we got even a second alone we couldn't keep our hands off each other. Her mouth ravaged over mine like she couldn't get enough, and I squeezed her to me as I tasted her, wishing this would never end and I would get to kiss Sophia Henley every day for the rest of my existence. Even if I did, it wouldn't be enough.

When she pulled away, her breasts heaved against my chest. "When did you know?" she asked quietly.

I took a deep breath and said, "I don't know. From the first moment I saw you. Always."

The way she looked at me... I'd never had anyone look at me like that before. Not any of my other girlfriends. Not Mia. Just Sophia.

I was okay with living in secret and hiding our love forever. I never thought I'd get a second chance at love. Sophia was all I ever wanted. This unbreakable connection between us would be enough for me.

But I didn't want that for her. I didn't want her to be married to a cripple. I didn't want her to suffer through never letting anyone know we were together, and never having kids. I didn't want her to lose her Familiar. I couldn't do that to her.

It didn't change the fact that I felt like I'd been waiting for her all my life, and in her, I thought I found the only person who matched me. Sophia was the one girl who could love a man without a soul.

Sophia trailed out of my arms. "Will I see you when we get back to school?" She swallowed. "Like this?"

I knew what she meant. "Yes. That's a promise." I gave her a quick peck on the lips again before she turned to open the door. Her fingers trailed away from mine. Esis gave me a salute and a wink, like I'd done good, before he vanished into the dorms.

"Bye, Liam," Sophia said quietly, and she closed the door. I waited for a moment.

"Goodnight, Sophia," I whispered long after she was gone. "I love you."

I wish I had the balls to say it to her face. But that was scary, and I had a lot to think about over break first before I ever went that far.

Sophia wanted a relationship. So did I. But I needed time to figure out if that was something that was worth the risk.

And... I had to go back to the hospital. Which sucked. Time for another IV in my arm and machines beeping all night. Yay me.

I hurried to the medical wing, because I'd been gone long enough. I shouldn't have been surprised when I saw Dad sitting on a bench outside, Tatum sleeping beside him. The bear's shoulders shook with loud snores as he dreamed.

Dad rose to his feet, but Tatum still slept. I felt pretty guilty as my father stomped toward me. He didn't look happy.

"How'd you know how to find me?" I asked.

Dad bluntly said, "I knew you had to come back eventually."

Well, he was right about that. No matter what I did, I'd always end up *back here* it seemed... in a hospital.

"You're supposed to be in bed." Dad's tone was heavy. He'd hardly left my bedside all week, which had been annoying as much as it had been endearing.

"I wanted to celebrate my Cup win," I said. "I took care of myself. I was fine."

I hoped he couldn't smell the booze on my breath, because if he did, he'd totally flip out. He'd taken it really hard that I almost died in the tournament, harder than even my mom had.

Dad gave a disapproving glance at my tie. "You're wearing red. I noticed Sophia had on blue."

Shit. I had hoped he hadn't seen her dress. Wearing the wrong *colors* was a big deal around here. How would people react if they knew Sophia and I had kissed, and were considering a relationship?

"It was just..." I shrugged. I didn't have a good answer. Dad sighed, and shook his head.

"Liam, about you and Sophia..." Dad started.

"It's not what it looks like." I quickly went to explain. "We're just friends, we're not—"

"That's not it." Dad cut me off. "The Water Elders *want* you to get close to Sophia."

It felt like a brick wall had smashed into my face. "What?" All the air rushed out of me. "Why?"

"Liam, listen." Dad put his hands on my shoulders firmly, to steady me. "I have to tell you something. Son, there might be a way to bring Nashoma back. The Water Elders have found a way, that, maybe... he can still be alive."

The sentence winded me. I was glad Dad steadied me, because I was weak on my feet. Tears sprang to my eyes. I couldn't control them. Pure desperation at the thought of getting Nashoma back, to make up for what I did, was screaming in my chest. A way to bring my Familiar back? A chance to restore my soul? It wasn't possible.

"Are you saying the Water Elders can bring Nashoma back to life?" The words sounded fake, even though I was sure that's what my dad was telling me. My hearing went all fuzzy and I got a little dizzy. This couldn't be real. I had to be dreaming.

"Yes. But, Liam, you don't understand. If you want Nashoma back, you're going to have to do something for the Water Council," he said, slowly so I could comprehend him.

"I don't care. What is it? I'll do anything," I said in a rush.

Dad's face sobered. His expression became grim as he said, "Liam, if you want Nashoma back, you're going to have to kill Sophia Henley."

END OF BOOK ONE

Continue on to read a special excerpt from Book Two: *The Water Legacy!*

HIDDEN LEGENDS

Read more from the Hidden Legends universe! Each Hidden Legends series takes place within the same world, but in separate and unique societies. Every series stands on its own, and they can be read in any order.

§♣

SHIFTERS, FAE, & SORCERESSES

University of Sorcery by Megan Linski

§♣

WITCHES, DEMONS, & REAPERS

College of Witchcraft by Alicia Rades

§♣

SUPERNATURAL PRISON

Prison for Supernatural Offenders by Megan Linski & Alicia Rades

§♣

Never miss a new release! Join our newsletter at www.hiddenlegendsbooks.com/fanclub/.

THE WATER LEGACY:
SNEAK PEEK

Liam - Several Months Earlier

My life was perfect, and I thought that would never change... until the day everything did.

I stood at the edge of a cliff, hundreds of feet above the raging ocean on the edge of the California coastline. The wind swept my hair back, and I could hear the harsh crashing of the waves on the rocky shore below. The ocean smelled amazing from up here, salty and pure. It was a hot, sunny day, not a cloud in the sky, perfect for the first day of summer. I could hear the rustling of the leaves as the breeze from the sea whispered through the forest.

A large castle made of white stone towered behind me, far above the woodland, stark against the towering mountains in the distance. Despite it being a mile off, it still looked huge and welcoming... it was home.

A black wolf stood at my side, a thin scar across one of his amber eyes, a hardened expression on his face. His coat was the color of dark coal, and he was so tall, his shoulder came up to my hip. His ears were perked forward, watching the water as if it were something for him to hunt.

"Ready for this, brother?" I asked, taking on a slightly cocky tone as I nudged my wolf.

He huffed. Nashoma was always so serious. I laughed and rubbed my hand over his head, scratching his ears.

"You know, it's my birthday. You could lighten up a little."

My touch caused his exterior to melt down. Nashoma barked, letting his tongue loll out of his mouth. His amber eyes glittered, and I grinned.

"Come on, then." I backed away from the cliff, and Nashoma followed. We walked until we were a good twenty feet from the cliff's edge, then stopped. My heartbeat picked up in deadly anticipation.

"No time like the present!" I said, and I bolted before he could answer. I ran at full speed toward the drop off, and Nashoma sprinted with me, side by side. Neither of us hesitated as we took a running start at the cliff...

And jumped.

My stomach bottomed out and became hollow as the feeling of weightlessness came upon me, and we started plummeting toward the ocean. I let out a *whoop* the minute my feet left solid ground, then started holding my breath.

This was the biggest fall we'd ever taken. We were at least three-hundred feet up. There was a risk we wouldn't make it. But I liked pushing things to the limit. There was something incredibly thrilling about always being on the edge of death. I *loved* it.

I glanced over. Nashoma was falling gracefully through the air, his legs held in an elegant pose. His face remained unfazed as we fell at high-speed, as if staring into the face of death just made him stare coolly back.

The ocean was approaching faster and faster. At this speed, we'd be smashed against the water if this didn't work. A thrill of exhilaration went through me as we sped downward, and soon, the surface drew too close.

But before I hit the water, I clenched my palms, and I felt a well of magic rise up within me. Instead of us smacking against the waves, the water rose up to meet us, soft tendrils spiraling out of the water, and they caught Nashoma and me, cradling us in their grasp before swinging backward and launching us even farther out to sea. We flew through the air again, this time at a lower height, and landed upon the water as it became a disk to catch our fall.

But we didn't sink. The water pushed us back to a vertical position, and it caught our feet, bubbling around us so that we were standing upon the water.

Before we could even gather our bearings, I opened my hands again and curled my fingers. The water beneath us became a funnel, swirling around Nashoma and me and sending us rocketing upward. When we reached the height I wanted, I forced the water to become a springboard for both of us, and it used pressure to launch us skyward. I could hear the water as it crashed back down to the surface below, and Nashoma and I went flying through the skies once more.

It was like time had ceased to exist, and everything was in slow-time. Nashoma was sailing over me, body poised like he was flying, while I performed a backflip. I closed my eyes and extended my arms wide, like I could fly, too, as we spun downward. A jolt of adrenaline shot through my body as I commanded the water to obey my every command and whim.

Like I said... I lived a perfect fucking life, and I loved every moment of it.

Nashoma grew close to me as we got near the water. I reached out and grabbed on to him, pulling him tightly to my body as we hit the surface. The waves became soft and broke our fall with just a thought from me, but this time, I allowed the water to submerge us deep within its depths. All around us, I saw the beautiful Familiars that the Elementai of my tribe were bonded to. All sorts of magical creatures swam throughout the ocean's depths... water monsters, with long necks and flat fins, swam peacefully besides giant multicolored fish and a blue sea dragon with fins for legs, wings, and a long, feathered tail.

Beside me, Nashoma had transformed into a water wolf. He was treading water, his feet webbed and his black coat turned to a translucent blue. His eyes had changed to an emerald green that resembled gemstones, and there was a thin green spine resembling that of a fish's that ran down his back from his neck to his tail.

He barked at me, and the sound became a bubble. I grinned at him. I had the best Familiar in the world.

A school of rainbow fish swam calmly in front of us, waving like a multicolored flag in the water. Nashoma chased after the school of fish like he did deer on land, and just as fast. When the school outran him, Nashoma opened his mouth, and a funnel of bubbles and water came jetting out at high-speed, making the fish scatter everywhere.

I chuckled, though it was hard to do while holding my breath. Beneath us, a curious sea serpent swam up to see what we were doing. Her scales were a mixture of pink and purple, and two large fins stuck out on the sides of her head like ears. Her black eyes glittered as she observed us without fear. She was young and unbonded, not much bigger than a car.

I skimmed my hand over the scales of the sea serpent, and she cooed within the ocean deep before she turned downward, most likely to go hunting at the bottom. I told the water to lift Nashoma and I upward, and we broke the surface.

When Nashoma was no longer underwater, he changed back into the black wolf I loved so much.

I leaned forward and flung my arms back behind me. The result was like a slingshot. The water sent us speeding forward at least a hundred miles an hour, waves tailing out behind us. The water supported our feet, and I swerved back and forth as we whizzed across the surface to determine direction, like I was surfing. Nashoma merely ran next to me like we were on land, the water rising to support each one of his footsteps.

I was almost out of breath with exhilaration. There was nothing better than being a Water Elementai. Not a damn thing.

We were near the beach now. I slowed us down, and we breathed heavily to catch our breath as the world spun around us. What a perfect way to start out the day.

"Hey, Liam!" I heard someone call my name, and I turned to see my younger brother, Ezra. Like me, Ezra was a Water Elementai, and he was waist-deep in a funnel of his own that held him above the ocean, though his funnel was obviously weaker than mine. He'd just graduated high school and would soon be attending Orenda Academy with me... something he hadn't stopped annoying me about since he'd got his acceptance letter.

"What's up?" I asked. I approached my brother. He was more or less my identical twin, except he was three years younger and his long black hair was a bit shorter than mine. Besides that, we shared the same brown skin, and his eyes were black, like mine.

Ezra was alone. He didn't have a Familiar yet. He wouldn't get one until he'd found one to bond with at Orenda. I'd only had Nashoma for nearly a year now, after we'd bonded late last fall. So far, it'd been the best year of my life, because of him. I told the water to glide me and Nashoma calmly over to him, and it obeyed.

"Where've you been? You've been gone all morning. Dad sent me to look for you," Ezra said as I approached.

I rolled my eyes. Dad could be over the top sometimes. "I'm twenty-one. I don't need a babysitter."

"Twenty-one *today*," Ezra reminded me. "Which is why Dad's probably freaking out. He thinks you're gonna go on a three-day bender with Jonah or something."

Which could totally happen, because that kind of thing could be expected when Jonah was involved. "Dad knows I can take care of myself," I said. "He doesn't need to be all paranoid. I'm responsible."

"Yeah, sure," Ezra said sarcastically, like he didn't believe it. He paused for a second before he added, "By the way, can you buy me some beer?"

I smirked. "That depends. Can you kick my ass to get it?"

"Oh, you're *on*." Ezra launched himself at me, and tackled me into the water. We sank under the deep and started wrestling together. Nashoma danced around us, barking in excitement as he watched the scrap.

But something weird happened. When I was messing around with Ezra, my muscles cramped, and I gasped, inhaling in a bit of water. Ezra noticed I was struggling and let go of me, and we both rose to the surface. We treaded water as I coughed, trying to regain my breath.

"Whoa. You okay?" Ezra backed off, looking concerned.

"Yeah." I recovered my breath. I wasn't very good at things that involved strength— I let my magic do the talking for me. To get back at Ezra for winning, I caused a large wave to rise silently behind him, then crash upon his head.

Ezra was pushed underwater. He broke the surface again, coughing and sputtering. "No fair!" he shouted. "Not everyone's as good as you, you know."

I snickered. Ezra thought I was showing off my magic, and maybe I was. I couldn't help it that I was talented.

We swam toward the beach, and Nashoma followed us, walking leisurely over the water. We reached the beach and walked upon the sand. The water left our bodies and clothes immediately, soaking onto the sand as we used our magic to dry us off. Nashoma shook his fur, and the water came splattering outward, leaving his fur dry and soft again.

"So what are you gonna do? Come back home?" Ezra asked.

Facing another one of my Dad's lectures about how *I was the first-born* and how *the future Water chief should be more responsible* didn't sound like something I wanted to do. "I'm meeting Jonah for lunch," I told him as we headed up the path toward town.

"I'll join you," Ezra said. "Dad will lose it if I come back without you."

There was a small bar that was still in the woods, on the edge of Kinpago. It was more or less an old hunting lodge that someone had converted into a restaurant.

My best friend, Jonah, was leaning against a tree on the outside of it. He was using his magic to play with a few leaves that had fallen on the ground in boredom, watching as they spiraled up and down on mini-tornadoes at his fingertips.

When he saw us coming, he pulled back his magic and let the leaves drop. Jonah didn't have a Familiar yet, though I felt like that time was getting close.

"About time," Jonah said as we approached. "I was worried my perfect complexion was gonna burn by the time you showed your pretty ass up."

I rolled my eyes. "Whatever you say, Jonah."

"Hey, boy!" Jonah said to Nashoma, and Nashoma barked in reply. "Look what I have for you!"

Jonah brought something out of his pants pocket. It was a tiny cupcake. He put it on the ground in front of Nashoma's paws. Nashoma barked and did a little dance when Jonah set the cupcake in front of him, spinning around in a few circles before he lunged forward and scarfed the dessert up.

"Hey, what the hell do I get?" I asked as Nashoma gobbled up the cupcake.

"A kiss, if you want it." Jonah leaned forward, his lips puckered obnoxiously. I shoved him away.

"Get out of here, asshole." I laughed.

We walked into the bar. It was a cozy place, but well-lit, with large windows and mismatched tables and chairs jostled against each other. There were all kinds of people in here— Toaqua like me, Yapluma, and Nivita, from the Earth tribe. I noticed the bar was absent of anyone Koigni... from the Fire tribe... and was grateful for that. You couldn't trust those types. All types of Familiars were in here. We had to navigate around a large stag's antlers, and apologized to a griffin as we stepped on its tail. A horse with a peacock tail moved out of the way so we could pass, and a strange creature that was half-deer, half-leopard growled as it started in on its salad, sharing it with her Earth Elementai.

This time of day, the place was packed. We had to pick a table in the middle of the room, because Jonah was so big and couldn't fit anywhere else. The three of us ordered buffalo burgers, and I started in on my first beer of my twenty-first birthday. Nashoma jumped onto a chair next to me, and I made sure to order him a steak, extra-rare.

"What do you want to do after this, Liam?" Ezra asked as he shoved a fistful of fries into his mouth. Nashoma had blood dripping down his front as he gnawed at his steak.

"I don't know," I replied. I was starving, and had already scarfed down my burger. "Go hiking, I guess."

"You *always* want to go hiking," Jonah whined. "Don't you ever get tired of looking at all the rocks and trees? It's like, the same thing."

I made a face at Jonah. I knew I grew up here, but there was something about this land that was incredible to me. This place was magical. It was like no matter how many times I'd walked around it, there was always something even more amazing to see.

"All you like looking at is man ass," I replied as a come-back. Ezra spit out his drink and laughed. Jonah didn't even bother rebuking me.

"You got that right," Jonah said as his eyes followed the back end of a Yapluma dude who left the bar. "You know me too well, Liam."

I shook my head. I liked girls, but I was quiet about it. Jonah took every opportunity he could to act horny around every male entity that was in a hundred mile radius. Thirsty didn't even come close to describing the way he behaved.

"Mom's making your special birthday dinner later. Can't miss that," Ezra reminded me.

"Not on your life." Mom's cooking was phenomenal, even if I would have to deal with a talk to Dad about tribal responsibilities once I got back home.

"And after that, we're going to get my man here *wasted*," Jonah sang, flinging an arm around my shoulders. "If you and Nashoma aren't completely hungover tomorrow, I've totally failed at my job as your bestie."

Nashoma and I eyed each other warily. If Jonah had his way, we'd be so drunk by the end of the night he'd have to carry us home. Or, more likely, hire a carriage to bring us back, because he would be just as intoxicated as we were.

We left the bar. A large female dragon waited outside of it. The dragon was gorgeous, with large horns and scales that looked like rubies. She belonged to one of the Professors at school, Professor Curt, who taught Dragonology. He must've been inside, eating. She bowed her head to us as we continued down the dirt path, but in the opposite direction of town.

My Familiar kept close to me. When Nashoma moved, he looked like a shadow gliding over the ground, silent, every step filled with intent. I couldn't wait for the day when he'd grow big enough to ride.

There were a group of Koigni in a clearing ahead, shooting fireballs at each other for practice. They barely noticed us as we walked by. We weren't important enough, I guess.

"Be careful, little brother," Jonah said as we passed them by. He leaned on Ezra to tease him. "Your magic's not strong enough to put their fire out if they attack. Stay by us. We'll keep you safe."

Ezra blushed, before his expression cleared. "Hey, Liam said that you couldn't manipulate air until *after* you got to Orenda!" Ezra protested. I smiled, and Jonah's expression became outraged.

When Jonah went to say something back, Nashoma opened his mouth. Another jet of water came out like a cannon, soaking him to the bone.

"Oh, I see how it is! No more cupcakes for you!" Jonah shouted as he tried shaking the water off his arms.

Nashoma's shoulders shook like he was laughing. He cackled, showing his large fangs.

Jonah caused a giant gust of wind to rise, drying him off quickly. It messed up his man-bun. Ezra and I were howling.

"Yeah, yeah. Fucking hilarious," Jonah muttered as he fixed his hair. He shot me a dirty look. "See how many secrets I tell you, now."

I chuckled. Jonah was being a bit ridiculous about Koigni— he was just using the rumors Ezra knew about them to try and scare my little brother. Sure, they had bad tempers, but members of the Fire tribe would never just randomly attack anyone.

...They hadn't for a long time, anyway.

I thought of something. "Jonah, I think I'm gonna ask Mia to come with us tonight," I said. "We should stop by her house and ask."

"Man, it's a guy's night!" Jonah complained. "Don't invite *her*."

Nashoma gave a growl of agreement, and Jonah nodded at him. Jonah and Nashoma had bonded over the fact they both despised Mia, but the two of them would have to get over it someday. Ezra stayed quiet.

I opened my mouth to respond, but something on the road caught my attention. A fellow Toaqua, Brittney, was struggling with a cart that had gotten stuck in a hole. Brittney's Familiar was a pink alicorn, a unicorn with fluffy wings, and she was hitched to the cart. The alicorn tried to pull it out as Brittney tugged, but the cart didn't move.

I hurried forward. "Here, let me help," I said. I lifted the cart out of the hole. As I did it, a sharp spasm ricocheted through my back. It wasn't much, but it made me gasp again, though I managed to set the cart down.

That was the second time that happened today. What the heck was going on with me? Nashoma narrowed his eyes and growled lowly, as if he'd felt something, too.

I didn't like the look he was giving me. It said he knew something I didn't.

"Thanks, Liam," Brittney said kindly. "But you didn't have to do that."

"Of course I did. You shouldn't have to do it by yourself," I told her. Behind me, Jonah groaned. Ezra watched carefully, taking notes. It went without saying that the second reason Ezra couldn't wait to get to Orenda was because there were plenty of girls around.

Brittney batted her eyelashes at me. "You're so sweet." Her expression lit up. "By the way, Mia wanted me to give you this. See you around."

Brittney handed me a note, then climbed back up on her cart, letting her alicorn pull it down the road once more.

"You're such a nice guy, Liam," Jonah said, sighing dramatically. "It makes the rest of us look bad."

"Well, yeah," I replied, not sure what else there was to say. What was the point of *not* being friendly? I couldn't imagine going around being rude and pissed off all the time.

I unfolded the note and read it quickly. My insides bottomed out. Mia couldn't hang out today— said she was busy, though she didn't clarify and she wished me a happy birthday.

"I guess it *is* going to be a guy's night. Mia can't come," I told them as I pocketed the note.

Jonah and Nashoma looked positively thrilled. I was a little disappointed, but that was okay. If Mia had things to do, I was okay with it, even if it was my birthday.

"Can I come instead?" Ezra said hopefully.

"Aw, sure," Jonah said, and he put Ezra in a headlock, ruffling his hair up. "I guess the little brother can tag along."

I wasn't really listening. I felt... different. Couldn't explain how. I noticed I felt tired. Kind of worn out. Maybe we shouldn't have gone on this walk. Nashoma watched me carefully, his head tilted a little to the side.

"Dude, I seriously can't wait to take Yapluma Magic II next semester," Jonah rambled. "There are gonna be *so* many hot guys in that class."

"I'm just so excited to go," Ezra said. "I've been hearing about Orenda my entire life, and now I finally get to be a student! I can't wait to learn how to use my magic!"

Jonah and Ezra kept talking about classes while we proceeded forward. I walked a few steps ahead with my hands in my pockets, thinking. The path led to the mountain range, and I had a sudden urge to climb it. By this time, the skies had darkened and grey clouds had appeared. The sun was gone, and it looked like it was going to rain soon.

"Let's climb up, guys," I said. "I bet the view is incredible from up there."

"Ugh, man, stop making me work," Jonah said, but he and Ezra followed me up the mountain path anyway.

When we rounded the side of the marked path, my eyes caught something strange. There was a small blue light, glowing about twenty feet or so below us within a cave carved into the mountainside. It was so small that you'd miss it if you didn't look closely. If I had to guess, it was magic.

Nashoma saw it, too. He crouched as close to the edge as he could, seemingly drawn to the small blue light, just like I was.

"Liam, we should turn back. It's going to rain soon," Ezra said, looking up.

"I can shield you from the rain if it comes down," I told him. I peered closer. What was that crazy light shining at the end of the mountain opening? I had to reach it. My eyes scanned the mountainside. There was a thin embankment by the opening, but it would be hard to get to. We'd have to slide down to get to it.

"Let's explore that cave down there," I offered. "I think there's something inside."

"I don't know, dude. That path looks dangerous," Jonah said, staring warily at the embankment. "I doubt we can make it down."

"Where's your sense of adventure?" I asked. "You could just fly us down there if you wanted."

"Fuck you," Jonah snapped back. "You know I don't like caves."

Most Yapluma didn't. I looked expectantly at Ezra, but he shook his head.

"Fine," I said. "I'll do it myself."

I jumped down the path and landed on the tiny embankment, walking carefully along the edge. If I slipped, I had better hope Jonah would catch me. Otherwise, I'd go falling down the mountainside. There wasn't enough water within the mountain that I could use it to break my fall.

Nashoma let out a tiny whine, like he was reluctant to come after me. But he'd follow me wherever I went, so he slid down the side of the mountain and joined me as I proceeded toward the cave opening.

The edge got thinner and thinner as I walked toward the cave, but that didn't slow my steps. The blue light was drawing me in, making it hard to think. It was like I was under some sort of spell. Nashoma was pretty far behind me, now. I'd gone ahead of him without thinking. A few rocks crumbled above me and spattered dirt down, but I wiped it away from my eyes and kept going.

"Liam, you need to come back!" Ezra sounded scared. "Those rocks don't look stable!"

"I'm fine!" I shouted back, ignoring him. That was the same moment I slipped. My right foot staggered forward, meeting nothing but air. I grabbed on to a root sticking out of the side of the mountain to try and stop my fall.

The root gave way, and I heard a loud cracking sound. Everything happened so fast that there wasn't enough time for Jonah to react to catch me, and I tumbled downward, landing in front of the cave opening.

I didn't get a chance to look inside and see where the blue light was coming from. I pushed myself to my feet as I heard Jonah and Ezra telling me to get out of the way. Multiple rocks from the side of the mountainside above had come loose and were rolling toward me in a landslide.

Those rocks were going to crush me. I glanced around frantically for an escape, but there was nowhere to go. My mind froze as several large boulders tumbled toward me at high speed.

There was no chance. I was going to die.

Liam, watch out!

I felt a pair of paws on my back, and I went tumbling down the side of the mountain. I felt air wrap around my body and lift me upward before I plummeted to my death. The air lifted me backward, pulling me upward until I landed face-first in the dirt.

Two pairs of shoes were in front of my face. Jonah and Ezra. He had flown me back to where they were standing.

That sentence still echoed in my ears. Someone had called my name. The sound had been deep, and male. I hadn't heard that voice before, couldn't place it, yet it sounded terribly intimate... like I'd been hearing that voice every day since before I'd been born. I staggered to my feet, dazed. Ezra and Jonah were both staring at me, their faces pale white and horrified.

... Where was Nashoma?

When I understood where the voice had come from, it felt like the weight of the world had been suddenly dropped on my head, crushing me.

The voice telling me to watch out had been my Familiar.

I let out an audible cry and spun around. The landslide had covered up the entrance of the cave and most of the embankment, making it so I couldn't see the entrance.

I couldn't see Nashoma, either.

"*Nashoma!*" I screamed. He didn't answer me. My scream bounced off the sides of the mountain and echoed through the trees, vibrating throughout the entire forest.

No. *No, no, no, no, no...*

I tried jumping off the embankment and racing to my Familiar, but Jonah grabbed me. He and Ezra each took an arm, trying to hold me back.

"Liam, it's not going to help!" Jonah shouted. He sounded panicked. Ezra said something about it being too dangerous, but I barely heard him.

Jonah was a big guy, and Ezra wasn't exactly tiny, but a freight train couldn't hold me back from getting to my Familiar now. I threw them both off and slid downward, until I reached the site of the landslide.

I started throwing boulders off of him. The rocks cut into my hands. I left large red streaks on the rocks as I sifted through them, my palms gushing blood. I didn't even fucking feel it. All I could feel was absolute terror as I tore through the rubble, hoping against hope he was okay, that he would make it through this.

I let out a cry of relief as I spotted his black fur, but it was short-lived as I heaved the last boulder off of him. Bones were poking through his fur in multiple places, and he was bleeding so much, from so many spots. He'd been crushed underneath the landslide. Nashoma was still breathing, but his amber eyes shone with a terrible agony. He was in awful pain, and it was all my fault. He couldn't even whine.

My hands skimmed over him, unsure of what to do or how to touch him, because I was pretty sure whatever I did would only torture him. "It's gonna be okay, brother. We're going to find someone to help, you're gonna make it..."

Soft footsteps landed beside me. It was Jonah and Ezra. They had followed me, even though it was dangerous for them to do so.

"Liam," Jonah said softly. His voice sounded choked. "It's... it's too late."

"No." They'd already accepted what I couldn't. Tears started dripping out of my eyes and onto Nashoma's fur. "We— we can still save him."

I heard sobs from behind me. Ezra was crying, too.

Hold me, Liam. Nashoma spoke to me. It was all he had the strength to say. His eyes pleaded with me to help.

I knew it would hurt him to pick him up, but it's what he wanted. I held my breath as I gently pushed my arms underneath Nashoma's broken body. I could feel all the shattered bones underneath my

434

hands. I cradled Nashoma's body against me and buried my face in his shoulder. His hot blood soaked my shirt and jeans.

"Nashoma, I'm so sorry," I gasped. "Please hold on. There has to be another way."

He weakly licked the side of my face. Nashoma panted heavily for a couple of seconds, gasping for breath. I could feel his heartbeat growing faint against my own. I prayed that the ancestors would make my heart stop, so his could keep going on.

But it didn't work. Nashoma slowly went stiff, curling against me and giving a last, ragged breath. I felt his heart stop as I was clutching him in my arms.

"Don't leave," I whispered weakly. But it was too late. He was already...

Something inside of me ripped. The warmth and acceptance Nashoma had created inside of me fled, like a part of myself I could no longer keep. A hole opened up inside of me, feeling cavernous, swallowing me up until I forgot who I was and I turned into a new person. Something awful grabbed my heart and changed it, turned it black and ill. It was something I'd never be able to repair, something I couldn't fix ever again. Who I'd been five minutes ago, I could never get back.

Nashoma was gone forever. He was *gone*. And with his death, I lost myself.

I mashed my face into Nashoma's body and wept. I dug my fingers into his fur and wailed as loudly as I possibly could, though I didn't mean to. It was something that just came out of me. Every breath felt like knives were stabbing into my lungs, and I hated each one, wished myself to stop breathing just like Nashoma had, though it didn't happen. I'd never felt something so agonizing in my life, not even when my grandfather had died.

I felt Jonah's hand on my shoulder trying to comfort me, and Ezra knelt by my side, but both of them felt so far away. I felt myself grow cold... like Nashoma would soon be.

Please, ancestors, let this be a dream. Let me wake up. I'll do anything.

But this wasn't a dream. This was my new reality— a reality I had created with one stupid mistake.

There was no point anymore. My purpose, my place in this world, my reason for existing... it had left when Nashoma went away.

I'd lost my soul. I no longer had it.

He died.

Continue The Water Legacy and see where Liam and Sophia's adventures lead next!

BONUS OFFERS

Find coloring pages, games, quizzes, and bonus content at www.
hiddenlegendsbooks.com.

Join the *Orenda Academy: Hidden Legends Fan Group* on Facebook for all
things Hidden Legends!

Check out the *Academy of Magical Creatures Official Playlist* on Spotify!

Never miss a new release! Join the Hidden Legends fan club at www.
hiddenlegendsbooks.com/fanclub.

ABOUT THE AUTHORS

Megan Linski (left) and Alicia Rades (right) are two best friends and the authors of the *Academy of Magical Creatures* series. Both are USA TODAY Bestselling Authors and award-winning novelists for teens and young adults. Megan Linski is a disabled author who loves laughter, adventure, and fantasy worlds. She is a proud member of Koigni House. Alicia Rades is a mother who enjoys exploring paranormal realms and trying new recipes. She is a champion from Toaqua House. Both girls love nature, animals, sexy romances, and eating cheese.

CPSIA information can be obtained
at www.ICGtesting.com
Printed in the USA
BVHW040009100223
658199BV00024B/88